TALES OF NARNIA

C. S. Lewis

TALES OF NARNIA

The Lion, the Witch and the Wardrobe

Prince Caspian

The Voyage of the *Dawn Treader*

COLLINS

William Collins Sons & Co Ltd
Sydney · Auckland · Toronto · Johannesburg

The Lion, the Witch and the Wardrobe
First published 1950 by Geoffrey Bles
First published by William Collins Sons & Co Ltd 1974
Copyright © C S Lewis Ptc Ltd 1950

Prince Caspian
First published 1951 by Geoffrey Bles
First published by William Collins Sons & Co Ltd 1974
Copyright © C S Lewis Ptc Ltd 1951

The Voyage of the Dawn Treader
First published 1952 by Geoffrey Bles
First published by William Collins Sons & Co Ltd 1974
Copyright © C S Lewis Ptc Ltd 1952

First published in this edition by
William Collins Sons & Co Ltd 1987

ISBN 0 00 183196 8

Printed and bound in Great Britain
by Mackays of Chatham Ltd, Kent.

CONTENTS

The Lion, the Witch and the Wardrobe

TO LUCY BARFIELD

My Dear Lucy,

I wrote this story for you, but when I began it I had not realized that girls grow quicker than books. As a result you are already too old for fairy tales, and by the time it is printed and bound you will be older still. But some day you will be old enough to start reading fairy tales again. You can then take it down from some upper shelf, dust it, and tell me what you think of it. I shall probably be too deaf to hear, and too old to understand, a word you say, but I shall still be

your affectionate Godfather,

C. S. LEWIS

CONTENTS

CHAPTER ONE

LUCY LOOKS INTO A WARDROBE

ONCE there were four children whose names were Peter, Susan, Edmund and Lucy. This story is about something that happened to them when they were sent away from London during the war because of the air-raids. They were sent to the house of an old Professor who lived in the heart of the country, ten miles from the nearest railway station and two miles from the nearest post office. He had no wife and he lived in a very large house with a housekeeper called Mrs Macready and three servants. (Their names were Ivy, Margaret and Betty, but they do not come into the story much.) He himself was a very old man with shaggy white hair which grew over most of his face as well as on his head, and they liked him almost at once; but on the first evening when he came out to meet them at the front door he was so odd-looking that Lucy (who was the youngest) was a little afraid of him, and Edmund (who was the next youngest) wanted to laugh and had to keep on pretending he was blowing his nose to hide it.

As soon as they had said good night to the Professor and gone upstairs on the first night, the boys came into the girls' room and they all talked it over.

"We've fallen on our feet and no mistake," said Peter. "This is going to be perfectly splendid. That old chap will let us do anything we like."

"I think he's an old dear," said Susan.

"Oh, come off it!" said Edmund, who was tired

and pretending not to be tired, which always made him bad-tempered. "Don't go on talking like that."

"Like what?" said Susan; "and anyway, it's time you were in bed."

"Trying to talk like Mother," said Edmund. "And who are you to say when I'm to go to bed? Go to bed yourself."

"Hadn't we all better go to bed?" said Lucy. "There's sure to be a row if we're heard talking here."

"No there won't," said Peter. "I tell you this is the sort of house where no one's going to mind what we do. Anyway, they won't hear us. It's about ten minutes' walk from here down to that dining-room, and any amount of stairs and passages in between."

"What's that noise?" said Lucy suddenly. It was a far larger house than she had ever been in before and the thought of all those long passages and rows of doors leading into empty rooms was beginning to make her feel a little creepy.

"It's only a bird, silly," said Edmund.

"It's an owl," said Peter. "This is going to be a wonderful place for birds. I shall go to bed now. I say, let's go and explore tomorrow. You might find anything in a place like this. Did you see those mountains as we came along? And the woods? There might be eagles. There might be stags. There'll be hawks."

"Badgers!" said Lucy.

"Foxes!" said Edmund.

"Rabbits!" said Susan.

But when next morning came there was a steady

rain falling, so thick that when you looked out of the window you could see neither the mountains nor the woods nor even the stream in the garden.

"Of course it *would* be raining!" said Edmund. They had just finished their breakfast with the Professor and were upstairs in the room he had set apart for them – a long, low room with two windows looking out in one direction and two in another.

"Do stop grumbling, Ed," said Susan. "Ten to one it'll clear up in an hour or so. And in the meantime we're pretty well off. There's a wireless and lots of books."

"Not for me," said Peter; "I'm going to explore in the house."

Everyone agreed to this and that was how the adventures began. It was the sort of house that you never seem to come to the end of, and it was full of unexpected places. The first few doors they tried led only into spare bedrooms, as everyone had expected that they would; but soon they came to a very long room full of pictures and there they found a suit of armour; and after that was a room all hung with green, with a harp in one corner; and then came three steps down and five steps up, and then a kind of little upstairs hall and a door that led out on to a balcony, and then a whole series of rooms that led into each other and were lined with books – most of them very old books and some bigger than a Bible in a church. And shortly after that they looked into a room that was quite empty except for one big wardrobe; the sort that has a looking-glass in the door. There was nothing else in the room at all except a dead blue-bottle on the window-sill.

"Nothing there!" said Peter, and they all trooped out again – all except Lucy. She stayed behind because she thought it would be worth while trying the door of the wardrobe, even though she felt almost sure that it would be locked. To her surprise

it opened quite easily, and two moth-balls dropped out.

Looking into the inside, she saw several coats hanging up – mostly long fur coats. There was nothing Lucy liked so much as the smell and feel of fur. She immediately stepped into the wardrobe and got in among the coats and rubbed her face against them, leaving the door open, of course, because she knew that it is very foolish to shut oneself into any wardrobe. Soon she went further in and found that there was a second row of coats hanging up behind the first one. It was almost quite dark in there and she kept her arms stretched out in front of her so as not to bump her face into the back of the wardrobe. She took a step further in – then two or three steps – always expecting to feel woodwork against the tips of her fingers. But she could not feel it.

"This must be a simply enormous wardrobe!" thought Lucy, going still further in and pushing the soft folds of the coats aside to make room for her. Then she noticed that there was something crunching under her feet. "I wonder is that more moth-balls?" she thought, stooping down to feel it with her hand. But instead of feeling the hard, smooth wood of the floor of the wardrobe, she felt something soft and powdery and extremely cold. "This is very queer," she said, and went on a step or two further.

Next moment she found that what was rubbing against her face and hands was no longer soft fur but something hard and rough and even prickly. "Why, it is just like branches of trees!" exclaimed Lucy. And then she saw that there was a light ahead of her; not a few inches away where the back of the wardrobe ought to have been, but a long way off. Something cold and soft was falling on her. A moment later she found that she was standing in the middle of a wood at night-time with snow under her feet and snowflakes falling through the air.

Lucy felt a little frightened, but she felt very inquisitive and excited as well. She looked back over her shoulder and there, between the dark tree-trunks, she could still see the open doorway of the wardrobe and even catch a glimpse of the empty room from which she had set out. (She had, of course, left the door open, for she knew that it is a

very silly thing to shut oneself into a wardrobe.) It seemed to be still daylight there. "I can always get back if anything goes wrong," thought Lucy. She began to walk forward, *crunch-crunch* over the snow and through the wood towards the other light. In about ten minutes she reached it and found it was a lamp-post. As she stood looking at it, wondering why there was a lamp-post in the middle of a wood and wondering what to do next, she heard a pitter patter of feet coming towards her. And soon after that a very strange person stepped out from among the trees into the light of the lamp-post.

He was only a little taller than Lucy herself and he carried over his head an umbrella, white with snow. From the waist upwards he was like a man, but his legs were shaped like a goat's (the hair on them was glossy black) and instead of feet he had goat's hoofs. He also had a tail, but Lucy did not notice this at first because it was neatly caught up over the arm that held the umbrella so as to keep it from trailing in the snow. He had a red woollen muffler round his neck and his skin was rather reddish too. He had a strange, but pleasant little face, with a short pointed beard and curly hair, and out of the hair there stuck two horns, one on each side of his forehead. One of his hands, as I have said, held the umbrella: in the other arm he carried several brown-paper parcels. What with the parcels and the snow it looked just as if he had been doing his Christmas shopping. He was a Faun. And when he saw Lucy he gave such a start of surprise that he dropped all his parcels.

"Goodness gracious me!" exclaimed the Faun.

CHAPTER TWO

WHAT LUCY FOUND THERE

"GOOD EVENING," said Lucy. But the Faun was so busy picking up its parcels that at first it did not reply. When it had finished it made her a little bow.

"Good evening, good evening," said the Faun. "Excuse me – I don't want to be inquisitive – but should I be right in thinking that you are a Daughter of Eve?"

"My name's Lucy," said she, not quite understanding him.

"But you are – forgive me – you are what they call a girl?" said the Faun.

"Of course I'm a girl," said Lucy.

"You are in fact Human?"

"Of course I'm human," said Lucy, still a little puzzled.

"To be sure, to be sure," said the Faun. "How stupid of me! But I've never seen a Son of Adam or a Daughter of Eve before. I am delighted. That is to say –" and then it stopped as if it had been going to say something it had not intended but had remembered in time. "Delighted, delighted," it went on. "Allow me to introduce myself. My name is Tumnus."

"I am very pleased to meet you, Mr Tumnus," said Lucy.

"And may I ask, O Lucy Daughter of Eve," said Mr Tumnus, "how you have come into Narnia?"

"Narnia? What's that?" said Lucy.

"This is the land of Narnia," said the Faun, "where

we are now; all that lies between the lamp-post and the great castle of Cair Paravel on the eastern sea. And you – you have come from the wild woods of the west?"

"I – I got in through the wardrobe in the spare room," said Lucy.

"Ah!" said Mr Tumnus in a rather melancholy voice, "if only I had worked harder at geography when I was a little Faun, I should no doubt know all about those strange countries. It is too late now."

"But they aren't countries at all," said Lucy, almost laughing. "It's only just back there – at least – I'm not sure. It is summer there."

"Meanwhile," said Mr Tumnus, "it is winter in Narnia, and has been for ever so long, and we shall both catch cold if we stand here talking in the snow. Daughter of Eve from the far land of Spare Oom where eternal summer reigns around the bright city of War Drobe, how would it be if you came and had tea with me?"

"Thank you very much, Mr Tumnus," said Lucy. "But I was wondering whether I ought to be getting back."

"It's only just round the corner," said the Faun, "and there'll be a roaring fire – and toast – and sardines – and cake."

"Well, it's very kind of you," said Lucy. "But I shan't be able to stay long."

"If you will take my arm, Daughter of Eve," said Mr Tumnus, "I shall be able to hold the umbrella over both of us. That's the way. Now – off we go."

And so Lucy found herself walking through the

wood arm in arm with this strange creature as if they had known one another all their lives.

They had not gone far before they came to a place where the ground became rough and there were rocks all about and little hills up and little hills down. At the bottom of one small valley Mr Tumnus turned suddenly aside as if he were going to walk straight into an unusually large rock, but at the last moment Lucy found he was leading her into the entrance of a cave. As soon as they were inside she found herself blinking in the light of a wood fire. Then Mr Tumnus stooped and took a flaming piece of wood out of the fire with a neat little pair of tongs, and lit a lamp. "Now we shan't be long," he said, and immediately put a kettle on.

Lucy thought she had never been in a nicer place. It was a little, dry, clean cave of reddish stone with a carpet on the floor and two little chairs ("one for me and one for a friend," said Mr Tumnus) and a table and a dresser and a mantelpiece over the fire and above that a picture of an old Faun with a grey beard. In one corner there was a door which Lucy thought must lead to Mr Tumnus's bedroom, and on one wall was a shelf full of books. Lucy looked at these while he was setting out the tea things. They had titles like *The Life and Letters of Silenus* or *Nymphs and Their Ways* or *Men, Monks and Gamekeepers; a Study in Popular Legend* or *Is Man a Myth?*

"Now, Daughter of Eve!" said the Faun.

And really it was a wonderful tea. There was a nice brown egg, lightly boiled, for each of them, and then sardines on toast, and then buttered toast, and then toast with honey, and then a sugar-topped cake. And when Lucy was tired of eating the Faun began to talk. He had wonderful tales to tell of life in the forest. He told about the midnight dances and how the Nymphs who lived in the wells and the Dryads who lived in the trees came out to dance with the Fauns; about long hunting parties after the milk-white stag who could give you wishes if you caught him; about feasting and treasure-seeking with the wild Red Dwarfs in deep mines and caverns far beneath the forest floor; and then about summer when the woods were green and old Silenus on his fat donkey would come to visit them, and sometimes Bacchus himself, and then the streams would run with wine instead of water and the whole forest would give itself up to jollification for weeks on end. "Not that it isn't always winter now," he added gloomily. Then to cheer himself up he took out from its case on the dresser a strange little flute that looked as if it were made of straw and began to play. And the tune he played made Lucy want to cry and laugh and dance and go to sleep all at the same time. It must have been hours later when she shook herself and said:

"Oh, Mr Tumnus – I'm so sorry to stop you, and I do love that tune – but really, I must go home. I only meant to stay for a few minutes."

"It's no good *now*, you know," said the Faun, laying down its flute and shaking its head at her very sorrowfully.

"No good?" said Lucy, jumping up and feeling rather frightened. "What do you mean? I've got to go home at once. The others will be wondering what has happened to me." But a moment later she asked, "Mr Tumnus! Whatever is the matter?" for the Faun's brown eyes had filled with tears and then the tears began trickling down its cheeks, and soon they were running off the end of its nose; and at last it covered its face with its hands and began to howl.

"Mr Tumnus! Mr Tumnus!" said Lucy in great distress. "Don't! Don't! What is the matter? Aren't you well? Dear Mr Tumnus, do tell me what is wrong." But the Faun continued sobbing as if its heart would break. And even when Lucy went over

and put her arms round him and lent him her hand-kerchief, he did not stop. He merely took the handker-chief and kept on using it, wringing it out with both hands whenever it got too wet to be any more use, so that presently Lucy was standing in a damp patch.

"Mr Tumnus!" bawled Lucy in his ear, shaking him. "Do stop. Stop it at once! You ought to be ashamed of yourself, a great big Faun like you. What on earth are you crying about?"

"Oh – oh – oh!" sobbed Mr Tumnus, "I'm crying because I'm such a bad Faun."

"I don't think you're a bad Faun at all," said Lucy. "I think you are a very good Faun. You are the nicest Faun I've ever met."

"Oh – oh – you wouldn't say that if you knew," replied Mr Tumnus between his sobs. "No, I'm a bad Faun. I don't suppose there ever was a worse Faun since the beginning of the world."

"But what have you done?" asked Lucy.

"My old father, now," said Mr Tumnus; "that's his picture over the mantelpiece. He would never have done a thing like this."

"A thing like what?" said Lucy.

"Like what I've done," said the Faun. "Taken service under the White Witch. That's what I am. I'm in the pay of the White Witch."

"The White Witch? Who is she?"

"Why, it is she that has got all Narnia under her thumb. It's she that makes it always winter. Always winter and never Christmas; think of that!"

"How awful!" said Lucy. "But what does she pay *you* for?"

"That's the worst of it," said Mr Tumnus with a deep groan. "I'm a kidnapper for her, that's what I am. Look at me, Daughter of Eve. Would you believe that I'm the sort of Faun to meet a poor innocent child in the wood, one that had never done me any harm, and pretend to be friendly with it, and invite it home to my cave, all for the sake of lulling it asleep and then handing it over to the White Witch?"

"No," said Lucy. "I'm sure you wouldn't do anything of the sort."

"But I have," said the Faun.

"Well," said Lucy rather slowly (for she wanted to be truthful and yet not be too hard on him), "well, that was pretty bad. But you're so sorry for it that I'm sure you will never do it again."

"Daughter of Eve, don't you understand?" said the Faun. "It isn't something I *have* done. I'm doing it now, this very moment."

"What do you mean?" cried Lucy, turning very white.

"You are the child," said Tumnus. "I had orders from the White Witch that if ever I saw a Son of Adam or a Daughter of Eve in the wood, I was to catch them and hand them over to her. And you are the first I ever met. And I've pretended to be your friend and asked you to tea, and all the time I've been meaning to wait till you were asleep and then go and tell *Her*."

"Oh, but you won't, Mr Tumnus," said Lucy. "You won't, will you? Indeed, indeed you really mustn't."

"And if I don't," said he, beginning to cry again, "she's sure to find out. And she'll have my tail cut off, and my horns sawn off, and my beard plucked out, and she'll wave her wand over my beautiful cloven hoofs and turn them into horrid solid hoofs like a wretched horse's. And if she is extra and specially angry she'll turn me into stone and I shall be only a statue of a Faun in her horrible house until the four thrones at Cair Paravel are filled – and goodness knows when that will happen, or whether it will ever happen at all."

"I'm very sorry, Mr Tumnus," said Lucy. "But please let me go home."

"Of course I will," said the Faun. "Of course I've got to. I see that now. I hadn't known what Humans were like before I met you. Of course I can't give you up to the Witch; not now that I know you. But we must be off at once. I'll see you back to the lamp-post. I suppose you can find your own way from there back to Spare Oom and War Drobe?"

"I'm sure I can," said Lucy.

"We must go as quietly as we can," said Mr

Tumnus. "The whole wood is full of *her* spies. Even some of the trees are on her side."

They both got up and left the tea things on the table, and Mr Tumnus once more put up his umbrella and gave Lucy his arm, and they went out into the snow. The journey back was not at all like the journey to the Faun's cave; they stole along as quickly as they could, without speaking a word, and Mr Tumnus kept to the darkest places. Lucy was relieved when they reached the lamp-post again.

"Do you know your way from here, Daughter of Eve?" said Tumnus.

Lucy looked very hard between the trees and could just see in the distance a patch of light that looked like daylight. "Yes," she said, "I can see the wardrobe door."

"Then be off home as quick as you can," said the Faun, "and – c-can you ever forgive me for what I meant to do?"

"Why, of course I can," said Lucy, shaking him heartily by the hand. "And I do hope you won't get into dreadful trouble on my account."

"Farewell, Daughter of Eve," said he. "Perhaps I may keep the handkerchief?"

"Rather!" said Lucy, and then ran towards the far off patch of daylight as quickly as her legs would carry her. And presently instead of rough branches brushing past her she felt coats, and instead of crunching snow under her feet she felt wooden boards, and all at once she found herself jumping out of the wardrobe into the same empty room from which the whole adventure had started. She shut the wardrobe door tightly behind her and looked around, panting for breath. It was still raining and she could hear the voices of the others in the passage.

"I'm here," she shouted. "I'm here. I've come back, I'm all right."

CHAPTER THREE

EDMUND AND THE WARDROBE

Lucy ran out of the empty room into the passage and found the other three.

"It's all right," she repeated, "I've come back."

"What on earth are you talking about, Lucy?" asked Susan.

"Why? said Lucy in amazement, "haven't you all been wondering where I was?"

"So you've been hiding, have you?" said Peter. "Poor old Lu, hiding and nobody noticed! You'll have to hide longer than that if you want people to start looking for you."

"But I've been away for hours and hours," said Lucy.

The others all stared at one another.

"Batty!" said Edmund, tapping his head. "Quite batty."

"What do you mean, Lu?" asked Peter.

"What I said," answered Lucy. "It was just after breakfast when I went into the wardrobe, and I've been away for hours and hours, and had tea, and all sorts of things have happened."

"Don't be silly, Lucy," said Susan. "We've only just come out of that room a moment ago, and you were there then."

"She's not being silly at all," said Peter, "she's just making up a story for fun, aren't you, Lu? And why shouldn't she?"

"No, Peter, I'm not," she said. "It's – it's a magic

wardrobe. There's a wood inside it, and it's snowing, and there's a Faun and a Witch and it's called Narnia; come and see."

The others did not know what to think, but Lucy was so excited that they all went back with her into the room. She rushed ahead of them, flung open the door of the wardrobe and cried, "Now! go in and see for yourselves."

"Why, you goose," said Susan, putting her head inside and pulling the fur coats apart, "it's just an ordinary wardrobe; look! there's the back of it."

Then everyone looked in and pulled the coats apart; and they all saw – Lucy herself saw – a perfectly ordinary wardrobe. There was no wood and no snow, only the back of the wardrobe, with hooks on it. Peter went in and rapped his knuckles on it to make sure that it was solid.

"A jolly good hoax, Lu," he said as he came out again; "you have really taken us in, I must admit. We half believed you."

"But it wasn't a hoax at all," said Lucy, "really and truly. It was all different a moment ago. Honestly it was. I promise."

"Come, Lu," said Peter, "that's going a bit far. You've had your joke. Hadn't you better drop it now?"

Lucy grew very red in the face and tried to say something, though she hardly knew what she was trying to say, and burst into tears.

For the next few days she was very miserable. She could have made it up with the others quite easily at any moment if she could have brought herself to say that the whole thing was only a story made up for fun. But Lucy was a very truthful girl and she knew that she was really in the right; and she could not bring herself to say this. The others who thought she was telling a lie, and a silly lie too, made her very unhappy. The two elder ones did this without meaning to do it, but Edmund could be spiteful, and on this occasion he was spiteful. He sneered and jeered at Lucy and kept on asking her if she'd found any other new countries in other cupboards all over the house. What made it worse was that these days ought to have been delightful. The weather was fine and they were out of doors from morning to night, bathing, fishing, climbing trees, and lying in the heather. But Lucy could not properly enjoy any of it. And so things went on until the next wet day.

That day, when it came to the afternoon and there was still no sign of a break in the weather, they decided to play hide-and-seek. Susan was "It" and as soon as the others scattered to hide, Lucy went to the room where the wardrobe was. She did not mean to hide in the wardrobe, because she knew that would only set the others talking again about the whole wretched business. But she did want to have one more look inside it; for by this time she was beginning to wonder herself whether Narnia and the Faun had not been a dream. The house was so large and complicated and full of hiding-places that she thought she would have time to have one look into the wardrobe and then hide somewhere else. But as soon as she reached it she heard steps in the passage outside, and then there was nothing for it but to jump into the wardrobe and hold the door closed behind her. She did not shut it properly because she knew that it is very silly to shut oneself into a wardrobe, even if it is not a magic one.

Now the steps she had heard were those of Edmund; and he came into the room just in time to see Lucy vanishing into the wardrobe. He at once decided to get into it himself – not because he thought it a particularly good place to hide but because he wanted to go on teasing her about her imaginary country. He opened the door. There were the coats hanging up as usual, and a smell of mothballs, and darkness and silence, and no sign of Lucy. "She thinks I'm Susan come to catch her," said Edmund to himself, "and so she's keeping very quiet in at the back." He jumped in and

shut the door, forgetting what a very foolish thing this is to do. Then he began feeling about for Lucy in the dark. He had expected to find her in a few seconds and was very surprised when he did not. He decided to open the door again and let in some light. But he could not find the door either. He didn't like this at all and began groping wildly in every direction; he even shouted out, "Lucy! Lu! Where are you? I know you're here."

There was no answer and Edmund noticed that his own voice had a curious sound – not the sound you expect in a cupboard, but a kind of open-air sound. He also noticed that he was unexpectedly cold; and then he saw a light.

"Thank goodness," said Edmund, "the door must have swung open of its own accord." He forgot all about Lucy and went towards the light, which he thought was the open door of the wardrobe. But instead of finding himself stepping out into the spare room he found himself stepping out from the shadow of some thick dark fir trees into an open place in the middle of a wood.

There was crisp, dry snow under his feet and more snow lying on the branches of the trees. Overhead there was pale blue sky, the sort of sky one sees on a fine winter day in the morning. Straight ahead of him he saw between the tree-trunks the sun, just rising, very red and clear. Everything was perfectly still, as if he were the only living creature in that country. There was not even a robin or a squirrel among the trees, and the wood stretched as far as he could see in every direction. He shivered.

He now remembered that he had been looking for Lucy; and also how unpleasant he had been to her about her "imaginary country" which now turned out not to have been imaginary at all. He thought that she must be somewhere quite close and so he shouted, "Lucy! Lucy! I'm here too – Edmund."

There was no answer.

"She's angry about all the things I've been saying lately," thought Edmund. And though he did not like to admit that he had been wrong, he also did not much like being alone in this strange, cold, quiet place; so he shouted again.

"I say, Lu! I'm sorry I didn't believe you. I see now you were right all along. Do come out. Make it Pax."

Still there was no answer.

"Just like a girl," said Edmund to himself, "sulking somewhere, and won't accept an apology." He looked round him again and decided he did not much like this place, and had almost made up his mind to go home, when he heard, very far off in the wood, a sound of bells. He listened and the sound came nearer and nearer and at last there swept into sight a sledge drawn by two reindeer.

The reindeer were about the size of Shetland ponies and their hair was so white that even the snow hardly looked white compared with them; their branching horns were gilded and shone like something on fire when the sunrise caught them. Their harness was of scarlet leather and covered with bells. On the sledge, driving the reindeer, sat a fat dwarf who would have been about three feet high if he had been standing. He was dressed in polar bear's fur and on his head he wore a red hood with a long gold tassel hanging down from its point; his huge beard covered his knees and served him instead of a rug. But behind him, on a much higher seat in the middle of the sledge sat a very different person – a great lady, taller than any woman that Edmund had ever seen. She also was covered in white fur up to her throat and held a long straight golden wand in her right hand and wore a golden crown on her head. Her face was white – not merely pale, but white like snow or paper or icing-sugar, except for her very red mouth. It was a beautiful face in other respects, but proud and cold and stern.

The sledge was a fine sight as it came sweeping to-wards Edmund with the bells jingling and the dwarf cracking his whip and the snow flying up on each side of it.

"Stop!" said the Lady, and the dwarf pulled the reindeer up so sharp that they almost sat down. Then they recovered themselves and stood champing their bits and blowing. In the frosty air the breath coming out of their nostrils looked like smoke.

"And what, pray, are you?" said the Lady, looking hard at Edmund.

"I'm – I'm – my name's Edmund," said Edmund rather awkwardly. He did not like the way she looked at him.

The Lady frowned, "Is that how you address a Queen?" she asked, looking sterner than ever.

"I beg your pardon, your Majesty, I didn't know," said Edmund.

"Not know the Queen of Narnia?" cried she. "Ha! You shall know us better hereafter. But I repeat — what are you?"

"Please, your Majesty," said Edmund, "I don't know what you mean. I'm at school — at least I was — it's the holidays now."

CHAPTER FOUR

TURKISH DELIGHT

"But what *are* you?" said the Queen again. "Are you a great overgrown dwarf that has cut off its beard?"

"No, your Majesty," said Edmund, "I never had a beard, I'm a boy."

"A boy!" said she. "Do you mean you are a Son of Adam?"

Edmund stood still, saying nothing. He was too confused by this time to understand what the question meant.

"I see you are an idiot, whatever else you may be," said the Queen. "Answer me, once and for all, or I shall lose my patience. Are you human?"

"Yes, your Majesty," said Edmund.

"And how, pray, did you come to enter my dominions?"

"Please, your Majesty, I came in through a wardrobe."

"A wardrobe? What do you mean?"

"I – I opened a door and just found myself here, your Majesty," said Edmund.

"Ha!" said the Queen, speaking more to herself than to him. "A door. A door from the world of men! I have heard of such things. This may wreck all. But he is only one, and he is easily dealt with." As she spoke these words she rose from her seat and looked Edmund full in the face, her eyes flaming; at the same moment she raised her wand. Edmund felt sure that she was going to do something dreadful but he seemed unable to move. Then, just as he gave himself up for lost, she appeared to change her mind.

"My poor child," she said in quite a different voice, "how cold you look! Come and sit with me here on the sledge and I will put my mantle round you and we will talk."

Edmund did not like this arrangement at all but he dared not disobey; he stepped on to the sledge and sat at her feet, and she put a fold of her fur mantle round him and tucked it well in.

"Perhaps something hot to drink?" said the Queen. "Should you like that?"

"Yes please, your Majesty," said Edmund, whose teeth were chattering.

The Queen took from somewhere among her wrappings a very small bottle which looked as if it were made of copper. Then, holding out her arm, she let one drop fall from it on the snow beside the sledge. Edmund saw the drop for a second in mid-air, shining like a diamond. But the moment it touched the snow there was a hissing sound and there stood a jewelled cup full of something that steamed. The dwarf immediately took this and handed it to Edmund with a bow and a smile; not a very nice smile. Edmund felt much better as he began to sip the hot drink. It was something he had never tasted before, very sweet and foamy and creamy, and it warmed him right down to his toes.

"It is dull, Son of Adam, to drink without eating," said the Queen presently. "What would you like best to eat?"

"Turkish Delight, please, your Majesty," said Edmund.

The Queen let another drop fall from her bottle on to the snow, and instantly there appeared a round box, tied with green silk ribbon, which, when opened, turned out to contain several pounds of the best Turkish Delight. Each piece was sweet and light to the very centre and Edmund had never tasted anything more delicious. He was quite warm now, and very comfortable.

While he was eating the Queen kept asking him questions. At first Edmund tried to remember that it is rude to speak with one's mouth full, but soon he forgot about this and thought only of trying to shovel down as much Turkish Delight as he could, and the more he ate the more he wanted to eat, and he never asked himself why the Queen should be so inquisitive. She got him to tell her that he had one brother and two sisters, and that one of his sisters had already been in Narnia and had met a Faun there, and that no one except himself and his brother and his sisters knew anything about Narnia. She seemed especially interested in the fact that there were four of them, and kept on coming back to it. "You are sure there are just four of you?" she asked. "Two Sons of Adam and two Daughters of Eve, neither more nor less?" and Edmund, with his mouth full of Turkish Delight, kept on saying, "Yes, I told you that before," and forgetting to call her "Your Majesty", but she didn't seem to mind now.

At last the Turkish Delight was all finished and Edmund was looking very hard at the empty box and wishing that she would ask him whether he would like some more. Probably the Queen knew quite well what he was thinking; for she knew, though Edmund did not, that this was enchanted Turkish Delight and that anyone who had once tasted it would want more and more of it, and would even, if they were allowed, go on eating it till they killed themselves. But she did not offer him any more. Instead, she said to him,

"Son of Adam, I should so much like to see your brother and your two sisters. Will you bring them to see me?"

"I'll try," said Edmund, still looking at the empty box.

"Because, if you did come again – bringing them with you of course – I'd be able to give you some more Turkish Delight. I can't do it now, the magic will only work once. In my own house it would be another matter."

"Why can't we go to your house now?" said Edmund. When he had first got on to the sledge he had been afraid that she might drive away with him to some unknown place from which he would not be able to get back; but he had forgotten about that fear now.

"It is a lovely place, my house," said the Queen. "I am sure you would like it. There are whole rooms full of Turkish Delight, and what's more, I have no children of my own. I want a nice boy whom I could bring up as a Prince and who would be King of Narnia when I am gone. While he was Prince he would wear a gold crown and eat Turkish Delight all day long; and you are much the cleverest and handsomest young man I've ever met. I think I would like to make you the Prince – some day, when you bring the others to visit me."

"Why not now?" said Edmund. His face had become very red and his mouth and fingers were sticky. He did not look either clever or handsome, whatever the Queen might say.

"Oh, but if I took you there now," said she, "I shouldn't see your brother and your sisters. I very much want to know your charming relations. You are to be the Prince and – later on – the King; that is understood. But you must have courtiers and nobles. I will make your brother a Duke and your sisters Duchesses."

"There's nothing special about *them*," said Edmund, "and, anyway, I could always bring them some other time."

"Ah, but once you were in my house," said the Queen, "you might forget all about them. You would be enjoying yourself so much that you wouldn't want the bother of going to fetch them. No. You must go back to your own country now and come to me another day, *with them*, you understand. It is no good coming without them."

"But I don't even know the way back to my own country," pleaded Edmund. "That's easy," answered the Queen. "Do you see that lamp?" She pointed with her wand and Edmund turned and saw the same lamp-post under which Lucy had met the Faun. "Straight on, beyond that, is the way to the World of Men. And now look the other way' — here she pointed in the opposite direction — "and tell me if you can see two little hills rising above the trees."

"I think I can," said Edmund.

"Well, my house is between those two hills. So next time you come you have only to find the lamp-post and look for those two hills and walk through the wood till you reach my house. But remember — you must bring the others with you. I might have to be very angry with you if you came alone."

"I'll do my best," said Edmund.

"And, by the way," said the Queen, "you needn't tell them about me. It would be fun to keep it a secret between us two, wouldn't it? Make it a surprise for them. Just bring them along to the two hills — a clever boy like you will easily think of some excuse for doing that — and when you come to my house you could just say "Let's see who lives here" or something like that. I am sure that would be best. If your sister has met one of the Fauns, she may have heard strange stories about me — nasty stories that might make her afraid to come to me. Fauns will say anything, you know, and now —"

"Please, please," said Edmund suddenly, "please couldn't I have just one piece of Turkish Delight to eat on the way home?"

"No, no," said the Queen with a laugh, "you must wait till next time." While she spoke, she signalled to the dwarf to drive on, but as the sledge swept away out of sight, the Queen waved to Edmund, calling out, "Next time! Next time! Don't forget. Come soon."

Edmund was still staring after the sledge when he heard someone calling his own name, and looking round he saw Lucy coming towards him from another part of the wood.

"Oh, Edmund!" she cried. "So you've got in too! Isn't it wonderful, and now –"

"All right," said Edmund, "I see you were right and it is a magic wardrobe after all. I'll say I'm sorry if you like. But where on earth have you been all this time? I've been looking for you everywhere."

"If I'd known you had got in I'd have waited for you," said Lucy, who was too happy and excited to notice how snappishly Edmund spoke or how flushed and strange his face was. "I've been having lunch with dear Mr Tumnus, the Faun, and he's very well and the White Witch has done nothing to him for letting me go, so he thinks she can't have found out and perhaps everything is going to be all right after all."

"The White Witch?" said Edmund; "who's she?"

"She is a perfectly terrible person," said Lucy. "She calls herself the Queen of Narnia though she has no right to be queen at all, and all the Fauns and Dryads and Naiads and Dwarfs and Animals – at least all the good ones – simply hate her. And she can turn people into stone and do all kinds of horrible things. And she has made a magic so that it is always winter in Narnia – always winter, but it never gets to Christmas. And she drives about on a sledge, drawn by reindeer, with her wand in her hand and a crown on her head."

Edmund was already feeling uncomfortable from having eaten too many sweets, and when he heard that the Lady he had made friends with was a dangerous witch he felt even more uncomfortable. But he still wanted to taste that Turkish Delight again more than he wanted anything else.

"Who told you all that stuff about the White Witch?" he asked.

"Mr Tumnus, the Faun," said Lucy.

"You can't always believe what Fauns say," said Edmund, trying to sound as if he knew far more about them than Lucy.

"Who said so?" asked Lucy.

"Everyone knows it," said Edmund; "ask anybody you like. But it's pretty poor sport standing here in the snow. Let's go home."

"Yes, let's," said Lucy. "Oh, Edmund, I *am* glad you've got in too. The others will have to believe in Narnia now that both of us have been there. What fun it will be!"

But Edmund secretly thought that it would not be as good fun for him as for her. He would have to admit that Lucy had been right, before all the others, and he felt sure the others would all be on the side of the Fauns and the animals; but he was already more than half on the side of the Witch. He did not know what he would say, or how he would keep his secret once they were all talking about Narnia.

By this time they had walked a good way. Then suddenly they felt coats around them instead of branches and next moment they were both standing outside the wardrobe in the empty room.

"I say," said Lucy, "you do look awful, Edmund. Don't you feel well?"

"I'm all right," said Edmund, but this was not true. He was feeling very sick.

"Come on then," said Lucy, "let's find the others. What a lot we shall have to tell them! And what wonderful adventures we shall have now that we're all in it together."

CHAPTER FIVE

BACK ON THIS SIDE OF THE DOOR

BECAUSE the game of hide-and-seek was still going on, it took Edmund and Lucy some time to find the others. But when at last they were all together (which happened in the long room, where the suit of armour was) Lucy burst out:

"Peter! Susan! It's all true. Edmund has seen it too. There *is* a country you can get to through the wardrobe. Edmund and I both got in. We met one another in there, in the wood. Go on, Edmund; tell them all about it."

"What's all this about, Ed?" said Peter.

And now we come to one of the nastiest things in this story. Up to that moment Edmund had been feeling sick, and sulky, and annoyed with Lucy for being right, but he hadn't made up his mind what to do. When Peter suddenly asked him the question he decided all at once to do the meanest and most spiteful thing he could think of. He decided to let Lucy down.

"Tell us, Ed," said Susan.

And Edmund gave a very superior look as if he were far older than Lucy (there was really only a year's difference) and then a little snigger and said, "Oh, yes, Lucy and I have been playing – pretending that all her story about a country in the wardrobe is true. Just for fun, of course. There's nothing there really."

Poor Lucy gave Edmund one look and rushed out of the room.

Edmund, who was becoming a nastier person every minute, thought that he had scored a great success, and went on at once to say, "There she goes again. What's the matter with her? That's the worst of young kids, they always —"

"Look here," said Peter, turning on him savagely, "shut up! You've been perfectly beastly to Lu ever since she started this nonsense about the wardrobe, and now you go playing games with her about it and setting her off again. I believe you did it simply out of spite."

"But it's all nonsense," said Edmund, very taken aback.

"Of course it's all nonsense," said Peter, "that's just the point. Lu was perfectly all right when we left home, but since we've been down here she seems to be either going queer in the head or else turning into a most frightful liar. But whichever it is, what good do you think you'll do by jeering and nagging at her one day and encouraging her the next?"

"I thought — I thought," said Edmund; but he couldn't think of anything to say.

"You didn't think anything at all," said Peter; "it's just spite. You've always liked being beastly to anyone smaller than yourself; we've seen that at school before now."

"Do stop it," said Susan; "it won't make things any better having a row between you two. Let's go and find Lucy."

It was not surprising that when they found Lucy, a good deal later, everyone could see that she had been crying. Nothing they could say to her made any difference. She stuck to her story and said:

"I don't care what you think, and I don't care what you say. You can tell the Professor or you can write to Mother or you can do anything you like. I know I've met a Faun in there and – I wish I'd stayed there and you are all beasts, beasts."

It was an unpleasant evening. Lucy was miserable and Edmund was beginning to feel that his plan wasn't working as well as he had expected. The two older ones were really beginning to think that Lucy was out of her mind. They stood in the passage talking about it in whispers long after she had gone to bed.

The result was the next morning they decided that they really would go and tell the whole thing to the Professor. "He'll write to Father if he thinks there is really something wrong with Lu," said Peter; "it's getting beyond us." So they went and knocked at the study door, and the Professor said "Come in," and got up and found chairs for them and said he was quite at their disposal. Then he sat listening to them with the tips of his fingers pressed together and never interrupting, till they had finished the whole story. After that he said nothing for quite a long time. Then he cleared his throat and said the last thing either of them expected:

"How do you know," he asked, "that your sister's story is not true?"

"Oh, but –" began Susan, and then stopped. Anyone could see from the old man's face that he was perfectly serious. Then Susan pulled herself together and said, "But Edmund said they had only been pretending."

"That is a point," said the Professor, "which

certainly deserves consideration; very careful consideration. For instance – if you will excuse me for asking the question – does your experience lead you to regard your brother or your sister as the more reliable? I mean, which is the more truthful?"

"That's just the funny thing about it, sir," said Peter. "Up ⁺ill now, I'd have said Lucy every time."

"And what do you think, my dear?" said the Professor, turning to Susan.

"Well," said Susan, "in general, I'd say the same as Peter, but this couldn't be true – all this about the wood and the Faun."

"That is more than I know," said the Professor, "and a charge of lying against someone whom you have always found truthful is a very serious thing; a very serious thing indeed."

"We were afraid it mightn't even be lying," said Susan; "we thought there might be something wrong with Lucy."

"Madness, you mean?" said the Professor quite coolly. "Oh, you can make your minds easy about that. One has only to look at her and talk to her to see that she is not mad."

"But then," said Susan, and stopped. She had never dreamed that a grown-up would talk like the Professor and didn't know what to think.

"Logic!" said the Professor half to himself. "Why don't they teach logic at these schools? There are only three possibilities. Either your sister is telling lies, or she is mad, or she is telling the truth. You know she doesn't tell lies and it is obvious that she is not mad. For the moment then and unless any further evidence turns up, we must assume that she is telling the truth."

Susan looked at him very hard and was quite sure from the expression on his face that he was not making fun of them.

"But how could it be true, sir?" said Peter.

"Why do you say that?" asked the Professor.

"Well, for one thing," said Peter, "if it was real why doesn't everyone find this country every time they go to the wardrobe? I mean, there was nothing there when we looked; even Lucy didn't pretend there was."

"What has that to do with it?" said the Professor.

"Well, sir, if things are real, they're there all the time."

"Are they?" said the Professor; and Peter did not know quite what to say.

"But there was no time," said Susan. "Lucy had had no time to have gone anywhere, even if there was such a place. She came running after us the very moment we were out of the room. It was less than a minute, and she pretended to have been away for hours."

"That is the very thing that makes her story so likely to be true," said the Professor. "If there really is a door in this house that leads to some other world (and I should warn you that this is a very strange house, and even I know very little about it) – if, I say, she had got into another world, I should not be at all surprised to find that the other world had a separate time of its own; so that however long you stayed there it would never take up any of *our* time. On the other hand, I don't think many girls of her age would invent that idea for themselves. If she had been pretending, she would have hidden for a reasonable time before coming out and telling her story."

"But do you really mean, sir," said Peter, "that

there could be other worlds – all over the place, just round the corner – like that?"

"Nothing is more probable," said the Professor, taking off his spectacles and beginning to polish them, while he muttered to himself, "I wonder what they *do* teach them at these schools."

"But what are we to do?" said Susan. She felt

that the conversation was beginning to get off the point.

"My dear young lady," said the Professor, suddenly looking up with a very sharp expression at both of them, "there is one plan which no one has yet suggested and which is well worth trying."

"What's that?" said Susan.

"We might all try minding our own business," said he. And that was the end of that conversation.

After this things were a good deal better for Lucy. Peter saw to it that Edmund stopped jeering at her, and neither she nor anyone else felt inclined to talk about the wardrobe at all. It had become a rather

alarming subject. And so for a time it looked as if all the adventures were coming to an end; but that was not to be.

This house of the Professor's – which even he knew so little about – was so old and famous that people from all over England used to come and ask permission to see over it. It was the sort of house that is mentioned in guide books and even in histories; and well it might be, for all manner of stories were told about it, some of them even stranger than the one I am telling you now. And when parties of sightseers arrived and asked to see the house, the Professor always gave them permission, and Mrs Macready, the housekeeper, showed them round, telling them about the pictures and the armour, and the rare books in the library. Mrs Macready was not fond of children, and did not like to be interrupted when she was telling visitors all the things she knew. She had said to Susan and Peter almost on the first morning (along with a good many other instructions), "And please remember you're to keep out of the way whenever I'm taking a party over the house."

"Just as if any of us would *want* to waste half the morning trailing round with a crowd of strange grown-ups!" said Edmund, and the other three thought the same. That was how the adventures began for the second time.

A few mornings later Peter and Edmund were looking at the suit of armour and wondering if they could take it to bits when the two girls rushed into the room and said, "Look out! Here comes the Macready and a whole gang with her."

"Sharp's the word," said Peter, and all four made off through the door at the far end of the room. But when they had got out into the Green Room and beyond it, into the Library, they suddenly heard voices ahead of them, and realized that Mrs

Macready must be bringing her party of sightseers up the back stairs – instead of up the front stairs as they had expected. And after that – whether it was that they lost their heads, or that Mrs Macready was trying to catch them, or that some magic in the house had come to life and was chasing them into Narnia – they seemed to find themselves being followed everywhere, until at last Susan said, "Oh bother those trippers! Here – let's get into the Wardrobe Room till they've passed. No one will follow us in there." But the moment they were inside they heard the voices in the passage – and then someone fumbling at the door – and then they saw the handle turning.

"Quick!" said Peter, "there's nowhere else," and flung open the wardrobe. All four of them bundled inside it and sat there, panting, in the dark. Peter held the door closed but did not shut it; for, of course, he remembered, as every sensible person does, that you should never never shut yourself up in a wardrobe.

CHAPTER SIX

INTO THE FOREST

"I wish the Macready would hurry up and take all these people away," said Susan presently, "I'm getting horribly cramped."

"And what a filthy smell of camphor!" said Edmund.

"I expect the pockets of these coats are full of it," said Susan, "to keep away the moths."

"There's something sticking into my back," said Peter.

"And isn't it cold?" said Susan.

"Now that you mention it, it is cold," said Peter, "and hang it all, it's wet too. What's the matter with this place? I'm sitting on something wet. It's getting wetter every minute." He struggled to his feet.

"Let's get out," said Edmund, "they've gone."

"O-o-oh!" said Susan suddenly, and everyone asked her what was the matter.

"I'm sitting against a tree," said Susan, "and look! It's getting light – over there."

"By jove, you're right," said Peter, "and look there – and there. It's trees all round. And this wet stuff is snow. Why, I do believe we've got into Lucy's wood after all."

And now there was no mistaking it and all four children stood blinking in the daylight of a winter day. Behind them were coats hanging on pegs, in front of them were snow-covered trees.

Peter turned at once to Lucy.

"I apologize for not believing you," he said, "I'm sorry. Will you shake hands?"

"Of course," said Lucy, and did.

"And now," said Susan, "what do we do next?"

"Do?" said Peter, "why, go and explore the wood, of course."

"Ugh!" said Susan, stamping her feet, "it's pretty cold. What about putting on some of these coats?"

"They're not ours," said Peter doubtfully.

"I am sure nobody would mind," said Susan; "it isn't as if we wanted to take them out of the house; we shan't take them even out of the wardrobe."

"I never thought of that, Su," said Peter. "Of course, now you put it that way, I see. No one could say you had bagged a coat as long as you leave it in the wardrobe where you found it. And I suppose this whole country is in the wardrobe."

They immediately carried out Susan's very sensible plan. The coats were rather too big for them so that they came down to their heels and looked more like royal robes than coats when they had put them on. But they all felt a good deal warmer and each thought the others looked better in their new get-up and more suitable to the landscape.

"We can pretend we are Arctic explorers," said Lucy.

"This is going to be exciting enough without pretending," said Peter, as he began leading the way forward into the forest. There were heavy darkish clouds overhead and it looked as if there might be more snow before night.

"I say," began Edmund presently, "oughtn't we to

be bearing a bit more to the left, that is, if we are aiming for the lamp-post?" He had forgotten for the moment that he must pretend never to have been in the wood before. The moment the words were out of his mouth he realized that he had given himself away. Everyone stopped; everyone stared at him. Peter whistled.

"So you really were here," he said, "that time Lu said she'd met you in here – and you made out she was telling lies."

There was a dead silence. "Well, of all the poisonous little beasts –" said Peter, and shrugged his shoulders and said no more. There seemed, indeed, no more to say, and presently the four resumed their journey; but Edmund was saying to himself, "I'll pay you all out for this, you pack of stuck-up, self-satisfied prigs."

"Where *are* we going anyway?" said Susan, chiefly for the sake of changing the subject.

"I think Lu ought to be the leader," said Peter; "goodness knows she deserves it. Where will you take us, Lu?"

"What about going to see Mr Tumnus?" said Lucy. "He's the nice Faun I told you about."

Everyone agreed to this and off they went walking briskly and stamping their feet. Lucy proved a good leader. At first she wondered whether she would be able to find the way, but she recognized an odd-looking tree on one place and a stump in another and brought them on to where the ground became uneven and into the little valley and at last to the very door of Mr Tumnus's cave. But there a terrible surprise awaited them.

The door had been wrenched off its hinges and broken to bits. Inside, the cave was dark and cold and had the damp feel and smell of a place that had not been lived in for several days. Snow had drifted in from the doorway and was heaped on the floor,

mixed with something black, which turned out to be the charred sticks and ashes from the fire. Someone had apparently flung it about the room and then stamped it out. The crockery lay smashed on the floor and the picture of the Faun's father had been slashed into shreds with a knife.

"This is a pretty good wash-out," said Edmund; "not much good coming here."

"What is this?" said Peter, stooping down. He had just noticed a piece of paper which had been nailed through the carpet to the floor.

"Is there anything written on it?" asked Susan.

"Yes, I think there is," answered Peter, "but I can't read it in this light. Let's get out into the open air."

They all went out in the daylight and crowded round Peter as he read out the following words:

The former occupant of these premises, the Faun Tumnus, is under arrest and awaiting his trial on a charge of High Treason against her Imperial Majesty Jadis, Queen of Narnia, Chatelaine of Cair Paravel, Empress of the Lone Islands, etc., also of comforting her said Majesty's enemies, harbouring spies and fraternizing with Humans.

> *signed* MAUGRIM, Captain of the Secret Police,
>
> LONG LIVE THE QUEEN!

The children stared at each other.

"I don't know that I'm going to like this place after all," said Susan.

"Who is this Queen, Lu?" said Peter. "Do you know anything about her?"

"She isn't a real queen at all," answered Lucy; "she's a horrible witch, the White Witch. Everyone – all the wood people – hate her. She has made an enchantment over the whole country so that it is always winter here and never Christmas."

"I – I wonder if there's any point in going on," said Susan. "I mean, it doesn't seem particularly safe here and it looks as if it won't be much fun either. And it's getting colder every minute, and we've brought nothing to eat. What about just going home?"

"Oh, but we can't, we can't," said Lucy suddenly; "don't you see? We can't just go home, not after this. It is all on my account that the poor Faun has got into this trouble. He hid me from the Witch and showed me the way back. That's what it means by comforting the Queen's enemies and fraternizing with Humans. We simply must try to rescue him."

"A lot *we* could do! said Edmund, "when we haven't even got anything to eat!"

"Shut up – you!" said Peter, who was still very angry with Edmund. "What do you think, Susan?"

"I've a horrid feeling that Lu is right," said Susan. "I don't want to go a step further and I wish we'd never come. But I think we must try to do something for Mr Whatever-his-name is – I mean the Faun."

"That's what I feel too," said Peter. "I'm worried about having no food with us. I'd vote for going back and getting something from the larder, only there doesn't seem to be any certainty of getting into this country again when once you've got out of it. I think we'll have to go on."

"So do I," said both the girls.

"If only we knew where the poor chap was imprisoned!" said Peter.

They were all still wondering what to do next, when Lucy said, "Look! There's a robin, with such a red breast. It's the first bird I've seen here. I say! – I wonder can birds talk in Narnia? It almost looks as if it wanted to say something to us." Then she turned to the Robin and said, "Please, can you tell us where Tumnus the Faun has been taken to?" As she said this she took a step towards the bird. It at once flew away but only as far as to the next tree. There it perched and looked at them very hard as if it understood all they had been saying. Almost without noticing that they had done so, the four children went a step or two nearer to it. At this the Robin flew away again to the next tree and once more looked at them very hard. (You couldn't have found a robin with a redder chest or a brighter eye.)

"Do you know," said Lucy, "I really believe he means us to follow him."

"I've an idea he does," said Susan. "What do you think, Peter?"

"Well, we might as well try it," answered Peter. The Robin appeared to understand the matter thoroughly. It kept going from tree to tree, always a few yards ahead of them, but always so near that they could easily follow it. In this way it led them on, slightly downhill. Wherever the Robin alighted a little shower of snow would fall off the branch. Presently the clouds parted overhead and the winter sun came out and the snow all around them grew dazzlingly bright. They had been travelling in this way for about half an hour, with the two girls in front, when Edmund said to Peter, "if you're not still too high and mighty to talk to me, I've something to say which you'd better listen to."

"What is it?" asked Peter.

"Hush! Not so loud," said Edmund; "there's no good frightening the girls. But have you realized what we're doing?"

"What?" said Peter, lowering his voice to a whisper.

"We're following a guide we know nothing about. How do we know which side that bird is on? Why shouldn't it be leading us into a trap?"

"That's a nasty idea. Still – a robin, you know. They're good birds in all the stories I've ever read. I'm sure a robin wouldn't be on the wrong side."

"It if comes to that, which *is* the right side? How do we know that the Fauns are in the right and the Queen (yes, I know we've been *told* she's a witch) is in the wrong? We don't really know anything about either."

"The Faun saved Lucy."

"He *said* he did. But how do we know? And there's another thing too. Has anyone the least idea of the way home from here?"

"Great Scott!" said Peter, "I hadn't thought of that."

"And no chance of dinner either," said Edmund.

CHAPTER SEVEN

A DAY WITH THE BEAVERS

WHILE the two boys were whispering behind, both the girls suddenly cried "Oh!" and stopped.

"The robin!" cried Lucy, "the robin. It's flown away." And so it had – right out of sight.

"And now what are we to do?" said Edmund, giving Peter a look which was as much as to say "What did I tell you?"

"Sh! Look!" said Susan.

"What?" said Peter.

"There's something moving among the trees over there to the left."

They all stared as hard as they could, and no one felt very comfortable.

"There it goes again," said Susan presently.

"I saw it that time too," said Peter. "It's still there. It's just gone behind that big tree."

"What is it?" asked Lucy, trying very hard not to sound nervous.

"Whatever it is," said Peter, "it's dodging us. It's something that doesn't want to be seen."

"Let's go home," said Susan. And then, though nobody said it out loud, everyone suddenly realized the same fact that Edmund had whispered to Peter at the end of the last chapter. They were lost.

"What's it like?" said Lucy.

"It's – it's a kind of animal," said Susan; and then, "Look! Look! Quick! There it is."

They all saw it this time, a whiskered furry face

which had looked out at them from behind a tree. But this time it didn't immediately draw back. Instead, the animal put its paw against its mouth just as humans put their finger on their lips when they are signalling to you to be quiet. Then it disappeared again. The children all stood holding their breath.

A moment later the stranger came out from behind the tree, glanced all round as if it were afraid someone was watching, said "Hush", made signs to them to join it in the thicker bit of wood where it was standing, and then once more disappeared.

"I know what it is," said Peter; "it's a beaver. I saw the tail."

"It wants us to go to it," said Susan, "and it is warning us not to make a noise."

"I know," said Peter. "The question is, are we to go to it or not? What do you think, Lu?"

"I think it's a nice beaver," said Lucy.

"Yes, but how do we *know*?" said Edmund.

"Shan't we have to risk it?" said Susan. "I mean,

it's no good just standing here and I feel I want some dinner."

At this moment the Beaver again popped its head out from behind the tree and beckoned earnestly to them.

"Come on," said Peter, "let's give it a try. All keep

close together. We ought to be a match for one beaver if it turns out to be an enemy."

So the children all got close together and walked up to the tree and in behind it, and there, sure enough, they found the Beaver; but it still drew back, saying to them in a hoarse throaty whisper, "Further in, come further in. Right in here. We're not safe in the open!"

Only when it had led them into a dark spot where four trees grew so close together that their boughs met and the brown earth and pine needles could be seen underfoot because no snow had been able to fall there, did it begin to talk to them.

"Are you the Sons of Adam and the Daughters of Eve?" it said.

"We're some of them," said Peter.

"S-s-s-sh!" said the Beaver, "not so loud please. We're not safe even here."

"Why, who are you afraid of?" said Peter. "There's no one here but ourselves."

"There are the trees," said the Beaver. "They're always listening. Most of them are on our side, but there *are* trees that would betray us to *her*; you know who I mean," and it nodded its head several times.

"If it comes to talking about sides," said Edmund, "how do we know you're a friend?"

"Not meaning to be rude, Mr Beaver," added Peter, "but you see, we're strangers."

"Quite right, quite right," said the Beaver. "Here is my token." With these words it held up to them a little white object. They all looked at it in surprise, till suddenly Lucy said, "Oh, of course. It's my handkerchief – the one I gave to poor Mr Tumnus."

"That's right," said the Beaver. "Poor fellow, he got wind of the arrest before it actually happened and handed this over to me. He said that if anything happened to him I must meet you here and take you on to –" Here the Beaver's voice sank into silence and it gave one or two very mysterious nods. Then signalling to the children to stand as close around it as they possibly could, so that their faces were actually tickled by its whiskers, it added in a low whisper –

"They say Aslan is on the move – perhaps has already landed."

And now a very curious thing happened. None of the children knew who Aslan was any more than you do; but the moment the Beaver had spoken these words everyone felt quite different. Perhaps it has sometimes happened to you in a dream that someone says something which you don't understand but in the dream it feels as if it had some enormous meaning – either a terrifying one which turns the whole dream into a nightmare or else a lovely meaning too lovely to put into words, which makes the dream so beautiful that you remember it all your life and are always wishing you could get into that dream again. It was like that now. At the name of Aslan each one of the children felt something jump in its inside. Edmund felt a sensation of mysterious horror. Peter felt suddenly brave and adventurous. Susan felt as if some delicious smell or some delightful strain of music had just floated by her. And Lucy got the feeling you have when you wake up in the morning and realize that it is the beginning of the holidays or the beginning of summer.

"And what about Mr Tumnus," said Lucy; "where is he?"

"S-s-s-sh," said the Beaver, "not here. I must bring you where we can have a real talk and also dinner."

No one except Edmund felt any difficulty about trusting the beaver now, and everyone, including Edmund, was very glad to hear the word "dinner".

They therefore all hurried along behind their new friend who led them at a surprisingly quick pace, and always in the thickest parts of the forest, for over an hour. Everyone was feeling very tired and very hungry when suddenly the trees began to get thinner in front of them and the ground to fall steeply downhill. A minute later they came out under the open sky (the sun was still shining) and found themselves looking down on a fine sight.

They were standing on the edge of a steep, narrow valley at the bottom of which ran – at least it would have been running if it hadn't been frozen – a fairly large river. Just below them a dam had been built across this river, and when they saw it everyone suddenly remembered that of course beavers are always making dams and felt quite sure that Mr Beaver had made this one. They also noticed that he now had a sort of modest expression on his face – the sort of look people have when you are visiting a garden they've made or reading a story they've written. So it was only common politeness when Susan said, "What a lovely dam!" And Mr Beaver didn't say "Hush" this time but "Merely a trifle! Merely a trifle! And it isn't really finished!"

Above the dam there was what ought to have been a deep pool but was now, of course, a level floor of dark green ice. And below the dam, much lower down, was more ice, but instead of being smooth this was all frozen into the foamy and wavy shapes in which the water had been rushing along at the very moment when the frost came. And where the water had been trickling over and spurting through the dam there was now a glittering wall of icicles, as if the side of the dam had been covered all over with flowers and wreaths and festoons of the purest sugar. And out in the middle, and partly on top of the dam was a funny little house shaped rather like an enormous beehive and from a hole in the roof smoke was going up, so that when you saw it (especially if you were hungry) you at once thought of cooking and became hungrier than you were before.

That was what the others chiefly noticed, but Edmund noticed something else. A little lower down the river there was another small river which came down another small valley to join it. And looking up that valley, Edmund could see two small hills, and he was almost sure they were the two hills which the White Witch had pointed out to him when he parted from her at the lamp-post that other day. And then between them, he thought, must be her palace, only a mile off or less. And he thought about Turkish Delight and about being a King ("And I wonder how Peter will like that?" he asked himself) and horrible ideas came into his head.

"Here we are," said Mr Beaver, "and it looks as if Mrs Beaver is expecting us. I'll lead the way. But be careful and don't slip."

The top of the dam was wide enough to walk on, though not (for humans) a very nice place to walk because it was covered with ice, and though the frozen pool was level with it on one side, there was a nasty drop to the lower river on the other. Along this route Mr Beaver led them in single file right out to the middle where they could look a long way up the river and a long way down it. And when they had reached the middle they were at the door of the house.

"Here we are, Mrs Beaver," said Mr Beaver, "I've found them. Here are the Sons and Daughters of Adam and Eve' – and they all went in.

The first thing Lucy noticed as she went in was a

burring sound, and the first thing she saw was a kind-looking old she-beaver sitting in the corner with a thread in her mouth working busily at her sewing machine, and it was from it that the sound came. She stopped her work and got up as soon as the children came in.

"So you've come at last!" she said, holding out both her wrinkled old paws. "At last! To think that ever I should live to see this day! The potatoes are on boiling and the kettle's singing and I daresay, Mr Beaver, you'll get us some fish."

"That I will," said Mr Beaver, and he went out of the house (Peter went with him), and across the ice of the deep pool to where he had a little hole in the ice which he kept open every day with his hatchet. They took a pail with them. Mr Beaver sat down quietly at the edge of the hole (he didn't seem to mind it being so chilly), looked hard into it, then suddenly shot in his paw, and before you could say Jack Robinson had

whisked out a beautiful trout. Then he did it all over again until they had a fine catch of fish.

Meanwhile the girls were helping Mrs Beaver to fill the kettle and lay the table and cut the bread and put the plates in the oven to heat and draw a huge jug of beer for Mr Beaver from a barrel which stood in one corner of the house, and to put on the frying-pan and get the dripping hot. Lucy thought the Beavers had a very snug little home though it was not at all like Mr Tumnus's cave. There were no books or pictures, and instead of beds there were bunks, like on board ship, built into the wall. And there were hams and strings of onions hanging from the roof, and against the walls were gum boots and oilskins and hatchets and pairs of shears and spades and trowels and things for carrying mortar in and fishing-rods and fishing-nets and sacks. And the cloth on the table, though very clean, was very rough.

Just as the frying-pan was nicely hissing Peter and Mr Beaver came in with the fish which Mr Beaver had already opened with his knife and cleaned out in the open air. You can think how good the new-caught fish smelled while they were frying and how the hungry children longed for them to be done and how very much hungrier still they had become before Mr Beaver said, "Now we're nearly ready." Susan drained the potatoes and then put them all back in the empty pot to dry on the side of the range while Lucy was helping Mrs Beaver to dish up the trout, so that in a very few minutes everyone was drawing up their stools (it was all three-legged stools in the Beavers' house except for Mrs Beaver's own special rocking-chair beside the fire) and preparing to enjoy themselves. There was a jug of creamy milk for the children (Mr Beaver stuck to beer) and a great big lump of deep yellow butter in the middle of the table from which everyone took as much as he wanted to go with his potatoes, and all the children thought

– and I agree with them – that there's nothing to beat
good freshwater fish if you eat it when it has been
alive half an hour ago and has come out of the pan

half a minute ago. And when they had finished the
fish Mrs Beaver brought unexpectedly out of the oven
a great and gloriously sticky marmalade roll, steam-

ing hot, and at the same time moved the kettle on to the fire, so that when they had finished the marmalade roll the tea was made and ready to be poured out. And when each person had got his (or her) cup of tea, each person shoved back his (or her) stool so as to be able to lean against the wall and gave a long sigh of contentment.

"And now," said Mr Beaver, pushing away his empty beer mug and pulling his cup of tea towards him, "if you'll just wait till I've got my pipe lit up and going nicely – why, now we can get to business. It's snowing again," he added, cocking his eye at the window. "That's all the better, because it means we shan't have any visitors; and if anyone should have been trying to follow you, why he won't find any tracks."

CHAPTER EIGHT

WHAT HAPPENED AFTER DINNER

"AND now," said Lucy, "do please tell us what's happened to Mr Tumnus."

"Ah, that's bad," said Mr Beaver, shaking his head. "That's a very, very bad business. There's no doubt he was taken off by the police. I got that from a bird who saw it done."

"But where's he been taken to?" asked Lucy.

"Well, they were heading northwards when they were last seen and we all know what that means."

"No, *we* don't," said Susan. Mr Beaver shook his head in a very gloomy fashion.

"I'm afraid it means they were taking him to her House," he said.

"But what'll they do to him, Mr Beaver?" gasped Lucy.

"Well," said Mr Beaver, "you can't exactly say for sure. But there's not many taken in there that ever comes out again. Statues. All full of statues they say it is – in the courtyard and up the stairs and in the hall. People she's turned" – (he paused and shuddered) "turned into stone."

"But, Mr Beaver," said Lucy, "can't we – I mean we *must* do something to save him. It's too dreadful and it's all on my account."

"I don't doubt you'd save him if you could, dearie," said Mrs Beaver, "but you've no chance of getting into that House against her will and ever coming out alive."

"Couldn't we have some stratagem?" said Peter. "I mean couldn't we dress up as something, or pretend to be – oh, pedlars or anything – or watch till she was gone out – or – oh, hang it all, there must be *some* way. This Faun saved my sister at his own risk, Mr Beaver. We can't just leave him to be – to be – to have that done to him."

"It's no good, Son of Adam," said Mr Beaver, "no good *your* trying, of all people. But now that Aslan is on the move –"

"Oh, yes! Tell us about Aslan!" said several voices at once; for once again that strange feeling – like the first signs of spring, like good news, had come over them.

"Who is Aslan?" asked Susan.

"Aslan?" said Mr Beaver. "Why, don't you know? He's the King. He's the Lord of the whole wood, but not often here, you understand. Never in my time or my father's time. But the word has reached us that he has come back. He is in Narnia at this moment. He'll settle the White Queen all right. It is he, not you, that will save Mr Tumnus."

"She won't turn him into stone too?" said Edmund.

"Lord love you, Son of Adam, what a simple thing to say!" answered Mr Beaver with a great laugh. "Turn *him* into stone? If she can stand on her two feet and look him in the face it'll be the most she can do and more than I expect of her. No, no. He'll put all to rights as it says in an old rhyme in these parts:

Wrong will be right, when Aslan comes in sight,
At the sound of his roar, sorrows will be no more,
When he bares his teeth, winter meets its death,
And when he shakes his mane, we shall have spring
again.

You'll understand when you see him."

"But shall we see him?" asked Susan.

"Why, Daughter of Eve, that's what I brought you here for. I'm to lead you where you shall meet him," said Mr Beaver.

"Is – is he a man?" asked Lucy.

"Aslan a man!" said Mr Beaver sternly. "Certainly not. I tell you he is the King of the wood and the son of the great Emperor-beyond-the-Sea. Don't you know who is the King of Beasts? Aslan is a lion – *the* Lion, the great Lion."

"Ooh!" said Susan, "I'd thought he was a man. Is he – quite safe? I shall feel rather nervous about meeting a lion."

"That you will, dearie, and no mistake," said Mrs Beaver; "if there's anyone who can appear before Aslan without their knees knocking, they're either braver than most or else just silly."

"Then he isn't safe?" said Lucy.

"Safe?" said Mr Beaver; "don't you hear what Mrs Beaver tells you? Who said anything about safe? 'Course he isn't safe. But he's good. He's the King, I tell you."

"I'm longing to see him," said Peter, "even if I do feel frightened when it comes to the point."

"That's right, Son of Adam," said Mr Beaver, bring-ing his paw down on the table with a crash that made all the cups and saucers rattle. "And so you shall. Word has been sent that you *are* to meet him, tomorrow if you can, at the Stone Table."

"Where's that?" said Lucy.

"I'll show you," said Mr Beaver. "It's down the river, a good step from here. I'll take you to it!"

"But meanwhile what about poor Mr Tumnus?" said Lucy.

"The quickest way you can help him is by going to meet Aslan," said Mr Beaver, "once he's with us, then we can begin doing things. Not that we don't need you too. For that's another of the old rhymes:

When Adam's flesh and Adam's bone
Sits at Cair Paravel in throne,
The evil time will be over and done.

So things must be drawing near their end now he's come and you've come. We've heard of Aslan coming into these parts before – long ago, nobody can say when. But there's never been any of your race here before."

"That's what I don't understand, Mr Beaver," said Peter, "I mean isn't the Witch herself human?"

"She'd like us to believe it," said Mr Beaver, "and it's on that that she bases her claim to be Queen. But she's no Daughter of Eve. She comes of your father Adam's" – (here Mr Beaver bowed) "your father Adam's first wife, her they called Lilith. And she was one of the Jinn. That's what she comes from on one side. And on the other she comes of the giants. No, no, there isn't a drop of real human blood in the Witch."

"That's why she's bad all through, Mr Beaver," said Mrs Beaver.

"True enough, Mrs Beaver," replied he, "there may be two views about humans (meaning no offence to the present company). But there's no two views about things that look like humans and aren't."

"I've known good Dwarfs," said Mrs Beaver.

"So've I, now you come to speak of it," said her husband, "but precious few, and they were the ones least like men. But in general, take my advice, when you meet anything that's going to be human and isn't yet, or used to be human once and isn't now, or ought to be human and isn't, you keep your eyes on it and feel for your hatchet. And that's why the Witch is always on the lookout for any humans in Narnia. She's been watching for you this many a year, and if she knew there were four of you she'd be more dangerous still."

"What's that to do with it?" asked Peter.

"Because of another prophecy," said Mr Beaver. "Down at Cair Paravel – that's the castle on the sea coast down at the mouth of this river which ought to be the capital of the whole country if all was as it should be – down at Cair Paravel there are four thrones and it's a saying in Narnia time out of mind that when two Sons of Adam and two Daughters of Eve sit in those four thrones, then it will be the end not only of the White Witch's reign but of her life, and that is why we had to be so cautious as we came along, for if she knew about you four, your lives wouldn't be worth a shake of my whiskers!"

All the children had been attending so hard to what Mr Beaver was telling them that they had noticed nothing else for a long time. Then during the moment of silence that followed his last remark, Lucy suddenly said:

"I say – where's Edmund?"

There was a dreadful pause, and then everyone began asking "Who saw him last? How long has he been missing? Is he outside? and then all rushed to the door and looked out. The snow was falling thickly and steadily, the green ice of the pool had vanished under a thick white blanket, and from where the little house

stood in the centre of the dam you could hardly see either bank. Out they went, plunging well over their ankles into the soft new snow, and went round the house in every direction. "Edmund! Edmund!" they called till they were hoarse. But the silently falling snow seemed to muffle their voices and there was not even an echo in answer.

"How perfectly dreadful!" said Susan as they at last came back in despair. "Oh, how I wish we'd never come."

"What on earth are we to do, Mr Beaver?" said Peter.

"Do?" said Mr Beaver, who was already putting on his snow-boots, "do? We must be off at once. We haven't a moment to spare!"

"We'd better divide into four search parties," said Peter, "and all go in different directions. Whoever finds him must come back here at once and —"

"Search parties, Son of Adam?" said Mr Beaver; "what for?"

"Why, to look for Edmund, of course!"

"There's no point in looking for him," said Mr Beaver.

"What do you mean?" said Susan. "He can't be far away yet. And we've got to find him. What do you mean when you say there's no use looking for him?"

"The reason there's no use looking," said Mr Beaver, "is that we know already where he's gone!" Everyone stared in amazement. "Don't you understand?" said Mr Beaver. "He's gone to *her*, to the White Witch. He has betrayed us all."

"Oh, surely — oh, really!" said Susan, "he can't have done that."

"Can't he?" said Mr Beaver, looking very hard at the three children, and everything they wanted to say died on their lips, for each felt suddenly quite certain inside that this was exactly what Edmund had done.

"But will he know the way?" said Peter.

"Has he been in this country before?" asked Mr Beaver. "Has he ever been here alone?"

"Yes," said Lucy, almost in a whisper. "I'm afraid he has."

"And did he tell you what he'd done or who he'd met?"

"Well, no, he didn't," said Lucy.

"Then mark my words," said Mr Beaver, "he has already met the White Witch and joined her side, and been told where she lives. I didn't like to mention it before (he being your brother and all) but the moment I set eyes on that brother of yours I said to myself 'Treacherous'. He had the look of one who has been with the Witch and eaten her food. You can always tell them if you've lived long in Narnia; something about their eyes."

"All the same," said Peter in a rather choking sort of voice, "we'll still have to go and look for him. He is our brother after all, even if he is rather a little beast. And he's only a kid."

"Go to the Witch's House?" said Mrs Beaver. "Don't you see that the only chance of saving either him or yourselves is to keep away from her?"

"How do you mean?" said Lucy.

"Why, all she wants is to get all four of you (she's thinking all the time of those four thrones at Cair Paravel). Once you were all four inside her House her job would be done – and there'd be four new statues in her collection before you'd had time to speak. But she'll keep him alive as long as he's the only one she's got, because she'll want to use him as a decoy; as bait to catch the rest of you with."

"Oh, can *no* one help us?" wailed Lucy.

"Only Aslan," said Mr Beaver, "we must go on and meet him. That's our only chance now."

"It seems to me, my dears," said Mrs Beaver, "that it

is very important to know just *when* he slipped away. How much he can tell her depends on how much he heard. For instance, had we started talking of Aslan before he left? If not, then we may do very well, for she won't know that Aslan has come to Narnia, or that we are meeting him, and will be quite off her guard as far as *that* is concerned."

"I don't remember his being here when we were talking about Aslan —" began Peter, but Lucy interrupted him.

"Oh yes, he was," she said miserably; "don't you remember, it was he who asked whether the Witch couldn't turn Aslan into stone too?"

"So he did, by Jove," said Peter; "just the sort of thing he would say, too!"

"Worse and worse," said Mr Beaver, "and the next thing is this. Was he still here when I told you that the place for meeting Aslan was the Stone Table?"

And of course no one knew the answer to this question.

"Because, if he was," continued Mr Beaver, "then she'll simply sledge down in that direction and get between us and the Stone Table and catch us on our way down. In fact we shall be cut off from Aslan."

"But that isn't what she'll do first," said Mrs Beaver, "not if I know her. The moment that Edmund tells her that we're all here she'll set out to catch us this very night, and if he's been gone about half an hour, she'll be here in about another twenty minutes."

"You're right, Mrs Beaver," said her husband, "we must all get away from here. There's not a moment to lose."

CHAPTER NINE

IN THE WITCH'S HOUSE

AND now of course you want to know what had happened to Edmund. He had eaten his share of the dinner, but he hadn't really enjoyed it because he was thinking all the time about Turkish Delight – and there's nothing that spoils the taste of good ordinary food half so much as the memory of bad magic food. And he had heard the conversation, and hadn't enjoyed it much either, because he kept on thinking that the others were taking no notice of him and trying to give him the cold shoulder. They weren't, but he imagined it. And then he had listened until Mr Beaver told them about Aslan and until he had heard the whole arrangement for meeting Aslan at the Stone Table. It was then that he began very quietly to edge himself under the curtain which hung over the door. For the mention of Aslan gave him a mysterious and horrible feeling just as it gave the others a mysterious and lovely feeling.

Just as Mr Beaver had been repeating the rhyme about *Adam's flesh and Adam's bone* Edmund had been very quietly turning the door-handle; and just before Mr Beaver had begun telling them that the White Witch wasn't really human at all but half a Jinn and half a giantess, Edmund had got outside into the snow and cautiously closed the door behind him.

You mustn't think that even now Edmund was quite so bad that he actually wanted his brother and sisters to be turned into stone. He did want Turkish

Delight and to be a Prince (and later a King) and to
pay Peter out for calling him a beast. As for what the
Witch would do with the others, he didn't want her to
be particularly nice to them – certainly not to put
them on the same level as himself; but he managed to
believe, or to pretend he believed, that she wouldn't
do anything very bad to them, "Because," he said to
himself, "all these people who say nasty things about
her are her enemies and probably half of it isn't true.
She was jolly nice to me, anyway, much nicer than
they are. I expect she is the rightful Queen really.
Anyway, she'll be better than that awful Aslan!" At
least, that was the excuse he made in his own mind
for what he was doing. It wasn't a very good excuse,
however, for deep down inside him he really knew
that the White Witch was bad and cruel.

The first thing he realized when he got outside and
found the snow falling all round him, was that he had
left his coat behind in the Beavers' house. And of
course there was no chance of going back to get it
now. The next thing he realized was that the daylight
was almost gone, for it had been nearly three o'clock
when they sat down to dinner and the winter days
were short. He hadn't reckoned on this; but he had to
make the best of it. So he turned up his collar and
shuffled across the top of the dam (luckily it wasn't so
slippery since the snow had fallen) to the far side of
the river.

It was pretty bad when he reached the far side. It
was growing darker every minute and what with that
and the snowflakes swirling all round him he could
hardly see three feet ahead. And then too there was

no road. He kept slipping into deep drifts of snow, and skidding on frozen puddles, and tripping over fallen tree-trunks, and sliding down steep banks, and barking his shins against rocks, till he was wet and cold and bruised all over. The silence and the

loneliness were dreadful. In fact I really think he might have given up the whole plan and gone back and owned up and made friends with the others, if he hadn't happened to say to himself, "When I'm King of Narnia the first thing I shall do will be to make some decent roads." And of course that set him off thinking about being a King and all the other things he would do and this cheered him up a good deal. He had just settled in his mind what sort of palace he would have and how many cars and all about his private cinema and where the principal railways would run and what laws he would make against beavers and dams and was putting the finishing touches to some schemes for keeping Peter in his place, when the weather changed. First the snow stopped. Then a wind sprang up and it became freezing cold. Finally, the clouds rolled away and the moon came out. It was a full moon and, shining on all that snow, it made everything almost as bright as day – only the shadows were rather confusing.

He would never have found his way if the moon hadn't come out by the time he got to the other river – you remember he had seen (when they first arrived at the Beavers') a smaller river flowing into the great one lower down. He now reached this and turned to follow it up. But the little valley down which it came was much steeper and rockier than the one he had just left and much overgrown with bushes, so that he could not have managed it at all in the dark. Even as it was, he got wet through for he had to stoop under branches and great loads of snow came sliding off on to his back. And every time this happened he thought more and more how he hated Peter – just as if all this had been Peter's fault.

But at last he came to a part where it was more level and the valley opened out. And there, on the other side of the river, quite close to him, in the middle of a little plain between two hills, he saw what must be the White Witch's House. And the moon was shining brighter than ever. The House was really a small castle. It seemed to be all towers; little towers with long pointed spires on them, sharp as needles. They looked like huge dunce's caps or sorcerer's caps. And they shone in the moonlight and their long shadows looked strange on the snow. Edmund began to be afraid of the House.

But it was too late to think of turning back now.

He crossed the river on the ice and walked up to the House. There was nothing stirring; not the slightest sound anywhere. Even his own feet made no noise on the deep newly fallen snow. He walked on and on, past corner after corner of the House, and past turret after turret to find the door. He had to go right round

to the far side before he found it. It was a huge arch but the great iron gates stood wide open.

Edmund crept up to the arch and looked inside into the courtyard, and there he saw a sight that nearly made his heart stop beating. Just inside the gate, with the moonlight shining on it, stood an enormous lion crouched as if it was ready to spring. And Edmund stood in the shadow of the arch, afraid to go on and afraid to go back, with his knees knocking together. He stood there so long that his teeth would have been chattering with cold even if they had not been chattering with fear. How long this really lasted I don't know, but it seemed to Edmund to last for hours.

Then at last he began to wonder why the lion was

standing so still – for it hadn't moved one inch since he first set eyes on it. Edmund now ventured a little nearer, still keeping in the shadow of the arch as much as he could. He now saw from the way the lion was standing that it couldn't have been looking at him at all. ("But supposing it turns its head?" thought Edmund.) In fact it was staring at something else – namely a little dwarf who stood with his back to it about four feet away. "Aha!" thought Edmund. "When it springs at the dwarf then will be my chance to escape." But still the lion never moved, nor did the dwarf. And now at last Edmund remembered what the others had said about the White Witch turning people into stone. Perhaps this was only a stone lion. And as soon as he had thought of that he noticed that the lion's back and the top of its head were covered with snow. Of course it must be only a statue! No living animal would have let itself get covered with snow. Then very slowly and with his heart beating as if it would burst, Edmund ventured to go up to the lion. Even now he hardly dared to touch it, but at last he put out his hand, very quickly, and did. It was cold stone. He had been frightened of a mere statue!

The relief which Edmund felt was so great that in spite of the cold he suddenly got warm all over right down to his toes, and at the same time there came into his head what seemed a perfectly lovely idea. "Probably," he thought, "this is the great Lion Aslan that they were all talking about. She's caught him already and turned him into stone. So *that's* the end of all their fine ideas about him! Pooh! Who's afraid of Aslan?"

And he stood there gloating over the stone lion, and presently he did something very silly and childish. He took a stump of lead pencil out of his pocket and scribbled a moustache on the lion's upper lip and then a pair of spectacles on its eyes. Then he said, "Yah! Silly old Aslan! How do you like being a stone? You thought yourself mighty fine, didn't you?" But in spite of the scribbles on it the face of the great stone beast still looked so terrible, and sad, and noble, staring up in the moonlight, that Edmund didn't really get any fun out of jeering at it. He turned away and began to cross the courtyard.

As he got into the middle of it he saw that there were dozens of statues all about – standing here and there rather as the pieces stand on a chess-board when it is half-way through the game. There were stone satyrs, and stone wolves, and bears and foxes and cat-a-mountains of stone. There were lovely stone shapes that looked like women but who were really the spirits of trees. There was the great shape of a centaur and a winged horse and a long lithe creature that Edmund took to be a dragon. They all looked so strange standing there perfectly life-like and also perfectly still, in the bright cold moonlight, that it was eerie work crossing the courtyard. Right in the very middle stood a huge shape like a man, but as tall as a tree, with a fierce face and a shaggy beard and a great club in its right hand. Even though he knew that it was only a stone giant and not a live one, Edmund did not like going past it.

He now saw that there was a dim light showing from a doorway on the far side of the courtyard. He went to it, there was a flight of stone steps going up to an open door. Edmund went up them. Across the threshold lay a great wolf.

"It's all right, it's all right," he kept saying to himself; "it's only a stone wolf. It can't hurt me", and he raised his leg to step over it. Instantly the huge

creature rose, with all the hair bristling along its back, opened a great, red mouth and said in a growling voice:

"Who's there? Who's there? Stand still, stranger, and tell me who you are."

"If you please, sir," said Edmund, trembling so that he could hardly speak, "my name is Edmund, and I'm

the Son of Adam that Her Majesty met in the wood
the other day and I've come to bring her the news that
my brother and sisters are now in Narnia – quite
close, in the Beavers' house. She – she wanted to see
them."

"I will tell Her Majesty," said the Wolf.
"Meanwhile, stand still on the threshold, as you value
your life." Then it vanished into the house.

Edmund stood and waited, his fingers aching with
cold and his heart pounding in his chest, and pre-
sently the grey wolf, Maugrim, the Chief of the
Witch's Secret Police, came bounding back and said,
"Come in! Come in! Fortunate favourite of the
Queen – or else not so fortunate."

And Edmund went in, taking great care not to
tread on the Wolf's paws.

He found himself in a long gloomy hall with many
pillars, full, as the courtyard had been, of statues. The
one nearest the door was a little faun with a very sad
expression on its face, and Edmund couldn't help
wondering if this might be Lucy's friend. The only
light came from a single lamp and close beside this sat
the White Witch.

"I'm come, your Majesty," said Edmund, rushing
eagerly forward.

"How dare you come alone?" said the Witch in a
terrible voice. "Did I not tell you to bring the others
with you?"

"Please, your Majesty," said Edmund, "I've done
the best I can. I've brought them quite close. They're
in the little house on top of the dam just up the river –
with Mr and Mrs Beaver."

A slow cruel smile came over the Witch's face.

"Is this all your news?" she asked.

"No, your Majesty," said Edmund, and proceeded to tell her all he had heard before leaving the Beavers' house.

"What! Aslan?" cried the Queen, "Aslan! Is this true? If I find you have lied to me —"

"Please, I'm only repeating what they said," stammered Edmund.

But the Queen, who was no longer attending to him, clapped her hands. Instantly the same dwarf whom Edmund had seen with her before appeared.

"Make ready our sledge," ordered the Witch, "and use the harness without bells."

CHAPTER TEN

THE SPELL BEGINS TO BREAK

Now we must go back to Mr and Mrs Beaver and the three other children. As soon as Mr Beaver said, "There's no time to lose," everyone began bundling themselves into coats, except Mrs Beaver, who started picking up sacks and laying them on the table and said: "Now, Mr Beaver, just reach down that ham. And here's a packet of tea, and there's sugar, and some matches. And if someone will get two or three loaves out of the crock over there in the corner."

"What *are* you doing, Mrs Beaver?" exclaimed Susan.

"Packing a load for each of us, dearie," said Mrs Beaver very coolly. "You didn't think we'd set out on a journey with nothing to eat, did you?"

"But we haven't time!" said Susan, buttoning the collar of her coat. "She may be here any minute."

"That's what I say," chimed in Mr Beaver.

"Get along with you all," said his wife. "Think it over, Mr Beaver. She can't be here for quarter of an hour at least."

"But don't we want as big a start as we can possibly get," said Peter, "if we're to reach the Stone Table before her?"

"You've got to remember *that*, Mrs Beaver," said Susan. "As soon as she has looked in here and finds we're gone she'll be off at top speed."

"That she will," said Mrs Beaver. "But we can't get

there before her whatever we do, for she'll be on a sledge and we'll be walking."

"Then – have we no hope?" said Susan.

"Now don't you get fussing, there's a dear," said Mrs Beaver, "but just get half a dozen clean handkerchiefs out of the drawer. 'Course we've got a hope. We can't get there *before* her but we can keep under cover and go by ways she won't expect and perhaps we'll get through."

"That's true enough, Mrs Beaver," said her husband. "But it's time we were out of this."

"And don't *you* start fussing either, Mr Beaver," said his wife. "There. That's better. There's five

loads and the smallest for the smallest of us: that's you, my dear," she added, looking at Lucy.

"Oh, do please come on," said Lucy.

"Well, I'm nearly ready now," answered Mrs Beaver at last, allowing her husband to help her into her snow-boots. "I suppose the sewing machine's too heavy to bring?"

"Yes. It *is*," said Mr Beaver. "A great deal too heavy. And you don't think you'll be able to use it while we're on the run, I suppose?"

"I can't abide the thought of that Witch fiddling with it," said Mrs Beaver, "and breaking it or stealing it, as likely as not."

"Oh, please, please, please, do hurry!" said the three children. And so at last they all got outside and Mr Beaver locked the door ("It'll delay her a bit," he said) and they set off, all carrying their loads over their shoulders.

The snow had stopped and the moon had come out when they began their journey. They went in single file – first Mr Beaver, then Lucy, then Peter, then Susan, and Mrs Beaver last of all. Mr Beaver led them across the dam and on to the right bank of the river and then along a very rough sort of path among the trees right down by the river-bank. The sides of the valley, shining in the moonlight, towered up far above them on either hand. "Best keep down here as much as possible," he said. "She'll have to keep to the top, for you couldn't bring a sledge down here."

It would have been a pretty enough scene to look at it through a window from a comfortable armchair; and even as things were, Lucy enjoyed it at first. But as they went on walking and walking – and walking – and as the sack she was carrying felt heavier and heavier, she began to wonder how she was going to keep up at all. And she stopped looking at the dazzling brightness of the frozen river with all its waterfalls of ice and at the white masses of the tree-tops and the great glaring moon and the countless stars and could only watch the little short legs of Mr Beaver going pad-pad-pad-pad through the snow in front of her as if they were never going to stop. Then the moon disappeared and the snow began to fall once more. And at last Lucy was so tired that she was almost asleep and walking at the same time when suddenly she found that Mr Beaver had turned away from the river-bank to the right and was leading them steeply uphill into the very thickest bushes. And then as she came fully awake she found that Mr Beaver was just vanishing into a little hole in the bank which had been almost hidden under the bushes until you were quite on top of it. In fact, by the time she realized what was happening, only his short flat tail was showing.

Lucy immediately stooped down and crawled in after him. Then she heard noises of scrambling and puffing and panting behind her and in a moment all five of them were inside.

"Wherever is this?" said Peter's voice, sounding tired and pale in the darkness. (I hope you know what I mean by a voice sounding pale.)

"It's an old hiding-place for beavers in bad times," said Mr Beaver, "and a great secret. It's not much of a place but we must get a few hours' sleep."

"If you hadn't all been in such a plaguey fuss when we were starting, I'd have brought some pillows," said Mrs Beaver.

It wasn't nearly such a nice cave as Mr Tumnus's, Lucy thought – just a hole in the ground but dry and earthy. It was very small so that when they all lay down they were all a bundle of clothes together, and what with that and being warmed up by their long

walk they were really rather snug. If only the floor of
the cave had been a little smoother! Then Mrs Beaver
handed round in the dark a little flask out of which
everyone drank something – it made one cough and
splutter a little and stung the throat, but it also made
you feel deliciously warm after you'd swallowed it –
and everyone went straight to sleep.

It seemed to Lucy only the next minute (though
really it was hours and hours later) when she woke up
feeling a little cold and dreadfully stiff and thinking
how she would like a hot bath. Then she felt a set of
long whiskers tickling her cheek and saw the cold
daylight coming in through the mouth of the cave.
But immediately after that she was very wide awake
indeed, and so was everyone else. In fact they were all
sitting up with their mouths and eyes wide open
listening to a sound which was the very sound they'd
all been thinking of (and sometimes imagining they
heard) during their walk last night. It was a sound of
jingling bells.

Mr Beaver was out of the cave like a flash the
moment he heard it. Perhaps you think, as Lucy
thought for a moment, that this was a very silly thing
to do? But it was really a very sensible one. He knew
he could scramble to the top of the bank among
bushes and brambles without being seen; and he
wanted above all things to see which way the Witch's
sledge went. The others all sat in the cave waiting
and wondering. They waited nearly five minutes.
Then they heard something that frightened them
very much. They heard voices. "Oh," thought Lucy,
"he's been seen. She's caught him!" Great was their

surprise when a little later, they heard Mr Beaver's voice calling to them from just outside the cave.

"It's all right," he was shouting. "Come out, Mrs Beaver. Come out, Sons and Daughters of Adam. It's all right! It isn't *Her*!" This was bad grammar of course, but that is how beavers talk when they are excited; I mean, in Narnia – in our world they usually don't talk at all.

So Mrs Beaver and the children came bundling out of the cave, all blinking in the daylight, and with earth all over them, and looking very frowsty and unbrushed and uncombed and with the sleep in their eyes.

"Come on!" cried Mr Beaver, who was almost dancing with delight. "Come and see! This is a nasty knock for the Witch! It looks as if her power is already crumbling."

"What *do* you mean, Mr Beaver?" panted Peter as they all scrambled up the steep bank of the valley together.

"Didn't I tell you," answered Mr Beaver, "that she'd made it always winter and never Christmas? Didn't I tell you? Well, just come and see!"

And then they were all at the top and did see.

It *was* a sledge, and it *was* reindeer with bells on their harness. But they were far bigger than the Witch's reindeer, and they were not white but brown. And on the sledge sat a person whom everyone knew the moment they set eyes on him. He was a huge man in a bright red robe (bright as hollyberries) with a hood that had fur inside it and a great white beard that fell like a foamy waterfall over his chest.

Everyone knew him because, though you see people
of his sort only in Narnia, you see pictures of them
and hear them talked about even in our world – the
world on this side of the wardrobe door. But when
you really see them in Narnia it is rather different.
Some of the pictures of Father Christmas in our world
make him look only funny and jolly. But now that the
children actually stood looking at him they didn't
find it quite like that. He was so big, and so glad, and
so real, that they all became quite still. They felt very
glad, but also solemn.

"I've come at last," said he. "She has kept me out
for a long time, but I have got in at last. Aslan is on
the move. The Witch's magic is weakening."

And Lucy felt running through her that deep shiver
of gladness which you only get if you are being solemn and still.

"And now," said Father Christmas, "for your
presents. There is a new and better sewing machine
for you, Mrs Beaver. I will drop it in your house as I
pass."

"If you please, sir," said Mrs Beaver, making a
curtsey. "It's locked up."

"Locks and bolts make no difference to me," said
Father Christmas. "And as for you, Mr Beaver, when
you get home you will find your dam finished and
mended and all the leaks stopped and a new sluice-
gate fitted."

Mr Beaver was so pleased that he opened his
mouth very wide and then found he couldn't say
anything at all.

"Peter, Adam's Son," said Father Christmas.

"Here, sir," said Peter.

"These are your presents," was the answer, "and they are tools not toys. The time to use them is perhaps near at hand. Bear them well." With these words he handed to Peter a shield and a sword. The shield was the colour of silver and across it there ramped a red lion, as bright as a ripe strawberry at the moment when you pick it. The hilt of the sword was of gold and it had a sheath and a sword belt and everything it needed, and it was just the right size and weight for Peter to use. Peter was silent and solemn as he received these gifts, for he felt they were a very serious kind of present.

"Susan, Eve's Daughter," said Father Christmas. "These are for you," and he handed her a bow and a quiver full of arrows and a little ivory horn. "You must use the bow only in great need," he said, "for I do not mean you to fight in the battle. It does not easily miss. And when you put this horn to your lips and blow it, then, wherever you are, I think help of some kind will come to you."

Last of all he said, "Lucy, Eve's Daughter," and Lucy came forward. He gave her a little bottle of what looked like glass (but people said afterwards that it was made of diamond) and a small dagger. "In this bottle," he said, "there is a cordial made of the juice of one of the fire-flowers that grow in the mountains of the sun. If you or any of your friends is hurt, a few drops of this will restore them. And the dagger is to defend yourself at great need. For you also are not to be in the battle."

"Why, sir?" said Lucy. "I think – I don't know – but I think I could be brave enough."

"That is not the point," he said. "But battles are ugly when women fight. And now" – here he suddenly looked less grave – "here is something for the moment for you all!" and he brought out (I suppose from the big bag at his back, but nobody quite saw him do it) a large tray containing five cups and saucers, a bowl of lump sugar, a jug of cream, and a great big teapot all sizzling and piping hot. Then he cried out "Merry Christmas! Long live the true King!" and cracked his whip, and he and the reindeer and the sledge and all were out of sight before anyone realized that they had started.

Peter had just drawn his sword out of its sheath and was showing it to Mr Beaver, when Mrs Beaver said:

"Now then, now then! Don't stand talking there till the tea's got cold. Just like men. Come and help to carry the tray down and we'll have breakfast. What a mercy I thought of bringing the bread-knife."

So down the steep bank they went and back to the cave, and Mr Beaver cut some of the bread and ham into sandwiches and Mrs Beaver poured out the tea and everyone enjoyed themselves. But long before they had finished enjoying themselves Mr Beaver said, "Time to be moving on now."

CHAPTER ELEVEN

ASLAN IS NEARER

EDMUND meanwhile had been having a most dis-appointing time. When the dwarf had gone to get the sledge ready he expected that the Witch would start being nice to him, as she had been at their last meeting. But she said nothing at all. And when at last Edmund plucked up his courage to say, "Please, your Majesty, could I have some Turkish Delight? You – you – said –" she answered, "Silence, fool!" Then she appeared to change her mind and said, as if to herself, "And yet it will not do to have the brat fainting on the way," and once more clapped her hands. Another dwarf appeared.

"Bring the human creature food and drink," she said.

The dwarf went away and presently returned bringing an iron bowl with some water in it and an iron plate with a hunk of dry bread on it. He grinned in a repulsive manner as he set them down on the floor beside Edmund and said:

"Turkish Delight for the little Prince. Ha! Ha! Ha!"

"Take it away," said Edmund sulkily. "I don't want dry bread." But the Witch suddenly turned on him with such a terrible expression on her face that he apologized and began to nibble at the bread, though it was so stale he could hardly get it down.

"You may be glad enough of it before you taste bread again," said the Witch.

While he was still chewing away the first dwarf
came back and announced that the sledge was ready.
The White Witch rose and went out, ordering
Edmund to go with her. The snow was again falling
as they came into the courtyard, but she took no
notice of that and made Edmund sit beside her on the

sledge. But before they drove off she called Maugrim
and he came bounding like an enormous dog to the
side of the sledge.

"Take with you the swiftest of your wolves and
go at once to the house of the Beavers," said the
Witch, "and kill whatever you find there. If they are
already gone, then make all speed to the Stone Table,
but do not be seen. Wait for me there in hiding. I
meanwhile must go many miles to the West before I
find a place where I can drive across the river. You
may overtake these humans before they reach the

Stone Table. You will know what to do if you find them!"

"I hear and obey, O Queen," growled the Wolf, and immediately he shot away into the snow and darkness, as quickly as a horse can gallop. In a few minutes he had called another wolf and was with him down on the dam sniffing at the Beavers' house. But of course they found it empty. It would have been a dreadful thing for the Beavers and the children if the night had remained fine, for the wolves would then have been able to follow their trail – and ten to one would have overtaken them before they had got to the cave. But now that the snow had begun again the scent was cold and even the footprints were covered up.

Meanwhile the dwarf whipped up the reindeer, and the Witch and Edmund drove out under the archway and on and away into the darkness and the cold. This was a terrible journey for Edmund, who had no coat. Before they had been going quarter of an hour all the front of him was covered with snow – he soon stopped trying to shake it off because, as quickly as he did that, a new lot gathered, and he was so tired. Soon he was wet to the skin. And oh, how miserable he was! It didn't look now as if the Witch intended to make him a King. All the things he had said to make himself believe that she was good and kind and that her side was really the right side sounded to him silly now. He would have given anything to meet the others at this moment – even Peter! The only way to comfort himself now was to try to believe that the whole thing was a dream and that he might wake up at any moment. And as they went on, hour after hour, it did come to seem like a dream.

This lasted longer than I could describe even if I wrote pages and pages about it. But I will skip on to the time when the snow had stopped and the morning had come and they were racing along in the daylight. And still they went on and on, with no sound but the everlasting swish of the snow and the creaking of the reindeer's harness. And then at last the Witch said, "What have we here? Stop!" and they did.

How Edmund hoped she was going to say something about breakfast! But she had stopped for quite a different reason. A little way off at the foot of a tree sat a merry party, a squirrel and his wife with their children and two satyrs and a dwarf and an old dog-fox, all on stools round a table. Edmund couldn't quite see what they were eating, but it smelled lovely and there seemed to be decorations of holly and he wasn't at all sure that he didn't see something like a plum pudding. At the moment when the sledge stopped, the Fox, who was obviously the oldest person present, had just risen to its feet, holding a glass in its right paw as if it was going to say something. But when the whole party saw the sledge stopping and who was in it, all the gaiety went out of their faces. The father squirrel stopped eating with his fork half-way to his mouth and one of the satyrs stopped with its fork actually in its mouth, and the baby squirrels squeaked with terror.

"What is the meaning of this?" asked the Witch Queen. Nobody answered.

"Speak, vermin!" she said again. "Or do you want

my dwarf to find you a tongue with his whip? What is the meaning of all this gluttony, this waste, this self-indulgence? Where did you get all these things?"

"Please, your Majesty," said the Fox, "we were given them. And if I might make so bold as to drink your Majesty's very good health – "

"Who gave them to you?" said the Witch.

"F-F-F-Father Christmas," stammered the Fox.

"What?" roared the Witch, springing from the sledge and taking a few strides nearer to the terrified animals. "He has not been here! He cannot have been here! How dare you – but no. Say you have been lying and you shall even now be forgiven."

At that moment one of the young squirrels lost its head completely.

"He has – he has – he has!" it squeaked, beating its little spoon on the table. Edmund saw the Witch bite her lips so that a drop of blood appeared on her white cheek. Then she raised her wand. "Oh, don't, don't, please don't," shouted Edmund, but even while he was shouting she had waved her wand and instantly where the merry party had been there were only statues of creatures (one with its stone fork fixed forever half-way to its stone mouth) seated round a stone table on which there were stone plates and a stone plum pudding.

"As for you," said the Witch, giving Edmund a stunning blow on the face as she re-mounted the sledge, "let that teach you to ask favour for spies and traitors. Drive on!" And Edmund for the first time in this story felt sorry for someone besides himself. It seemed so pitiful to think of those little stone figures sitting there all the silent days and all the dark nights, year after year, till the moss grew on them and at last even their faces crumbled away.

Now they were steadily racing on again. And soon Edmund noticed that the snow which splashed against them as they rushed through it was much wetter than it had been all last night. At the same time he noticed that he was feeling much less cold. It was also becoming foggy. In fact every minute it grew foggier and warmer. And the sledge was not running nearly as well as it had been running up till now. At first he thought this was because the reindeer were tried, but soon he saw that that couldn't be the real reason. The sledge jerked, and skidded and kept on jolting as if it had struck against stones. And however the dwarf whipped the poor reindeer the sledge went slower and slower. There also seemed to be a curious noise all round them, but the noise of their driving and jolting and the dwarf's shouting at the reindeer prevented Edmund from hearing what it was, until suddenly the sledge stuck so fast that it wouldn't go on at all. When that happened there was a moment's silence. And in that silence Edmund could at last listen to the other noise properly. A strange, sweet, rustling, chattering noise – and yet not so strange, for he'd heard it before – if only he could remember where! Then all at once he did remember. It was the noise of running water. All round them though out of sight, there were streams, chattering, murmuring, bubbling, splashing and even (in the distance) roaring. And his heart gave a great leap (though he hardly knew why) when he realized that the frost was over. And much nearer there was a drip-drip-drip from the branches of all the trees. And then, as he looked at one tree he saw a great load of snow slide off it and for the first time since he had entered Narnia he saw the dark green of a fir tree. But he hadn't time to listen or watch any longer, for the Witch said:

"Don't sit staring, fool! Get out and help."

And of course Edmund had to obey. He stepped out into the snow – but it was really only slush by now – and began helping the dwarf to get the sledge out of the muddy hole it had got into. They got it out in the end, and by being very cruel to the reindeer the dwarf managed to get it on the move again, and they drove a little further. And now the snow was really melting in earnest and patches of green grass were beginning to appear in every direction. Unless you have looked at a world of snow as long as Edmund had been looking at it, you will hardly be able to

imagine what a relief those green patches were after the endless white. Then the sledge stopped again.

"It's no good, your Majesty," said the dwarf. "We can't sledge in this thaw."

"Then we must walk," said the Witch.

"We shall never overtake them walking," growled the dwarf. "Not with the start they've got."

"Are you my councillor or my slave?" said the Witch. "Do as you're told. Tie the hands of the human creature behind it and keep hold of the end of the rope. And take your whip. And cut the harness of the reindeer; they'll find their own way home."

The dwarf obeyed, and in a few minutes Edmund found himself being forced to walk as fast as he could

with his hands tied behind him. He kept on slipping
in the slush and mud and wet grass, and every time he
slipped the dwarf gave him a curse and sometimes a
flick with the whip. The Witch walked behind the
dwarf and kept on saying, "Faster! Faster!"

Every moment the patches of green grew bigger
and the patches of snow grew smaller. Every moment
more and more of the trees shook off their robes of
snow. Soon, wherever you looked, instead of white
shapes you saw the dark green of firs or the black
prickly branches of bare oaks and beeches and elms.
Then the mist turned from white to gold and presently cleared away altogether. Shafts of delicious
sunlight struck down on to the forest floor and overhead you could see a blue sky between the tree tops.

Soon there were more wonderful things happening.
Coming suddenly round a corner into a glade of silver
birch trees Edmund saw the ground covered in all
directions with little yellow flowers – celandines. The
noise of water grew louder. Presently they actually
crossed a stream. Beyond it they found snowdrops
growing.

"Mind your own business!" said the dwarf when
he saw that Edmund
had turned his head to
look at them; and he
gave the rope a vicious
jerk.

But of course this
didn't prevent Edmund
from seeing. Only five
minutes later he noticed

a dozen crocuses growing
round the foot of an old
tree – gold and purple and
white. Then came a sound
even more delicious than
the sound of the water.
Close beside the path they
were following a bird suddenly chirped from the
branch of a tree. It was
answered by the chuckle of another bird a little
further off. And then, as if that had been a signal,
there was chattering and chirruping in every
direction, and then a moment of full song, and within
five minutes the whole wood was ringing with birds'
music, and wherever Edmund's eyes turned he saw
birds alighting on branches, or sailing overhead or
chasing one another or having their little quarrels or
tidying up their feathers with their beaks.

"Faster! Faster!" said the Witch.

There was no trace of the fog now. The sky became
bluer and bluer, and now there were white clouds
hurrying across it from time to time. In the wide
glades there were primroses. A light breeze sprang up
which scattered drops of moisture from the swaying
branches and carried cool, delicious scents against the
faces of the travellers. The trees began to come fully
alive. The larches and birches were covered with
green, the laburnums with gold. Soon the beech trees
had put forth their delicate, transparent leaves. As the
travellers walked under them the light also became
green. A bee buzzed across their path.

"This is no thaw," said the dwarf, suddenly stopping. "This is *Spring*. What are we to do? Your winter has been destroyed, I tell you! This is Aslan's doing."

"If either of you mention that name again," said the Witch, "he shall instantly be killed."

CHAPTER TWELVE

PETER'S FIRST BATTLE

WHILE the dwarf and the White Witch were saying this, miles away the Beavers and the children were walking on hour after hour into what seemed a delicious dream. Long ago they had left the coats behind them. And by now they had even stopped saying to one another, "Look! there's a kingfisher," or "I say, bluebells!" or "What was that lovely smell?" or "Just listen to that thrush!" They walked on in silence drinking it all in, passing through patches of warm sunlight into cool, green thickets and out again into wide mossy glades where tall elms raised the leafy roof far overhead, and then into dense masses of flowering currant and among hawthorn bushes where the sweet smell was almost overpowering.

They had been just as surprised as Edmund when they saw the winter vanishing and the whole wood passing in a few hours or so from January to May. They hadn't even known for certain (as the Witch did) that this was what would happen when Aslan came to Narnia. But they all knew that it was her spells which had produced the endless winter; and therefore they all knew when this magic spring began that something had gone wrong, and badly wrong, with the Witch's schemes. And after the thaw had been going on for some time they all realized that the Witch would no longer be able to use her sledge. After that they didn't hurry so much and they allowed themselves more rests and longer ones. They were pretty tired by now of course; but not what I'd call bitterly tired – only slow and feeling very dreamy and quiet inside as one does when one is coming to the end of a long day in the open. Susan had a slight blister on one heel.

They had left the course of the big river some time ago; for one had to turn a little to the right (that meant a little to the south) to reach the place of the Stone Table. Even if this had not been their way they couldn't have kept to the river valley once the thaw began, for with all that melting snow the river was soon in flood – a wonderful, roaring, thundering yellow flood – and their path would have been under water.

And now the sun got low and the light got redder and the shadows got longer and the flowers began to think about closing.

"Not long now," said Mr Beaver, and began leading them uphill across some very deep, springy moss (it felt nice under their tired feet) in a place where only tall trees grew, very wide apart. The climb, coming at the end of the long day, made them all pant and blow. And just as Lucy was wondering whether she could really get to the top without another long rest, suddenly they *were* at the top. And this is what they saw.

They were on a green open space from which you could look down on the forest spreading as far as one could see in every direction – except right ahead. There, far to the East, was something twinkling and moving. "By gum!" whispered Peter to Susan, "the sea!" In the very middle of this open hill-top was the

Stone Table. It was a great grim slab of grey stone supported on four upright stones. It looked very old; and it was cut all over with strange lines and figures that might be the letters of an unknown language. They gave you a curious feeling when you looked at them. The next thing they saw was a pavilion pitched on one side of the open place. A wonderful pavilion it was – and especially now when the light of the setting sun fell upon it – with sides of what looked like yellow silk and cords of crimson and tent-pegs of ivory; and high above it on a pole a banner which bore a red rampant lion fluttering in the breeze which was blowing in their faces from the far-off sea. While they were looking at this they heard a sound of music on their right; and turning in that direction they saw what they had come to see.

Aslan stood in the centre of a crowd of creatures who had grouped themselves round him in the shape of a half-moon. There were Tree-Women there and Well-Women (Dryads and Naiads as they used to be called in our world) who had stringed instruments; it was they who had made the music. There were four great centaurs. The horse part of them was like huge English farm horses, and the man part was like stern but beautiful giants. There was also a unicorn, and a bull with the head of a man, and a pelican, and an eagle, and a great Dog. And next to Aslan stood two leopards of whom one carried his crown and the other his standard.

But as for Aslan himself, the Beavers and the children didn't know what to do or say when they saw him. People who have not been in Narnia

sometimes think that a thing cannot be good and terrible at the same time. If the children had ever thought so, they were cured of it now. For when they tried to look at Aslan's face they just caught a glimpse of the golden mane and the great, royal, solemn, overwhelming eyes; and then they found they couldn't look at him and went all trembly.

"Go on," whispered Mr Beaver.

"No," whispered Peter, "you first."

"No, Sons of Adam before animals," whispered Mr Beaver back again.

"Susan," whispered Peter, "What about you? Ladies first."

"No, you're the eldest," whispered Susan. And of course the longer they went on doing this the more awkward they felt. Then at last Peter realized that it was up to him. He drew his sword and raised it to the salute and hastily saying to the others "Come on. Pull yourselves together," he advanced to the Lion and said:

"We have come – Aslan."

"Welcome, Peter, Son of Adam," said Aslan. "Welcome, Susan and Lucy, Daughters of Eve. Welcome He-Beaver and She-Beaver."

His voice was deep and rich and somehow took the fidgets out of them. They now felt glad and quiet and it didn't seem awkward to them to stand and say nothing.

"But where is the fourth?" asked Aslan.

"He has tried to betray them and joined the White Witch, O Aslan," said Mr Beaver. And then something made Peter say,

"That was partly my fault, Aslan. I was angry with him and I think that helped him to go wrong."

And Aslan said nothing either to excuse Peter or to blame him but merely stood looking at him with his great unchanging eyes. And it seemed to all of them that there was nothing to be said.

"Please – Aslan," said Lucy, "can anything be done to save Edmund?"

"All shall be done," said Aslan. "But it may be harder than you think." And then he was silent again for some time. Up to that moment Lucy had been thinking how royal and strong and peaceful his face looked; now it suddenly came into her head that he looked sad as well. But next minute that expression was quite gone. The Lion shook his mane and clapped his paws together ("Terrible paws," thought Lucy, "if he didn't know how to velvet them!") and said,

"Meanwhile, let the feast be prepared. Ladies, take these Daughters of Eve to the pavilion and minister to them."

When the girls had gone Aslan laid his paw – and though it was velveted it was very heavy – on Peter's shoulder and said, "Come, Son of Adam, and I will show you a far-off sight of the castle where you are to be King."

And Peter with his sword still drawn in his hand went with the Lion to the eastern edge of the hilltop. There a beautiful sight met their eyes. The sun was setting behind their backs. That meant that the whole country below them lay in the evening light – forest and hills and valleys and, winding away like a silver snake, the lower part of the great river. And beyond all this, miles away, was the sea, and beyond the sea the sky, full of clouds which were just turning rose colour with the reflection of the sunset. But just where the land of Narnia met the sea – in fact, at the mouth of the great river – there was something on a little hill, shining. It was shining because it was a castle and of course the sunlight was reflected from all the windows which looked towards Peter and the sunset; but to Peter it looked like a great star resting on the seashore.

"That, O Man," said Aslan, "is Cair Paravel of the four thrones, in one of which you must sit as King. I show it to you because you are the first-born and you will be High King over all the rest."

And once more Peter said nothing, for at that moment a strange noise woke the silence suddenly. It was like a bugle, but richer.

"It is your sister's horn," said Aslan to Peter in a low voice; so low as to be almost a purr, if it is not disrespectful to think of a Lion purring.

For a moment Peter did not understand. Then, when he saw all the other creatures start forward and heard Aslan say with a wave of his paw, "Back! Let the Prince win his spurs," he did understand, and set off running as hard as he could to the pavilion. And there he saw a dreadful sight.

The Naiads and Dryads were scattering in every direction. Lucy was running towards him as fast as her short legs would carry her and her face was as white as paper. Then he saw Susan make a dash for a tree, and swing herself up, followed by a huge grey beast. At first Peter thought it was a bear. Then he saw that it looked like an Alsatian, though it was far too big to be a dog. Then he realized that it was a wolf – a wolf standing on its hind legs, with its front paws against the tree-trunk, snapping and snarling. All the hair on its back stood up on end. Susan had not been able to get higher than the second big branch. One of her legs hung down so that her foot was only an inch or two above the snapping teeth. Peter wondered why she did not get higher or at least take a better grip; then he realized that she was just going to faint and that if she fainted she would fall off.

Peter did not feel very brave; indeed, he felt he was going to be sick. But that made no difference to what he had to do. He rushed straight up to the monster and aimed a slash of his sword at its side. That stroke never reached the Wolf. Quick as lightning it turned round, its eyes flaming, and its mouth wide open in a howl of anger. If it had not been so angry that it simply had to howl it would have got him by the throat at once. As it was – though all this happened too quickly for Peter to think at all – he had just time to duck down and plunge his sword, as hard as he could, between the brute's forelegs into its heart. Then came a horrible, confused moment like something in a nightmare. He was tugging and pulling and the Wolf seemed neither alive nor dead, and its bared teeth knocked against his forehead, and everything was blood and heat and hair. A moment later he found that the monster lay dead and he had drawn his sword out of it and was straightening his back and rubbing the sweat off his face and out of his eyes. He felt tired all over.

Then, after a bit, Susan came down the tree. She and Peter felt pretty shaky when they met and I won't say there wasn't kissing and crying on both sides. But in Narnia no one thinks any the worse of you for that.

"Quick! Quick!" shouted the voice of Aslan. "Centaurs! Eagles! I see another wolf in the thickets. There – behind you. He has just darted away. After him, all of you. He will be going to his mistress. Now is your chance to find the Witch and rescue the fourth Son of Adam." And instantly with a thunder of hoofs and beating of wings a dozen or so of the swiftest creatures disappeared into the gathering darkness.

Peter, still out of breath, turned and saw Aslan close at hand.

"You have forgotten to clean your sword," said Aslan.

It was true. Peter blushed when he looked at the bright blade and saw it all smeared with the Wolf's hair and blood. He stooped down and wiped it quite clean on the grass, and then wiped it quite dry on his coat.

"Hand it to me and kneel, Son of Adam," said Aslan. And when Peter had done so he struck him with the flat of the blade and said, "Rise up, Sir Peter Wolf's-Bane. And, whatever happens, never forget to wipe your sword."

CHAPTER THIRTEEN

DEEP MAGIC FROM THE
DAWN OF TIME

Now we must get back to Edmund. When he had been made to walk far further than he had ever known that anybody *could* walk, the Witch at last halted in a dark valley all overshadowed with fir trees and yew trees. Edmund simply sank down and lay on his face doing nothing at all and not even caring what was going to happen next provided they would let him lie still. He was too tired even to notice how hungry and thirsty he was. The Witch and the dwarf were talking close beside him in low tones.

"No," said the dwarf, "it is no use now, O Queen. They must have reached the Stone Table by now."

"Perhaps the Wolf will smell us out and bring us news," said the Witch.

"It cannot be good news if he does," said the dwarf.

"Four thrones in Cair Paravel," said the Witch. "How if only three were filled? That would not fulfil the prophecy."

"What difference would that make now that *He* is here?" said the dwarf. He did not dare, even now, to mention the name of Aslan to his mistress.

"He may not stay long. And then — we would fall upon the three at Cair."

"Yet it might be better," said the dwarf, "to keep this one" (here he kicked Edmund) "for bargaining with."

"Yes! and have him rescued," said the Witch scornfully.

"Then," said the dwarf, "we had better do what we have to do at once."

"I would like to have it done on the Stone Table itself," said the Witch. "That is the proper place. That is where it has always been done before."

"It will be a long time now before the Stone Table can again be put to its proper use," said the dwarf.

"True," said the Witch; and then, "Well, I will begin."

At that moment with a rush and a snarl a Wolf rushed up to them.

"I have seen them. They are all at the Stone Table, with Him. They have killed my captain, Maugrim. I was hidden in the thickets and saw it all. One of the Sons of Adam killed him. Fly! Fly!"

"No," said the Witch. "There need be no flying. Go quickly. Summon all our people to meet me here as speedily as they can. Call out the giants and the werewolves and the spirits of those trees who are on our side. Call the Ghouls, and the Boggles, the Ogres and the Minotaurs. Call the Cruels, the Hags, the Spectres, and the people of the Toadstools. We will fight. What? Have I not still my wand? Will not their ranks turn into stone even as they come on? Be off quickly, I have a little thing to finish here while you are away."

The great brute bowed its head, turned, and galloped away.

"Now!" she said, "we have no table – let me see. We had better put it against the trunk of a tree."

Edmund found himself being roughly forced to his feet. Then the dwarf set him with his back against a tree and bound him fast. He saw the Witch take off her outer mantle. Her arms were bare underneath it and terribly white. Because they were so very white he could see them, but he could not see much else, it was so dark in this valley under the dark trees.

"Prepare the victim," said the Witch. And the dwarf undid Edmund's collar and folded back his shirt at the neck. Then he took Edmund's hair and pulled his head back so that he had to raise his chin. After that Edmund heard a strange noise – whizz – whizz – whizz. For a moment he couldn't think what

it was. Then he realized. It was the sound of a knife being sharpened.

At that very moment he heard loud shouts from every direction – a drumming of hoofs and a beating of wings – a scream from the Witch – confusion all round him. And then he found he was being untied. Strong arms were round him and he heard big, kind voices saying things like –

"Let him lie down – give him some wine – drink this – steady now – you'll be all right in a minute."

Then he heard the voices of people who were not talking to him but to one another. And they were saying things like "Who's got the Witch?" "I thought you had her." "I didn't see her after I knocked the knife out of her hand – I was after the dwarf – do you mean to say she's escaped?" "– A chap can't mind everything at once – what's that? Oh, sorry, it's only an old stump!" But just at this point Edmund went off in a dead faint.

Presently the centaurs and unicorns and deer and birds (they were of course the rescue party which Aslan had sent in the last chapter) all set off to go back to the Stone Table, carrying Edmund with them. But if they could have seen what happened in that valley after they had gone, I think they might have been surprised.

It was perfectly still and presently the moon grew bright; if you had been there you would have seen the moonlight shining on an old tree-stump and on a fair-sized boulder. But if you had gone on looking you would gradually have begun to think there was something odd about both the stump and the boulder. And next you would have thought that the stump did look really remarkably like a little fat man crouching on the ground. And if you had watched long enough you would have seen the stump walk across to the boulder and the boulder sit up and begin talking to the stump; for in reality the stump and the boulder were simply the Witch and the dwarf. For it was part of her magic that she could make things look like what they aren't, and she had the presence of mind to do so at the very moment when the knife was knocked out of her hand. She had kept hold of her wand, so it had been kept safe, too.

When the other children woke up next morning (they had been sleeping on piles of cushions in the pavilion) the first thing they heard – from Mrs Beaver – was that their brother had been rescued and brought into camp late last night; and was at that moment with Aslan. As soon as they had breakfasted they all went out, and there they saw Aslan and Edmund walking together in the dewy grass, apart from the rest of the court. There is no need to tell you (and no one ever heard) what Aslan was saying, but it was a conversation which Edmund never forgot. As the others drew nearer Aslan turned to meet them, bringing Edmund with him.

"Here is your brother," he said, "and – there is no need to talk to him about what is past."

Edmund shook hands with each of the others and said to each of them in turn, "I'm sorry," and everyone said, "That's all right." And then everyone wanted very hard to say something which would make it quite clear that they were all friends with him again – something ordinary and natural – and of course no one could think of anything in the world to say. But before they had time to feel really awkward one of the leopards approached Aslan and said,

"Sire, there is a messenger from the enemy who craves audience."

"Let him approach," said Aslan.

The leopard went away and soon returned leading the Witch's dwarf.

"What is your message, Son of Earth?" asked Aslan.

"The Queen of Narnia and Empress of the Lone Islands desires a safe conduct to come and speak with you," said the dwarf, "on a matter which is as much to your advantage as to hers."

"Queen of Narnia, indeed!" said Mr Beaver. "Of all the cheek —"

"Peace, Beaver," said Aslan. "All names will soon be restored to their proper owners. In the meantime we will not dispute about them. Tell your mistress, Son of Earth, that I grant her safe conduct on condition that she leaves her wand behind her at that great oak."

This was agreed to and two leopards went back with the dwarf to see that the conditions were properly carried out. "But supposing she turns the two leopards into stone?" whispered Lucy to Peter. I think the same idea had occurred to the leopards themselves; at any rate, as they walked off their fur was all standing up on their backs and their tails were bristling — like a cat's when it sees a strange dog.

"It'll be all right," whispered Peter in reply. "He wouldn't send them if it weren't."

A few minutes later the Witch herself walked out on to the top of the hill and came straight across and stood before Aslan. The three children who had not seen her before felt shudders running down their backs at the sight of her face; and there were low growls among all the animals present. Though it was bright sunshine everyone felt suddenly cold. The only two people present who seemed to be quite at their ease were Aslan and the Witch herself. It was the oddest thing to see those two faces – the golden face and the dead-white face – so close together. Not that the Witch looked Aslan exactly in his eyes; Mrs Beaver particularly noticed this.

"You have a traitor there, Aslan," said the Witch. Of course everyone present knew that she meant Edmund. But Edmund had got past thinking about himself after all he'd been through and after the talk he'd had that morning. He just went on looking at Aslan. It didn't seem to matter what the Witch said.

"Well," said Aslan. "His offence was not against you."

"Have you forgotten the Deep Magic?" asked the Witch.

"Let us say I have forgotten it," answered Aslan gravely. "Tell us of this Deep Magic."

"Tell you?" said the Witch, her voice growing suddenly shriller. "Tell you what is written on that very Table of Stone which stands beside us? Tell you what is written in letters deep as a spear is long on the fire-stones on the Secret Hill? Tell you what is engraved on the sceptre of the Emperor-beyond-the-Sea? You at least know the Magic which the Emperor put into Narnia at the very beginning. You know that every traitor belongs to me as my lawful prey and that for every treachery I have a right to a kill."

"Oh," said Mr Beaver. "So *that's* how you came to imagine yourself a queen – because you were the Emperor's hangman. I see."

"Peace, Beaver," said Aslan, with a very low growl.

"And so," continued the Witch, "that human creature is mine. His life is forfeit to me. His blood is my property."

"Come and take it then," said the Bull with the man's head in a great bellowing voice.

"Fool," said the Witch with a savage smile that was almost a snarl, "do you really think your master can rob me of my rights by mere force? He knows the Deep Magic better than that. He knows that unless I have blood as the Law says all Narnia will be overturned and perish in fire and water."

"It is very true," said Aslan, "I do not deny it."

"Oh, Aslan!" whispered Susan in the Lion's ear, "can't we – I mean, you won't, will you? Can't we do something about the Deep Magic? Isn't there something you can work against it?"

"Work against the Emperor's Magic?" said Aslan, turning to her with something like a frown on his face. And nobody ever made that suggestion to him again.

Edmund was on the other side of Aslan, looking all the time at Aslan's face. He felt a choking feeling and wondered if he ought to say something; but a moment later he felt that he was not expected to do anything except to wait, and do what he was told.

"Fall back, all of you," said Aslan, "and I will talk to the Witch alone."

They all obeyed. It was a terrible time this – waiting and wondering while the Lion and the Witch talked earnestly together in low voices. Lucy said, "Oh, Edmund!" and began to cry. Peter stood with

his back to the others looking out at the distant sea.
The Beavers stood holding each other's paws with
their heads bowed. The centaurs stamped uneasily
with their hoofs. But everyone became perfectly still
in the end, so that you noticed even small sounds like
a bumble-bee flying past, or the birds in the forest
down below them, or the wind rustling the leaves.
And still the talk between Aslan and the White Witch
went on.

At last they heard Aslan's voice, "You can all come

back," he said. "I have settled the matter. She has
renounced the claim on your brother's blood." And
all over the hill there was a noise as if everyone had
been holding their breath and had now begun breathing again, and then a murmur of talk.

The Witch was just turning away with a look of
fierce joy on her face when she stopped and said,

"But how do I know this promise will be kept?"

"Haa-a-arrh!" roared Aslan, half rising from his throne; and his great mouth opened wider and wider and the roar grew louder and louder, and the Witch, after staring for a moment with her lips wide apart, picked up her skirts and fairly ran for her life.

CHAPTER FOURTEEN

THE TRIUMPH OF THE WITCH

As soon as the Witch had gone Aslan said, "We must move from this place at once, it will be wanted for other purposes. We shall encamp tonight at the Fords of Beruna."

Of course everyone was dying to ask him how he had arranged matters with the witch; but his face was stern and everyone's ears were still ringing with the sound of his roar and so nobody dared.

After a meal, which was taken in the open air on the hill-top (for the sun had got strong by now and dried the grass), they were busy for a while taking the pavilion down and packing things up. Before two o'clock they were on the march and set off in a north-easterly direction, walking at an easy pace for they had not far to go.

During the first part of the journey Aslan explained to Peter his plan of campaign. "As soon as she has finished her business in these parts," he said, "the Witch and her crew will almost certainly fall back to her House and prepare for a siege. You may or may not be able to cut her off and prevent her from reaching it." He then went on to outline two plans of battle – one for fighting the Witch and her people in the wood and another for assaulting her castle. And all the time he was advising Peter how to conduct the operations, saying things like, "You must put your Centaurs in such and such a place" or "You must post scouts to see that she doesn't do so-and-so," till at last Peter said,

"But you will be there yourself, Aslan."

"I can give you no promise of that," answered the Lion. And he continued giving Peter his instructions.

For the last part of the journey it was Susan and Lucy who saw most of him. He did not talk very much and seemed to them to be sad.

It was still afternoon when they came down to a place where the river valley had widened out and the river was broad and shallow. This was the Fords of Beruna and Aslan gave orders to halt on this side of the water. But Peter said,

"Wouldn't it be better to camp on the far side – for fear she should try a night attack or anything?"

Aslan, who seemed to have been thinking about something else, roused himself with a shake of his magnificent mane and said, "Eh? What's that?" Peter said it all over again.

"No," said Aslan in a dull voice, as if it didn't matter. "No. She will not make an attack to-night." And then he sighed deeply. But presently he added, "All the same it was well thought of. That is how a soldier ought to think. But it doesn't really matter." So they proceeded to pitch their camp.

Aslan's mood affected everyone that evening. Peter was feeling uncomfortable too at the idea of fighting the battle on his own; the news that Aslan might not be there had come as a great shock to him. Supper that evening was a quiet meal. Everyone felt how different it had been last night or even that morning. It was as if the good times, having just begun, were already drawing to their end.

This feeling affected Susan so much that she

couldn't get to sleep when she went to bed. And after she had lain counting sheep and turning over and over she heard Lucy give a long sigh and turn over just beside her in the darkness.

"Can't you get to sleep either?" said Susan.

"No," said Lucy. "I thought you were asleep. I say, Susan!"

"What?"

"I've a most horrible feeling – as if something were hanging over us."

"Have you? Because, as a matter of fact, so have I."

"Something about Aslan," said Lucy. "Either some dreadful thing is going to happen to him, or something dreadful that he's going to do."

"There's been something wrong with him all afternoon," said Susan. "Lucy! What was that he said about not being with us at the battle? You don't think he could be stealing away and leaving us tonight, do you?"

"Where is he now?" said Lucy. "Is he here in the pavilion?"

"I don't think so."

"Susan! let's go outside and have a look round. We might see him."

"All right. Let's," said Susan; "we might just as well be doing that as lying awake here."

Very quietly the two girls groped their way among the other sleepers and crept out of the tent. The moonlight was bright and everything was quite still except for the noise of the river chattering over the stones. Then Susan suddenly caught Lucy's arm and said, "Look!" On the far side of the camping ground, just where the trees began, they saw the Lion slowly walking away from them into the wood. Without a word they both followed him.

He led them up the steep slope out of the river valley and then slightly to the right – apparently by the very same route which they had used that afternoon in coming from the Hill of the Stone Table. On and on he led them, into dark shadows and out into pale moonlight, getting their feet wet with the heavy dew. He looked somehow different from the Aslan they knew. His tail and his head hung low and he walked slowly as if he were very, very tired. Then, when they were crossing a wide open place where there where no shadows for them to hide in, he stopped and looked round. It was no good trying to run away so they came towards him. When they were closer he said,

"Oh, children, children, why are you following me?"

"We couldn't sleep," said Lucy – and then felt sure that she need say no more and that Aslan knew all they had been thinking.

"Please, may we come with you – wherever you're going?" asked Susan.

"Well –" said Aslan, and seemed to be thinking. Then he said, "I should be glad of company tonight. Yes, you may come, if you will promise to stop when I tell you, and after that leave me to go on alone."

"Oh, thank you, thank you. And we will," said the two girls.

Forward they went again and one of the girls walked on each side of the Lion. But how slowly he walked! And his great, royal head drooped so that his nose nearly touched the grass. Presently he stumbled and gave a low moan.

"Aslan! Dear Aslan!" said Lucy, "what is wrong? Can't you tell us?"

"Are you ill, dear Aslan?" asked Susan.

"No," said Aslan. "I am sad and lonely. Lay your hands on my mane so that I can feel you are there and let us walk like that."

And so the girls did what they would never have dared to do without his permission, but what they had longed to do ever since they first saw him — buried their cold hands in the beautiful sea of fur and stroked it and, so doing, walked with him. And presently they saw that they were going with him up the slope of the hill on which the Stone Table stood. They went up at the side where the trees came furthest up, and when they got to the last tree (it was one that had some bushes about it) Aslan stopped and said,

"Oh, children, children. Here you must stop. And whatever happens, do not let yourselves be seen. Farewell."

And both the girls cried bitterly (though they hardly knew why) and clung to the Lion and kissed his mane and his nose and his paws and his great, sad eyes. Then he turned from them and walked out on to the top of the hill. And Lucy and Susan, crouching in the bushes, looked after him, and this is what they saw.

A great crowd of people were standing all round the Stone Table and though the moon was shining many of them carried torches which burned with

evil-looking red flames and black smoke. But such people! Ogres with monstrous teeth, and wolves, and bull-headed men; spirits of evil trees and poisonous plants; and other creatures whom I won't describe because if I did the grown-ups would probably not let you read this book – Cruels and Hags and Incubuses, Wraiths, Horrors, Efreets, Sprites, Orknies, Wooses, and Ettins. In fact here were all those who were on the Witch's side and whom the Wolf had summoned at her command. And right in the middle, standing by the Table, was the Witch herself.

A howl and a gibber of dismay went up from the creatures when they first saw the great Lion pacing towards them, and for a moment even the Witch seemed to be struck with fear. Then she recovered herself and gave a wild fierce laugh.

"The fool!" she cried. "The fool has come. Bind him fast."

Lucy and Susan held their breaths waiting for Aslan's roar and his spring upon his enemies. But it never came. Four Hags, grinning and leering, yet also (at first) hanging back and half afraid of what they had to do, had approached him. "Bind him, I say!" repeated the White Witch. The Hags made a dart at him and shrieked with triumph when they found that he made no resistance at all. Then others – evil dwarfs and apes – rushed in to help them, and between them they rolled the huge Lion over on his back and tied all his four paws together, shouting and cheering as if they had done something brave, though, had the Lion chosen, one of those paws could have been the death of them all. But he made no noise, even when the enemies, straining and tugging, pulled the cords so tight that they cut into his flesh. Then they began to drag him towards the Stone Table.

"Stop!" said the Witch. "Let him first be shaved."

Another roar of mean laughter went up from her followers as an ogre with a pair of shears came forward and squatted down by Aslan's head. Snip-snip-snip went the shears and masses of curling gold began to fall to the ground. Then the ogre stood back and the children, watching from their hiding-place, could see the face of Aslan looking all small and different without its mane. The enemies also saw the difference.

"Why, he's only a great cat after all!" cried one.

"Is *that* what we were afraid of?" said another.

And they surged round Aslan, jeering at him, saying things like "Puss, Puss! Poor Pussy," and "How many mice have you caught today, Cat?" and "Would you like a saucer of milk, Pussums?"

"Oh, how *can* they?" said Lucy, tears streaming down her cheeks. "The brutes, the brutes!" for now that the first shock was over the shorn face of Aslan looked to her braver, and more beautiful, and more patient than ever.

"Muzzle him!" said the Witch. And even now, as they worked about his face putting on the muzzle, one bite from his jaws would have cost two or three of them their hands. But he never moved. And this seemed to enrage all that rabble. Everyone was at him now. Those who had been afraid to come near him even after he was bound began to find their courage, and for a few minutes the two girls could not even see him – so thickly was he surrounded by the whole crowd of creatures kicking him, hitting him, spitting on him, jeering at him.

At last the rabble had had enough of this. They began to drag the bound and muzzled Lion to the Stone Table, some pulling and some pushing. He was so huge that even when they got him there it took all their efforts to hoist him on to the surface of it. Then there was more tying and tightening of cords.

"The cowards! The cowards!" sobbed Susan. "Are they *still* afraid of him, even now?"

When once Aslan had been tied (and tied so that he was really a mass of cords) on the flat stone, a hush fell on the crowd. Four Hags, holding four torches, stood at the corners of the Table. The Witch bared her arms as she had bared them the previous night when it had been Edmund instead of Aslan. Then she began to whet her knife. It looked to the children, when the gleam of the torchlight fell on it, as if the knife were made of stone, not of steel, and it was of a strange and evil shape.

As last she drew near. She stood by Aslan's head. Her face was working and twitching with passion, but his looked up at the sky, still quiet, neither angry nor afraid, but a little sad. Then, just before she gave the blow, she stooped down and said in a quivering voice,

"And now, who has won? Fool, did you think that by all this you would save the human traitor? Now I will kill you instead of him as our pact was and so the Deep Magic will be appeased. But when you are dead what will prevent me from killing him as well? And who will take him out of my hand *then*? Understand that you have given me Narnia forever, you have lost your own life and you have not saved his. In that knowledge, despair and die."

The children did not see the actual moment of the killing. They couldn't bear to look and had covered their eyes.

CHAPTER FIFTEEN

DEEPER MAGIC FROM BEFORE THE DAWN OF TIME

WHILE the two girls still crouched in the bushes with their hands over their faces, they heard the voice of the Witch calling out,

"Now! Follow me all and we will set about what remains of this war! It will not take us long to crush the human vermin and the traitors now that the great Fool, the great Cat, lies dead."

At this moment the children were for a few seconds in very great danger. For with wild cries and a noise of skirling pipes and shrill horns blowing, the whole of that vile rabble came sweeping off the hill-top and down the slope right past their hiding-place. They felt the Spectres go by them like a cold wind and they felt the ground shake beneath them under the galloping feet of the Minotaurs; and overhead there went a flurry of foul wings and a blackness of vultures and giant bats. At any other time they would have trembled with fear; but now the sadness and shame and horror of Aslan's death so filled their minds that they hardly thought of it.

As soon as the wood was silent again Susan and Lucy crept out onto the open hill-top. The moon was getting low and thin clouds were passing across her, but still they could see the shape of the Lion lying dead in his bonds. And down they both knelt in the wet grass and kissed his cold face and stroked his beautiful fur – what was left of it – and cried till they could cry no more. And then they looked at each other and held each other's hands for mere loneliness and cried again; and then again were silent. At last Lucy said,

"I can't bear to look at that horrible muzzle. I wonder could we take if off?"

So they tried. And after a lot of working at it (for their fingers were cold and it was now the darkest part of the night) they succeeded. And when they saw his face without it they burst out crying again and kissed it and fondled it and wiped away the blood and the foam as well as they could. And it was all more lonely and hopeless and horrid than I know how to describe.

"I wonder could we untie him as well?" said Susan presently. But the enemies, out of pure spitefulness, had drawn the cords so tight that the girls could make nothing of the knots.

I hope no one who reads this book has been quite as miserable as Susan and Lucy were that night; but if you have been – if you've been up all night and cried till you have no more tears left in you – you will know that there comes in the end a sort of quietness. You feel as if nothing was ever going to happen again. At any rate that was how it felt to these two. Hours and hours seemed to go by in this dead calm, and they hardly noticed that they were getting colder and colder. But at last Lucy noticed two other things. One was that the sky on the east side of the hill was a little less dark than it had been an hour ago. The other was some tiny movement going on in the grass at her feet. At first she took no interest in this. What did it matter? Nothing mattered now! But at last she saw that whatever-it-was had begun to move up the upright stones of the Stone Table. And now whatever-they-were were moving about on Aslan's body. She peered closer. They were little grey things.

"Ugh!" said Susan from the other side of the Table. "How beastly! There are horrid little mice crawling over him. Go away, you little beasts." And she raised her hand to frighten them away.

"Wait!" said Lucy, who had been looking at them more closely still. "Can you see what they're doing?"

Both girls bent down and stared.

"I do believe –" said Susan. "But how queer! They're nibbling away at the cords!"

"That's what I thought," said Lucy. "I think they're friendly mice. Poor little things – they don't realize he's dead. They think it'll do some good untying him."

It was quite definitely lighter by now. Each of the girls noticed for the first time the white face of the other. They could see the mice nibbling away; dozens and dozens, even hundreds, of little field mice. And at last, one by one, the ropes were all gnawed through.

The sky in the east was whitish by now and the stars were getting fainter – all except one very big one

low down on the eastern horizon. They felt colder than they had been all night. The mice crept away again.

The girls cleared away the remains of the gnawed ropes. Aslan looked more like himself without them. Every moment his dead face looked nobler, as the light grew and they could see it better.

In the wood behind them a bird gave a chuckling sound. It had been so still for hours and hours that it startled them. Then another bird answered it. Soon there were birds singing all over the place.

It was quite definitely early morning now, not late night.

"I'm so cold," said Lucy.

"So am I," said Susan. "Let's walk about a bit."

They walked to the eastern edge of the hill and looked down. The one big star had almost disappeared. The country all looked dark grey, but beyond, at the very end of the world, the sea showed pale. The sky began to turn red. They walked to and fro more times than they could count between the dead Aslan and the eastern ridge, trying to keep warm; and oh, how tired their legs felt. Then at last, as they stood for a moment looking out towards the sea and Cair Paravel (which they could now just make out) the red turned to gold along the line where the sea and the sky met and very slowly up came the edge of the sun. At that moment they heard from behind them a loud noise – a great cracking, deafening noise as if a giant had broken a giant's plate.

"What's that?" said Lucy, clutching Susan's arm.

"I – I feel afraid to turn round," said Susan; "something awful is happening."

"They're doing something worse to *Him*," said Lucy. "Come on!" And she turned, pulling Susan round with her.

The rising of the sun had made everything look so different – all colours and shadows were changed – that for a moment they didn't see the important thing. Then they did. The Stone Table was broken into two pieces by a great crack that ran down it from end to end; and there was no Aslan.

"Oh, oh, oh!" cried the two girls, rushing back to the Table.

"Oh, it's *too* bad," sobbed Lucy; "they might have left the body alone."

"Who's done it?" cried Susan. "What does it mean? Is it magic?"

"Yes!" said a great voice behind their backs. "It is more magic." They looked round. There, shining in the sunrise, larger than they had seen him before,

shaking his mane (for it had apparently grown again) stood Aslan himself.

"Oh, Aslan!" cried both the children, staring up at him, almost as much frightened as they were glad.

"Aren't you dead then, dear Aslan?" said Lucy.

"Not now," said Aslan.

"You're not − not a − ?" asked Susan in a shaky voice. She couldn't bring herself to say the word *ghost*. Aslan stooped his golden head and licked her forehead. The warmth of his breath and a rich sort of smell that seemed to hang about his hair came all over her.

"Do I look it?" he said.

"Oh, you're real, you're real! Oh, Aslan!" cried Lucy, and both girls flung themselves upon him and covered him with kisses.

"But what does it all mean?" asked Susan when they were somewhat calmer.

"It means," said Aslan, "that though the Witch knew the Deep Magic, there is a magic deeper still which she did not know. Her knowledge goes back only to the dawn of time. But if she could have looked a little further back, into the stillness and the darkness before Time dawned, she would have read there a different incantation. She would have known that when a willing victim who had committed no treachery was killed in a traitor's stead, the Table would crack and Death itself would start working backwards. And now —"

"Oh yes. Now?" said Lucy, jumping up and clapping her hands.

"Oh, children," said the Lion, "I feel my strength coming back to me. Oh, children, catch me if you can!" He stood for a second, his eyes very bright, his limbs quivering, lashing himself with his tail. Then he made a leap high over their heads and landed on the other side of the Table. Laughing, though she didn't know why, Lucy scrambled over it to reach him. Aslan leaped again. A mad chase began. Round and round the hill-top he led them, now hopelessly out of their reach, now letting them almost catch his tail, now diving between them, now tossing them in the air with his huge and beautifully velveted paws and catching them again, and now stopping unexpectedly so that all three of them rolled over together in a happy laughing heap of fur and arms and legs. It was such a romp as no one has ever had except in Narnia; and whether it was more like playing with a thunderstorm or playing with a kitten Lucy could never make up her mind. And the funny thing was that when all three finally lay together panting in the sun the girls no longer felt in the least tired or hungry or thirsty.

"And now," said Aslan presently, "to business. I feel I am going to roar. You had better put your fingers in your ears."

And they did. And Aslan stood up and when he opened his mouth to roar his face became so terrible that they did not dare to look at it. And they saw all the trees in front of him bend before the blast of his roaring as grass bends in a meadow before the wind. Then he said,

"We have a long journey to go. You must ride on me." And he crouched down and the children climbed on to his warm, golden back, and Susan sat first, holding on tightly to his mane and Lucy sat behind holding on tightly to Susan. And with a great heave he rose underneath them and then shot off, faster than any horse could go, down hill and into the thick of the forest.

That ride was perhaps the most wonderful thing that happened to them in Narnia. Have you ever had a gallop on a horse? Think of that; and then take away the heavy noise of the hoofs and the jingle of the bits and imagine instead the almost noiseless padding of the great paws. Then imagine instead of the black or grey or chestnut back of the horse the soft roughness of golden fur, and the mane flying back in the wind. And then imagine you are going about twice as fast as the fastest racehorse. But this is a mount that doesn't need to be guided and never grows tired. He rushes on and on, never missing his footing, never hesitating, threading his way with perfect skill between tree trunks, jumping over bush and briar and the smaller streams, wading the larger, swimming the largest of all. And you are riding not on a road nor in a park nor even on the downs, but right across Narnia, in spring, down solemn avenues of beech and across sunny glades of oak, through wild orchards of snow-white cherry trees, past roaring waterfalls and mossy rocks and echoing caverns, up windy slopes alight with gorse bushes, and across the shoulders of heathery mountains and along giddy ridges and down, down, down again into wild valleys and out into acres of blue flowers.

It was nearly midday when they found themselves looking down a steep hillside at a castle – a little toy castle it looked from where they stood – which seemed to be all pointed towers. But the Lion was rushing down at such a speed that it grew larger every moment and before they had time even to ask themselves what it was they were already on a level with it. And now it no longer looked like a toy castle but rose frowning in front of them. No face looked over the battlements and the gates were fast shut. And Aslan, not at all slacking his pace, rushed straight as a bullet towards it.

"The Witch's home!" he cried. "Now, children, hold tight."

Next moment the whole world seemed to turn

upside down, and the children felt as if they had left their insides behind them; for the Lion had gathered himself together for a greater leap than any he had yet made and jumped – or you may call it flying rather than jumping – right over the castle wall. The two girls, breathless but unhurt, found themselves tumbling off his back in the middle of a wide stone courtyard full of statues.

CHAPTER SIXTEEN

WHAT HAPPENED ABOUT
THE STATUES

"What an extraordinary place!" cried Lucy. "All those stone animals – and people too! It's – it's like a museum."

"Hush," said Susan, "Aslan's doing something."

He was indeed. He had bounded up to the stone lion and breathed on him. Then without waiting a moment he whisked round – almost as if he had been a cat chasing its tail – and breathed also on the stone dwarf, which (as you remember) was standing a few feet from the lion with his back to it. Then he pounced on a tall stone dryad which stood beyond the dwarf, turned rapidly aside to deal with a stone rabbit on his right, and rushed on to two centaurs. But at that moment Lucy said,

"Oh, Susan! Look! Look at the lion."

I expect you've seen someone put a lighted match to a bit of newspaper which is propped up in a grate against an unlit fire. And for a second nothing seems to have happened; and then you notice a tiny streak of flame creeping along the edge of the newspaper. It was like that now. For a second after Aslan had breathed upon him the stone lion looked just the same. Then a tiny streak of gold began to run along his white marble back – then it spread – then the colour seemed to lick all over him as the flame licks all over a bit of paper – then, while his hindquarters were still obviously stone, the lion shook his mane and all the heavy, stone folds rippled into living hair. Then he opened a great red mouth, warm and living, and gave a prodigious yawn. And now his hind legs had come to life. He lifted one of them and scratched himself. Then, having caught sight of Aslan, he went bounding after him and frisking round him whimpering with delight and jumping up to lick his face.

Of course the children's eyes turned to follow the lion; but the sight they saw was so wonderful that they soon forgot about *him*. Everywhere the statues were coming to life. The courtyard looked no longer like a museum; it looked more like a zoo. Creatures were running after Aslan and dancing round him till he was almost hidden in the crowd. Instead of all that deadly white the courtyard was now a blaze of colours; glossy chestnut sides of centaurs, indigo horns of unicorns, dazzling plumage of birds, reddy-brown of foxes, dogs and satyrs, yellow stockings and crimson hoods of dwarfs; and the birch-girls in silver, and the beech-girls in fresh, transparent green, and the larch-girls in green so bright that it was almost yellow. And instead of the deadly silence the whole place rang with the sound of happy roarings, brayings, yelpings, barkings, squealings, cooings, neighings, stampings, shouts, hurrahs, songs and laughter.

"Oh!" said Susan in a different tone. "Look! I wonder – I mean, is it safe?"

Lucy looked and saw that Aslan had just breathed on the feet of the stone giant.

"It's all right!" shouted Aslan joyously. "Once the feet are put right, all the rest of him will follow."

"That wasn't exactly what I meant," whispered

Susan to Lucy. But it was too late to do anything about it now even if Aslan would have listened to her. The change was already creeping up the Giant's legs. Now he was moving his feet. A moment later he lifted his club off his shoulder, rubbed his eyes and said,

"Bless me! I must have been asleep. Now! Where's that dratted little Witch that was running about on the ground. Somewhere just by my feet it was." But when everyone had shouted up to him to explain what had really happened, and when the Giant had put his hand to his ear and got them to repeat it all again so that at last he understood, then he bowed down till his head was no further off than the top of a haystack and touched his cap repeatedly to Aslan, beaming all over his honest ugly face. (Giants of any sort are now so rare in England and so few giants are good-tempered that ten to one you have never seen a giant when his face is beaming. It's a sight well worth looking at.)

"Now for the inside of this house!" said Aslan. "Look alive, everyone. Up stairs and down stairs and in my lady's chamber! Leave no corner unsearched. You never know where some poor prisoner may be concealed."

And into the interior they all rushed and for several minutes the whole of that dark, horrible, fusty old castle echoed with the opening of windows and with everyone's voices crying out at once, "Don't forget the dungeons – Give us a hand with this door! – Here's another little winding stair – Oh! I say. Here's a poor kangaroo. Call Aslan – Phew! How it smells in here – Look out for trap-doors – Up here! There are a whole lot more on the landing!" But the best of all was when Lucy came rushing upstairs shouting out,

"Aslan! Aslan! I've found Mr Tumnus. Oh, do come quick."

A moment later Lucy and the little Faun were holding each other by both hands and dancing round and round for joy. The little chap was none the worse for having been a statue and was of course very interested in all she had to tell him.

But at last the ransacking of the Witch's fortress was ended. The whole castle stood empty with every door and window open and the light and the sweet spring air flooding into all the dark and evil places which needed them so badly. The whole crowd of liberated statues surged back into the courtyard. And it was then that someone (Tumnus, I think) first said,

"But how are we going to get out?" for Aslan had got in by a jump and the gates were still locked.

"That'll be all right," said Aslan; and then, rising on his hind-legs, he bawled up at the Giant. "Hi! You up there," he roared. "What's your name?"

"Giant Rumblebuffin, if it please your honour," said the Giant, once more touching his cap.

"Well then, Giant Rumblebuffin," said Aslan, "just let us out of this, will you?"

"Certainly, your honour. It will be a pleasure," said Giant Rumblebuffin. "Stand well away from the gates, all you little 'uns." Then he strode to the gate himself and bang – bang – bang – went his huge club. The gates creaked at the first blow, cracked at the second, and shivered at the third. Then he tackled the towers on each side of them and after a few minutes of crashing and thudding both the towers and a good bit of the wall on each side went thundering down in a mass of hopeless rubble; and when the dust cleared it was odd, standing in that dry, grim, stony yard, to see through the gap all the grass and waving trees and sparkling streams of the forest, and the blue hills beyond that and beyond them the sky.

"Blowed if I ain't all in a muck sweat," said the Giant, puffing like the largest railway engine. "Comes of being out of condition. I suppose neither of you young ladies has such a thing as a pocket-handkerchee about you?"

"Yes, I have," said Lucy, standing on tip-toes and holding her handkerchief up as far as she could reach.

"Thank you, Missie," said Giant Rumblebuffin, stooping down. Next moment Lucy got rather a fright for she found herself caught up in mid-air between the Giant's finger and thumb. But just as she was getting near his face he suddenly started and then put her gently back on the ground muttering, "Bless me! I've picked up the little girl instead. I beg your pardon, Missie, I thought you *was* the handkerchee!"

"No, no," said Lucy laughing, "here it is!" This time he managed to get it but it was only about the same size to him that a saccharine tablet would be to you, so that when she saw him solemnly rubbing it to and fro across his great red face, she said, "I'm afraid it's not much use to you, Mr Rumblebuffin."

"Not at all. Not at all," said the giant politely. "Never met a nicer handkerchee. So fine, so handy. So – I don't know how to describe it."

"What a nice giant he is!" said Lucy to Mr Tumnus.

"Oh yes," replied the Faun. "All the Buffins always were. One of the most respected of all the giant families in Narnia. Not very clever, perhaps (I never knew a giant that was), but an old family. With traditions, you know. If he'd been the other sort she'd never have turned him into stone."

At this point Aslan clapped his paws together and called for silence.

"Our day's work is not yet over," he said, "and if the Witch is to be finally defeated before bed-time we must find the battle at once."

"And join in, I hope, sir!" added the largest of the Centaurs.

"Of course," said Aslan. "And now! Those who can't keep up — that is, children, dwarfs, and small animals — must ride on the backs of those who can — that is, lions, centaurs, unicorns, horses, giants and eagles. Those who are good with their noses must come in front with us lions to smell out where the battle is. Look lively and sort yourselves."

And with a great deal of bustle and cheering they did. The most pleased of the lot was the other lion who kept running about everywhere pretending to be very busy but really in order to say to everyone he met. "Did you hear what he said? *Us Lions.* That means him and me. *Us Lions.* That's what I like about Aslan. No side, no stand-off-ishness. *Us Lions.* That meant him and me." At least he went on saying this till Aslan had loaded him up with three dwarfs, one dryad, two rabbits, and a hedgehog. That steadied him a bit.

When all were ready (it was a big sheep-dog who actually helped Aslan most in getting them sorted into their proper order) they set out through the gap in the castle wall. At first the lions and dogs went nosing about in all directions. But then suddenly one great hound picked up the scent and gave a bay. There was no time lost after that. Soon all the dogs and lions and wolves and other hunting animals were going at full speed with their noses to the ground, and all the others, streaked out for about half a mile behind them, were following as fast as they could. The noise was like an English fox-hunt only better because every now and then with the music of the hounds was mixed the roar of the other lion and sometimes the far deeper and more awful roar of Aslan himself. Faster and faster they went as the scent became easier and easier to follow. And then, just as they came to the last curve in a narrow, winding valley, Lucy heard above all these noises another noise – a different one, which gave her a queer feeling inside. It was a noise of shouts and shrieks and of the clashing of metal against metal.

Then they came out of the narrow valley and at once she saw the reason. There stood Peter and Edmund and all the rest of Aslan's army fighting desperately against the crowd of horrible creatures whom she had seen last night; only now, in the daylight, they looked even stranger and more evil and more deformed. There also seemed to be far more of them. Peter's army – which had their backs to her –

looked terribly few. And there were statues dotted all over the battlefield, so apparently the Witch had been using her wand. But she did not seem to be using it now. She was fighting with her stone knife. It was Peter she was fighting – both of them going at it so hard that Lucy could hardly make out what was happening; she only saw the stone knife and Peter's sword flashing so quickly that they looked like three knives and three swords. That pair were in the centre. On each side the line stretched out. Horrible things were happening wherever she looked.

"Off my back, children," shouted Aslan. And they both tumbled off. Then with a roar that shook all Narnia from the western lamp-post to the shores of the eastern sea the great beast flung himself upon the White Witch. Lucy saw her face lifted towards him for one second with an expression of terror and amazement. Then Lion and Witch had rolled over together but with the Witch underneath; and at the same moment all war-like creatures whom Aslan had led from the Witch's house rushed madly on the enemy lines, dwarfs with their battleaxes, dogs with teeth, the Giant with his club (and his feet also crushed dozens of the foe), unicorns with their horns, centaurs with swords and hoofs. And Peter's tired army cheered, and the newcomers roared, and the enemy squealed and gibbered till the wood re-echoed with the din of that onset.

CHAPTER SEVENTEEN

THE HUNTING OF THE WHITE STAG

THE battle was all over a few minutes after their arrival. Most of the enemy had been killed in the first charge of Aslan and his companions; and when those who were still living saw that the Witch was dead they either gave themselves up or took to flight. The next thing that Lucy knew was that Peter and Aslan were shaking hands. It was strange to her to see Peter looking as he looked now – his face was so pale and stern and he seemed so much older.

"It was all Edmund's doing, Aslan," Peter was saying. "We'd have been beaten if it hadn't been for him. The Witch was turning our troops into stone right and left. But nothing would stop him. He fought his way through three ogres to where she was just turning one of your leopards into a statue. And when he reached her he had sense to bring his sword smashing down on her wand instead of trying to go for her directly and simply getting made a statue himself for his pains. That was the mistake all the rest were making. Once her wand was broken we began to have some chance – if we hadn't lost so many already. He was terribly wounded. We must go and see him."

They found Edmund in charge of Mrs Beaver a little way back from the fighting line. He was covered with blood, his mouth was open, and his face a nasty green colour.

"Quick, Lucy," said Aslan.

And then, almost for the first time, Lucy remem-

bered the precious cordial that had been given her for
a Christmas present. Her hands trembled so much
that she could hardly undo the stopper, but she
managed it in the end and poured a few drops into
her brother's mouth.

"There are other people wounded," said Aslan
while she was still looking eagerly into Edmund's pale
face and wondering if the cordial would have any
result.

"Yes, I know," said Lucy crossly. "Wait a minute."

"Daughter of Eve," said Aslan in a graver voice,
"others also are at the point of death. Must *more*
people die for Edmund?"

"I'm sorry, Aslan," said Lucy, getting up and going
with him. And for the next half-hour they were busy
– she attending to the wounded while he restored
those who had been turned into stone. When at last
she was free to come back to Edmund she found him
standing on his feet and not only healed of his
wounds but looking better than she had seen him
look – oh, for ages; in fact ever since his first term at
that horrid school which was where he had begun to
go wrong. He had become his real old self again and
could look you in the face. And there on the field of
battle Aslan made him a knight.

"Does he know," whispered Lucy to Susan, "what
Aslan did for him? Does he know what the arrangement with the Witch really was?"

"Hush! No. Of course not," said Susan.

"Oughtn't he to be told?" said Lucy.

"Oh, surely not," said Susan. "It would be too
awful for him. Think how you'd feel if you were he."

"All the same I think he ought to know," said Lucy. But at that moment they were interrupted.

That night they slept where they were. How Aslan provided food for them all I don't know; but somehow or other they found themselves all sitting down on the grass to a fine high tea at about eight o'clock. Next day they began marching eastward down the

side of the great river. And the next day after that, at about teatime, they actually reached the mouth. The castle of Cair Paravel on its little hill towered up above them; before them were the sands, with rocks and little pools of salt water, and seaweed, and the smell of the sea and long miles of bluish-green waves breaking for ever and ever on the beach. And oh, the cry of the sea-gulls! Have you heard it? Can you remember?

That evening after tea the four children all managed to get down to the beach again and get their shoes and stockings off and feel the sand between their toes. But next day was more solemn. For then, in the Great Hall of Cair Paravel – that wonderful hall with the ivory roof and the west wall hung with peacock's feathers and the eastern door which looks towards the sea, in the presence of all their friends and to the sound of trumpets, Aslan solemnly crowned them and led them to the four thrones amid deafening shouts of, "Long Live King Peter! Long Live Queen Susan! Long Live King Edmund! Long Live Queen Lucy!"

"Once a king or queen in Narnia, always a king or queen. Bear it well, Sons of Adam! Bear it well, Daughters of Eve!" said Aslan.

And through the eastern door, which was wide open, came the voices of the mermen and the mermaids swimming close to the shore and singing in honour of their new Kings and Queens.

So the children sat on their thrones and sceptres were put into their hands and they gave rewards and honours to all their friends, to Tumnus the Faun, and to the Beavers, and Giant Rumblebuffin, to the leopards, and the good centaurs, and the good dwarfs, and to the lion. And that night there was a great feast in Cair Paravel, and revelry and dancing, and gold flashed and wine flowed, and answering to the music inside, but stranger, sweeter, and more piercing, came the music of the sea people.

But amidst all these rejoicings Aslan himself quietly slipped away. And when the Kings and Queens noticed that he wasn't there they said nothing about it. For Mr Beaver had warned them, "He'll be coming and going," he had said. "One day you'll see him and another you won't. He doesn't like being tied down – and of course he has other countries to attend to. It's quite all right. He'll often drop in. Only you mustn't press him. He's wild, you know. Not like a *tame* lion."

And now, as you see, this story is nearly (but not quite) at an end. These two Kings and two Queens governed Narnia well, and long and happy was their reign. At first much of their time was spent in seeking out the remnants of the White Witch's army and destroying them, and indeed for a long time there would be news of evil things lurking in the wilder parts of the forest – a haunting here and a killing there, a glimpse of a werewolf one month and a rumour of a hag the next. But in the end all that foul brood was stamped out. And they made good laws and kept the peace and saved good trees from being unnecessarily cut down, and liberated young dwarfs and young satyrs from being sent to school, and generally stopped busybodies and interferers and encouraged ordinary people who wanted to live and let live. And they drove back the fierce giants (quite a different sort from Giant Rumblebuffin) on the north of Narnia when these ventured across the frontier. And they entered into friendship and alliance with countries beyond the sea and paid them visits of state and received visits of state from them. And they themselves grew and changed as the years passed over them. And Peter became a tall and deep-chested man and a great warrior, and he was called King Peter the Magnificent. And Susan grew into a tall and gracious woman with black hair that fell almost to her feet and the kings of the countries beyond the sea began to send ambassadors asking for her hand in marriage. And she was called Susan the Gentle. Edmund was a graver and quieter man than Peter, and great in council and judgement. He was called King Edmund the Just. But as for Lucy, she was always gay and golden-haired, and all princes in those parts desired her to be their Queen, and her own people called her Queen Lucy the Valiant.

So they lived in great joy and if ever they remembered their life in this world it was only as one remembers a dream. And one year it fell out that Tumnus (who was a middle-aged Faun by now and beginning to be stout) came down river and brought them news that the White Stag had once more appeared in his parts – the White Stag who would give you wishes if you caught him. So these two Kings and two Queens with the principal members of their court, rode a-hunting with horns and hounds in the Western Woods to follow the White Stag. And they had not hunted long before they had a sight of him. And he led them a great pace over rough and smooth and through thick and thin, till the horses of all the courtiers were tired out and these four were still following. And they saw the stag enter into a thicket where their horses could not follow. Then said King Peter (for they talked in quite a different style now, having been Kings and Queens for so long), "Fair Consorts, let us now alight from our horses and follow this beast into the thicket; for in all my days I never hunted a nobler quarry."

"Sir," said the others, "even so let us do."

So they alighted and tied their horses to trees and went on into the thick wood on foot. And as soon as they had entered it Queen Susan said,

"Fair friends, here is a great marvel, for I seem to see a tree of iron."

"Madam," said King Edmund, "if you look well

upon it you shall see it is a pillar of iron with a lantern set on the top thereof."

"By the Lion's Mane, a strange device," said King Peter, "to set a lantern here where the trees cluster so thick about it and so high above it that if it were lit it should give light to no man!"

"Sir," said Queen Lucy. "By likelihood when this post and this lamp were set here there were smaller trees in the place, or fewer, or none. For this is a young wood and the iron post is old." And they stood looking upon it. Then said King Edmund,

"I know not how it is, but this lamp on the post worketh upon me strangely. It runs in my mind that I have seen the like before; as it were in a dream, or in the dream of a dream."

"Sir," answered they all, "it is even so with us also."

"And more," said Queen Lucy, "for it will not go out of my mind that if we pass this post and lantern either we shall find strange adventures or else some great change of our fortunes."

"Madam," said King Edmund, "the like fore-boding stirreth in my heart also."

"And in mine, fair brother," said King Peter.

"And in mine too," said Queen Susan. "Wherefore by my counsel we shall lightly return to our horses and follow this White Stag no further."

"Madam," said King Peter, "therein I pray thee to have me excused. For never since we four were Kings and Queens in Narnia have we set our hands to any high matter, as battles, quests, feats of arms, acts of justice, and the like, and then given over; but always what we have taken in hand, the same we have achieved."

"Sister," said Queen Lucy, "my royal brother speaks rightly. And it seems to me we should be shamed if for any fearing or foreboding we turned back from following so noble a beast as now we have in chase."

"And so say I," said King Edmund. "And I have such desire to find the signification of this thing that I would not by my good will turn back for the richest jewel in all Narnia and all the islands."

"Then in the name of Aslan," said Queen Susan, "if ye will all have it so, let us go on and take the adventure that shall fall to us."

So these Kings and Queens entered the thicket, and before they had gone a score of paces they all remembered that the thing they had seen was called a lamppost, and before they had gone twenty more they noticed that they were making their way not through branches but through coats. And next moment they all came tumbling out of a wardrobe door into the empty room, and they were no longer Kings and Queens in their hunting array but just Peter, Susan, Edmund and Lucy in their old clothes. It was the same day and the same hour of the day on which they had all gone into the wardrobe to hide. Mrs Macready and the visitors were still talking in the passage; but luckily they never came into the empty room and so the children weren't caught.

And that would have been the very end of the story if it hadn't been that they felt they really must explain to the Professor why four of the coats out of his wardrobe were missing. And the Professor, who was a very remarkable man, didn't tell them not to be silly or not to tell lies, but believed the whole story. "No," he said, "I don't think it will be any good trying to go back through the wardrobe door to get the coats. You won't get into Narnia again by *that* route. Nor would the coats be much use by now if you did! Eh? What's that? Yes, of course you'll get back to Narnia again some day. Once a King in Narnia, always a King in Narnia. But don't go trying to use the same route twice. Indeed, don't *try* to get there at all. It'll happen when you're not looking for it. And don't talk too much about it even among yourselves. And don't mention it to anyone else unless you find that they've had adventures of the same sort themselves. What's that? How will you know? Oh, you'll *know* all right. Odd things they say – even their looks – will let the secret out. Keep your eyes open. Bless me, what *do* they teach them at these schools?

And that is the very end of the adventure of the wardrobe. But if the Professor was right it was only the beginning of the adventures of Narnia.

Prince Caspian

TO MARY CLARE HAVARD

CONTENTS

CHAPTER ONE

THE ISLAND

ONCE there were four children whose names were Peter, Susan, Edmund, and Lucy, and it has been told in another book called *The Lion, the Witch and the Wardrobe* how they had a remarkable adventure. They had opened the door of a magic wardrobe and found themselves in a quite different world from ours, and in that different world they had become Kings and Queens in a country called Narnia. While they were in Narnia they seemed to reign for years and years; but when they came back through the door and found themselves in England again, it all seemed to have taken no time at all. At any rate, no one noticed that they had ever been away, and they never told anyone except one very wise grown-up.

That had all happened a year ago, and now all four of them were sitting on a seat at a railway station with trunks and playboxes piled up round them. They were, in fact, on their way back to school. They had travelled together as far as this station, which was a junction; and here, in a few minutes, one train would arrive and take the girls away to one school, and in about half an hour another train would arrive and the boys would go off to another school. The first part of the journey, when they were all together, always seemed to be part of the holidays; but now when they would be saying good-bye and going different ways so soon, everyone felt that the holidays were really over and everyone felt their term-time feelings beginning again, and they were all rather gloomy and no one could think of anything to say. Lucy was going to boarding school for the first time.

It was an empty, sleepy, country station and there was hardly anyone on the platform except themselves. Suddenly Lucy gave a sharp little cry, like someone who has been stung by a wasp.

"What's up, Lu?" said Edmund – and then suddenly broke off and made a noise like "Ow!"

"What on earth –" began Peter, and then he too suddenly changed what he had been going to say. Instead, he said, "Susan, let go! What are you doing? Where are you dragging me to?"

"I'm not touching you," said Susan. "Someone is pulling *me*. Oh – oh – oh – stop it!"

Everyone noticed that all the others' faces had gone very white.

"I felt just the same," said Edmund in a breathless voice. "As if I were being dragged along. A most frightful pulling – ugh! it's beginning again."

"Me too," said Lucy. "Oh, I can't bear it."

"Look sharp!" shouted Edmund. "All catch hands and keep together. This is magic – I can tell by the feeling. Quick!"

"Yes," said Susan. "Hold hands. Oh, I do wish it would stop – oh!"

Next moment the luggage, the seat, the platform, and the station had completely vanished. The four children, holding hands and panting, found themselves standing in a woody place – such a woody place that branches were sticking into them and there was hardly room to move. They all rubbed their eyes and took a deep breath.

"Oh, Peter!" exclaimed Lucy. "Do you think we can possibly have got back to Narnia?"

"It might be anywhere," said Peter. "I can't see a yard in

all these trees. Let's try to get into the open – if there is any open."

With some difficulty, and with some stings from nettles and pricks from thorns, they struggled out of the thicket. Then they had another surprise. Everything became much brighter, and after a few steps they found themselves at the edge of the wood, looking down on a sandy beach. A few yards away a very calm sea was falling on the sand with such tiny ripples that it made hardly any sound. There was no land in sight and no clouds in the sky. The sun was about where it ought to be at ten o'clock in the morning, and the sea was a dazzling blue. They stood sniffing in the sea-smell.

"By Jove!" said Peter. "This is good enough."

Five minutes later everyone was barefooted and wading in the cool clear water.

"This is better than being in a stuffy train on the way back to Latin and French and Algebra!" said Edmund. And then for quite a long time there was no more talking, only splashing and looking for shrimps and crabs.

"All the same," said Susan presently, "I suppose we'll have to make some plans. We shall want something to eat before long."

"We've got the sandwiches Mother gave us for the journey," said Edmund. "At least I've got mine."

"Not me," said Lucy. "Mine were in my little bag."

"So were mine," said Susan.

"Mine are in my coat-pocket, there on the beach," said Peter. "That'll be two lunches among four. This isn't going to be such fun."

"At present," said Lucy, "I want something to drink more than something to eat."

Everyone else now felt thirsty, as one usually is after wading in salt water under a hot sun.

"It's like being shipwrecked," remarked Edmund. "In the books they always find springs of clear, fresh water on the island. We'd better go and look for them."

"Does that mean we have to go back into all that thick wood?" said Susan.

"Not a bit of it," said Peter. "If there are streams they're bound to come down to the sea, and if we walk along the beach we're bound to come to them."

They all now waded back and went first across the smooth, wet sand and then up to the dry, crumbly sand that sticks to one's toes, and began putting on their shoes and socks. Edmund and Lucy wanted to leave them behind and do their exploring with bare feet, but Susan said this would be a mad thing to do. "We might never find them again," she pointed out, "and we shall want them if we're still here when night comes and it begins to be cold."

When they were dressed again they set out along the shore with the sea on their left hand and the wood on their right. Except for an occasional seagull it was a very quiet place. The wood was so thick and tangled that they could hardly see into it at all; and nothing in it moved – not a bird, not even an insect.

Shells and seaweed and anemones, or tiny crabs in rock-pools, are all very well, but you soon get tired of them if you are thirsty. The children's feet, after the change from the cool water, felt hot and heavy. Susan and Lucy had raincoats to carry. Edmund had put down his coat on the station seat just before the magic overtook them, and he and Peter took it in turns to carry Peter's great-coat.

Presently the shore began to curve round to the right.

About quarter of an hour later, after they had crossed a rocky ridge which ran out into a point, it made quite a sharp turn. Their backs were now to the part of the sea which had met them when they first came out of the wood, and now, looking ahead, they could see across the water another shore, thickly wooded like the one they were exploring.

"I wonder, is that an island or do we join on to it presently?" said Lucy.

"Don't know," said Peter and they all plodded on in silence.

The shore that they were walking on drew nearer and nearer to the opposite shore, and as they came round each promontory the children expected to find the place where the two joined. But in this they were disappointed. They came to some rocks which they had to climb and from the top they could see a fair way ahead and – "Oh bother!" said Edmund, "it's no good. We shan't be able to get to those other woods at all. We're on an island!"

It was true. At this point the channel between them and the opposite coast was only about thirty or forty yards wide; but they could now see that this was its narrowest place. After that, their own coast bent round to the right again and they could see open sea between it and the mainland. It was obvious that they had already come much more than half-way round the island.

"Look!" said Lucy suddenly. "What's that?" She pointed to a long, silvery, snake-like thing that lay across the beach.

"A stream! A stream!" shouted the others, and, tired as they were, they lost no time in clattering down the rocks and racing to the fresh water. They knew that the stream would be better to drink farther up, away from the beach, so they went at once to the spot where it came out of the wood. The trees were as thick as ever, but the stream had made itself a deep course between high mossy banks so that by stooping you could follow it up in a sort of tunnel of leaves. They dropped on their knees by the first brown, dimly pool and drank and drank, and dipped their faces in the water, and then dipped their arms in up to the elbow.

"Now," said Edmund, "what about those sandwiches?"

"Oh, hadn't we better save them?" said Susan. "We may need them far worse later on."

"I do wish," said Lucy, "now that we're not thirsty, we could go on feeling as not-hungry as we did when we *were* thirsty."

"But what about those sandwiches?" repeated Edmund. "There's no good saving them till they go bad. You've got to remember it's a good deal hotter here than in England and we've been carrying them about in pockets for hours." So they got out the two packets and divided them into four portions, and nobody had quite enough, but it was a great deal better than nothing. Then they talked about their plans for the next meal. Lucy wanted to go back to the sea and catch shrimps, until someone pointed out that they had no nets. Edmund said they must gather gulls' eggs from the rocks, but when they came to think of it they couldn't remember having seen any gulls' eggs and wouldn't be able to cook them if they found any. Peter thought to himself that unless they had some stroke of luck they would soon be glad to eat eggs raw, but he didn't see any point in saying this out loud. Susan said it was a pity they had eaten the sandwiches so soon. One or two tempers very nearly got lost at this stage. Finally Edmund said:

"Look here. There's only one thing to be done. We must explore the wood. Hermits and knights-errant and people like that always manage to live somehow if they're in a forest. They find roots and berries and things."

"What sort of roots?" asked Susan.

"I always thought it meant roots of trees," said Lucy.

"Come on," said Peter, "Ed is right. And we must try to do something. And it'll be better than going out into the glare and the sun again."

So they all got up and began to follow the stream. It was very hard work. They had to stoop under branches and climb over branches, and they blundered through great masses of stuff like rhododendrons and tore their clothes and got their feet wet in the stream; and still there was no noise at all except the noise of the stream and the noises they were making themselves. They were beginning to get very tired of it when they noticed a delicious smell, and then a flash of bright colour high above them at the top of the right bank.

"I say!" exclaimed Lucy. "I do believe that's an apple tree."

It was. They panted up the steep bank, forced their way through some brambles, and found themselves standing round an old tree that was heavy with large yellowish-golden apples as firm and juicy as you could wish to see.

"And this is not the only tree," said Edmund with his mouth full of apple. "Look there – and there."

"Why, there are dozens of them," said Susan, throwing away the core of her first apple and picking her second. "This must have been an orchard – long, long ago, before the place went wild and the wood grew up."

"Then this was once an inhabited island," said Peter.

"And what's that?" said Lucy, pointing ahead.

"By Jove, it's a wall," said Peter. "An old stone wall."

Pressing their way between the laden branches they reached the wall. It was very old, and broken down in places, with moss and wallflowers growing on it, but it was higher than all but the tallest trees. And when they came quite close to it they found a great arch which must once have had a gate in it but was now almost filled up with the largest of all the apple trees. They had to break some of the branches to get past, and when they had done so they all blinked because the daylight became suddenly much brighter. They found themselves in a wide open place with walls all round it. In here there were no trees, only level grass and daisies, and ivy, and grey walls. It was a bright, secret, quiet place, and rather sad; and all four stepped out into the middle of it, glad to be able to straighten their backs and move their limbs freely.

CHAPTER TWO

THE ANCIENT TREASURE HOUSE

"This wasn't a garden," said Susan presently. "It was a castle and this must have been the courtyard."

"I see what you mean," said Peter. "Yes. That is the remains of a tower. And there is what used to be a flight of steps going up to the top of the walls. And look at those other steps – the broad, shallow ones – going up to that doorway. It must have been the door into the great hall."

"Ages ago, by the look of it," said Edmund.

"Yes, ages ago," said Peter. "I wish we could find out who the people were that lived in this castle; and how long ago."

"It gives me a queer feeling," said Lucy.

"Does it, Lu?" said Peter, turning and looking hard at her. "Because it does the same to me. It is the queerest thing that has happened this queer day. I wonder where we are and what it all means?"

While they were talking they had crossed the courtyard and gone through the other doorway into what had once been the hall. This was now very like the courtyard, for the roof had long since disappeared and it was merely another space of grass and daisies, except that it was shorter and narrower and the walls were higher. Across the far end there was a kind of terrace about three feet higher than the rest.

"I wonder, was it really the hall?" said Susan. "What is that terrace kind of thing?"

"Why, you silly," said Peter (who had become strangely

excited), "don't you see? That was the dais where the High Table was, where the King and the great lords sat. Anyone would think you had forgotten that we ourselves were once Kings and Queens and sat on a dais just like that, in our great hall."

"In our castle of Cair Paravel," continued Susan in a dreamy and rather sing-song voice, "at the mouth of the great river of Narnia. How could I forget?"

"How it all comes back!" said Lucy. "We could pretend we were in Cair Paravel now. This hall must have been very like the great hall we feasted in."

"But unfortunately without the feast," said Edmund. "It's getting late, you know. Look how long the shadows are. And have you noticed that it isn't so hot?"

"We shall need a camp-fire if we've got to spend the night here," said Peter. "I've got matches. Let's go and see if we can collect some dry wood."

Everyone saw the sense of this, and for the next half-hour they were busy. The orchard through which they had first come into the ruins turned out not to be a good place for firewood. They tried the other side of the castle, passing out of the hall by a little side door into a maze of stony humps and hollows which must once have been passages and smaller rooms but was now all nettles and wild roses. Beyond this they found a wide gap in the castle wall and stepped through it into a wood of darker and bigger trees where they found dead branches and rotten wood and sticks and dry leaves and fir-cones in plenty. They went to and fro with bundles until they had a good pile on the dais. At the fifth journey they found the well, just outside the hall, hidden in weeds, but clean and fresh and deep when they had cleared these away.

The remains of a stone pavement ran half-way round it. Then the girls went out to pick some more apples and the boys built the fire, on the dais and fairly close to the corner between two walls, which they thought would be the snuggest and warmest place. They had great difficulty in lighting it and used a lot of matches, but they succeeded in the end. Finally, all four sat down with their backs to the wall and their faces to the fire. They tried roasting some of the apples on the ends of sticks. But roast apples are not much good without sugar, and they are too hot to eat with your fingers till they are too cold to be worth eating. So they had to content themselves with raw apples, which, as Edmund said, made one realize that school suppers weren't so bad after all – "I shouldn't mind a good thick slice of bread and margarine this minute," he added. But the spirit of adventure was rising in them all, and no one really wanted to be back at school.

Shortly after the last apple had been eaten, Susan went

out to the well to get another drink. When she came back she was carrying something in her hand.

"Look," she said in a rather choking kind of voice. "I found it by the well." She handed it to Peter and sat down. The others thought she looked and sounded as if she might be going to cry. Edmund and Lucy eagerly bent forward to see what was in Peter's hand – a little, bright thing that gleamed in the firelight.

"Well, I'm – I'm jiggered," said Peter, and his voice also sounded queer. Then he handed it to the others.

All now saw what it was – a little chess-knight, ordinary in size but extraordinarily heavy because it was made of pure gold; and the eyes in the horse's head were two tiny little rubies – or rather one was, for the other had been knocked out.

"Why!" said Lucy, "it's exactly like one of the golden chessmen we used to play with when we were Kings and Queens at Cair Paravel."

"Cheer up, Su," said Peter to his other sister.

"I can't help it," said Susan. "It brought back – oh, such lovely times. And I remembered playing chess with fauns and good giants, and the mer-people singing in the sea, and my beautiful horse – and – and –"

"Now," said Peter in a quite different voice, "it's about time we four started using our brains."

"What about?" asked Edmund.

"Have none of you guessed where we are?" said Peter.

"Go on, go on," said Lucy. "I've felt for hours that there was some wonderful mystery hanging over this place."

"Fire ahead, Peter," said Edmund. "We're all listening."

"We are in the ruins of Cair Paravel itself," said Peter.

"But, I say," replied Edmund. "I mean, how do you make that out? This place has been ruined for ages. Look at all those big trees growing right up to the gates. Look at the very stones. Anyone can see that nobody has lived here for hundreds of years."

"I know," said Peter. "That is the difficulty. But let's leave that out for the moment. I want to take the points one by one. First point: this hall is exactly the same shape and size as the hall at Cair Paravel. Just picture a roof on this, and a coloured pavement instead of grass, and tapestries on the walls, and you get our royal banqueting hall."

No one said anything.

"Second point," continued Peter. "The castle well is exactly where our well was, a little to the south of the great hall; and it is exactly the same size and shape."

Again there was no reply.

"Third point: Susan has just found one of our old chessmen – or something as like one of them as two peas."

Still nobody answered.

"Fourth point. Don't you remember – it was the very day before the ambassadors came from the King of Calormen – don't you remember planting the orchard outside the north gate of Cair Paravel? The greatest of all the wood-people, Pomona herself, came to put good spells on it. It was those very decent little chaps the moles who did the actual digging. Can you have forgotten that funny old Lilygloves, the chief mole, leaning on his spade and saying, 'Believe me, your Majesty, you'll be glad of these fruit trees one day.' And by Jove he was right."

"I do! I do!" said Lucy, and clapped her hands.

"But look here, Peter," said Edmund. "This must be all rot. To begin with, we didn't plant the orchard slap up against the gate. We wouldn't have been such fools."

"No, of course not," said Peter. "But it has grown up to the gate since."

"And for another thing," said Edmund, "Cair Paravel wasn't on an island."

"Yes, I've been wondering about that. But it was a what-do-you-call-it, a peninsula. Jolly nearly an island. Couldn't it have been made an island since our time? Somebody has dug a channel."

"But half a moment!" said Edmund. "You keep on saying *since our time*. But it's only a year ago since we came back from Narnia. And you want to make out that in one year castles have fallen down, and great forests have grown up, and little trees we saw planted ourselves have turned into a big old orchard, and goodness knows what else. It's all impossible."

"There's one thing," said Lucy. "If this is Cair Paravel there ought to be a door at this end of the dais. In fact we ought to be sitting with our backs against it at this moment. You know – the door that led down to the treasure chamber."

"I suppose there *isn't* a door," said Peter, getting up.

The wall behind them was a mass of ivy.

"We can soon find out," said Edmund, taking up one of the sticks that they had laid ready for putting on the fire. He began beating the ivied wall. Tap-tap went the stick against the stone; and again, tap-tap; and then, all at once, boom-boom, with a quite different sound, a hollow, wooden sound.

"Great Scott!" said Edmund.

"We must clear this ivy away," said Peter.

"Oh, do let's leave it alone," said Susan. "We can try it in the morning. If we've got to spend the night here I don't want an open door at my back and a great big black hole that anything might come out of, besides the draught and the damp. And it'll soon be dark."

"Susan! How can you?" said Lucy with a reproachful glance. But both the boys were too much excited to take any notice of Susan's advice. They worked at the ivy with their hands and with Peter's pocket-knife till the knife broke. After that they used Edmund's. Soon the whole place where they had been sitting was covered with ivy; and at last they had the door cleared.

"Locked, of course," said Peter.

"But the wood's all rotten," said Edmund. "We can pull it to bits in no time, and it will make extra firewood. Come on."

It took them longer than they expected and, before they had done, the great hall had grown dusky and the first star or two had come out overhead. Susan was not the only one who felt a slight shudder as the boys stood above the pile of splintered wood, rubbing the dirt off their hands and staring into the cold, dark opening they had made.

"Now for a torch," said Peter.

"Oh, what *is* the good?" said Susan. "And as Edmund said —"

"I'm not saying it now," Edmund interrupted. "I still don't understand, but we can settle that later. I suppose you're coming down, Peter?"

"We must," said Peter. "Cheer up, Susan. It's no good behaving like kids now that we are back in Narnia.

You're a Queen here. And anyway no one could go to sleep with a mystery like this on their minds."

They tried to use long sticks as torches but this was not a success. If you held them with the lighted end up they went out, and if you held them the other way they scorched your hand and the smoke got in your eyes. In the end they had to use Edmund's electric torch; luckily it had been a birthday present less than a week ago and the battery was almost new. He went first, with the light. Then came Lucy, then Susan, and Peter brought up the rear.

"I've come to the top of the steps," said Edmund.

"Count them," said Peter.

"One – two – three," said Edmund, as he went cautiously down, and so up to sixteen. "And this is the bottom," he shouted back.

"Then it really must be Cair Paravel," said Lucy. "There were sixteen." Nothing more was said till all four were standing in a knot together at the foot of the stairway. Then Edmund flashed his torch slowly round.

"O – o – o – oh!!" said all the children at once.

For now all knew that it was indeed the ancient treasure chamber of Cair Paravel where they had once reigned as Kings and Queens of Narnia. There was a kind of path up the middle (as it might be in a greenhouse), and along each side at intervals stood rich suits of armour, like knights guarding the treasures. In between the suits of armour, and on each side of the path, were shelves covered with precious things – necklaces and arm rings and finger rings and golden bowls and dishes and long tusks of ivory, brooches and coronets and chains of gold, and heaps of unset stones lying piled anyhow as if they were marbles or potatoes – diamonds, rubies, carbuncles, emeralds, topazes, and amethysts. Under the shelves stood great chests of oak strengthened with iron bars and heavily padlocked. And it was bitterly cold, and so still that they could hear themselves breathing, and the treasures were so covered with dust that unless they had realized where they were and remembered most of the things, they would hardly have known they were treasures. There was something sad and a little frightening about the place, because it all seemed so forsaken and long ago. That was why nobody said anything for at least a minute.

Then, of course, they began walking about and picking things up to look at. It was like meeting very old friends. If you had been there you would have heard them saying things like, "Oh look! Our coronation rings – do you remember first wearing this? – Why, this is the little brooch we all thought was lost – I say, isn't that the armour you wore in the great tournament in the Lone Islands? – do you remember the dwarf making that for me? – do you remember drinking out of that horn? – do you remember, do you remember?"

But suddenly Edmund said, "Look here. We mustn't waste the battery: goodness knows how often we shall need it. Hadn't we better take what we want and get out again?"

"We must take the gifts," said Peter. For long ago at a Christmas in Narnia he and Susan and Lucy had been given certain presents which they valued more than their whole kingdom. Edmund had had no gift, because he was not with them at the time. (This was his own fault, and you can read about it in the other book.)

They all agreed with Peter and walked up the path to the wall at the far end of the treasure chamber, and there, sure enough, the gifts were still hanging. Lucy's was the smallest for it was only a little bottle. But the bottle was made of diamond instead of glass, and it was still more than half full of the magical cordial which would heal almost every wound and every illness. Lucy said nothing and looked very solemn as she took her gift down from its place and slung the belt over her shoulder and once more felt the bottle at her side where it used to hang in the old days. Susan's gift had been a bow and arrows and a horn. The bow was still there, and the ivory quiver, full of well-feathered arrows, but – "Oh, Susan," said Lucy. "Where's the horn?"

"Oh bother, bother, bother," said Susan after she had thought for a moment. "I remember now. I took it with me the last day of all, the day we went hunting the White Stag. It must have got lost when we blundered back into that other place – England, I mean."

Edmund whistled. It was indeed a shattering loss; for this was an enchanted horn and, whenever you blew it, help was certain to come to you, wherever you were.

"Just the sort of thing that might come in handy in a place like this," said Edmund.

"Never mind," said Susan, "I've still got the bow." And she took it.

"Won't the string be perished, Su?" said Peter.

But whether by some magic in the air of the treasure chamber or not, the bow was still in working order. Archery and swimming were the things Susan was good at. In a moment she had bent the bow and then she gave one little pluck to the string. It twanged: a chirruping twang that vibrated through the whole room. And that one small noise brought back the old days to the children's minds more than anything that had happened yet. All the battles and hunts and feasts came rushing into their heads together.

Then she unstrung the bow again and slung the quiver at her side.

Next, Peter took down his gift – the shield with the great red lion on it, and the royal sword. He blew, and rapped them on the floor, to get off the dust. He fitted the shield on his arm and slung the sword by his side. He was afraid at first that it might be rusty and stick to the sheath. But it was not so. With one swift motion he drew it and held it up, shining in the torchlight.

"It is my sword Rhindon," he said; "with it I killed the Wolf." There was a new tone in his voice, and the others

all felt that he was really Peter the High King again. Then, after a little pause, everyone remembered that they must save the battery.

They climbed the stair again and made up a good fire and lay down close together for warmth. The ground was very hard and uncomfortable, but they fell asleep in the end.

CHAPTER THREE

THE DWARF

THE worst of sleeping out of doors is that you wake up so
dreadfully early. And when you wake you have to get up
because the ground is so hard that you are uncomfortable.
And it makes matters worse if there is nothing but apples
for breakfast and you have had nothing but apples for
supper the night before. When Lucy had said – truly
enough – that it was a glorious morning, there did not
seem to be anything else nice to be said. Edmund said what
everyone was feeling, "We've simply got to get off this
island."

When they had drunk from the well and splashed their
faces they all went down the stream again to the shore and
stared at the channel which divided them from the
mainland.

"We'll have to swim," said Edmund.

"It would be all right for Su," said Peter (Susan had won
prizes for swimming at school). "But I don't know about
the rest of us." By "the rest of us" he really meant Edmund
who couldn't yet do two lengths at the school baths, and
Lucy, who could hardly swim at all.

"Anyway," said Susan, "there may be currents. Father
says it's never wise to bathe in a place you don't know."

"But, Peter," said Lucy, "look here. I know I can't swim
for nuts at home – in England, I mean. But couldn't we all
swim long ago – if it was long ago – when we were Kings
and Queens in Narnia? We could ride then too, and do all
sorts of things. Don't you think –?"

"Ah, but we were sort of grown-up then," said Peter.

"We reigned for years and years and learned to do things. Aren't we just back at our proper ages again now?"

"Oh!" said Edmund in a voice which made everyone stop talking and listen to him.

"I've just seen it all," he said.

"Seen what?" asked Peter.

"Why, the whole thing," said Edmund. "You know what we were puzzling about last night, that it was only a year ago since we left Narnia but everything looks as if no one had lived in Cair Paravel for hundreds of years? Well, don't you see? You know that, however long we seemed to have lived in Narnia, when we got back through the wardrobe it seemed to have taken no time at all?"

"Go on," said Susan. "I think I'm beginning to understand."

"And that means," continued Edmund, "that, once you're out of Narnia, you have no idea how Narnian time is going. Why shouldn't hundreds of years have gone past in Narnia while only one year has passed for us in England?"

"By Jove, Ed," said Peter. "I believe you've got it. In that sense it really was hundreds of years ago that we lived in Cair Paravel. And now we're coming back to Narnia just as if we were Crusaders or Anglo-Saxons or Ancient Britons or someone coming back to modern England?"

"How excited they'll be to see us —" began Lucy, but at the same moment everyone else said, "Hush!" or "Look!" For now something was happening.

There was a wooded point on the mainland a little to their right, and they all felt sure that just beyond that point must be the mouth of the river. And now, round that point there came into sight a boat. When it had cleared the point,

it turned and began coming along the channel towards
them. There were two people on board, one rowing, the
other sitting in the stern and holding a bundle that
twitched and moved as if it were alive. Both these people
seemed to be soldiers. They had steel caps on their heads
and light shirts of chain-mail. Their faces were bearded and
hard. The children drew back from the beach into the
wood and watched without moving a finger.

"This'll do," said the soldier in the stern when the boat
had come about opposite to them.

"What about tying a stone to his feet, Corporal?" said
the other, resting on his oars.

"Garn!" growled the other. "We don't need that, and we
haven't brought one. He'll drown sure enough without a
stone, as long as we've tied the cords right." With these
words he rose and lifted his bundle. Peter now saw that it
was really alive and was in fact a Dwarf, bound hand and
foot but struggling as hard as he could. Next moment he
heard a twang just beside his ear, and all at once the soldier
threw up his arms, dropping the Dwarf into the bottom of

the boat, and fell over into the water. He floundered away to the far bank and Peter knew that Susan's arrow had struck on his helmet. He turned and saw that she was very pale but was already fitting a second arrow to the string. But it was never used. As soon as he saw his companion fall, the other soldier, with a loud cry, jumped out of the boat on the far side, and he also floundered through the water (which was apparently just in his depth) and disappeared into the woods of the mainland.

"Quick! Before she drifts!" shouted Peter. He and Susan, fully dressed as they were, plunged in, and before the water was up to their shoulders their hands were on the side of the boat. In a few seconds they had hauled her to the bank and lifted the Dwarf out, and Edmund was busily engaged in cutting his bonds with the pocket knife. (Peter's sword would have been sharper, but a sword is very inconvenient for this sort of work because you can't hold it anywhere lower than the hilt.) When at last the Dwarf was free, he sat up, rubbed his arms and legs, and exclaimed:

"Well, whatever they say, you don't *feel* like ghosts."

Like most Dwarfs he was very stocky and deep-chested. He would have been about three feet high if he had been standing up, and an immense beard and whiskers of coarse red hair left little of his face to be seen except a beak-like nose and twinkling black eyes.

"Anyway," he continued, "ghosts or not, you've saved my life and I'm extremely obliged to you."

"But why should we be ghosts?" asked Lucy.

"I've been told all my life," said the Dwarf, "that these woods along the shore were as full of ghosts as they were of trees. That's what the story is. And that's why, when they want to get rid of anyone, they usually bring him

down here (like they were doing with me) and say they'll
leave him to the ghosts. But I always wondered if they
didn't really drown 'em or cut their throats. I never quite
believed in the ghosts. But those two cowards you've just
shot believed all right. They were more frightened of taking
me to my death than I was of going!"

"Oh," said Susan. "So that's why they both ran away."

"Eh? What's that?" said the Dwarf.

"They got away," said Edmund. "To the mainland."

"I wasn't shooting to kill, you know," said Susan. She
would not have liked anyone to think she could miss at
such a short range.

"Hm," said the Dwarf. "That's not so good. That may
mean trouble later on. Unless they hold their tongues for
their own sake."

"What were they going to drown you for?" asked
Peter.

"Oh, I'm a dangerous criminal, I am," said the Dwarf
cheerfully. "But that's a long story. Meantime, I was
wondering if perhaps you were going to ask me to

breakfast? You've no idea what an appetite it gives one, being executed."

"There's only apples," said Lucy dolefully.

"Better than nothing, but not so good as fresh fish," said the Dwarf. "It looks as if I'll have to ask you to breakfast instead. I saw some fishing tackle in that boat. And anyway, we must take her round to the other side of the

island. We don't want anyone from the mainland coming down and seeing her."

"I ought to have thought of that myself," said Peter.

The four children and the Dwarf went down to the water's edge, pushed off the boat with some difficulty, and scrambled aboard. The Dwarf at once took charge. The oars were of course too big for him to use, so Peter rowed and the Dwarf steered them north along the channel and presently eastward round the tip of the island. From here the children could see right up the river, and all the bays and headlands of the coast beyond it. They thought they could recognize bits of it, but the woods, which had grown up since their time, made everything look very different.

When they had come round into open sea on the east of the island, the Dwarf took to fishing. They had an excellent catch of pavenders, a beautiful rainbow-coloured fish which they all remembered eating in Cair Paravel in the old days. When they had caught enough they ran the boat up into a little creek and moored her to a tree. The Dwarf, who was a most capable person (and, indeed, though one meets bad Dwarfs, I never heard of a Dwarf who was a fool), cut the fish open, cleaned them, and said:

"Now, what we want next is some firewood."

"We've got some up at the castle," said Edmund.

The Dwarf gave a low whistle. "Beards and bedsteads!" he said. "So there really is a castle, after all?"

"It's only a ruin," said Lucy.

The Dwarf stared round at all four of them with a very curious expression on his face. "And who on earth – ?" he began, but then broke off and said, "No matter. Breakfast first. But one thing before we go on. Can you lay your hand on your hearts and tell me I'm really alive? Are you sure I wasn't drowned and we're not all ghosts together?"

When they had all reassured him, the next question was how to carry the fish. They had nothing to string them on and no basket. They had to use Edmund's hat in the end because no one else had a hat. He would have made much more fuss about this if he had not by now been so ravenously hungry.

At first the Dwarf did not seem very comfortable in the

castle. He kept looking round and sniffing and saying, "H'm. Looks a bit spooky after all. Smells like
ghosts, too." But he cheered up when it came to lighting
the fire and showing them how to roast the fresh pavenders
in the embers. Eating hot fish with no forks, and one
pocket knife between five people, is a messy business
and there were several burnt fingers before the meal was
ended; but, as it was now nine o'clock and they had been
up since five, nobody minded the burns so much as you
might have expected. When everyone had finished off with
a drink from the well and an apple or so, the Dwarf produced a pipe about the size of his own arm, filled it,
lit it, blew a great cloud of fragrant smoke, and said,
"Now."

"You tell us your story first," said Peter. "And then we'll
tell you ours."

"Well," said the Dwarf, "as you've saved my life it is
only fair you should have your own way. But I hardly
know where to begin. First of all I'm a messenger of King
Caspian's."

"Who's he?" asked four voices all at once.

"Caspian the Tenth, King of Narnia, and long may he
reign!" answered the Dwarf. "That is to say, he ought to be
King of Narnia and we hope he will be. At present he is
only King of us Old Narnians – "

"What do you mean by *old* Narnians, please?" asked
Lucy.

"Why, that's us," said the Dwarf. "We're a kind of
rebellion, I suppose."

"I see," said Peter. "And Caspian is the chief Old
Narnian."

"Well, in a manner of speaking," said the Dwarf,

scratching his head. "But he's really a New Narnian himself, a Telmarine, if you follow me."

"I don't," said Edmund.

"It's worse than the Wars of the Roses," said Lucy.

"Oh dear," said the Dwarf. "I'm doing this very badly. Look here: I think I'll have to go right back to the beginning and tell you how Caspian grew up in his uncle's court and how he comes to be on our side at all. But it'll be a long story."

"All the better," said Lucy. "We love stories."

So the Dwarf settled down and told his tale. I shall not give it to you in his words, putting in all the children's questions and interruptions, because it would take too long and be confusing, and, even so, it would leave out some points that the children only heard later. But the gist of the story, as they knew it in the end, was as follows.

CHAPTER FOUR

THE DWARF TELLS OF PRINCE CASPIAN

PRINCE CASPIAN lived in a great castle in the centre of Narnia with his uncle, Miraz, the King of Narnia, and his aunt, who had red hair and was called Queen Prunaprismia. His father and mother were dead and the person whom Caspian loved best was his nurse, and though (being a prince) he had wonderful toys which would do almost anything but talk, he liked best the last hour of the day when the toys had all been put back in their cupboards and Nurse would tell him stories.

He did not care much for his uncle and aunt, but about twice a week his uncle would send for him and they would walk up and down together for half an hour on the terrace at the south side of the castle. One day, while they were doing this, the King said to him,

"Well, boy, we must soon teach you to ride and use a sword. You know that your aunt and I have no children, so it looks as if you might have to be King when I'm gone. How shall you like that, eh?"

"I don't know, Uncle," said Caspian.

"Don't know, eh?" said Miraz. "Why, I should like to know what more anyone could wish for!"

"All the same, I *do* wish," said Caspian.

"What do you wish?" asked the King.

"I wish – I wish – I wish I could have lived in the Old Days," said Caspian. (He was only a very little boy at the time.)

Up till now King Miraz had been talking in the tiresome way that some grown-ups have, which makes it quite clear that they are not really interested in what you are saying, but now he suddenly gave Caspian a very sharp look.

"Eh? What's that?" he said. "What old days do you mean?"

"Oh, don't you know, Uncle?" said Caspian. "When everything was quite different. When all the animals could talk, and there were nice people who lived in the streams and the trees. Naiads and Dryads they were called. And there were Dwarfs. And there were lovely little Fauns in all the woods. They had feet like goats. And —"

"That's all nonsense, for babies," said the King sternly. "Only fit for babies, do you hear? You're getting too old for that sort of stuff. At your age you ought to be thinking of battles and adventures, not fairy tales."

"Oh, but there *were* battles and adventures in those days," said Caspian. "Wonderful adventures. Once there was a White Witch and she made herself Queen of the whole country. And she made it so that it was always winter. And then two boys and two girls came from somewhere and so they killed the Witch and they were made Kings and Queens of Narnia, and their names were Peter and Susan and Edmund and Lucy. And so they reigned for ever so long and everyone had a lovely time, and it was all because of Aslan —"

"Who's he?" said Miraz. And if Caspian had been a very little older, the tone of his uncle's voice would have warned him that it would be wiser to shut up. But he babbled on,

"Oh, don't you know?" he said. "Aslan is the great Lion who comes from over the sea."

"Who has been telling you all this nonsense?" said the King in a voice of thunder. Caspian was frightened and said nothing.

"Your Royal Highness," said King Miraz, letting go of Caspian's hand, which he had been holding till now, "I insist upon being answered. Look me in the face. Who has been telling you this pack of lies?"

"N – Nurse," faltered Caspian, and burst into tears.

"Stop that noise," said his uncle, taking Caspian by the shoulders and giving him a shake. "Stop it. And never let me catch you talking – or *thinking* either – about all those silly stories again. There never were those Kings and Queens. How could there be two Kings at the same time? And there's no such person as Aslan. And there are no such things as lions. And there never was a time when animals could talk. Do you hear?"

"Yes, Uncle," sobbed Caspian.

"Then let's have no more of it," said the King. Then he called to one of the gentlemen-in-waiting who were standing at the far end of the terrace and said in a cold voice, "Conduct His Royal Highness to his apartments and send His Royal Highness's nurse to me AT ONCE."

Next day Caspian found what a terrible thing he had done, for Nurse had been sent away without even being allowed to say good-bye to him, and he was told he was to have a Tutor.

Caspian missed his nurse very much and shed many tears; and because he was so miserable, he thought about the old stories of Narnia far more than before. He dreamed of Dwarfs and Dryads every night and tried very hard to make the dogs and cats in the castle talk to him. But the dogs only wagged their tails and the cats only purred.

Caspian felt sure that he would hate the new Tutor, but when the new Tutor arrived about a week later he turned out to be the sort of person it is almost impossible not to like. He was the smallest, and also the fattest, man Caspian had ever seen. He had a long, silvery, pointed beard which came down to his waist, and his face, which was brown and covered with wrinkles, looked very wise, very ugly, and very kind. His voice was grave and his eyes were merry so that, until you got to know him really well, it was hard to know when he was joking and when he was serious. His name was Doctor Cornelius.

Of all his lessons with Doctor Cornelius the one that Caspian liked best was History. Up till now, except for Nurse's stories, he had known nothing about the History of Narnia, and he was very surprised to learn that the royal family were newcomers in the country.

"It was your Highness's ancestor, Caspian the First," said Doctor Cornelius, "who first conquered Narnia and made it his kingdom. It was he who brought all your nation into the country. You are not native Narnians at all. You are all Telmarines – that is, you all came from the Land of Telmar, far beyond the Western Mountains. That is why Caspian the First is called Caspian the Conqueror."

"Please, Doctor," asked Caspian one day, "who lived in Narnia before we all came here out of Telmar?"

"No men – or very few – lived in Narnia before the Telmarines took it," said Doctor Cornelius.

"Then who did my great-great-grandcesters conquer?"

"*Whom*, not *who*, your Highness," said Doctor Cornelius. "Perhaps it is time to turn from History to Grammar."

"Oh please, not yet," said Caspian. "I mean, wasn't

there a battle? Why is he called Caspian the Conqueror if there was nobody to fight with him?"

"I said there were very few *men* in Narnia," said the Doctor, looking at the little boy very strangely through his great spectacles.

For a moment Caspian was puzzled and then suddenly his heart gave a leap. "Do you mean," he gasped, "that there were other things? Do you mean it was like in the stories? Were there –?"

"Hush!" said Doctor Cornelius, laying his head very close to Caspian's. "Not a word more. Don't you know your Nurse was sent away for telling you about Old Narnia? The King doesn't like it. If he found me telling you secrets, you'd be whipped and I should have my head cut off."

"But why?" asked Caspian.

"It is high time we turned to Grammar now," said Doctor Cornelius in a loud voice. "Will your Royal Highness be pleased to open Pulverulentus Siccus at the fourth page of his *Grammatical garden or the Arbour of Accidence pleasantlie open'd to Tender Wits?*"

After that it was all nouns and verbs till lunchtime, but I don't think Caspian learned much. He was too excited. He felt sure that Doctor Cornelius would not have said so much unless he meant to tell him more sooner or later.

In this he was not disappointed. A few days later his Tutor said, "Tonight I am going to give you a lesson in Astronomy. At dead of night two noble planets, Tarva and Alambil, will pass within one degree of each other. Such a conjunction has not occurred for two hundred years, and your Highness will not live to see it again. It will be best if you go to bed a little earlier than usual. When the time of the conjunction draws near I will come and wake you."

This didn't seem to have anything to do with Old Narnia, which was what Caspian really wanted to hear about, but getting up in the middle of the night is always interesting and he was moderately pleased. When he went to bed that night, he thought at first that he would not be able to sleep; but he soon dropped off and it seemed only a few minutes before he felt someone gently shaking him.

He sat up in bed and saw that the room was full of moonlight. Doctor Cornelius, muffled in a hooded robe and holding a small lamp in his hand, stood by the bedside.

Caspian remembered at once what they were going to do. He got up and put on some clothes. Athough it was a summer night he felt colder than he had expected and was quite glad when the Doctor wrapped him in a robe like his own and gave him a pair of warm, soft buskins for his feet. A moment later, both muffled so that they could hardly be seen in the dark corridors, and both shod so that they made almost no noise, master and pupil left the room.

Caspian followed the Doctor through many passages and up several staircases, and at last, through a little door in a turret, they came out upon the leads. On one side were the battlements, on the other a steep roof; below them, all shadowy and shimmery, the castle gardens; above them, stars and moon. Presently they came to another door, which led into the great central tower of the whole castle: Doctor Cornelius unlocked it and they began to climb the dark winding stair of the tower. Caspian was becoming excited; he had never been allowed up this stair before.

It was long and steep, but when they came out on the roof of the tower and Caspian had got his breath, he felt that it had been well worth it. Away on his right he could see, rather indistinctly, the Western Mountains. On his left was the gleam of the Great River, and everything was so quiet that he could hear the sound of the waterfall at Beaversdam, a mile away. There was no difficulty in picking out the two stars they had come to see. They hung rather low in the southern sky, almost as bright as two little moons and very close together.

"Are they going to have a collision?" he asked in an awe-struck voice.

"Nay, dear Prince," said the Doctor (and he too spoke in a whisper). "The great lords of the upper sky know the steps of their dance too well for that. Look well upon them. Their meeting is fortunate and means some great good for the sad realm of Narnia. Tarva, the Lord of Victory, salutes Alambil, the Lady of Peace. They are just coming to their nearest."

"It's a pity that tree gets in the way," said Caspian. "We'd really see better from the West Tower, though it is not so high."

Doctor Cornelius said nothing for about two minutes, but stood still with his eyes fixed on Tarva and Alambil. Then he drew a deep breath and turned to Caspian.

"There," he said. "You have seen what no man now alive has seen, nor will see again. And you are right. We should have seen it even better from the smaller tower. I brought you here for another reason."

Caspian looked up at him, but the Doctor's hood concealed most of his face.

"The virtue of this tower," said Doctor Cornelius, "is that we have six empty rooms beneath us, and a long stair, and the door at the bottom of the stair is locked. We cannot be overheard."

"Are you going to tell me what you wouldn't tell me the other day?" said Caspian.

"I am," said the Doctor. "But remember. You and I must never talk about these things except here – on the very top of the Great Tower."

"No. That's a promise," said Caspian. "But do go on, please."

"Listen," said the Doctor. "All you have heard about Old Narnia is true. It is not the land of Men. It is the country of Aslan, the country of the Waking Trees and Visible Naiads, of Fauns and Satyrs, of Dwarfs and Giants, of the gods and the Centaurs, of Talking Beasts. It was against these that the first Caspian fought. It is you Telmarines who silenced the beasts and the trees and the fountains, and who killed and drove away the Dwarfs and Fauns, and are now trying to cover up even the memory of them. The King does not allow them to be spoken of."

"Oh, I do wish we hadn't," said Caspian. "And I *am* glad it was all true, even if it is all over."

"Many of your race wish that in secret," said Doctor Cornelius.

"But, Doctor," said Caspian, "why do you say *my* race? After all, I suppose you're a Telmarine too."

"Am I?" said the Doctor.

"Well, you're a Man anyway," said Caspian.

"Am I?" repeated the Doctor in a deeper voice, at the same moment throwing back his hood so that Caspian could see his face clearly in the moonlight.

All at once Caspian realized the truth and felt that he ought to have realized it long before. Doctor Cornelius was so small, and so fat, and had such a very long beard. Two thoughts came into his head at the same moment. One was a thought of terror – "He's not a real man, not a man at all, he's a *Dwarf*, and he's brought me up here to kill me." The other was sheer delight – "There are real Dwarfs still, and I've seen one at last."

"So you've guessed it in the end," said Doctor Cornelius. "Or guessed it nearly right. I'm not a pure Dwarf. I have human blood in me too. Many Dwarfs escaped in the great battles and lived on, shaving their beards and wearing high-heeled shoes and pretending to be men. They have mixed with your Telmarines. I am one of those, only a half-Dwarf, and if any of my kindred, the true Dwarfs, are still alive anywhere in the world, doubtless they would despise me and call me a traitor. But never in all these years have we forgotten our own people and all the other happy creatures of Narnia, and the long-lost days of freedom."

"I'm – I'm sorry, Doctor," said Caspian. "It wasn't my fault, you know."

"I am not saying these things in blame of you, dear Prince," answered the Doctor. "You may well ask why I say them at all. But I have two reasons. Firstly, because my old heart has carried these secret memories so long that it aches with them and would burst if I did not whisper them to you. But secondly, for this: that when you become King you may help us, for I know that you also, Telmarine though you are, love the Old Things."

"I do, I do," said Caspian. "But how can I help?"

"You can be kind to the poor remnants of the Dwarf people, like myself. You can gather learned magicians and try to find a way of awaking the trees once more. You can search through all the nooks and wild places of the land to see if any Fauns or Talking Beasts or Dwarfs are perhaps still alive in hiding."

"Do you think there are any?" asked Caspian eagerly.

"I don't know – I don't know," said the Doctor with a deep sigh. "Sometimes I am afraid there can't be. I have been looking for traces of them all my life. Sometimes I have thought I heard a Dwarf-drum in the mountains. Sometimes at night, in the woods, I thought I had caught a glimpse of Fauns and Satyrs dancing a long way off; but when I came to the place, there was never anything there. I have often despaired; but something always happens to start me hoping again. I don't know. But at least you can try to be a King like the High King Peter of old, and not like your uncle."

"Then it's true about the Kings and Queens too, and about the White Witch?" said Caspian.

"Certainly it is true," said Cornelius. "Their reign was the Golden Age in Narnia and the land has never forgotten them."

"Did they live in this castle, Doctor?"

"Nay, my dear," said the old man. "This castle is a thing of yesterday. Your great-great-grandfather built it. But when the two sons of Adam and the two daughters of Eve were made Kings and Queens of Narnia by Aslan himself, they lived in the castle of Cair Paravel. No man alive has seen that blessed place and perhaps even the ruins of it have now vanished. But we believe it was far from here, down at the mouth of the Great River, on the very shore of the sea."

"Ugh!" said Caspian with a shudder. "Do you mean in

the Black Woods? Where all the – the – you know, the ghosts live?"

"Your Highness speaks as you have been taught," said the Doctor. "But it is all lies. There are no ghosts there. That is a story invented by the Telmarines. Your Kings are in deadly fear of the sea because they can never quite forget that in all stories Aslan comes from over the sea. They don't want to go near it and they don't want anyone else to go near it. So they have let great woods grow up to cut their people off from the coast. But because they have quarrelled with the trees they are afraid of the woods. And because they are afraid of the woods they imagine that they are full of ghosts. And the Kings and great men, hating both the sea and the wood, partly believe these stories, and partly encourage them. They feel safer if no one in Narnia dares to go down to the coast and look out to sea – towards Aslan's land and the morning and the eastern end of the world."

There was a deep silence between them for a few minutes. Then Doctor Cornelius said, "Come. We have been here long enough. It is time to go down and to bed."

"Must we?" said Caspian. "I'd like to go on talking about these things for hours and hours and hours."

"Someone might begin looking for us, if we did that," said Doctor Cornelius.

CHAPTER FIVE

CASPIAN'S ADVENTURE IN
THE MOUNTAINS

AFTER this, Caspian and his Tutor had many more secret conversations on the top of the Great Tower, and at each conversation Caspian learned more about Old Narnia, so that thinking and dreaming about the old days, and longing that they might come back, filled nearly all his spare hours. But of course he had not many hours to spare, for now his education was beginning in earnest. He learned sword-fighting and riding, swimming and diving, how to shoot with the bow and play on the recorder and the theorbo, how to hunt the stag and cut him up when he was dead, besides Cosmography, Rhetoric, Heraldry, Versification, and of course History, with a little Law, Physic, Alchemy, and Astronomy. Of Magic he learned only the theory, for Doctor Cornelius said the practical part was not proper study for princes. "And I myself," he added, "am only a very imperfect magician and can do only the smallest experiments." Of Navigation ("Which is a noble and heroical art," said the Doctor) he was taught nothing, because King Miraz disapproved of ships and the sea.

He also learned a great deal by using his own eyes and ears. As a little boy he had often wondered why he disliked his aunt, Queen Prunaprismia; he now saw that it was because she disliked him. He also began to see that Narnia was an unhappy country. The taxes were high and the laws were stern and Miraz was a cruel man.

After some years there came a time when the Queen seemed to be ill and there was a great deal of bustle and pother about her in the castle and doctors came and the courtiers whispered. This was in early summertime. And one night, while all this fuss was going on, Caspian was unexpectedly wakened by Doctor Cornelius after he had been only a few hours in bed.

"Are we going to do a little Astronomy, Doctor?" said Caspian.

"Hush!" said the Doctor. "Trust me and do exactly as I tell you. Put on all your clothes; you have a long journey before you."

Caspian was very surprised, but he had learned to have confidence in his Tutor and he began doing what he was told at once. When he was dressed the Doctor said, "I have a wallet for you. We must go into the next room and fill it with victuals from your Highness's supper table."

"My gentlemen-in-waiting will be there," said Caspian.

"They are fast asleep and will not wake," said the Doctor. "I am a very minor magician but I *can* at least contrive a charmed sleep."

They went into the antechamber and there, sure enough, the two gentlemen-in-waiting were, sprawling on chairs and snoring hard. Doctor Cornelius quickly cut up the remains of a cold chicken and some slices of venison and put them, with bread and an apple or so and a little flask of good wine, into the wallet which he then gave to Caspian. It fitted on by a strap over Caspian's shoulder, like a satchel you would use for taking books to school.

"Have you your sword?" asked the Doctor.

"Yes," said Caspian.

"Then put this mantle over all to hide the sword and the wallet. That's right. And now we must go to the Great Tower and talk."

When they had reached the top of the Tower (it was a cloudy night, not at all like the night when they had seen the conjunction of Tarva and Alambil) Doctor Cornelius said,

"Dear Prince, you must leave this castle at once and go to seek your fortune in the wide world. Your life is in danger here."

"Why?" asked Caspian.

"Because you are the true King of Narnia: Caspian the Tenth, the true son and heir of Caspian the Ninth. Long life to your Majesty' – and suddenly, to Caspian's great surprise, the little man dropped down on one knee and kissed his hand.

"What does it all mean? I don't understand," said Caspian.

"I wonder you have never asked me before," said the Doctor, "why, being the son of King Caspian, you are not King Caspian yourself. Everyone except your Majesty knows that Miraz is a usurper. When he first began to rule he did not even pretend to be the King: he called himself Lord Protector. But then your royal mother died, the good Queen and the only Telmarine who was ever kind to me. And then, one by one, all the great lords, who had known your father, died or disappeared. Not by accident, either. Miraz weeded them out. Belisar and Uvilas were shot with arrows on a hunting party: by chance, it was pretended. All the great house of the Passarids he sent to fight giants on the northern frontier till one by one they fell. Arlian and Erimon and a dozen more he executed for treason on a false charge. The two brothers of Beaversdam he shut up as madmen. And finally he persuaded the seven noble lords, who alone among all the Telmarines did not fear the sea, to sail away and look for new lands beyond the Eastern Ocean, and, as he intended, they never came back. And when there was no one left who could speak a word for you, then his flatterers (as he had instructed them) begged him to become King. And of course he did."

"Do you mean he now wants to kill me too?" said Caspian.

"That is almost certain," said Doctor Cornelius.

"But why now?" said Caspian. "I mean, why didn't he do it long ago if he wanted to? And what harm have I done him?"

"He has changed his mind about you because of something that happened only two hours ago. The Queen has had a son."

"I don't see what that's got to do with it," said Caspian.

"Don't see!" exclaimed the Doctor. "Have all my lessons in History and Politics taught you no more than that? Listen. As long as he had no children of his own, he was willing enough that you should be King after he died. He may not have cared much about you, but he would rather you should have the throne than a stranger. Now that he has a son of his own he will want his own son to be the next King. You are in the way. He'll clear you out of the way."

"Is he really as bad as that?" said Caspian. "Would he really murder me?"

"He murdered your Father," said Doctor Cornelius.

Caspian felt very queer and said nothing.

"I can tell you the whole story," said the Doctor. "But not now. There is no time. You must fly at once."

"You'll come with me?" said Caspian.

"I dare not," said the Doctor. "It would make your

danger greater. Two are more easily tracked than one. Dear Prince, dear King Caspian, you must be very brave. You must go alone and at once. Try to get across the southern border to the court of King Nain of Archenland. He will be good to you."

"Shall I never see you again?" said Caspian in a quavering voice.

"I hope so, dear King," said the Doctor. "What friend have I in the wide world except your Majesty? And I have a little magic. But in the meantime, speed is everything. Here are two gifts before you go. This is a little purse of gold – alas, all the treasure in this castle should be your own by rights. And here is something far better."

He put in Caspian's hands something which he could hardly see but which he knew by the feel to be a horn.

"That," said Doctor Cornelius, "is the greatest and most sacred treasure of Narnia. Many terrors I endured, many spells did I utter, to find it, when I was still young. It is the magic horn of Queen Susan herself which she left behind her when she vanished from Narnia at the end of the Golden Age. It is said that whoever blows it shall have strange help – no one can say how strange. It may have the power to call Queen Lucy and King Edmund and Queen Susan and High King Peter back from the past, and they will set all to rights. It may be that it will call up Aslan himself. Take it, King Caspian: but do not use it except at your greatest need. And now, haste, haste, haste. The little door at the very bottom of the Tower, the door into the garden, is unlocked. There we must part."

"Can I get my horse Destrier?" said Caspian.

"He is already saddled and waiting for you just at the corner of the orchard."

During the long climb down the winding staircase Cornelius whispered many more words of direction and advice. Caspian's heart was sinking, but he tried to take it all in. Then came the fresh air in the garden, a fervent handclasp with the Doctor, a run across the lawn, a welcoming whinny from Destrier, and so King Caspian the Tenth left the castle of his fathers. Looking back, he saw fireworks going up to celebrate the birth of the new prince.

All night he rode southward, choosing by-ways and bridle paths through woods as long as he was in country that he knew; but afterwards he kept to the high road. Destrier was as excited as his master at this unusual journey, and Caspian, though tears had come into his eyes at saying good-bye to Doctor Cornelius, felt brave and, in a way, happy, to think that he was King Caspian riding to seek adventures, with his sword on his left hip and Queen Susan's magic horn on his right. But when day came, with a sprinkle of rain, and he looked about him and saw on every side unknown woods, wild heaths, and blue mountains, he thought how large and strange the world was and felt frightened and small.

As soon as it was full daylight he left the road and found an open grassy place amid a wood where he could rest. He took off Destrier's bridle and let him graze, ate some cold chicken and drank a little wine, and presently fell asleep. It was late afternoon when he awoke. He ate a morsel and continued his journey, still southward, by many unfrequented lanes. He was now in a land of hills, going up and down, but always more up than down. From every ridge he could see the mountains growing bigger and blacker ahead. As the evening closed in, he was riding their lower slopes. The wind rose. Soon rain fell in torrents.

Destrier became uneasy; there was thunder in the air. And now they entered a dark and seemingly endless pine forest, and all the stories Caspian had ever heard of trees being unfriendly to Man crowded into his mind. He remembered that he was, after all, a Telmarine, one of the race who cut down trees wherever they could and were at war with all wild things; and though he himself might be

unlike other Telmarines, the trees could not be expected to know this.

Nor did they. The wind became a tempest, the woods roared and creaked all round them. There came a crash. A tree fell right across the road just behind him. "Quiet, Destrier, quiet!" said Caspian, patting his horse's neck; but he was trembling himself and knew that he had escaped death by an inch. Lightning flashed and a great crack of thunder seemed to break the sky in two just overhead.

Destrier bolted in good earnest. Caspian was a good rider, but he had not the strength to hold him back. He kept his seat, but he knew that his life hung by a thread during the wild career that followed. Tree after tree rose up before them in the dusk and was only just avoided. Then, almost too suddenly to hurt (and yet it did hurt him too) something struck Caspian on the forehead and he knew no more.

When he came to himself he was lying in a firelit place with bruised limbs and a bad headache. Low voices were speaking close at hand.

"And now," said one, "before it wakes up we must decide what to do with it."

"Kill it," said another. "We can't let it live. It would betray us."

"We ought to have killed it at once, or else let it alone," said a third voice. "We can't kill it now. Not after we've taken it in and bandaged its head and all. It would be murdering a guest."

"Gentlemen," said Caspian in a feeble voice, "whatever you do to me, I hope you will be kind to my poor horse."

"Your horse had taken flight long before we found you," said the first voice – a curiously husky, earthy voice, as Caspian now noticed.

"Now don't let it talk you round with its pretty words," said the second voice. "I still say –"

"Horns and halibuts!" exclaimed the third voice. "Of course we're not going to murder it. For shame, Nikabrik. What do you say, Trufflehunter? What shall we do with it?"

"I shall give it a drink," said the first voice, presumably

Trufflehunter's. A dark shape approached the bed. Caspian felt an arm slipped gently under his shoulders – if it was exactly an arm. The shape somehow seemed wrong. The face that bent towards him seemed wrong too. He got the impression that it was very hairy and very long nosed, and there were odd white patches on each side of it. "It's a mask of some sort," thought Caspian. "Or perhaps I'm in a fever and imagining it all." A cupful of something sweet and hot was set to his lips and he drank. At that moment one of the others poked the fire. A blaze sprang up and Caspian almost screamed with the shock as the sudden light revealed the face that was looking into his own. It was not a man's face but a badger's, though larger and friendlier and more intelligent than the face of any badger he had seen before. And it had certainly been talking. He saw, too, that he was on a bed of heather, in a cave. By the fire sat two little bearded men, so much wilder and shorter and hairier and thicker than Doctor Cornelius that he knew them at once for real Dwarfs, ancient Dwarfs with not a drop of human blood in their veins. And Caspian knew that he had found the Old Narnians at last. Then his head began to swim again.

In the next few days he learned to know them by names.

The Badger was called Trufflehunter; he was the oldest and kindest of the three. The Dwarf who had wanted to kill Caspian was a sour Black Dwarf (that is, his hair and beard were black, and thick and hard like horsehair). His name was Nikabrik. The other Dwarf was a Red Dwarf with hair rather like a Fox's and he was called Trumpkin.

"And now," said Nikabrik on the first evening when Caspian was well enough to sit up and talk, "we still have to decide what to do with this Human. You two think you've done it a great kindess by not letting me kill it. But I suppose the upshot is that we have to keep it a prisoner for life. I'm certainly not going to let it go alive – to go back to its own kind and betray us all."

"Bulbs and bolsters! Nikabrik," said Trumpkin. "Why need you talk so unhandsomely? It isn't the creature's fault that it bashed its head against a tree outside our hole. And I don't think it looks like a traitor."

"I say," said Caspian, "you haven't yet found out whether I *want* to go back. I don't. I want to stay with you – if you'll let me. I've been looking for people like you all my life."

"That's a likely story," growled Nikabrik. "You're a Telmarine and a Human, aren't you? Of course you want to go back to your own kind."

"Well, even if I did, I couldn't," said Caspian. "I was flying for my life when I had my accident. The King wants to kill me. If you'd killed me, you'd have done the very thing to please him."

"Well now," said Trufflehunter, "you don't say so!"

"Eh?" said Trumpkin. "What's that? What have you been doing, Human, to fall foul of Miraz at your age?"

"He's my uncle," began Caspian, when Nikabrik jumped up with his hand on his dagger.

"There you are!" he cried. "Not only a Telmarine but close kin and heir to our greatest enemy. Are you still mad enough to let this creature live?" He would have stabbed Caspian then and there, if the Badger and Trumpkin had not got in the way and forced him back to his seat and held him down.

"Now, once and for all, Nikabrik," said Trumpkin. "Will you contain yourself, or must Trufflehunter and I sit on your head?"

Nikabrik sulkily promised to behave, and the other two asked Caspian to tell his whole story. When he had done so there was a moment's silence.

"This is the queerest thing I ever heard," said Trumpkin.

"I don't like it," said Nikabrik. "I didn't know there were stories about us still told among the Humans. The less they know about us the better. That old nurse, now. She'd better have held her tongue. And it's all mixed up with that Tutor: a renegade Dwarf. I hate 'em. I hate 'em worse than the Humans. You mark my words – no good will come of it."

"Don't you go talking about things you don't understand, Nikabrik," said Trufflehunter. "You Dwarfs are as forgetful and changeable as the Humans themselves. I'm a beast, I am, and a Badger what's more. We don't change. We hold on. I say great good will come of it. This is the true King of Narnia we've got here: a true King, coming back to true Narnia. And we beasts remember, even if Dwarfs forget, that Narnia was never right except when a son of Adam was King."

"Whistles and whirligigs! Trufflehunter," said

Trumpkin. "You don't mean you want to give the country to Humans?"

"I said nothing about that," answered the Badger. "It's not Men's country (who should know that better than me?) but it's a country for a man to be King of. We badgers have long enough memories to know that. Why, bless us all, wasn't the High King Peter a Man?"

"Do you believe all those old stories?" asked Trumpkin.

"I tell you, we don't change, we beasts," said Trufflehunter. "We don't forget. I believe in the High King Peter and the rest that reigned at Cair Paravel, as firmly as I believe in Aslan himself."

"As firmly as *that*, I dare say," said Trumpkin. "But who believes in Aslan nowadays?"

"I do," said Caspian. "And if I hadn't believed in him before, I would now. Back there among the Humans the people who laughed at Aslan would have laughed at stories about Talking Beasts and Dwarfs. Sometimes I did wonder if there really was such a person as Aslan: but then sometimes I wondered if there were really people like you. Yet there you are."

"That's right," said Trufflehunter. "You're right, King Caspian. And as long as you will be true to Old Narnia you shall be *my* King, whatever they say. Long life to your Majesty."

"You make me sick, Badger," growled Nikabrik. "The High King Peter and the rest may have been Men, but they were a different sort of Men. This is one of the cursed Telmarines. He has *hunted* beasts for sport. Haven't you, now?" he added, rounding suddenly on Caspian.

"Well, to tell you the truth, I have," said Caspian. "But they weren't Talking Beasts."

"It's all the same thing," said Nikabrik.

"No, no, no," said Trufflehunter. "You know it isn't. You know very well that the beasts in Narnia nowadays are different and are no more than the poor dumb, witless creatures you'd find in Calormen or Telmar. They're smaller too. They're far more different from us than the half-Dwarfs are from you."

There was a great deal more talk, but it all ended with the agreement that Caspian should stay and even the promise that, as soon as he was able to go out, he should be taken to see what Trumpkin called "the Others"; for apparently in these wild parts all sorts of creatures from the Old Days of Narnia still lived on in hiding.

CHAPTER SIX

THE PEOPLE THAT LIVED IN HIDING

Now began the happiest times that Caspian had ever known. On a fine summer morning when the dew lay on the grass he set off with the Badger and the two Dwarfs, up through the forest to a high saddle in the mountains and down on to their sunny southern slopes where one looked across the green wolds of Archenland.

"We will go first to the Three Bulgy Bears," said Trumpkin.

They came in a glade to an old hollow oak tree covered with moss, and Trufflehunter tapped with his paw three times on the trunk and there was no answer. Then he tapped again and a woolly sort of voice from inside said, "Go away. It's not time to get up yet." But when he tapped the third time there was a noise like a small earthquake from inside and a sort of door opened and out came three brown bears, very bulgy indeed and blinking their little eyes. And when everything had been explained to them (which took a long time because they were so sleepy) they said, just as Trufflehunter had said, that a son of Adam ought to be King of Narnia and all kissed Caspian – very wet, snuffly kisses they were – and offered him some honey. Caspian did not really want honey, without bread, at that time in the morning, but he thought it polite to accept. It took him a long time afterwards to get unsticky.

After that they went on till they came among tall beech trees and Trufflehunter called out, "Pattertwig! Pattertwig! Pattertwig!" and almost at once, bounding down from branch to branch till he was just above their heads, came the most magnificent red squirrel that Caspian had ever seen. He was for bigger than the ordinary dumb squirrels which he had sometimes seen in the castle gardens; indeed he was nearly the size of a terrier and the moment you looked in his face you saw that he could talk. Indeed the difficulty was to get him to stop talking, for, like all squirrels, he was a chatterer. He welcomed Caspian at once and asked if he would like a nut and Caspian said thanks, he would. But as Pattertwig went bounding away to fetch it, Trufflehunter whispered in Caspian's ear, "Don't look. Look the other way. It's very bad manners among squirrels to watch anyone going to his store or to look as if you wanted to know where it was." Then Pattertwig came back with the nut and Caspian ate it and after that Pattertwig asked if he could take any messages to other friends. "For I can go nearly everywhere without setting foot to ground," he said. Trufflehunter and the Dwarfs thought this a very good idea and gave Pattertwig messages to all sorts of people with queer names telling them all to come to a feast and council on Dancing Lawn at midnight three nights ahead. "And you'd better tell the three Bulgies too," added Trumpkin. "We forgot to mention it to them."

Their next visit was to the Seven Brothers of Shuddering

Wood. Trumpkin led the way back to the saddle and then down eastward on the northern slope of the mountains till they came to a very solemn place among rocks and fir trees. They went very quietly and presently Caspian could feel the ground shake under his feet as if someone were hammering down below. Trumpkin went to a flat stone about the size of the top of a water-butt, and stamped on it with his foot. After a long pause it was moved away by someone or something underneath, and there was a dark, round hole with a good deal of heat and steam coming out of it and in the middle of the hole the head of a Dwarf very like Trumpkin himself. There was a long talk here and the dwarf seemed more suspicious than the Squirrel or the Bulgy Bears had been, but in the end the whole party were invited to come down. Caspian found himself descending a dark stairway into the earth, but when he came to the bottom he saw firelight. It was the light of a furnace. The whole place was a smithy. A subterranean stream ran past on one side of it. Two Dwarfs were at the bellows, another was holding a piece of red-hot metal on the anvil with a pair of tongs, a fourth was hammering it, and two, wiping their horny little hands on a greasy cloth, were coming forward to meet the visitors. It took some time to satisfy them that Caspian was a friend and not an enemy, but when they did, they all cried, "Long live the King," and their gifts were noble – mail shirts and helmets and swords for Caspian and Trumpkin and Nikabrik. The Badger could have had the same if he had liked, but he said he was a beast, he was, and if his claws and teeth could not keep his skin whole, it wasn't worth keeping. The workmanship of the arms was far finer than any Caspian had ever seen, and he gladly accepted the Dwarf-made sword instead of his own, which looked, in comparison, as feeble as a toy and as clumsy as a stick. The seven brothers (who were all Red Dwarfs) promised to come to the feast at Dancing Lawn.

A little farther on, in a dry, rocky ravine they reached the cave of five Black Dwarfs. They looked suspiciously at Caspian, but in the end the eldest of them said, "If he is against Miraz, we'll have him for King." And the next oldest said, "Shall we go farther up for you, up to the crags? There's an Ogre or two and a Hag that we could introduce you to, up there."

"Certainly not," said Caspian.

"I should think not, indeed," said Trufflehunter. "We want none of that sort on our side." Nikabrik disagreed with this, but Trumpkin and the Badger overruled him. It gave Caspian a shock to realize that the horrible creatures out of the old stories, as well as the nice ones, had some descendants in Narnia still.

"We should not have Aslan for friend if we brought in *that* rabble," said Trufflehunter as they came away from the cave of the Black Dwarfs.

"Oh, Aslan!" said Trumpkin, cheerily but contemptuously. "What matters much more is that you wouldn't have me."

"Do *you* believe in Aslan?" said Caspian to Nikabrik.

"I'll believe in anyone or anything," said Nikabrik, "that'll batter these cursed Telmarine barbarians to pieces or drive them out of Narnia. Anyone or anything, Aslan *or* the White Witch, do you understand?"

"Silence, silence," said Trufflehunter. "You do not know what you are saying. She was a worse enemy than Miraz and all his race."

"Not to Dwarfs, she wasn't," said Nikabrik.

Their next visit was a pleasanter one. As they came lower down, the mountains opened out into a great glen or wooded gorge with a swift river running at the bottom. The open places near the river's edge were a mass of foxgloves and wild roses and the air was buzzing with bees. Here Trufflehunter called again, "Glenstorm! Glenstorm!" and after a pause Caspian heard the sound of hoofs. It grew louder till the valley trembled and at last, breaking and trampling the thickets, there came in sight the noblest creatures that Caspian had yet seen, the great Centaur Glenstorm and his three sons. His flanks were glossy chestnut and the beard that covered his broad chest was golden-red. He was a prophet and a star-gazer and knew what they had come about.

"Long live the King," he cried. "I and my sons are ready for war. When is the battle to be joined?"

Up till now neither Caspian nor the others had really been thinking of a war. They had some vague idea, perhaps, of an occasional raid on some Human farmstead or of attacking a party of hunters, if it ventured too far into these southern wilds. But, in the main, they had thought only of living to themselves in woods and caves and building up an attempt at Old Narnia in hiding. As soon as Glenstorm had spoken everyone felt much more serious.

"Do you mean a real war to drive Miraz out of Narnia?" asked Caspian.

"What else?" said the Centaur. "Why else does your Majesty go clad in mail and girt with sword?"

"Is it possible, Glenstorm?" said the Badger.

"The time is ripe," said Glenstorm. "I watch the skies,

Badger, for it is mine to watch, as it is yours to remember. Tarva and Alambil have met in the halls of high heaven, and on earth a son of Adam has once more arisen to rule and name the creatures. The hour has struck. Our council at the Dancing Lawn must be a council of war." He spoke in such a voice that neither Caspian nor the others hesitated for a moment: it now seemed to them quite possible that they might win a war and quite certain that they must wage one.

As it was now past the middle of the day, they rested with the Centaurs and ate such food as the centaurs provided – cakes of oaten meal, and apples, and herbs, and wine, and cheese.

The next place they were to visit was quite near at hand, but they had to go a long way round in order to avoid a region in which Men lived. It was well into the afternoon before they found themselves in level fields, warm between hedgerows. There Trufflehunter called at the mouth of a little hole in a green bank and out popped the last thing Caspian expected – a Talking Mouse. He was of course bigger than a common mouse, well over a foot high when he stood on his hind legs, and with ears nearly as long as (though broader than) a rabbit's. His name was Reepicheep and he was a gay and martial mouse. He wore a tiny little rapier at his side and twirled his long whiskers as if they were a moustache. "There are twelve of us, Sire," he said with a dashing and graceful bow, "and I place all the resources of my people unreservedly at your Majesty's disposal." Caspian tried hard (and unsuccessfully) not to laugh, but he couldn't help thinking that Reepicheep and all his people could very easily be put in a washing basket and carried home on one's back.

It would take too long to mention all the creatures whom Caspian met that day – Clodsley Shovel the Mole, the three Hardbiters (who were badgers like Trufflehunter), Camillo the Hare, and Hogglestock the Hedgehog. They rested at last beside a well at the edge of a wide and level circle of grass, bordered with tall elms which now threw long shadows across it, for the sun was setting, the daisies closing, and the rooks flying home to bed. Here they supped on food they had brought with them and Trumpkin lit his pipe (Nikabrik was not a smoker).

"Now," said the Badger, "if only we could wake the spirits of these trees and this well, we should have done a good day's work."

"Can't we?" said Caspian.

"No," said Trufflehunter. "We have no power over them. Since the Humans came into the land, felling forests and defiling streams, the Dryads and Naiads have sunk into a deep sleep. Who knows if ever they will stir again? And that is a great loss to our side. The Telmarines are horribly afraid of the woods, and once the Trees moved in anger, our enemies would go mad with fright and be chased out of Narnia as quick as their legs could carry them."

"What imaginations you Animals have!" said Trumpkin, who didn't believe in such things. "But why stop at Trees and Waters? Wouldn't it be even nicer if the stones started throwing themselves at old Miraz?"

The Badger only grunted at this, and after that there was such a silence that Caspian had nearly dropped off to sleep

when he thought he heard a faint musical sound from the depth of the woods at his back. Then he thought it was only a dream and turned over again; but as soon as his ear touched the ground he felt or heard (it was hard to tell which) a faint beating or drumming. He raised his head. The beating noise at once became fainter, but the music returned, clearer this time. It was like flutes. He saw that Trufflehunter was sitting up staring into the wood. The moon was bright; Caspian had been asleep longer than he thought. Nearer and nearer came the music, a tune wild and yet dreamy, and the noise of many light feet, till at last, out from the wood into the moonlight, came dancing shapes such as Caspian had been thinking of all his life. They were not much taller than dwarfs, but far slighter and more graceful. Their curly heads had little horns, the upper part of their bodies gleamed naked in the pale light, but their legs and feet were those of goats.

"Fauns!" cried Caspian, jumping up, and in a moment they were all round him. It took next to no time to explain the whole situation to them and they accepted Caspian at once. Before he knew what he was doing he found himself joining in the dance. Trumpkin, with heavier and jerkier movements, did likewise and even Trufflehunter hopped and lumbered about as best he could. Only Nikabrik stayed where he was, looking on in silence. The Fauns footed it all round Caspian to their reedy pipes. Their strange faces, which seemed mournful and merry all at once, looked into his; dozens of Fauns, Mentius and Obentinus and Dumnus, Voluns, Voltinus, Girbius, Nimienus, Nausus, and Oscuns. Pattertwig had sent them all.

When Caspian awoke next morning he could hardly believe that it had not all been a dream; but the grass was covered with little cloven hoof-marks.

CHAPTER SEVEN

OLD NARNIA IN DANGER

THE place where they had met the Fauns was, of course, Dancing Lawn itself, and here Caspian and his friends remained till the night of the great Council. To sleep under the stars, to drink nothing but well water and to live chiefly on nuts and wild fruit, was a strange experience for Caspian after his bed with silken sheets in a tapestried chamber at the castle, with meals laid out on gold and silver dishes in the anteroom, and attendants ready at his call. But he had never enjoyed himself more. Never had sleep been more refreshing nor food tasted more savoury, and he began already to harden and his face wore a kinglier look.

When the great night came, and his various strange subjects came stealing into the lawn by ones and twos and threes or by sixes and sevens — the moon then shining almost at her full — his heart swelled as he saw their numbers and heard their greetings. All whom he had met were there: Bulgy Bears and Red Dwarfs and Black Dwarfs, Moles and Badgers, Hares and Hedgehogs, and others whom he had not yet seen — five Satyrs as red as foxes, the whole contingent of Talking Mice, armed to the teeth and following a shrill trumpet, some Owls, the Old Raven of Ravenscaur. Last of all (and this took Caspian's breath away), with the Centaurs came a small but genuine Giant, Wimbleweather of Deadman's Hill, carrying on his back a basketful of rather sea-sick Dwarfs who had accepted his offer of a lift and were now wishing they had walked instead.

The Bulgy Bears were very anxious to have the feast first and leave the council till afterwards: perhaps till tomorrow. Reepicheep and his Mice said that councils and feasts could both wait, and proposed storming Miraz in his own castle that very night. Pattertwig and the other Squirrels said they could talk and eat at the same time, so why not have the council and feast all at once? The Moles proposed throwing up entrenchments round the Lawn before they did anything else. The Fauns thought it would be better to begin with a solemn dance. The Old Raven, while agreeing with the Bears that it would take too long to have a full council before supper, begged to be allowed to give a brief address to the whole company. But Caspian and the Centaurs and the Dwarfs overruled all these suggestions and insisted on holding a real council of war at once.

When all the other creatures had been persuaded to sit down quietly in a great circle, and when (with more difficulty) they had got Pattertwig to stop running to and fro and saying "Silence! Silence, everyone, for the King's speech", Caspian, feeling a little nervous, got up. "Narnians!" he began, but he never got any further, for at that very moment Camillo the Hare said, "Hush! There's a Man somewhere near."

They were all creatures of the wild, accustomed to being hunted, and they all became still as statues. The beasts all turned their noses in the direction which Camillo had indicated.

"Smells like Man and yet not quite like Man," whispered Trufflehunter.

"It's getting steadily nearer," said Camillo.

"Two badgers and you three Dwarfs, with your

bows at the ready, go softly off to meet it," said Caspian.

"We'll settle 'un," said a Black Dwarf grimly, fitting a shaft to his bowstring.

"Don't shoot if it is alone," said Caspian. "Catch it."

"Why?" asked the Dwarf.

"Do as you're told," said Glenstorm the Centaur.

Everyone waited in silence while the three Dwarfs and two Badgers trotted stealthily across to the trees on the north-west side of the Lawn. Then came a sharp dwarfish cry, "Stop! Who goes there?" and a sudden spring. A moment later a voice, which Caspian knew well, could he heard saying, "All right, all right, I'm unarmed. Take my wrists if you like, worthy Badgers, but don't bite right through them. I want to speak to the King."

"Doctor Cornelius!" cried Caspian with joy, and rushed forward to greet his old tutor. Everyone else crowded round.

"Pah!" said Nikabrik. "A renegade Dwarf. A half-and-halfer! Shall I pass my sword through its throat?"

"Be quiet, Nikabrik," said Trumpkin. "The creature can't help its ancestry."

"This is my greatest friend and the saviour of my life," said Caspian. "And anyone who doesn't like his company may leave my army: at once. Dearest doctor, I *am* glad to see you again. How ever did you find us out?"

"By a little use of simple magic, your Majesty," said the Doctor, who was still puffing and blowing from having walked so fast. "But there's no time to go into that now. We must all fly from this place at once. You are already betrayed and Miraz is on the move. Before midday tomorrow you will be surrounded."

"Betrayed!" said Caspian. "And by whom?"

"Another renegade Dwarf, no doubt," said Nikabrik.

"By your horse Destrier," said Doctor Cornelius. "The poor brute knew no better. When you were knocked off, of course, he went dawdling back to his stable in the castle. Then the secret of your flight was known. I made myself scarce, having no wish to be questioned about it in Miraz's torture chamber. I had a pretty good guess from my crystal as to where I should find you. But all day – that was the day before yesterday – I saw Miraz's tracking parties out in the woods. Yesterday I learned that his army is out. I don't think some of your – um – pure-blooded Dwarfs have as much woodcraft as might be expected. You've left tracks all over the place. Great carelessness. At any rate something has warned Miraz that Old Narnia is not so dead as he had hoped, and he is on the move."

"Hurrah!" said a very shrill and small voice from somewhere at the Doctor's feet. "Let them come! All I ask is that the King will put me and my people in the front."

"What on earth?" said Doctor Cornelius. "Has your Majesty got grasshoppers – or mosquitoes – in your army?" Then after stooping down and peering carefully through his spectacles, he broke into a laugh.

"By the Lion," he swore, "it's a mouse. Signior Mouse, I desire your better acquaintance. I am honoured by meeting so valiant a beast."

"My friendship you shall have, learned Man," piped Reepicheep. "And any Dwarf – or Giant – in the army who does not give you good language shall have my sword to reckon with."

"Is there time for this foolery?" asked Nikabrik. "What are our plans? Battle or flight?"

"Battle if need be," said Trumpkin. "But we are hardly ready for it yet, and this is no very defensible place."

"I don't like the idea of running away," said Caspian.

"Hear him! Hear him!" said the Bulgy Bears. "Whatever we do, don't let's have any *running*. Especially not before supper; and not too soon after it neither."

"Those who run first do not always run last," said the Centaur. "And why should we let the enemy choose our position instead of choosing it ourselves? Let us find a strong place."

"That's wise, your Majesty, that's wise," said Truffle-hunter.

"But where are we to go?" asked several voices.

"Your Majesty," said Doctor Cornelius, "and all you variety of creatures, I think we must fly east and down the river to the great woods. The Telmarines hate that region. They have always been afraid of the sea and of something that may come over the sea. That is why they have let the great woods grow up. If traditions speak true, the ancient Cair Paravel was at the river-mouth. All that part is friendly to us and hateful to our enemies. We must go to Aslan's How."

"Aslan's How?" said several voices. "We do not know what it is."

"It lies within the skirts of the Great Woods and it is a huge mound which Narnians raised in very ancient times over a very magical place, where there stood – and perhaps still stands – a very magical Stone. The Mound is all hollowed out within into galleries and caves, and the Stone is in the central cave of all. There is room in the mound for all our stores, and those of us who have most need of cover and are most accustomed to underground life can be lodged in the caves. The rest of us can lie in the wood. At a pinch all of us (except this worthy Giant) could retreat into the Mound itself, and there we should be beyond the reach of every danger except famine."

"It is a good thing we have a learned man among us," said Trufflehunter; but Trumpkin muttered under his breath, "Soup and celery! I wish our leaders would think less about these old wives' tales and more about victuals and arms." But all approved of Cornelius's proposal and

that very night, half an hour later, they were on the march. Before sunrise they arrived at Aslan's How.

It was certainly an awesome place, a round green hill on top of another hill, long since grown over with trees, and one little, low doorway leading into it. The tunnels inside were a perfect maze till you got to know them, and they were lined and roofed with smooth stones, and on the stones, peering in the twilight, Caspian saw strange characters and snaky patterns, and pictures in which the form of a Lion was repeated again and again. It all seemed to belong to an even older Narnia than the Narnia of which his nurse had told him.

It was after they had taken up their quarters in and around the How that fortune began to turn against them. King Miraz's scouts soon found their new lair, and he and his army arrived on the edge of the woods. And as so often happens, the enemy turned out stronger than they had reckoned. Caspian's heart sank as he saw company after company arriving. And though Miraz's men may have been afraid of going into the wood, they were even more afraid of Miraz, and with him in command they carried battle deeply into it and sometimes almost to the How itself. Caspian and other captains of course made many sorties into the open country. Thus there was fighting on most days and sometimes by night as well; but Caspian's party had on the whole the worst of it.

At last there came a night when everything had gone as badly as possible, and the rain which had been falling heavily all day had ceased at nightfall only to give place to raw cold. That morning Caspian had arranged what was his biggest battle yet, and all had hung their hopes on it. He, with most of the Dwarfs, was to have fallen on the King's right wing at daybreak, and then, when they were heavily engaged, Giant Wimbleweather, with the Centaurs and some of the fiercest beasts, was to have broken out from another place and endeavoured to cut the King's right off from the rest of the army. But it had all failed. No one had warned Caspian (because no one in these later days of Narnia remembered) that Giants are not at all clever. Poor Wimbleweather, though as brave as a lion, was a true Giant in that respect. He had broken out at the wrong time and from the wrong place, and both his party and

Caspian's had suffered badly and done the enemy little harm. The best of the Bears had been hurt, a Centaur terribly wounded, and there were few in Caspian's party who had not lost blood. It was a gloomy company that huddled under the dripping trees to eat their scanty supper.

The gloomiest of all was Giant Wimbleweather. He knew it was all his fault. He sat in silence shedding big tears which collected on the end of his nose and then fell off with a huge splash on the whole bivouac of the Mice, who had just been beginning to get warm and drowsy. They all jumped up, shaking the water out of their ears and wringing their little blankets, and asked the Giant in shrill but forcible voices whether he thought they weren't wet enough without this sor of thing. And then other people woke up and told the Mice they had been enrolled as scouts and not as a concert party, and asked why they couldn't keep quiet. And Wimbleweather tiptoed away to find some place where he could be miserable in peace and stepped on somebody's tail and somebody (they said afterwards it was a fox) bit him. And so everyone was out of temper.

But in the secret and magical chamber at the heart of the How, King Caspian, with Cornelius and the Badger and Nikabrik and Trumpkin, were at council. Thick pillars of ancient workmanship supported the roof. In the centre was the Stone itself – a stone table, split right down the centre, and covered with what had once been writing of some kind: but ages of wind and rain and snow had almost worn them away in old times when the Stone Table had stood on the hilltop, and the Mound had not yet been built above it. They were not using the Table nor sitting round it: it was too magic a thing for any common use. They sat on logs a little way from it, and between them was a rough wooden table, on which stood a rude clay lamp lighting up their pale faces and throwing big shadows on the walls.

"If your Majesty is ever to use the Horn," said Trufflehunter, "I think the time has now come." Caspian had of course told them of his treasure several days ago.

"We are certainly in great need," answered Caspian. "But it is hard to be sure we are at our greatest. Supposing there came an even worse need and we had already used it?"

"By that argument," said Nikabrik, "your Majesty will never use it until it is too late."

"I agree with that," said Doctor Cornelius.

"And what do you think, Trumpkin?" asked Caspian.

"Oh, as for me," said the Red Dwarf, who had been listening with complete indifference, "your Majesty knows

I think the Horn – and that bit of broken stone over there – and your great King Peter – and your Lion Aslan – are all eggs in moonshine. It's all one to me when your Majesty blows the Horn. All I insist on is that the army is told nothing about it. There's no good raising hopes of magical help which (as I think) are sure to be disappointed."

"Then in the name of Aslan we will wind Queen Susan's Horn," said Caspian.

"There is one thing, Sire," said Doctor Cornelius, "that should perhaps be done first. We do not know what form the help will take. It might call Aslan himself from oversea. But I think it is more likely to call Peter the High King and his mighty consorts down from the high past. But in either case, I do not think we can be sure that the help will come to this very spot –"

"You never said a truer word," put in Trumpkin.

"I think," went on the learned man, "that they – or he – will come back to one or other of the Ancient Places of Narnia. This, where we now sit, is the most ancient and most deeply magical of all, and here, I think, the answer is likeliest to come. But there are two others. One is Lantern Waste, up-river, west of Beaversdam, where the Royal Children first appeared in Narnia, as the records tell. The other is down at the river-mouth, where their castle of Cair Paravel once stood. And if Aslan himself comes, that would be the best place for meeting him too, for every story says that he is the son of the great Emperor-over-the-Sea, and over the sea he will pass. I should like very much to send messengers to both places, to Lantern Waste and the river-mouth, to receive them – or him – or it."

"Just as I thought," muttered Trumpkin. "The first

result of all this foolery is not to bring us help but to lose us two fighters."

"Who would you think of sending, Doctor Cornelius?" asked Caspian.

"Squirrels are best for getting through enemy country without being caught," said Trufflehunter.

"All *our* squirrels (and we haven't many)," said Nikabrik, "are rather flighty. The only one I'd trust on a job like that would be Pattertwig."

"Let it be Pattertwig, then," said King Caspian. "And who for our other messenger? I know you'd go, Trufflehunter, but you haven't the speed. Nor you, Doctor Cornelius."

"I *won't* go," said Nikabrik. "With all these Humans and beasts about, there must be a Dwarf here to see that the Dwarfs are fairly treated."

"Thimbles and thunderstorms!" cried Trumpkin in a rage. "Is that how you speak to the King? Send me, Sire, I'll go."

"But I thought you didn't believe in the Horn, Trumpkin," said Caspian.

"No more I do, your Majesty. But what's that got to do with it? I might as well die on a wild goose chase as die here. You are my King. I know the difference between giving advice and taking orders. You've had my advice, and now it's the time for orders."

"I will never forget this, Trumpkin," said Caspian. "Send for Pattertwig, one of you. And when shall I blow the Horn?"

"I would wait for sunrise, your Majesty," said Doctor Cornelius. "That sometimes has an effect in operations of White Magic."

A few minutes later Pattertwig arrived and had his task explained to him. As he was, like many squirrels, full of courage and dash and energy and excitement and mischief (not to say conceit), he no sooner heard it than he was eager to be off. It was arranged that he should run for Lantern Waste while Trumpkin made the shorter journey to the river-mouth. After a hasty meal they both set off with the fervent thanks and good wishes of the King, the Badger, and Cornelius.

CHAPTER EIGHT

HOW THEY LEFT THE ISLAND

"AND SO," said Trumpkin (for, as you have realized, it was he who had been telling all this story to the four children, sitting on the grass in the ruined hall of Cair Paravel) – "and so I put a crust or two in my pocket, left behind all weapons but my dagger, and took to the woods in the grey of the morning. I'd been plugging away for many hours when there came a sound that I'd never heard the like of in my born days. Eh, I won't forget that. The whole air was full of it, loud as thunder but far longer, cool and sweet as music over water, but strong enough to shake the woods. And I said to myself, 'If that's not the Horn, call me a rabbit.' And a moment later I wondered why he hadn't blown it sooner –"

"What time was it?" asked Edmund.

"Between nine and ten of the clock," said Trumpkin.

"Just when we were at the railway station!" said all the children, and looked at one another with shining eyes.

"Please go on," said Lucy to the Dwarf.

"Well, as I was saying, I wondered, but I went on as hard as I could pelt. I kept on all night – and then, when it was half light this morning, as if I'd no more sense than a Giant, I risked a short cut across open country to cut off a big loop of the river, and was caught. Not by the army, but by a pompous old fool who has charge of a little castle which is Miraz's last stronghold towards the coast. I needn't tell you they got no true tale out of me, but I was a Dwarf and that was enough. But, lobsters and lollipops! it is a good thing the seneschal *was* a pompous fool. Anyone else would have run me through there and then. But nothing would do for him short of a grand execution: sending me down 'to the ghosts' in the full ceremonial way. And then this young lady" (he nodded at Susan) "does her bit of archery – and it was pretty shooting, let me tell you – and here we are. And without my armour, for of course they took that." He knocked out and refilled his pipe.

"Great Scott!" said Peter. "So it was the horn – your own horn, Su – that dragged us all off that seat on the platform yesterday morning! I can hardly believe it; yet it all fits in."

"I don't know why you shouldn't believe it," said Lucy, "if you believe in magic at all. Aren't there lots of stories about magic forcing people out of one place – out of one world – into another? I mean, when a magician in *The Arabian Nights* calls up a Jinn, it has to come. We had to come, just like that."

"Yes," said Peter, "I suppose what makes it feel so queer is that in the stories it's always someone in our world who does the calling. One doesn't really think about where the Jinn's coming *from*."

"And now we know what it feels like for the Jinn," said Edmund with a chuckle. "Golly! It's a bit uncomfortable to know that *we* can be whistled for like that. It's worse than what Father says about living at the mercy of the telephone."

"But we want to be here, don't we," said Lucy, "if Aslan wants us?"

"Meanwhile," said the Dwarf, "what are we to do? I suppose I'd better go back to King Caspian and tell him no help has come."

"No help?" said Susan. "But it *has* worked. And here we are."

"Um – um – yes, to be sure. I see that," said the Dwarf, whose pipe seemed to be blocked (at any rate he made himself very busy cleaning it). "But – well – I mean –"

"But don't you yet see who we are?" shouted Lucy. "You *are* stupid."

"I suppose you are the four children out of the old stories," said Trumpkin. "And I'm very glad to meet you of course. And it's very interesting, no doubt. But – no offence?' – and he hesitated again.

"Do get on and say whatever you're going to say," said Edmund.

"Well, then – no offence," said Trumpkin. "But, you know, the King and Trufflehunter and Doctor Cornelius were expecting – well, if you see what I mean, help. To put it in another way, I think they'd been imagining you as great warriors. As it is – we're awfully fond of children and all that, but just at the moment, in the middle of a war – but I'm sure you understand."

"You mean you think we're no good," said Edmund, getting red in the face.

"Now pray don't be offended," interrupted the Dwarf. "I assure you, my dear little friends – "

"*Little* from you is really a bit too much," said Edmund, jumping up. "I suppose you don't believe we won the Battle of Beruna? Well, you can say what you like about me because I know –"

"There's no good losing our tempers," said Peter. "Let's fit him out with fresh armour and fit ourselves out from the treasure chamber, and have a talk after that."

"I don't quite see the point –" began Edmund, but Lucy

whispered in his ear, "Hadn't we better do what Peter says? He is the High King, you know. And I think he has an idea." So Edmund agreed and by the aid of his torch they all, including Trumpkin, went down the steps again into the dark coldness and dusty splendour of the treasure house.

The Dwarf's eyes glistened as he saw the wealth that lay on the shelves (though he had to stand on tiptoes to do so) and he muttered to himself, "It would never do to let Nikabrik see this; never." They found easily enough a mail shirt for him, a sword, a helmet, a shield, a bow and quiverful of arrows, all of dwarfish size. The helmet was of copper, set with rubies, and there was gold on the hilt of the sword: Trumpkin had never seen, much less carried, so much wealth in all his life. The children also put on mail shirts and helmets; a sword and shield were found for Edmund and a bow for Lucy – Peter and Susan were of course already carrying their gifts. As they came back up the stairway, jingling in their mail, and already looking and feeling more like Narnians and less like schoolchildren, the two boys were behind, apparently making some plan. Lucy heard Edmund say, "No, let me do it. It will be more of a sucks for him if I win, and less of a let-down for us all if I fail."

"All right, Ed," said Peter.

When they came out into the daylight Edmund turned to the Dwarf very politely and said, "I've got something to ask you. Kids like us don't often have the chance of meeting a great warrior like you. Would you have a little fencing match with me? It would be frightfully decent."

"But, lad," said Trumpkin, "these swords are sharp."

"I know," said Edmund. "But I'll never get anywhere

near you and you'll be quite clever enough to disarm me without doing me any damage."

"It's a dangerous game," said Trumpkin. "But since you make such a point of it, I'll try a pass or two."

Both swords were out in a moment and the three others jumped off the dais and stood watching. It was well worth it. It was not like the silly fighting you see with broad swords on the stage. It was not even like the rapier fighting which you sometimes see rather better done. This was real broad-sword fighting. The great thing is to slash at your enemy's legs and feet because they are the part that have no armour. And when he slashes at yours you jump with both feet off the ground so that his blow goes under them. This gave the Dwarf an advantage because Edmund, being much taller, had to be always stooping. I don't think Edmund would have had a chance if he had fought Trumpkin twenty-four hours earlier. But the air of Narnia had been working upon him ever since they arrived on the island, and all his old battles came back to him, and his arms and fingers remembered their old skill. He was King Edmund once more. Round and round the two combatants circled, stroke after stroke they gave, and Susan (who never could learn to like this sort of thing) shouted out, "Oh, *do* be careful." And then, so quickly that no one (unless they knew, as Peter did) could quite see how it happened, Edmund flashed his sword round with a peculiar twist, the Dwarf's sword flew out of his grip, and Trumpkin was wringing his empty hand as you do after a "sting" from a cricket-bat.

"Not hurt, I hope, my dear little friend?" said Edmund, panting a little and returning his own sword to its sheath.

"I see the point," said Trumpkin drily. "You know a trick I never learned."

"That's quite true," put in Peter. "The best swordsman in the world may be disarmed by a trick that's new to him. I think it's only fair to give Trumpkin a chance at something else. Will you have a shooting match with my sister? There are no tricks in archery, you know."

"Ah, you're jokers, you are," said the Dwarf. "I begin to

see. As if I didn't know how she can shoot, after what happened this morning. All the same, I'll have a try." He spoke gruffly, but his eyes brightened, for he was a famous bowman among his own people.

All five of them came out into the courtyard.

"What's to be the target?" asked Peter.

"I think that apple hanging over the wall on the branch there would do," said Susan.

"That'll do nicely, lass," said Trumpkin. "You mean the yellow one near the middle of the arch?"

"No, not that," said Susan. "The red one up above – over the battlement."

The Dwarf's face fell. "Looks more like a cherry than an apple," he muttered, but he said nothing out loud.

They tossed up for first shot (greatly to the interest of Trumpkin, who had never seen a coin tossed before) and Susan lost. They were to shoot from the top of the steps that led from the hall into the courtyard. Everyone could see from the way the Dwarf took his position and handled his bow that he knew what he was about.

Twang went the string. It was an excellent shot. The tiny apple shook as the arrow passed, and a leaf came fluttering down. Then Susan went to the top of the steps and strung her bow. She was not enjoying her match half so much as Edmund had enjoyed his; not because she had any doubt about hitting the apple but because Susan was so tender-hearted that she almost hated to beat someone who had been beaten already. The Dwarf watched her keenly as she drew the shaft to her ear. A moment later, with a little soft thump which they could all hear in that quiet place, the apple fell to the grass with Susan's arrow in it.

"Oh, well done, Su," shouted the other children.

"It wasn't really any better than yours," said Susan to the Dwarf. "I think there was a tiny breath of wind as you shot."

"No, there wasn't," said Trumpkin. "Don't tell me. I

know when I am fairly beaten. I won't even say that the scar of my last wound catches me a bit when I get my arm well back —"

"Oh, are you wounded?" asked Lucy. "Do let me look."

"It's not a sight for little girls," began Trumpkin, but then he suddenly checked himself. "There I go talking like a fool again," he said. "I suppose you're as likely to be a great surgeon as your brother was to be a great swordsman or your sister to be a great archer." He sat down on the steps and took off his hauberk and slipped down his little shirt, showing an arm hairy and muscular (in proportion) as a sailor's though not much bigger than a child's. There was a clumsy bandage on the shoulder which Lucy proceeded to unroll. Underneath, the cut looked very nasty and there was a good deal of swelling. "Oh, poor Trumpkin," said Lucy. "How horrid." Then she carefully dripped on to it one single drop of the cordial from her flask.

"Hullo. Eh? What have you done?" said Trumpkin. But however he turned his head and squinted and whisked his beard to and fro, he couldn't quite see his own shoulder. Then he felt it as well as he could, getting his arms and fingers into very difficult positions as you do when you're trying to scratch a place that is just out of reach. Then he swung his arm and raised it and tried the muscles, and finally jumped to his feet crying, "Giants and junipers! It's cured! It's as good as new." After that he burst into a great laugh and said, "Well, I've made as big a fool of myself as ever a Dwarf did. No offence, I hope? My humble duty to your Majesties all — humble duty. And thanks for my life, my cure, my breakfast — and my lesson."

The children all said it was quite all right and not to mention it.

"And now," said Peter, "if you've really decided to believe in us —"

"I have," said the Dwarf.

"It's quite clear what we have to do. We must join King Caspian at once."

"The sooner the better," said Trumpkin. "My being such a fool has already wasted about an hour."

"It's about two days' journey, the way you came," said Peter. "For us, I mean. We can't walk all day and night like you Dwarfs." Then he turned to the others. "What Trumpkin calls Aslan's How is obviously the Stone Table itself. You remember it was about half a day's march, or a little less, from there down to the Fords of Beruna —"

"Beruna's Bridge, we call it," said Trumpkin.

"There was no bridge in our time," said Peter. "And then from Beruna down to here was another day and a bit. We used to get home about teatime on the second day, going easily. Going hard, we could do the whole thing in a day and a half perhaps."

"But remember it's all woods now," said Trumpkin, "and there are enemies to dodge."

"Look here," said Edmund, "need we go by the same way that Our Dear Little Friend came?"

"No more of that, your Majesty, if you love me," said the Dwarf.

"Very well," said Edmund. "May I say our D.L.F.?"

"Oh, Edmund," said Susan. "Don't keep *on* at him like that."

"That's all right, lass — I mean your Majesty," said

Trumpkin with a chuckle. "A jibe won't raise a blister."
(And after that they often called him the D.L.F. till they'd
almost forgotten what it meant.)

"As I was saying," continued Edmund, "we needn't go
that way. Why shouldn't we row a little south till we come
to Glasswater Creek and row up it? That brings us up
behind the Hill of the Stone Table, and we'll be safe while
we're at sea. If we start at once, we can be at the head of
Glasswater before dark, get a few hours' sleep, and be with
Caspian pretty early tomorrow."

"What a thing it is to know the coast," said Trumpkin.
"None of us know anything about Glasswater."

"What about food?" asked Susan.

"Oh, we'll have to do with apples," said Lucy. "Do let's
get on. We've done nothing yet, and we've been here nearly
two days."

"And anyway, no one's going to have my hat for a fish-
basket again," said Edmund.

They used one of the raincoats as a kind of bag and put a
good many apples in it. Then they all had a good long
drink at the well (for they would meet no more fresh water
till they landed at the head of the Creek) and went down
to the boat. The children were sorry to leave Cair
Paravel, which, even in ruins, had begun to feel like home
again.

"The D.L.F. had better steer," said Peter, "and Ed and I
will take an oar each. Half a moment, though. We'd better
take off our mail: we're going to be pretty warm before
we're done. The girls had better be in the bows and shout
directions to the D.L.F. because he doesn't know the way.
You'd better get us a fair way out to sea till we've passed the
island."

And soon the green, wooded coast of the island was falling away behind them, and its little bays and headlands were beginning to look flatter, and the boat was rising and falling in the gentle swell. The sea began to grow bigger around them and, in the distance, bluer, but close round the boat it was green and bubbly. Everything smelled salt and there was no noise except the swishing of water and the clop-clop of water against the sides and the splash of the oars and the jolting noise of the rowlocks. The sun grew hot.

It was delightful for Lucy and Susan in the bows, bending over the edge and trying to get their hands in the sea which they could never quite reach. The bottom, mostly pure, pale sand but with occasional patches of purple seaweed, could be seen beneath them.

"It's like old times," said Lucy. "Do you remember our voyage to Terebinthia – and Galma – and Seven Isles – and the Lone Islands?"

"Yes," said Susan, "and our great ship the *Splendour Hyaline*, with the swan's head at her prow and the carved swan's wings coming back almost to her waist?"

"And the silken sails, and the great stern lanterns?"

"And the feasts on the poop and the musicians."

"Do you remember when we had the musicians up in the rigging playing flutes so that it sounded like music out of the sky?"

Presently Susan took over Edmund's oar and he came forward to join Lucy. They had passed the island now and stood closer in to the shore – all wooded and deserted. They would have thought it very pretty if they had not remembered the time when it was open and breezy and full of merry friends.

"Phew! This is pretty gruelling work," said Peter.

"Can't I row for a bit?" said Lucy.

"The oars are too big for you," said Peter shortly, not because he was cross but because he had no strength to spare for talking.

CHAPTER NINE

WHAT LUCY SAW

SUSAN and the two boys were bitterly tired with rowing before they rounded the last headland and began the final pull up Glasswater itself, and Lucy's head ached from the long hours of sun and the glare on the water. Even Trumpkin longed for the voyage to be over. The seat on which he sat to steer had been made for men, not Dwarfs, and his feet did not reach the floor-boards; and everyone knows how uncomfortable that is even for ten minutes. And as they all grew more tired, their spirits fell. Up till now the children had only been thinking of how to get to Caspian. Now they wondered what they would do when they found him, and how a handful of Dwarfs and woodland creatures could defeat an army of grown-up Humans.

Twilight was coming on as they rowed slowly up the windings of Glasswater Creek – a twilight which deepened as the banks drew closer together and the overhanging trees began almost to meet overhead. It was very quiet in here as the sound of the sea died away behind them; they could even hear the trickle of the little streams that poured down from the forest into Glasswater.

They went ashore at last, far too tired to attempt lighting a fire; and even a supper of apples (though most of them felt that they never wanted to see an apple again) seemed better than trying to catch or shoot anything. After a little silent munching they all huddled down together in the moss and dead leaves between four large beech trees.

Everyone except Lucy went to sleep at once. Lucy, being far less tired, found it hard to get comfortable. Also, she had forgotten till now that all Dwarfs snore. She knew that one of the best ways of getting to sleep is to stop trying, so she opened her eyes. Through a gap in the bracken and branches she could just see a patch of water in the Creek and the sky above it. Then, with a thrill of memory, she saw again, after all those years, the bright Narnian stars. She had once known them better than the stars of our own world, because as a Queen in Narnia she had gone to bed much later than as a child in England. And there they were – at least, three of the summer constellations could be seen from where she lay: the Ship, the Hammer, and the Leopard. "Dear old Leopard," she murmured happily to herself.

Instead of getting drowsier she was getting more awake – with an odd, night-time, dreamish kind of wakefulness. The Creek was growing brighter. She knew now that the moon was on it, though she couldn't see the moon. And now she began to feel that the whole forest was coming awake like herself. Hardly knowing why she did it, she got up quickly and walked a little distance away from their bivouac.

"This is lovely," said Lucy to herself. It was cool and fresh; delicious smells were floating everywhere.

Somewhere close by she heard the twitter of a nightingale beginning to sing, then stopping, then beginning again. It was a little lighter ahead. She went towards the light and came to a place where there were fewer trees, and whole patches or pools of moonlight, but the moonlight and the shadows so mixed that you could hardly be sure where anything was or what it was. At the same moment the nightingale, satisfied at last with his tuning up, burst into full song.

Lucy's eyes began to grow accustomed to the light, and she saw the trees that were nearest her more distinctly. A great longing for the old days when the trees could talk in Narnia came over her. She knew exactly how each of these trees would talk if only she could wake them, and what sort of human form it would put on. She looked at a silver birch: it would have a soft, showery voice and would look like a slender girl, with hair blown all about her face, and fond of dancing. She looked at the oak: he would be a wizened, but hearty old man with a frizzled beard and warts on his face and hands, and hair growing out of the warts. She looked at the beech under which she was standing. Ah! – she would be the best of all. She would be a gracious goddess, smooth and stately, the lady of the wood.

"Oh, Trees, Trees, Trees," said Lucy (though she had not been intending to speak at all). "Oh, Trees, wake, wake, wake. Don't you remember it? Don't you remember *me*? Dryads and Hamadryads, come out, come to me."

Though there was not a breath of wind they all stirred about her. The rustling noise of the leaves was almost like words. The nightingale stopped singing as if to listen to it.

Lucy felt that at any moment she would begin to understand what the trees were trying to say. But the moment did not come. The rustling died away. The nightingale resumed its song. Even in the moonlight the wood looked more ordinary again. Yet Lucy had the feeling (as you sometimes have when you are trying to remember a name or a date and almost get it, but it vanishes before you really do) that she had just missed something: as if she

had spoken to the trees a split second too soon or a split second too late, or used all the right words except one, or put in one word that was just wrong.

Quite suddenly she began to feel tired. She went back to the bivouac, snuggled down between Susan and Peter, and was asleep in a few minutes.

It was a cold and cheerless waking for them all next morning, with a grey twilight in the wood (for the sun had not yet risen) and everything damp and dirty.

"Apples, heigh-ho," said Trumpkin with a rueful grin. "I must say you ancient kings and queens don't overfeed your courtiers!"

They stood up and shook themselves and looked about. The trees were thick and they could see no more than a few yards in any direction.

"I suppose your Majesties know the way all right?" said the Dwarf.

"I don't," said Susan. "I've never seen these woods in my life before. In fact I thought all along that we ought to have gone by the river."

"Then I think you might have said so at the time," answered Peter, with pardonable sharpness.

"Oh, don't take any notice of her," said Edmund. "She always is a wet blanket. You've got that pocket compass of yours, Peter, haven't you? Well, then, we're as right as rain. We've only got to keep on going north-west – cross that little river, the what-do-you-call-it? – the Rush –"

"I know," said Peter. "The one that joins the big river at the Fords of Beruna, or Beruna's Bridge, as the D.L.F. calls it."

"That's right. Cross it and strike uphill, and we'll be at the Stone Table (Aslan's How, I mean) by eight or nine o'clock. I hope King Caspian will give us a good breakfast!"

"I hope you're right," said Susan. "I can't remember all that at all."

"That's the worst of girls," said Edmund to Peter and the Dwarf. "They never carry a map in their heads."

"That's because our heads have something inside them," said Lucy.

At first things seemed to be going pretty well. They

even thought they had struck an old path; but if you know anything about woods, you will know that one is always finding imaginary paths. They disappear after about five minutes and then you think you have found another (and hope it is not another but more of the same one) and it also disappears, and after you have been well lured out of your right direction you realize that none of them were paths at all. The boys and the Dwarf, however, were used to woods and were not taken in for more than a few seconds.

They had plodded on for about half an hour (three of them very stiff from yesterday's rowing) when Trumpkin suddenly whispered, "Stop." They all stopped. "There's something following us," he said in a low voice. "Or rather, something keeping up with us: over there on the left." They all stood still, listening and staring till their ears and eyes ached. "You and I'd better each have an arrow on the string," said Susan to Trumpkin. The Dwarf nodded, and when both bows were ready for action the party went on again.

They went a few dozen yards through fairly open woodland, keeping a sharp look-out. Then they came to a place where the undergrowth thickened and they had to pass nearer to it. Just as they were passing the place, there came a sudden something that snarled and flashed, rising out from the breaking twigs like a thunderbolt. Lucy was knocked down and winded, hearing the twang of a bowstring as she fell. When she was able to take notice of things again, she saw a great grim-looking grey bear lying dead with Trumpkin's arrow in its side.

"The D.L.F. beat you in *that* shooting match, Su," said

Peter, with a slightly forced smile. Even he had been shaken by this adventure.

"I – I left it too late," said Susan, in an embarrassed voice. "I was so afraid it might be, you know – one of our kind of bears, a *talking* bear." She hated killing things.

"That's the trouble of it," said Trumpkin, "when most of the beasts have gone enemy and gone dumb, but there are still some of the other kind left. You never know, and you daren't wait to see."

"Poor old Bruin," said Susan. "You don't think he *was*?"

"Not he," said the Dwarf. "I saw the face and I heard the snarl. He only wanted Little Girl for his breakfast. And talking of breakfast, I didn't want to discourage your Majesties when you said you hoped King Caspian would give you a good one: but meat's precious scarce in camp. And there's good eating on a bear. It would be a shame to leave the carcass without taking a bit, and it won't delay us more than half an hour. I dare say you two youngsters – Kings, I should say – know how to skin a bear?"

"Let's go and sit down a fair way off," said Susan to Lucy. "I know what a horrid messy business *that* will be." Lucy shuddered and nodded. When they had sat down she said: "Such a horrible idea has come into my head, Su."

"What's that?"

"Wouldn't it be dreadful if some day, in our own world, at home, men started going wild inside, like the animals here, and still looked like men, so that you'd never know which were which?"

"We've got enough to bother about here and now in

Narnia," said the practical Susan, "without imagining things like that."

When they rejoined the boys and the Dwarf, as much as they thought they could carry of the best meat had been cut off. Raw meat is not a nice thing to fill one's pockets with, but they folded it up in fresh leaves and made the best of it. They were all experienced enough to know that they would feel quite differently about these squashy and unpleasant parcels when they had walked long enough to be really hungry.

On they trudged again (stopping to wash three pairs of hands that needed it in the first stream they passed) until the sun rose and the birds began to sing, and more flies than they wanted were buzzing in the bracken. The stiffness from yesterday's rowing began to wear off. Everybody's spirits rose. The sun grew warmer and they took their helmets off and carried them.

"I suppose we *are* going right?" said Edmund about an hour later.

"I don't see how we can go wrong as long as we don't bear too much to the left," said Peter. "If we bear too much to the right, the worst that can happen is wasting a little time by striking the great River too soon and not cutting off the corner."

And again they trudged on with no sound except the thud of their feet and the jingle of their chain shirts.

"Where's this bally Rush got to?" said Edmund a good deal later.

"I certainly thought we'd have struck it by now," said Peter. "But there's nothing to do but keep on." They both knew that the Dwarf was looking anxiously at them, but he said nothing.

And still they trudged on and their mail shirts began to feel very hot and heavy.

"What on earth?" said Peter suddenly.

They had come, without seeing it, almost to the edge of a small precipice from which they looked down into a gorge with a river at the bottom. On the far side the cliffs rose much higher. None of the party except Edmund (and perhaps Trumpkin) was a rock climber.

"I'm sorry," said Peter. "It's my fault for coming this way. We're lost. I've never seen this place in my life before."

The Dwarf gave a low whistle between his teeth.

"Oh, do let's go back and go the other way," said Susan. "I knew all along we'd get lost in these woods."

"Susan!" said Lucy, reproachfully, "don't nag at Peter like that. It's so rotten, and he's doing all he can."

"And don't you snap at Su like that, either," said Edmund. "I think she's quite right."

"Tubs and tortoiseshells!" exclaimed Trumpkin. "If we've got lost coming, what chance have we of finding our way back? And if we're to go back to the Island and begin all over again – even supposing we could – we might as well give the whole thing up. Miraz will have finished with Caspian before we get there at that rate."

"You think we ought to go on?" said Lucy.

"I'm not sure the High King *is* lost," said Trumpkin. "What's to hinder this river being the Rush?"

"Because the Rush is not in a gorge," said Peter, keeping his temper with some difficulty.

"Your Majesty says *is*," replied the Dwarf, "but oughtn't you to say *was*? You knew this country hundreds – it may be a thousand – years ago. Mayn't it have changed? A landslide might have pulled off half the side of that hill, leaving bare rock, and there are your precipices beyond the gorge. Then the Rush might go on deepening its course year after year till you get the little precipices this side. Or there might have been an earthquake, or anything."

"I never thought of that," said Peter.

"And anyway," continued Trumpkin, "even if this is not the Rush, it's flowing roughly north and so it must

fall into the Great River anyway. I think I passed something that might have been it, on my way down. So if we go downstream, to our right, we'll hit the Great River. Perhaps not so high as we'd hoped, but at least we'll be no worse off than if you'd come my way."

"Trumpkin, you're a brick," said Peter. "Come on, then. Down this side of the gorge."

"Look! Look! Look!" cried Lucy.

"Where? What?" said everyone.

"The Lion," said Lucy. "Aslan himself. Didn't you

see?" Her face had changed completely and her eyes shone.

"Do you really mean –?" began Peter.

"Where did you think you saw him?" asked Susan.

"Don't talk like a grown-up," said Lucy, stamping her foot. "I didn't *think* I saw him. I saw him."

"Where, Lu?" asked Peter.

"Right up there between those mountain ashes. No, this side of the gorge. And up, not down. Just the opposite of the way you want to go. And he wanted us to go where he was – up there."

"How do you know that was what he wanted?" asked Edmund.

"He – I – I just know," said Lucy, "by his face."

The others all looked at each other in puzzled silence.

"Her Majesty may well have seen a lion," put in Trumpkin. "There are lions in these woods, I've been told. But it needn't have been a friendly and talking lion any more than the bear was a friendly and talking bear."

"Oh, don't be so stupid," said Lucy. "Do you think I don't know Aslan when I see him?"

"He'd be a pretty elderly lion by now," said Trumpkin, "if he's one you knew when you were here before! And if it could be the same one, what's to prevent him having gone wild and witless like so many others?"

Lucy turned crimson and I think she would have flown at Trumpkin, if Peter had not laid his hand on her arm. "The D.L.F. doesn't understand. How could he? You must just take it, Trumpkin, that we do really know about Aslan; a little bit about him, I mean. And you mustn't talk about him like that again. It isn't lucky for one thing: and it's all nonsense for another. The only question is whether Aslan was really there."

"But I know he was," said Lucy, her eyes filling with tears.

"Yes, Lu, but we don't, you see," said Peter.

"There's nothing for it but a vote," said Edmund.

"All right," replied Peter. "You're the eldest, D.L.F. What do you vote for? Up or down?"

"Down," said the Dwarf. "I know nothing about Aslan. But I do know that if we turn left and follow the gorge up, it might lead us all day before we found a place where we could cross it. Whereas if we turn right and go down, we're bound to reach the Great River in about a couple of hours. And if there *are* any real lions about, we want to go away from them, not towards them."

"What do you say, Susan?"

"Don't be angry, Lu," said Susan, "but I do think we should go down. I'm dead tired. Do let's get out of this wretched wood into the open as quick as we can. And none of us except you saw *anything*."

"Edmund?" said Peter.

"Well, there's just this," said Edmund, speaking quickly and turning a little red. "When we first discovered Narnia a year ago – or a thousand years ago, whichever it is – it was Lucy who discovered it first and none of us would believe her. I was the worst of the lot, I know. Yet she was right after all. Wouldn't it be fair to believe her this time? I vote for going up."

"Oh, Ed!" said Lucy and seized his hand.

"And now it's your turn, Peter," said Susan, "and I do hope –"

"Oh, shut up, shut up and let a chap think,"

interrupted Peter. "I'd much rather not have to vote."

"You're the High King," said Trumpkin sternly.

"Down," said Peter after a long pause. "I know Lucy may be right after all, but I can't help it. We must do one or the other."

So they set off to their right along the edge, downstream. And Lucy came last of the party, crying bitterly.

CHAPTER TEN

THE RETURN OF THE LION

To keep along the edge of the gorge was not so easy as it had looked. Before they had gone many yards they were confronted with young fir woods growing on the very edge, and after they had tried to go through these, stooping and pushing for about ten minutes, they realized that, in there, it would take them an hour to do half a mile. So they came back and out again and decided to go round the fir wood. This took them much farther to their right than they wanted to go, far out of sight of the cliffs and out of sound of the river, till they began to be afraid they had lost it altogether. Nobody knew the time, but it was getting to the hottest part of the day.

When they were able at last to go back to the edge of the gorge (nearly a mile below the point from which they had started) they found the cliffs on their side of it a good deal lower and more broken. Soon they found a way down into the gorge and continued the journey at the river's edge. But first they had a rest and a long drink. No one was talking any more about breakfast, or even dinner, with Caspian.

They may have been wise to stick to the Rush instead of going along the top. It kept them sure of their direction: and ever since the fir wood they had all been afraid of being forced too far out of their course and losing themselves in the wood. It was an old and pathless forest, and you could not keep anything like a straight course in it. Patches of hopeless brambles, fallen trees, boggy places and dense undergrowth would be always getting in your way. But the gorge of the Rush was not at all a nice place for travelling either. I mean, it was not a nice place for people in a hurry. For an afternoon's ramble ending in a picnic tea it would have been delightful. It had everything you could want on an occasion of that sort – rumbling waterfalls, silver cascades, deep, amber-coloured pools, mossy rocks, and deep moss on the banks in which you could sink over your ankles, every kind of fern, jewel-like dragon flies, sometimes a hawk overhead and once (Peter and Trumpkin both thought) an eagle. But of course what

the children and the Dwarf wanted to see as soon as possible was the Great River below them, and Beruna, and the way to Aslan's How.

As they went on, the Rush began to fall more and more steeply. Their journey became more and more of a climb and less and less of a walk – in places even a dangerous climb over slippery rock with a nasty drop into dark chasms, and the river roaring angrily at the bottom.

You may be sure they watched the cliffs on their left eagerly for any sign of a break or any place where they could climb them; but those cliffs remained cruel. It was maddening, because everyone knew that if once they were out of the gorge on that side, they would have only a smooth slope and a fairly short walk to Caspian's head-quarters.

The boys and the Dwarf were now in favour of lighting a fire and cooking their bear-meat. Susan didn't want this; she only wanted, as she said, "to get *on* and finish it and get out of these beastly woods". Lucy was far too tired and miserable to have any opinion about anything. But as there was no dry wood to be had, it mattered very little what anyone thought. The boys began to wonder if raw meat was really as nasty as they had always been told. Trumpkin assured them it was.

Of course, if the children had attempted a journey like this a few days ago in England, they would have been knocked up. I think I have explained before how Narnia was altering them. Even Lucy was by now, so to speak, only one-third of a little girl going to boarding school for the first time, and two-thirds of Queen Lucy of Narnia.

"At last!" said Susan.

"Oh, hurray!" said Peter.

The river gorge had just made a bend and the whole view spread out beneath them. They could see open country stretching before them to the horizon and, between it and them, the broad silver ribbon of the Great River. They could see the specially broad and shallow place which had once been the Fords of Beruna but was now spanned by a long, many-arched bridge. There was a little town at the far end of it.

"By Jove," said Edmund. "We fought the Battle of Beruna just where that town is!"

This cheered the boys more than anything. You can't help feeling stronger when you look at a place where you won a glorious victory not to mention a kingdom, hundreds of years ago. Peter and Edmund were soon so busy talking about the battle that they forgot their sore feet and the heavy drag of their mail shirts on their shoulders. The Dwarf was interested too.

They were all getting on at a quicker pace now. The going became easier. Though there were still sheer cliffs on their left, the ground was becoming lower on their right. Soon it was no longer a gorge at all, only a valley. There were no more waterfalls and presently they were in fairly thick woods again.

Then – all at once – *whizz*, and a sound rather like the stroke of a woodpecker. The children were still wondering where (ages ago) they had heard a sound just like that and why they disliked it so, when Trumpkin shouted, "Down', at the same moment forcing Lucy (who happened to be next to him) flat down into the bracken. Peter, who had been looking up to see if he could spot a squirrel, had seen what it was – a long cruel arrow had sunk into a tree trunk just above his head. As he pulled Susan down and dropped himself, another came rasping over his shoulder and struck the ground at his side.

"Quick! Quick! Get back! *Crawl*!" panted Trumpkin.

They turned and wriggled along uphill, under the

bracken amid clouds of horribly buzzing flies. Arrows whizzed round them. One struck Susan's helmet with a sharp ping and glanced off. They crawled quicker. Sweat poured off them. Then they ran, stooping nearly double. The boys held their swords in their hands for fear they would trip them up.

It was heart-breaking work – all uphill again, back over the ground they had already travelled. When they felt that they really couldn't run any more, even to save their lives,

they all dropped down in the damp moss beside a waterfall and behind a big boulder, panting. They were surprised to see how high they had already got.

They listened intently and heard no sound of pursuit.

"So *that's* all right," said Trumpkin, drawing a deep breath. "They're not searching the wood. Only sentries, I expect. But it means that Miraz has an outpost down there. Bottles and battledores! though, it was a near thing."

"I ought to have my head smacked for bringing us this way at all," said Peter.

"On the contrary, your Majesty," said the Dwarf. "For one thing it wasn't you, it was your royal brother, King Edmund, who first suggested going by Glasswater."

"I'm afraid the D.L.F.'s right," said Edmund, who had quite honestly forgotten this ever since things began going wrong.

"And for another," continued Trumpkin, "if we'd gone my way, we'd have walked straight into that new outpost, most likely; or at least had just the same trouble avoiding it. I think this Glasswater route has turned out for the best."

"A blessing in disguise," said Susan.

"Some disguise!" said Edmund.

"I suppose we'll have to go right up the gorge again now," said Lucy.

"Lu, you're a hero," said Peter. "That's the nearest you've got today to saying *I told you so*. Let's get on."

"And as soon as we're well up into the forest," said Trumpkin, "whatever anyone says, I'm going to light a fire and cook supper. But we must get well away from here."

There is no need to describe how they toiled back up the gorge. It was pretty hard work, but oddly enough everyone felt more cheerful. They were getting their second wind; and the word *supper* had had a wonderful effect.

They reached the fir wood which had caused them so much trouble while it was still daylight, and bivouacked in a hollow just above it. It was tedious gathering the firewood; but it was grand when the fire blazed up and they began producing the damp and smeary parcels of bear-meat which would have been so very unattractive to anyone who had spent the day indoors. The Dwarf had splendid ideas about cookery. Each apple (they still had a few of these) was wrapped up in bear's meat – as if it was to be apple dumpling with meat instead of pastry, only much thicker – and spiked on a sharp stick and then roasted. And the juice of the apple worked all through the meat, like apple sauce with roast pork. Bear that has lived too much on other animals is not very nice, but bear that has had plenty of honey and fruit is excellent, and this turned out to be that sort of bear. It was a truly glorious meal. And, of course, no washing up – only lying back and watching the smoke from Trumpkin's pipe and stretching one's tired legs and chatting. Everyone felt quite hopeful now about finding King Caspian tomorrow and defeating Miraz in a few days. It may not have been sensible of them to feel like this, but they did.

They dropped off to sleep one by one, but all pretty quickly.

Lucy woke out of the deepest sleep you can imagine, with the feeling that the voice she liked best in the world had been calling her name. She thought at first it was her father's voice, but that did not seem quite right. Then she thought it was Peter's voice, but that did not seem to fit either. She did not want to get up; not because she was still tired – on the contrary she was wonderfully rested and all the aches had gone from her bones – but because she felt so extremely happy and comfortable. She was looking straight up at the Narnian moon, which is larger than ours, and at the starry sky, for the place where they had bivouacked was comparatively open.

"Lucy," came the call again, neither her father's voice nor Peter's. She sat up, trembling with excitement but not with fear. The moon was so bright that the whole forest landscape around her was almost as clear as day, though it looked wilder. Behind her was the fir wood; away to her right the jagged cliff-tops on the far side of the gorge; straight ahead, open grass to where a glade of trees began about a bow-shot away. Lucy looked very hard at the trees of that glade.

"Why, I do believe they're moving," she said to herself. "They're walking about."

She got up, her heart beating wildly, and walked towards them. There was certainly a noise in the glade, a noise such as trees make in a high wind, though there was no wind tonight. Yet it was not exactly an ordinary tree-noise either. Lucy felt there was a tune in it, but she could not catch the tune any more than she had been able to catch the words when the trees had so nearly talked to her the night before. But there was, at least, a lilt; she felt her own feet wanting to dance as she got nearer. And now there was no doubt that the trees were really moving – moving in and out through one another as if in a complicated country dance. ("And I suppose," thought Lucy, "when trees dance, it must be a very, very country dance indeed.') She was almost among them now.

The first tree she looked at seemed at first glance to be not a tree at all but a huge man with a shaggy beard and great bushes of hair. She was not frightened: she had seen such things before. But when she looked again he was only a tree, though he was still moving. You couldn't see whether he had feet or roots, of course, because when trees move they don't walk on the surface of the earth; they wade in it as we do in water. The same thing happened with every tree she looked at. At one moment they seemed to be the friendly, lovely giant and giantess forms which the tree-people put on when some good magic has called them into full life: next moment they all looked like trees again. But when they looked like trees, it was like strangely human trees, and when they looked like people, it was like strangely branchy and leafy people – and all the time that queer lilting, rustling, cool, merry noise.

"They are almost awake, not quite," said Lucy. She knew she herself was wide awake, wider than anyone usually is.

She went fearlessly in among them, dancing herself as she leaped this way and that to avoid being run into by these huge partners. But she was only half interested in them. She wanted to get beyond them to something else; it was from beyond them that the dear voice had called.

She soon got through them (half wondering whether she had been using her arms to push branches aside, or to take hands in a Great Chain with big dancers who stooped to reach her) for they were really a ring of trees round a central open place. She stepped out from among their shifting confusion of lovely lights and shadows.

A circle of grass, smooth as a lawn, met her eyes, with dark trees dancing all round it. And then – oh joy! For *he* was there: the huge Lion, shining white in the moonlight, with his huge black shadow underneath him.

But for the movement of his tail he might have been a stone lion, but Lucy never thought of that. She never stopped to think whether he was a friendly lion or not. She rushed to him. She felt her heart would burst if she lost a moment. And the next thing she knew was that she was kissing him and putting her arms as far round his neck as

she could and burying her face in the beautiful rich silkiness of his mane.

"Aslan, Aslan. Dear Aslan," sobbed Lucy. "At last."

The great beast rolled over on his side so that Lucy fell, half sitting and half lying between his front paws. He bent forward and just touched her nose with his tongue. His warm breath came all round her. She gazed up into the large wise face.

"Welcome, child," he said.

"Aslan," said Lucy, "you're bigger."

"That is because you are older, little one," answered he.

"Not because you are?"

"I am not. But every year you grow, you will find me bigger."

For a time she was so happy that she did not want to speak. But Aslan spoke.

"Lucy," he said, "we must not lie here for long. You have work in hand, and much time has been lost today."

"Yes, wasn't it a shame?" said Lucy. "*I* saw you all right. They wouldn't believe me. They're all so –"

From somewhere deep inside Aslan's body there came the faintest suggestion of a growl.

"I'm sorry," said Lucy, who understood some of his moods. "I didn't mean to start slanging the others. But it wasn't my fault anyway, was it?"

The Lion looked straight into her eyes.

"Oh, Aslan," said Lucy. "You don't mean it was? How could I – I couldn't have left the others and come up to you alone, how could I? Don't look at me like that . . . oh well, I suppose I *could*. Yes, and it wouldn't have been alone, I know, not if I was with you. But what would have been the good?"

Aslan said nothing.

"You mean," said Lucy rather faintly, "that it would have turned out all right – somehow? But how? Please, Aslan! Am I not to know?"

"To know what *would* have happened, child?" said Aslan. "No. Nobody is ever told that."

"Oh dear," said Lucy.

"But anyone can find out what *will* happen," said Aslan. "If you go back to the others now, and wake them up; and tell them you have seen me again; and that you must all get up at once and follow me – what will happen? There is only one way of finding out."

"Do you mean that is what you want me to do?" gasped Lucy.

"Yes, little one," said Aslan.

"Will the others see you too?" asked Lucy.

"Certainly not at first," said Aslan. "Later on, it depends."

"But they won't believe me!" said Lucy.

"It doesn't matter," said Aslan.

"Oh dear, oh dear," said Lucy. "And I was so pleased at finding you again. And I thought you'd let me stay. And I thought you'd come roaring in and frighten all the enemies away – like last time. And now everything is going to be horrid."

"It is hard for you, little one," said Aslan. "But things never happen the same way twice. It has been hard for us all in Narnia before now."

Lucy buried her head in his mane to hide from his face. But there must have been magic in his mane. She could feel lion-strength going into her. Quite suddenly she sat up.

"I'm sorry, Aslan," she said. "I'm ready now."

"Now you are a lioness," said Aslan. "And now all Narnia will be renewed. But come. We have no time to lose."

He got up and walked with stately, noiseless paces back to the belt of dancing trees through which she had just come: and Lucy went with him, laying a rather tremulous hand on his mane. The trees parted to let them through and for one second assumed their human forms completely. Lucy had a glimpse of tall and lovely wood-gods and wood-goddesses all bowing to the Lion; next moment they were trees again, but still bowing, with such graceful sweeps of branch and trunk that their bowing was itself a kind of dance.

"Now, child," said Aslan, when they had left the trees behind them, "I will wait here. Go and wake the others and tell them to follow. If they will not, then you at least must follow me alone."

It is a terrible thing to have to wake four people, all older than yourself and all very tired, for the purpose of telling them something they probably won't believe and making them do something they certainly won't like. "I mustn't think about it, I must just do it," thought Lucy.

She went to Peter first and shook him. "Peter," she whispered in his ear, "wake up. Quick. Aslan is here. He says we've got to follow him at once."

"Certainly, Lu. Whatever you like," said Peter unexpectedly. This was encouraging, but as Peter instantly rolled round and went to sleep again it wasn't much use.

Then she tried Susan. Susan did really wake up, but only to say in her most annoying grown-up voice, "You've been dreaming, Lucy. Go to sleep again."

She tackled Edmund next. It was very difficult to wake

him, but when at last she had done it he was really awake
and sat up.

"Eh?" he said in a grumpy voice. "What are you talking
about?"

She said it all over again. This was one of the worst parts
of her job, for each time she said it, it sounded less
convincing.

"Aslan!" said Edmund, jumping up. "Hurray! Where?"

Lucy turned back to where she could see the Lion
waiting, his patient eyes fixed upon her. "There," she said,
pointing.

"Where?" asked Edmund again.

"There. There. Don't you see? Just this side of the trees."

Edmund stared hard for a while and then said, "No.
There's nothing there. You've got dazzled and muddled
with the moonlight. One does, you know. I thought I saw
something for a moment myself. It's only an optical
what-do-you-call-it."

"I can see him all the time," said Lucy. "He's looking
straight at us."

"Then why can't I see him?"

"He said you mightn't be able to."

"Why?"

"I don't know. That's what he said."

"Oh, bother it all," said Edmund. "I do wish you
wouldn't keep on seeing things. But I suppose we'll have to
wake the others."

CHAPTER ELEVEN

THE LION ROARS

WHEN the whole party was finally awake Lucy had to tell her story for the fourth time. The blank silence which followed it was as discouraging as anything could be.

"I can't see anything," said Peter after he had stared his eyes sore. "Can you, Susan?"

"No, of course I can't," snapped Susan. "Because there isn't anything to see. She's been dreaming. Do lie down and go to sleep, Lucy."

"And I do hope," said Lucy in a tremulous voice, "that you will all come with me. Because – because I'll have to go with him whether anyone else does or not."

"Don't talk nonsense, Lucy," said Susan. "Of course you can't go off on your own. Don't let her, Peter. She's being downright naughty."

"I'll go with her, if she *must* go," said Edmund. "She's been right before."

"I know she has," said Peter. "And she may have been right this morning. We certainly had no luck going down the gorge. Still – at this hour of the night. And why should Aslan be invisible to us? He never used to be. It's not like him. What does the D.L.F. say?"

"Oh, I say nothing at all," answered the Dwarf. "If you all go, of course, I'll go with you; and if your party splits up, I'll go with the High King. That's my duty to him and King Caspian. But, if you ask my private opinion, I'm a plain dwarf who doesn't think there's much chance of finding a road by night where you couldn't find one by day. And I have no use for magic lions which are talking lions and don't talk, and friendly lions though they don't do us any good, and whopping big lions though nobody can see them. It's all bilge and beanstalks as far as I can see."

"He's beating his paw on the ground for us to hurry," said Lucy. "We must go *now*. At least I must."

"You've no right to try to force the rest of us like that. It's four to one and you're the youngest," said Susan.

"Oh, come on," growled Edmund. "We've got to go. There'll be no peace till we do." He fully intended to back Lucy up, but he was annoyed at losing his night's sleep and was making up for it by doing everything as sulkily as possible.

"On the march, then," said Peter, wearily fitting his arm into his shield-strap and putting his helmet on. At any other time he would have said something nice to Lucy, who was his favourite sister, for he knew how wretched she must be feeling, and he knew that, whatever had happened, it was not her fault. But he couldn't help being a little annoyed with her all the same.

Susan was the worst. "Supposing *I* started behaving like Lucy," she said. "I might threaten to stay here whether the rest of you went on or not. I jolly well think I shall."

"Obey the High King, your Majesty," said Trumpkin, "and let's be off. If I'm not to be allowed to sleep, I'd as soon march as stand here talking."

And so at last they got on the move. Lucy went first, biting her lip and trying not to say all the things she thought of saying to Susan. But she forgot them when she fixed her eyes on Aslan. He turned and walked at a slow pace about thirty yards ahead of them. The others had only Lucy's directions to guide them, for Aslan was not only invisible to them but silent as well. His big cat-like paws made no noise on the grass.

He led them to the right of the dancing trees – whether they were still dancing nobody knew, for Lucy had her eyes on the Lion and the rest had their eyes on Lucy – and nearer the edge of the gorge. "Cobbles and kettledrums!" thought Trumpkin. "I hope this madness isn't going to end in a moonlight climb and broken necks."

For a long way Aslan went along the top of the precipices. Then they came to a place where some little trees grew right on the edge. He turned and disappeared among them. Lucy held her breath, for it looked as if he had plunged over the cliff; but she was too busy keeping him in sight to stop and think about this. She quickened her pace and was soon among the trees herself. Looking down, she could see a steep and narrow path going slantwise down into the gorge between rocks, and Aslan descending it. He turned and looked at her with his happy eyes. Lucy clapped her hands and began to scramble down after him. From behind her she heard the voices of the others shouting, "Hi! Lucy! Look out, for goodness' sake. You're right on the edge of the gorge. Come back – " and then, a moment later, Edmund's voice saying, "No, she's right. There *is* a way down."

Half-way down the path Edmund caught up with her.

"Look!" he said in great excitement. "Look! What's that shadow crawling down in front of us?"

"It's *his* shadow," said Lucy.

"I do believe you're right, Lu," said Edmund. "I can't think how I didn't see it before. But where is he?"

"With his shadow, of course. Can't you see him?"

"Well, I almost thought I did – for a moment. It's such a rum light."

"Get on, King Edmund, get on," came Trumpkin's voice from behind and above: and then, farther behind and still nearly at the top, Peter's voice saying, "Oh, buck up, Susan. Give me your hand. Why, a baby could get down here. And do stop grousing."

In a few minutes they were at the bottom and the roaring of water filled their ears. Treading delicately, like a cat, Aslan stepped from stone to stone across the stream. In the middle he stopped, bent down to drink, and as he raised his shaggy head, dripping from the water, he turned to face them again. This time Edmund saw him. "Oh, Aslan!" he cried, darting forward. But the Lion whisked round and began padding up the slope on the far side of the Rush.

"Peter, Peter," cried Edmund. "Did you see?"

"I saw something," said Peter. "But it's so tricky in this moonlight. On we go, though, and three cheers for Lucy. I don't feel half so tired now, either."

Aslan without hesitation led them to their left, farther up the gorge. The whole journey was odd and dream-like – the roaring stream, the wet grey grass, the glimmering cliffs which they were approaching, and always the glorious, silently pacing Beast ahead. Everyone except Susan and the Dwarf could see him now.

Presently they came to another steep path, up the face of the farther precipices. These were far higher than the ones they had just descended, and the journey up them was a long and tedious zig-zag. Fortunately the Moon shone right above the gorge so that neither side was in shadow.

Lucy was nearly blown when the tail and hind legs of Aslan disappeared over the top: but with one last effort she scrambled after him and came out, rather shaky-legged and breathless, on the hill they had been trying to reach ever since they left Glasswater. The long gentle slope (heather and grass and a few very big rocks that shone white in the moonlight) stretched up to where it vanished in a glimmer of trees about half a mile away. She knew it. It was the hill of the Stone Table.

With a jingling of mail the others climbed up behind her. Aslan glided on before them and they walked after him.

"Lucy," said Susan in a very small voice.

"Yes?" said Lucy.

"I see him now. I'm sorry."

"That's all right."

"But I've been far worse than you know. I really believed it was him – he, I mean – yesterday. When he warned us not to go down to the fir wood. And I really believed it was him tonight, when you woke us up. I mean, deep down inside. Or I could have, if I'd let myself. But I just wanted to get out of the woods and – and – oh, I don't know. And what ever am I to say to him?"

"Perhaps you won't need to say much," suggested Lucy.

Soon they reached the trees and through them the children could see the Great Mound, Aslan's How, which had been raised over the Table since their days.

"Our side don't keep very good watch," muttered Trumpkin. "We ought to have been challenged before now –"

"Hush!" said the other four, for now Aslan had stopped and turned and stood facing them, looking so majestic that they felt as glad as anyone can who feels afraid, and as afraid as anyone can who feels glad. The boys strode forward: Lucy made way for them: Susan and the Dwarf shrank back.

"Oh, Aslan," said King Peter, dropping on one knee and raising the Lion's heavy paw to his face, "I'm so glad. And I'm so sorry. I've been leading them wrong ever since we started and especially yesterday morning."

"My dear son," said Aslan.

Then he turned and welcomed Edmund. "Well done," were his words.

Then, after an awful pause, the deep voice said, "Susan." Susan made no answer but the others thought she was crying. "You have listened to fears, child," said Aslan. "Come, let me breathe on you. Forget them. Are you brave again?"

"A little, Aslan," said Susan.

"And now!" said Aslan in a much louder voice with just a hint of roar in it, while his tail lashed his flanks. "And now, where is this little Dwarf, this famous swordsman and archer, who doesn't believe in lions? Come here, son of Earth, come HERE!" – and the last word was no longer the hint of a roar but almost the real thing.

"Wraiths and wreckage!" gasped Trumpkin in the ghost of a voice. The children, who knew Aslan well enough to see that he liked the Dwarf very much, were not disturbed; but it was quite another thing for Trumpkin, who had never seen a lion before, let alone this Lion. He did the only sensible thing he could have done; that is, instead of bolting, he tottered towards Aslan.

Aslan pounced. Have you ever seen a very young kitten being carried in the mother cat's mouth? It was like that. The Dwarf, hunched up in a little, miserable ball, hung from Aslan's mouth. The Lion gave him one shake and all his armour rattled like a tinker's pack and then – hey-presto – the Dwarf flew up in the air. He was as safe as if he had been in bed, though he did not feel so. As he came down the huge velvety paws caught him as gently as a

mother's arms and set him (right way up, too) on the ground.

"Son of Earth, shall we be friends?" asked Aslan.

"Ye – he – he – hes," panted the Dwarf, for it had not yet got its breath back.

"Now," said Aslan. "The Moon is setting. Look behind you: there is the dawn beginning. We have no time to lose. You three, you sons of Adam and son of Earth, hasten into the Mound and deal with what you will find there."

The Dwarf was still speechless and neither of the boys dared to ask if Aslan would follow them. All three drew their swords and saluted, then turned and jingled away into the dusk. Lucy noticed that there was no sign of weariness in their faces: both the High King and King Edmund looked more like men than boys.

The girls watched them out of sight, standing close beside Aslan. The light was changing. Low down in the east, Aravir, the morning star of Narnia, gleamed like a little moon. Aslan, who seemed larger than before, lifted his head, shook his mane, and roared.

The sound, deep and throbbing at first like an organ beginning on a low note, rose and became louder, and then far louder again, till the earth and air were shaking with it. It rose up from that hill and floated across all Narnia. Down in Miraz's camp men woke, stared palely in one another's faces, and grasped their weapons. Down below that in the Great River, now at its coldest hour, the heads and shoulders of the nymphs, and the great weedy-bearded head of the river-god, rose from the water. Beyond it, in every field and wood, the alert ears of rabbits rose from their holes, the sleepy heads of birds came out from under wings, owls hooted, vixens barked, hedgehogs grunted, the trees stirred. In towns and villages mothers pressed babies close to their breasts, staring with wild eyes, dogs whimpered, and men leaped up groping for lights. Far away on the northern frontier the mountain giants peered from the dark gateways of their castles.

What Lucy and Susan saw was a dark something coming to them from almost every direction across the hills. It looked first like a black mist creeping on the ground, then like the stormy waves of a black sea rising higher and higher as it came on, and then, at last, like what it was – woods on the move. All the trees of the world appeared to be rushing towards Aslan. But as they drew nearer they looked less like trees, and when the whole crowd, bowing and curtsying and waving thin long arms to Aslan, were all around Lucy, she saw that it was a crowd of human shapes. Pale birch-girls were tossing their heads, willow-women pushed back their hair from their brooding faces to gaze on Aslan, the queenly beeches stood still and adored

him, shaggy oak-men, lean and melancholy elms, shock-headed hollies (dark themselves, but their wives all bright with berries) and gay rowans, all bowed and rose again, shouting, "Aslan, Aslan!" in their various husky or creaking or wave-like voices.

The crowd and the dance round Aslan (for it had become a dance once more) grew so thick and rapid that Lucy was confused. She never saw where certain other people came from who were soon capering about among the trees. One was a youth, dressed only in a fawn-skin, with vine-leaves wreathed in his curly hair. His face would have been almost too pretty for a boy's, if it had not looked so extremely wild. You felt, as Edmund said when he saw him a few days later, "There's a chap who might do anything – absolutely anything." He seemed to have a great many names – Bromios, Bassareus, and the Ram were three of them. There were a lot of girls with him, as wild as he. There was even, unexpectedly, someone on a donkey. And everybody was laughing: and everybody was shouting out, "Euan, euan, eu-oi-oi-oi."

"Is it a Romp, Aslan?" cried the youth. And apparently it was. But nearly everyone seemed to have a different idea as to what they were playing. It may have been Tig, but Lucy never discovered who was It. It was rather like Blind Man's Buff, only everyone behaved as if they were blindfolded. It was not unlike Hunt the Slipper, but the slipper was never found. What made it more complicated was that the man on the donkey, who was old and enormously fat, began calling out at once, "Refreshments! Time for refreshments," and falling off his donkey and being bundled on to it again by the others, while the donkey was under the impression that the whole thing was a circus and tried to give a display of walking on its hind legs. And all the time there were more and more vine leaves everywhere. And soon not only leaves but vines. They were climbing up everything. They were running up the legs of the tree people and circling round their necks. Lucy put up her hands to push back her hair and found she was pushing back vine branches. The donkey was a mass of them. His tail was completely entangled and something dark was nodding between his ears. Lucy looked again and saw it was a bunch of grapes. After that it was mostly grapes – overhead and underfoot and all around.

"Refreshments! Refreshments," roared the old man.

Everyone began eating, and whatever hothouses your people may have, you have never tasted such grapes. Really good grapes, firm and tight on the outside, but bursting into cool sweetness when you put them into your mouth, were one of the things the girls had never had quite enough of before. Here, there were more than anyone could possibly want, and no table-manners at all. One saw sticky and stained fingers everywhere, and, though mouths were full, the laughter never ceased nor the yodelling cries of *Euan, euan, eu-oi-oi-oi-oi*, till all of a sudden everyone felt at the same moment that the game (whatever it was), and the feast, ought to be over, and everyone flopped down breathless on the ground and turned their faces to Aslan to hear what he would say next.

At that moment the sun was just rising and Lucy remembered something and whispered to Susan,

"I say, Su, I know who they are."

"Who?"

"The boy with the wild face is Bacchus and the old one on the donkey is Silenus. Don't you remember Mr Tumnus telling us about them long ago?"

"Yes, of course. But I say, Lu –"

"What?"

"I wouldn't have felt safe with Bacchus and all his wild girls if we'd met them without Aslan."

"I should think not," said Lucy.

CHAPTER TWELVE

SORCERY AND SUDDEN VENGEANCE

MEANWHILE Trumpkin and the two boys arrived at the
dark little stone archway which led into the inside of the
Mound, and two sentinel badgers (the white patches on
their cheeks were all Edmund could see of them) leaped up
with bared teeth and asked them in snarling voices, "Who
goes there?"

"Trumpkin," said the Dwarf. "Bringing the High King
of Narnia out of the far past."

The badgers nosed at the boys' hands. "At last," they
said. "At last."

"Give us a light, friends," said Trumpkin.

The badgers found a torch just inside the arch and Peter
lit it and handed it to Trumpkin. "The D.L.F. had better
lead," he said. "We don't know our way about this place."

Trumpkin took the torch and went ahead into the dark
tunnel. It was a cold, black, musty place, with an occasional bat fluttering in the torchlight, and plenty of
cobwebs. The boys, who had been mostly in the open air
since that morning at the railway station, felt as if they
were going into a trap or a prison.

"I say, Peter," whispered Edmund. "Look at those carv-
ings on the walls. Don't they look old? And yet we're older
than that. When we were last here, they hadn't been
made."

"Yes," said Peter. "That makes one think."

The Dwarf went on ahead and then turned to the right,
and then to the left, and then down some steps, and then to
the left again. Then at last they saw a light ahead – light

from under a door. And now for the first time they heard voices, for they had come to the door of the central chamber. The voices inside were angry ones. Someone was talking so loudly that the approach of the boys and the Dwarf had not been heard.

"Don't like the sound of that," whispered Trumpkin to Peter. "Let's listen for a moment." All three stood perfectly still on the outside of the door.

"You know well enough," said a voice ("That's the

King," whispered Trumpkin), "why the Horn was not blown at sunrise this morning. Have you forgotten that Miraz fell upon us almost before Trumpkin had gone, and we were fighting for our lives for the space of three hours and more? I blew it when first I had a breathing space."

"I'm not likely to forgot it," came the angry voice, "when my Dwarfs bore the brunt of the attack and one in five of them fell." ("That's Nikabrik," whispered Trumpkin.)

"For shame, Dwarf," came a thick voice ("Trufflehunter's," said Trumpkin). "We all did as much as the Dwarfs and none more than the King."

"Tell that tale your own way for all I care," answered

Nikabrik. "But whether it was that the Horn was blown too late, or whether there was no magic in it, no help has come. You, you great clerk, you master magician, you know-all; are you still asking us to hang our hopes on Aslan and King Peter and all the rest of it?"

"I must confess – I cannot deny it – that I am deeply disappointed in the result of the operation," came the answer. ("That'll be Doctor Cornelius," said Trumpkin.)

"To speak plainly," said Nikabrik, "your wallet's empty, your eggs addled, your fish uncaught, your promises broken. Stand aside then and let others work. And that is why –"

"The help will come," said Trufflehunter. "I stand by Aslan. Have patience, like us beasts. The help will come. It may be even now at the door."

"Pah!" snarled Nikabrik. "You badgers would have us wait till the sky falls and we can all catch larks. I tell you we *can't* wait. Food is running short; we lose more than we can afford at every encounter; our followers are slipping away."

"And why?" asked Trufflehunter. "I'll tell you why. Because it is noised among them that we have called on the Kings of old and the Kings of old have not answered. The last words Trumpkin spoke before he went (and went, most likely, to his death) were, 'If you must blow the Horn, do not let the army know why you blow it or what you hope from it.' But that same evening everyone seemed to know."

"You'd better have shoved your grey snout in a hornets' nest, Badger, than suggest that I am the blab," said Nikabrik. "Take it back, or –"

"Oh, stop it, both of you," said King Caspian. "I want

to know what it is that Nikabrik keeps on hinting we should do. But before that, I want to know who those two strangers are whom he has brought into our council and who stand there with their ears open and their mouths shut."

"They are friends of mine," said Nikabrik. "And what better right have you yourself to be here than that you are a friend of Trumpkin's and the Badger's? And what right has that old dotard in the black gown to be here except that he is your friend? Why am I to be the only one who can't bring in his friends?"

"His Majesty is the King to whom you have sworn allegiance," said Trufflehunter sternly.

"Court manners, court manners," sneered Nikabrik. "But in this hole we may talk plainly. You know — and he knows — that this Telmarine boy will be king of nowhere and nobody in a week unless we can help him out of the trap in which he sits."

"Perhaps," said Cornelius, "your new friends would like to speak for themselves? You there, who and what are you?"

"Worshipful Master Doctor," came a thin, whining voice. "So please you, I'm only a poor old woman, I am, and very obliged to his Worshipful Dwarfship for his friendship, I'm sure. His Majesty, bless his handsome face, has no need to be afraid of an old woman that's nearly doubled up with the rheumatics and hasn't two sticks to put under her kettle. I have some poor little skill — not like yours, Master Doctor, of course — in small spells and cantrips that I'd be glad to use against our enemies if it was agreeable to all concerned. For I hate 'em. Oh yes. No one hates better than me."

"That is all most interesting and – er – satisfactory," said Doctor Cornelius. "I think I now know what you are, Madam. Perhaps your other friend, Nikabrik, would give some account of himself?"

A dull, grey voice at which Peter's flesh crept replied, "I'm hunger. I'm thirst. Where I bite, I hold till I die, and even after death they must cut out my mouthful from my enemy's body and bury it with me. I can fast a hundred years and not die. I can lie a hundred nights on the ice and not freeze. I can drink a river of blood and not burst. Show me your enemies."

"And it is in the presence of these two that you wish to disclose your plan?" said Caspian.

"Yes," said Nikabrik. "And by their help that I mean to execute it."

There was a minute or two during which Trumpkin and the boys could hear Caspian and his two friends speaking in low voices but could not make out what they were saying. Then Caspian spoke aloud.

"Well, Nikabrik," he said, "we will hear your plan."

There was a pause so long that the boys began to wonder if Nikabrik was ever going to begin; when he did, it was in a lower voice, as if he himself did not much like what he was saying.

"All said and done," he muttered, "none of us knows the truth about the ancient days in Narnia. Trumpkin believed none of the stories. I was ready to put them to the trial. We tried first the Horn and it has failed. If there ever was a High King Peter and a Queen Susan and a King Edmund and a Queen Lucy, then either they have not heard us, or they cannot come, or they are our enemies –"

"Or they are on the way," put in Trufflehunter.

"You can go on saying that till Miraz has fed us all to his dogs. As I was saying, we have tried one link in the chain of old legends, and it has done us no good. Well. But when your sword breaks, you draw your dagger. The stories tell of other powers beside the ancient Kings and Queens. How if we could call *them* up?"

"If you mean Aslan," said Trufflehunter, "it's all one calling on him and on the Kings. They were his servants. If he will not send them (but I make no doubt he will), is he more likely to come himself?"

"No. You're right there," said Nikabrik. "Aslan and the Kings go together. Either Aslan is dead, or he is not on our side. Or else something stronger than himself keeps him back. And if he did come – how do we know he'd be our friend? He was not always a good friend to Dwarfs by all that's told. Not even to all beasts. Ask the Wolves. And anyway, he was in Narnia only once that I ever heard of, and he didn't stay long. You may drop Aslan out of the reckoning. I was thinking of someone else."

There was no answer, and for a few minutes it was so still that Edmund could hear the wheezy and snuffling breath of the Badger.

"Who do you mean?" said Caspian at last.

"I mean a power so much greater than Aslan's that it held Narnia spellbound for years and years, if the stories are true."

"The White Witch!" cried three voices all at once, and from the noise Peter guessed that three people had leaped to their feet.

"Yes," said Nikabrik very slowly and distinctly, "I mean the Witch. Sit down again. Don't all take fright at a name as if you were children. We want power: and we want a power that will be on our side. As for power, do not the stories say that the Witch defeated Aslan, and bound him, and killed him on that very stone which is over there, just beyond the light?"

"But they also say that he came to life again," said the Badger sharply.

"Yes, they *say*," answered Nikabrik, "but you'll notice that we hear precious little about anything he did afterwards. He just fades out of the story. How do you explain that, if he really came to life? Isn't it much more likely that he didn't, and that the stories say nothing more about him because there was nothing more to say?"

"He established the Kings and Queens," said Caspian.

"A King who has just won a great battle can usually establish himself without the help of a performing lion," said Nikabrik. There was a fierce growl, probably from Trufflehunter.

"And anyway," Nikabrik continued, "what came of the Kings and their reign? They faded too. But it's very different with the Witch. They say she ruled for a hundred years: a hundred years of winter. There's power, if you like. There's something practical."

"But, heaven and earth!" said the King, "haven't we always been told that she was the worst enemy of all? Wasn't she a tyrant ten times worse than Miraz?"

"Perhaps," said Nikabrik in a cold voice. "Perhaps she *was* for you humans, if there were any of you in those days. Perhaps she was for some of the beasts. She stamped out the Beavers, I dare say; at least there are none of them in Narnia now. But she got on all right with us Dwarfs. I'm a Dwarf and I stand by my own people. *We're* not afraid of the Witch."

"But you've joined with us," said Trufflehunter.

"Yes, and a lot of good it has done my people, so far," snapped Nikabrik. "Who is sent on all the dangerous raids? The Dwarfs. Who goes short when the rations fail? The Dwarfs. Who –?"

"Lies! All lies!" said the Badger.

"And so," said Nikabrik, whose voice now rose to a scream, "if you can't help my people, I'll go to someone who can."

"Is this open treason, Dwarf?" asked the King.

"Put that sword back in its sheath, Caspian," said Nikabrik. "Murder at council, eh? Is that your game? Don't be fool enough to try it. Do you think I'm afraid of you? There's three on my side, and three on yours."

"Come on, then," snarled Trufflehunter, but he was immediately interrupted.

"Stop, stop, stop," said Doctor Cornelius. "You go on too fast. The Witch is dead. All the stories agree on that. What does Nikabrik mean by calling on the Witch?"

That grey and terrible voice which had spoken only once before said, "Oh, *is* she?"

And then the shrill, whining voice began, "Oh, bless his heart, his dear little Majesty needn't mind about the White Lady – that's what *we* call her – being dead. The Worshipful Master Doctor is only making game of a poor old woman like me when he says that. Sweet Master Doctor, learned Master Doctor, who ever heard of a witch that really died? You can always get them back."

"Call her up," said the grey voice. "We are all ready. Draw the circle. Prepare the blue fire."

Above the steadily increasing growl of the Badger and

Cornelius's sharp "What?" rose the voice of King Caspian like thunder.

"So that is your plan, Nikabrik! Black sorcery and the calling up of an accursed ghost. And I see who your companions are – a Hag and a Wer-Wolf!"

The next minute or so was very confused. There was an animal roaring, a clash of steel; the boys and Trumpkin rushed in; Peter had a glimpse of a horrible, grey, gaunt creature, half man and half wolf, in the very act of leaping

upon a boy about his own age, and Edmund saw a badger and a Dwarf rolling on the floor in a sort of cat fight. Trumpkin found himself face to face with the Hag. Her nose and chin stuck out like a pair of nut-crackers, her dirty grey hair was flying about her face and she had just got Doctor Cornelius by the throat. At one slash of Trumpkin's sword her head rolled on the floor. Then the light was knocked over and it was all swords, teeth, claws, fists, and boots for about sixty seconds. Then silence.

"Are you all right, Ed?"

"I – I think so," panted Edmund. "I've got that brute Nikabrik, but he's still alive."

"Weights and water-bottles!" came an angry voice. "It's *me* you're sitting on. Get off. You're like a young elephant."

"Sorry, D.L.F.," said Edmund. "Is that better?"

"Ow! No!" bellowed Trumpkin. "You're putting your boot in my mouth. Go away."

"Is King Caspian anywhere?" asked Peter.

"I'm here," said a rather faint voice. "Something bit me."

They all heard the noise of someone striking a match. It was Edmund. The little flame showed his face, looking pale and dirty. He blundered about for a little, found the candle (they were no longer using the lamp, for they had run out of oil), set it on the table, and lit it. When the flame rose clear, several people scrambled to their feet. Six faces blinked at one another in the candlelight.

"We don't seem to have any enemies left," said Peter. "There's the Hag, dead." (He turned his eyes quickly away from her.) "And Nikabrik, dead too. And I suppose this thing is a Wer-Wolf. It's so long since I've seen one. Wolf's head and man's body. That means he was just turning from man into wolf at the moment he was killed. And you, I suppose, are King Caspian?"

"Yes," said the other boy. "But I've no idea who you are."

"It's the High King, King Peter," said Trumpkin.

"Your Majesty is very welcome," said Caspian.

"And so is *your* Majesty," said Peter. "I haven't come to take your place, you know, but to put you into it."

"Your Majesty," said another voice at Peter's elbow. He turned and found himself face to face with the Badger.

Peter leaned forward, put his arms round the beast and kissed the furry head: it wasn't a girlish thing for him to do, because he was the High King.

"Best of badgers," he said. "You never doubted us all through."

"No credit to me, your Majesty," said Trufflehunter. "I'm a beast and we don't change. I'm a badger, what's more, and we hold on."

"I am sorry for Nikabrik," said Caspian, "though he hated me from the first moment he saw me. He had gone sour inside from long suffering and hating. If we had won quickly he might have become a good Dwarf in the days of peace. I don't know which of us killed him. I'm glad of that."

"You're bleeding," said Peter.

"Yes, I'm bitten," said Caspian. "It was that – that wolf thing." Cleaning and bandaging the wound took a long time, and when it was done Trumpkin said, "Now. Before everything else we want some breakfast."

"But not here," said Peter.

"No," said Caspian with a shudder. "And we must send someone to take away the bodies."

"Let the vermin be flung into a pit," said Peter. "But the Dwarf we will give to his people to be buried in their own fashion."

They breakfasted at last in another of the dark cellars of Aslan's How. It was not such a breakfast as they would have chosen, for Caspian and Cornelius were thinking of venison pasties, and Peter and Edmund of buttered eggs and hot coffee, but what everyone got was a little bit of cold bear-meat (out of the boys' pockets), a lump of hard cheese, an onion, and a mug of water. But, from the way they fell to, anyone would have supposed it was delicious.

CHAPTER THIRTEEN

THE HIGH KING IN COMMAND

"Now," said Peter, as they finished their meal, "Aslan and the girls (that's Queen Susan and Queen Lucy, Caspian) are somewhere close. We don't know when he will act. In his time, no doubt, not ours. In the meantime he would like us to do what we can on our own. You say, Caspian, we are not strong enough to meet Miraz in pitched battle."

"I'm afraid not, High King," said Caspian. He was liking Peter very much, but was rather tongue-tied. It was much stranger for him to meet the great Kings out of the old stories than it was for them to meet him.

"Very well, then," said Peter, "I'll send him a challenge to single combat." No one had thought of this before.

"Please," said Caspian, "could it not be me? I want to avenge my father."

"You're wounded," said Peter. "And anyway, wouldn't he just laugh at a challenge from you? I mean, we have seen that you are a king and a warrior but he thinks of you as a kid."

"But, Sire," said the Badger, who sat very close to Peter and never took his eyes off him. "Will he accept a challenge even from you? He knows he has the stronger army."

"Very likely he won't," said Peter, "but there's always the chance. And even if he doesn't, we shall spend the best part of the day sending heralds to and fro and all that. By then Aslan may have done something. And at least I can inspect the army and strengthen the position. I will send the challenge. In fact I will write it at once. Have you pen and ink, Master Doctor?"

"A scholar is never without them, your Majesty," answered Doctor Cornelius.

"Very well, I will dictate," said Peter. And while the Doctor spread out a parchment and opened his ink-horn and sharpened his pen, Peter leant back with half-closed eyes and recalled to his mind the language in which he had written such things long ago in Narnia's golden age.

"Right," he said at last. "And now, if you are ready, Doctor?"

Doctor Cornelius dipped his pen and waited. Peter dictated as follows:

"*Peter, by the gift of Aslan, by election, by prescription, and by conquest, High King over all Kings in Narnia, Emperor of the Lone Islands and Lord of Cair Paravel, Knight of the Most Noble Order of the Lion, to Miraz, Son of Caspian the Eighth, sometime Lord Protector of Narnia and now styling himself King of Narnia, Greeting.* Have you got that?"

"*Narnia, comma, greeting,*" muttered the Doctor. "Yes, Sire."

"Then begin a new paragraph," said Peter. "*For to prevent the effusion of blood, and for the avoiding all other inconveniences likely to grow from the wars now levied in our realm of Narnia, it is our pleasure to adventure our royal person on behalf of our trusty and well-beloved Caspian in clean wager of battle to prove upon your Lordship's body that the said Caspian is lawful King under us in Narnia both by our gift and by the laws of the Telmarines, and your Lordship twice guilty of treachery both in withholding the dominion of Narnia from the said*

Caspian and in the most abhominable, – don't forget to spell it with an H, Doctor – bloody, and unnatural murder of your kindly lord and brother King Caspian Ninth of that name. Wherefore we most heartily provoke, challenge, and defy your Lordship to the said combat and monomachy, and have sent these letters by the hand of our well beloved and royal brother Edmund, sometime King under us in Narnia, Duke of Lantern Waste and Count of the Western March, Knight of the Noble Order of the Table, to whom we have given full power of determining with your Lordship all the conditions of the said battle. Given at our lodging in Aslan's How this XII day of the month Greenroof in the first year of Caspian Tenth of Narnia.

"That ought to do," said Peter, drawing a deep breath. "And now we must send two others with King Edmund. I think the Giant ought to be one."

"He's – he's not very clever, you know," said Caspian.

"Of course not," said Peter. "But any giant looks impressive if only he will keep quiet. And it will cheer him up. But who for the other?"

"Upon my word," said Trumpkin, "if you want someone who can kill with looks, Reepicheep would be the best."

"He would indeed, from all I hear," said Peter with a laugh. "If only he wasn't so small. They wouldn't even see him till he was close!"

"Send Glenstorm, Sire," said Trufflehunter. "No one ever laughed at a Centaur."

An hour later two great lords in the army of Miraz, the Lord Glozelle and the Lord Sopespian, strolling along their lines and picking their teeth after breakfast, looked up and saw coming down to them from the wood the Centaur and Giant Wimbleweather, whom they had seen before in battle, and between them a figure they could not recognize. Nor indeed would the other boys at Edmund's school have recognized him if they could have seen him at that moment. For Aslan had breathed on him at their meeting and a kind of greatness hung about him.

"What's to do?" said the Lord Glozelle. "An attack?"

"A parley, rather," said Sopespian. "See, they carry green branches. They are coming to surrender most likely."

"He that is walking between the Centaur and the Giant has no look of surrender in his face," said Glozelle. "Who can he be? It is not the boy Caspian."

"No indeed," said Sopespian. "This is a fell warrior, I warrant you, wherever the rebels have got him from. He is (in your Lordship's private ear) a kinglier man than ever Miraz was. And what mail he wears! None of our smiths can make the like."

"I'll wager my dappled Pomely he brings a challenge, not a surrender," said Glozelle.

"How then?" said Sopespian. "We hold the enemy in our fist here. Miraz would never be so hair-brained as to throw away his advantage on a combat."

"He might be brought to it," said Glozelle in a much lower voice.

"Softly," said Sopespian. "Step a little aside here out of earshot of those sentries. Now. Have I taken your Lordship's meaning aright?"

"If the King undertook wager of battle," whispered Glozelle, "why, either he would kill or be killed."

"So," said Sopespian, nodding his head.

"And if he killed we should have won this war."

"Certainly. And if not?"

"Why, if not, we should be as able to win it without the King's grace as with him. For I need not tell your Lordship that Miraz is no very great captain. And after that, we should be both victorious and kingless."

"And it is your meaning, my Lord, that you and I could hold this land quite as conveniently without a King as with one?"

Glozelle's face grew ugly. "Not forgetting," said he, "that it was we who first put him on the throne. And in all the years that he has enjoyed it, what fruits have come our way? What gratitude has he shown us?"

"Say no more," answered Sopespian. "But look – here comes one to fetch us to the King's tent."

When they reached Miraz's tent they saw Edmund and his two companions seated outside it and being entertained with cakes and wine, having already delivered the challenge, and withdrawn while the King was considering it. When they saw them thus at close quarters the two Telmarine lords thought all three of them very alarming.

Inside, they found Miraz, unarmed and finishing his breakfast. His face was flushed and there was a scowl on his brow.

"There!" he growled, flinging the parchment across the table to them. "See what a pack of nursery tales our jackanapes of a nephew has sent us."

"By your leave, Sire," said Glozelle. "If the young warrior whom we have just seen outside is the King Edmund mentioned in the writing, then I would not call him a nursery tale but a very dangerous knight."

"King Edmund, pah!" said Miraz. "Does your Lordship believe those old wives' fables about Peter and Edmund and the rest?"

"I believe my eyes, your Majesty," said Glozelle.

"Well, this is to no purpose," said Miraz, "but as touching the challenge, I suppose there is only one opinion between us?"

"I suppose so, indeed, Sire," said Glozelle.

"And what is that?" asked the King.

"Most infallibly to refuse it," said Glozelle. "For though I have never been called a coward, I must plainly say that to meet that young man in battle is more than my heart would serve me for. And if (as is likely) his brother, the High King, is more dangerous than he – why, on your life, my Lord King, have nothing to do with him."

"Plague on you!" cried Miraz. "It was not that sort of council I wanted. Do you think I am asking you if I should be afraid to meet this Peter (if there is such a man)? Do you think I fear him? I wanted your counsel on the policy of the matter; whether we, having the advantage, should hazard it on a wager of battle."

"To which I can only answer, your Majesty," said Glozelle, "that for all reasons the challenge should be refused. There is death in the strange knight's face."

"There you are again!" said Miraz, now thoroughly angry. "Are you trying to make it appear that I am as great a coward as your Lordship?"

"Your Majesty may say your pleasure," said Glozelle sulkily.

"You talk like an old woman, Glozelle," said the King. "What say you, my Lord Sopespian?"

"Do not touch it, Sire," was the reply. "And what your Majesty says of the policy of the thing comes in very happily. It gives your Majesty excellent grounds for a refusal without any cause for questioning your Majesty's honour or courage."

"Great Heaven!" exclaimed Miraz, jumping to his feet. "Are *you* also bewitched today? Do you think I am *looking* for grounds to refuse it? You might as well call me coward to my face."

The conversation was going exactly as the two lords wished, so they said nothing.

"I see what it is," said Miraz, after staring at them as if his eyes would start out of his head, "you are as lily-livered as hares yourselves and have the effrontery to imagine my heart after the likeness of yours! Grounds for a refusal, indeed! Excuses for not fighting! Are you soldiers? Are you Telmarines? Are you men? And if I do refuse it (as all good reasons of captaincy and martial policy urge me to do) you will think, and teach others to think, I was afraid. Is it not so?"

"No man of your Majesty's age," said Glozelle, "would be called coward by any wise soldier for refusing the combat with a great warrior in the flower of his youth."

"So I'm to be a dotard with one foot in the grave, as well as a dastard," roared Miraz. "I'll tell you what it is, my Lords. With your womanish counsels (ever shying from the true point, which is one of policy) you have done the very opposite of your intent. I had meant to refuse it. But I'll accept it. Do you hear, accept it! I'll not be shamed because some witchcraft or treason has frozen both your bloods."

"We beseech your Majesty –" said Glozelle, but Miraz had flung out of the tent and they could hear him bawling out his acceptance to Edmund.

The two lords looked at one another and chuckled quietly.

"I knew he'd do it if he were properly chafed," said Glozelle. "But I'll not forget he called me coward. It shall be paid for."

There was a great stirring at Aslan's How when the news came back and was communicated to the various creatures. Edmund, with one of Miraz's captains, had already marked out the place for the combat, and ropes and stakes had been put round it. Two Telmarines were to stand at two of the corners, and one in the middle of one side, as marshals of the lists. Three marshals for the other two corners and the other side were to be furnished by the High King. Peter was just explaining to Caspian that he could not be one, because his right to the throne was what they were fighting about, when suddenly a thick, sleepy voice said, "Your Majesty, please." Peter turned and there stood the eldest of the Bulgy Bears.

"If you please, your Majesty," he said, "I'm a bear, I am."

"To be sure, so you are, and a good bear too, I don't doubt," said Peter.

"Yes," said the Bear. "But it was always a right of the bears to supply one marshal of the lists."

"Don't let him," whispered Trumpkin to Peter. "He's a good creature, but he'll shame us all. He'll go to sleep and he *will* suck his paws. In front of the enemy too."

"I can't help that," said Peter. "Because he's quite right. The Bears had that privilege. I can't imagine how it has been remembered all these years, when so many other things have been forgotten."

"Please, your Majesty," said the Bear.

"It is your right," said Peter. "And you shall be one of the marshals. But you *must* remember not to suck your paws."

"Of course not," said the Bear in a very shocked voice.

"Why, you're doing it this minute!" bellowed Trumpkin.

The Bear whipped his paw out of his mouth and pretended he hadn't heard.

"Sire!" came a shrill voice from near the ground.

"Ah – Reepicheep!" said Peter after looking up and down and round as people usually did when addressed by the Mouse.

"Sire," said Reepicheep. "My life is ever at your command, but my honour is my own. Sire, I have among my people the only trumpeter in your Majesty's army. I had thought, perhaps, we might have been sent with the challenge. Sire, my people are grieved. Perhaps if it were your pleasure that I should be a marshal of the lists, it would content them."

A noise not unlike thunder broke out from somewhere overhead at this point, as Giant Wimbleweather burst into one of those not very intelligent laughs to which the nicer sorts of Giant are so liable. He checked himself at once and looked as grave as a turnip by the time Reepicheep discovered where the noise came from.

"I am afraid it would not do," said Peter very gravely. "Some humans are afraid of mice –"

"I had observed it, Sire," said Reepicheep.

"And it would not be quite fair to Miraz," Peter continued, "to have in sight anything that might abate the edge of his courage."

"Your Majesty is the mirror of honour," said the Mouse with one of his admirable bows. "And on this matter we have but a single mind. . . . I thought I heard someone laughing just now. If anyone present wishes to make me the subject of his wit, I am very much at his service – with my sword – whenever he has leisure."

An awful silence followed this remark, which was

broken by Peter saying, "Giant Wimbleweather and the
Bear and the Centaur Glenstorm shall be our marshals.
The combat will be at two hours after noon. Dinner at
noon precisely."

"I say," said Edmund as they walked away, "I suppose
it *is* all right. I mean, I suppose you can beat him?"

"That's what I'm fighting him to find out," said Peter.

CHAPTER FOURTEEN

HOW ALL WERE VERY BUSY

A LITTLE before two o'clock Trumpkin and the Badger sat with the rest of the creatures at the wood's edge looking across at the gleaming line of Miraz's army which was about two arrow-shots away. In between, a square space of level grass had been staked for the combat. At the two far corners stood Glozelle and Sopespian with drawn swords. At the near corners were Giant Wimbleweather and the Bulgy Bear, who in spite of all their warnings was sucking his paws and looking, to tell the truth, uncommonly silly. To make up for this, Glenstorm on the right of the lists, stock-still except when he stamped a hind hoof occasionally on the turf, looked much more imposing than the Telmarine baron who faced him on the left. Peter had just shaken hands with Edmund and the Doctor, and was now walking down to the combat. It was like the moment before the pistol goes at an important race, but very much worse.

"I wish Aslan had turned up before it came to this," said Trumpkin.

"So do I," said Trufflehunter. "But look behind you."

"Crows and crockery!" muttered the Dwarf as soon as he had done so. "What are they? Huge people – beautiful people – like gods and goddesses and giants. Hundreds and thousands of them, closing in behind us. What are they?"

"It's the Dryads and Hamadryads and Silvans," said Trufflehunter. "Aslan has waked them."

"Humph!" said the Dwarf. "That'll be very useful if the

enemy try any treachery. But it won't help the High King very much if Miraz proves handier with his sword."

The Badger said nothing, for now Peter and Miraz were entering the lists from opposite ends, both on foot, both in chain shirts, with helmets and shields. They advanced till they were close together. Both bowed and seemed to speak, but it was impossible to hear what they said. Next moment the two swords flashed in the sunlight. For a second the clash could be heard but it was immediately drowned because both armies began shouting like crowds at a football match.

"Well done, Peter, oh, well done!" shouted Edmund as he saw Miraz reel back a whole pace and a half. "Follow it up, quick!" And Peter did, and for a few seconds it looked as if the fight might be won. But then Miraz pulled himself together — began to make real use of his height and weight. "Miraz! Miraz! The King! The King!" came the roar of the Telmarines. Caspian and Edmund grew white with sickening anxiety.

"Peter is taking some dreadful knocks," said Edmund.

"Hullo!" said Caspian. "What's happening now?"

"Both falling apart," said Edmund. "A bit blown, I expect. Watch. Ah, now they're beginning again, more scientifically this time. Circling round and round, feeling each other's defences."

"I'm afraid this Miraz knows his work," muttered the Doctor. But hardly had he said this when there was such a clapping and baying and throwing up of hoods among the Old Narnians that it was nearly deafening.

"What was it? What was it?" asked the Doctor. "My old eyes missed it."

"The High King has pricked him in the arm-pit," said

Caspian, still clapping. "Just where the arm-hole of the hauberk let the point through. First blood."

"It's looking ugly again now, though," said Edmund. "Peter's not using his shield properly. He must be hurt in the left arm."

It was only too true. Everyone could see that Peter's shield hung limp. The shouting of the Telmarines redoubled.

"You've seen more battles than I," said Caspian. "Is there any chance now?"

"Precious little," said Edmund. "I suppose he might *just* do it. With luck."

"Oh, why did we let it happen at all?" said Caspian.

Suddenly all the shouting on both sides died down. Edmund was puzzled for a moment. Then he said, "Oh, I see. They've both agreed to a rest. Come on, Doctor. You and I may be able to do something for the High King." They ran down to the lists and Peter came outside the ropes to meet them, his face red and sweaty, his chest heaving.

"Is your left arm wounded?" asked Edmund.

"It's not exactly a wound," Peter said. "I got the full weight of his shoulder on my shield — like a load of bricks — and the rim of the shield drove into my wrist. I don't think it's broken, but it might be a sprain. If you could tie it up very tight I think I could manage."

While they were doing this, Edmund asked anxiously, "What do you think of him, Peter?"

"Tough," said Peter. "Very tough. I have a chance if I can keep him on the hop till his weight and short wind come against him — in this hot sun too. To tell the truth, I haven't much chance else. Give my love to — to everyone at home, Ed, if he gets me. Here he comes into the lists again.

So long, old chap. Good-bye, Doctor. And I say, Ed, say something specially nice to Trumpkin. He's been a brick."

Edmund couldn't speak. He walked back with the Doctor to his own lines with a sick feeling in his stomach.

But the new bout went well. Peter now seemed to be able to make some use of his shield, and he certainly made good use of his feet. He was almost playing Tig with Miraz now, keeping out of range, shifting his ground, making the enemy work.

"Coward!" booed the Telmarines. "Why don't you stand up to him? Don't you like it, eh? Thought you'd come to fight, not dance. Yah!"

"Oh, I do hope he won't listen to them," said Caspian.

"Not he," said Edmund. "You don't know him – Oh!" – for Miraz had got in a blow at last, on Peter's helmet. Peter staggered, slipped sideways, and fell on one knee. The roar of the Telmarines rose like the noise of the sea. "Now, Miraz," they yelled. "Now. Quick! Quick! Kill him." But indeed there was no need to egg the usurper on. He was on top of Peter already. Edmund bit his lips till the blood came, as the sword flashed down on Peter. It looked as if it would slash off his head. Thank heavens! it had glanced down his right shoulder. The Dwarf-wrought mail was sound and did not break.

"Great Scott!" cried Edmund. "He's up again. Peter, go it, Peter."

"I couldn't see what happened," said the Doctor. "How did he do it?"

"Grabbed Miraz's arm as it came down," said Trumpkin, dancing with delight. "There's a man for you! Uses his enemy's arm as a ladder. The High King! The High King! Up, Old Narnia!"

"Look," said Trufflehunter. "Miraz is angry. It is good."

They were certainly at it hammer and tongs now: such a flurry of blows that it seemed impossible for either not to be killed. As the excitement grew, the shouting almost died away. The spectators were holding their breath. It was most horrible and most magnificent.

A great shout arose from the Old Narnians. Miraz was down – not struck by Peter, but face downwards, having tripped on a tussock. Peter stepped back, waiting for him to rise.

"Oh bother, bother, bother," said Edmund to himself. "Need he be as gentlemanly as all that? I suppose he must. Comes of being a Knight *and* a High King. I suppose it is what Aslan would like. But that brute will be up again in a minute and then –"

But "that brute" never rose. The Lords Glozelle and Sopespian had their own plans ready. As soon as they saw their King down they leaped into the lists crying, "Treachery! Treachery! The Narnian traitor has stabbed him in the back while he lay helpless. To arms! To arms, Telmar!"

Peter hardly understood what was happening. He saw two big men running towards him with drawn swords. Then the third Telmarine had leaped over the ropes on his left. "To arms, Narnia! Treachery!" Peter shouted. If all three had set upon him at once he would never have spoken again. But Glozelle stopped to stab his own King dead where he lay: "That's for your insult, this morning," he whispered as the blade went home. Peter swung to face Sopespian, slashed his legs from under him and, with the back-cut of the same stroke, walloped off his head. Edmund was now at his side crying, "Narnia, Narnia! The Lion!" The whole Telmarine army was rushing towards them. But now the Giant was stamping forward, stooping low and swinging his club. The Centaurs charged. *Twang, twang* behind and *hiss, hiss* overhead came the archery of Dwarfs. Trumpkin was fighting at his left. Full battle was joined.

"Come back, Reepicheep, you little ass!" shouted Peter. "You'll only be killed. This is no place for mice." But the ridiculous little creatures were dancing in and out among the feet of both armies, jabbing with their swords. Many a Telmarine warrior that day felt his foot suddenly pierced as if by a dozen skewers, hopped on one leg cursing the pain, and fell as often as not. If he fell, the mice finished him off; if he did not, someone else did.

But almost before the Old Narnians were really warmed to their work they found the enemy giving way. Tough-looking warriors turned white, gazed in terror not on the Old Narnians but on something behind them, and then flung down their weapons, shrieking, "The Wood! The Wood! The end of the world!"

But soon neither their cries nor the sound of weapons could be heard any more, for both were drowned in the ocean-like roar of the Awakened Trees as they plunged through the ranks of Peter's army, and then on, in pursuit of the Telmarines. Have you ever stood at the edge of a great wood on a high ridge when a wild south-wester broke over it in full fury on an autumn evening? Imagine that sound. And then imagine that the wood, instead of being fixed to one place, was rushing *at* you; and was no longer trees but huge people; yet still like trees because their long arms waved like branches and their heads tossed and leaves fell round them in showers. It was like that for the Telmarines. It was a little alarming even for the

Narnians. In a few minutes all Miraz's followers were running down to the Great River in the hope of crossing the bridge to the town of Beruna and there defending themselves behind ramparts and closed gates.

They reached the river, but there was no bridge. It had disappeared since yesterday. Then utter panic and horror fell upon them and they all surrendered.

But what had happened to the bridge?

Early that morning, after a few hours' sleep, the girls had

waked, to see Aslan standing over them and to hear his voice saying, "We will make holiday." They rubbed their eyes and looked round them. The trees had all gone but could still be seen moving away towards Aslan's How in a dark mass. Bacchus and the Maenads – his fierce, madcap girls – and Silenus were still with them. Lucy, fully rested, jumped up. Everyone was awake, everyone was laughing, flutes were playing, cymbals clashing. Animals, not Talking Animals, were crowding in upon them from every direction.

"What is it, Aslan?" said Lucy, her eyes dancing and her feet wanting to dance.

"Come, children," said he. "Ride on my back again today."

"Oh, lovely!" cried Lucy, and both girls climbed on to the warm golden back as they had done no one knew how many years before. Then the whole party moved off – Aslan leading, Bacchus and his Maenads leaping, rushing, and turning somersaults, the beasts frisking round them, and Silenus and his donkey bringing up the rear.

They turned a little to the right, raced down a steep hill, and found the long Bridge of Beruna in front of them. Before they had begun to cross it, however, up out of the water came a great wet, bearded head, larger than a man's, crowned with rushes. It looked at Aslan and out of its mouth a deep voice came.

"Hail, Lord," it said. "Loose my chains."

"Who on earth is *that*?" whispered Susan.

"I think it's the river-god, but hush," said Lucy.

"Bacchus," said Aslan. "Deliver him from his chains."

"That means the bridge, I expect," thought Lucy. And so it did. Bacchus and his people splashed forward into the shallow water, and a minute later the most curious things began happening. Great, strong trunks of ivy came curling up all the piers of the bridge, growing as quickly as a fire grows, wrapping the stones round, splitting, breaking, separating them. The walls of the bridge turned into hedges gay with hawthorn for a moment and then disappeared as the whole thing with a rush and a rumble collapsed into the swirling water. With much splashing, screaming, and laughter the revellers waded or swam or danced across the ford ("Hurrah! It's the Ford of Beruna again now!" cried the girls) and up the bank on the far side and into the town.

Everyone in the streets fled before their faces. The first house they came to was a school: a girls' school, where a lot of Narnian girls, with their hair done very tight and ugly tight collars round their necks and thick tickly stockings on their legs, were having a history lesson. The sort of "History" that was taught in Narnia under Miraz's rule was duller than the truest history you ever read and less true than the most exciting adventure story.

"If you don't attend, Gwendolen," said the mistress, "and stop looking out of the window, I shall have to give you an order-mark."

"But please, Miss Prizzle –" began Gwendolen.

"Did you hear what I said, Gwendolen?" asked Miss Prizzle.

"But please, Miss Prizzle," said Gwendolen, "there's a LION!"

"Take two order-marks for talking nonsense," said Miss Prizzle. "And now –" A roar interrupted her. Ivy came curling in at the windows of the classroom. The walls became a mass of shimmering green, and leafy branches arched overhead where the ceiling had been. Miss Prizzle found she was standing on grass in a forest glade. She clutched at her desk to steady herself, and found that the desk was a rose-bush. Wild people such as she had never even imagined were crowding round her. Then she saw the Lion, screamed and fled, and with her fled her class, who were mostly dumpy, prim little girls with fat legs. Gwendolen hesitated.

"You'll stay with us, sweetheart?" said Aslan.

"Oh, *may* I? Thank you, thank you," said Gwendolen. Instantly she joined hands with two of the Maenads, who whirled her round in a merry dance and helped her take off some of the unnecessary and uncomfortable clothes that she was wearing.

Wherever they went in the little town of Beruna it was the same. Most of the people fled, a few joined them. When they left the town they were a larger and a merrier company.

They swept on across the level fields on the north bank, or left bank, of the river. At every farm animals came out to join them. Sad old donkeys who had never known joy grew suddenly young again; chained dogs broke their chains; horses kicked their carts to pieces and came trotting along with them – clop-clop – kicking up the mud and whinnying.

At a well in a yard they met a man who was beating a boy. The stick burst into flower in the man's hand. He tried to drop it, but it stuck to his hand. His arm became a branch, his body the trunk of a tree, his feet took root. The boy, who had been crying a moment before, burst out laughing and joined them.

At a little town half-way to Beaversdam, where two rivers met, they came to another school, where a tired-looking girl was teaching arithmetic to a number of boys who looked very like pigs. She looked out of the window and saw the divine revellers singing up the street and a stab of joy went through her heart. Aslan stopped right under the window and looked up at her.

"Oh, don't, don't," she said. "I'd love to. But I mustn't. I

must stick to my work. And the children would be frightened if they saw you."

"Frightened?" said the most pig-like of the boys. "Who's she talking to out of the window? Let's tell the inspector she talks to people out of the window when she ought to be teaching us."

"Let's go and see who it is," said another boy, and they all came crowding to the window. But as soon as their mean little faces looked out, Bacchus gave a great cry of *Euan, euoi-oi-oi-oi* and the boys all began howling with fright and trampling one another down to get out of the door and jumping out of the windows. And it was said afterwards (whether truly or not) that those particular little boys were never seen again, but that there were a lot of very fine little pigs in that part of the country which had never been there before.

"Now, Dear Heart," said Aslan to the Mistress: and she jumped down and joined them.

At Beaversdam they re-crossed the river and came east again along the southern bank. They came to a little cottage where a child stood in the doorway crying. "Why are you crying, my love?" asked Aslan. The child, who had never seen a picture of a lion, was not afraid of him. "Auntie's very ill," she said. "She's going to die." Then Aslan went to go in at the door of the cottage, but it was too small for him. So, when he had got his head through, he pushed with his shoulders (Lucy and Susan fell off when he did this) and lifted the whole house up and it fell backwards and apart. And there, still in her bed, though the bed was now in the open air, lay a little old woman who looked as if she had Dwarf blood in her. She was at death's door, but when she opened her eyes and saw the bright, hairy head of the lion staring into her face, she did not scream or faint. She said, "Oh, Aslan! I knew it was true. I've been waiting for this all my life. Have you come to take me away?"

"Yes, Dearest," said Aslan. "But not the long journey yet." And as he spoke, like the flush creeping along the underside of a cloud at sunrise, the colour came back to her white face and her eyes grew bright and she sat up and said, "Why, I do declare I feel *that* better. I think I could take a little breakfast this morning."

"Here you are, mother," said Bacchus, dipping a pitcher in the cottage well and handing it to her. But what was in it now was not water but the richest wine, red as red-currant jelly, smooth as oil, strong as beef, warming as tea, cool as dew.

"Eh, you've done something to our well," said the old woman. "That makes a nice change, that does." And she jumped out of bed.

"Ride on me," said Aslan, and added to Susan and Lucy, "You two queens will have to run now."

"But we'd like that just as well," said Susan. And off they went again.

And so at last, with leaping and dancing and singing, with music and laughter and roaring and barking and neighing, they all came to the place where Miraz's army stood flinging down their swords and holding up their hands, and Peter's army, still holding their weapons and breathing hard, stood round them with stern and glad faces. And the first thing that happened was that the old woman slipped off Aslan's back and ran across to Caspian and they embraced one another; for she was his old nurse.

CHAPTER FIFTEEN

ASLAN MAKES A DOOR IN THE AIR

AT the sight of Aslan the cheeks of the Telmarine soldiers became the colour of cold gravy, their knees knocked together, and many fell on their faces. They had not believed in lions and this made their fear greater. Even the Red Dwarfs, who knew that he came as a friend, stood with open mouths and could not speak. Some of the Black Dwarfs, who had been of Nikabrik's party, began to edge away. But all the Talking Beasts surged round the Lion, with purrs and grunts and squeaks and whinneys of delight, fawning on him with their tails, rubbing against him, touching him reverently with their noses and going to and fro under his body and between his legs. If you have ever seen a little cat loving a big dog whom it knows and trusts, you will have a pretty good picture of their behaviour. Then Peter, leading Caspian, forced his way through the crowd of animals.

"This is Caspian, Sir," he said. And Caspian knelt and kissed the Lion's paw.

"Welcome, Prince," said Aslan. "Do you feel yourself sufficient to take up the Kingship of Narnia?"

"I – I don't think I do, Sir," said Caspian. "I'm only a kid."

"Good," said Aslan. "If you had felt yourself sufficient, it would have been a proof that you were not. Therefore, under us and under the High King, you shall be King of Narnia, Lord of Cair Paravel, and Emperor of the Lone Islands. You and your heirs while your race lasts. And your coronation – but what have we here?" For at that

moment a curious little procession was approaching –
eleven Mice, six of whom carried between them something on a litter made of branches, but the litter was no
bigger than a large atlas. No one has ever seen mice more
woebegone than these. They were plastered with mud –
some with blood too – and their ears were down and their
whiskers drooped and their tails dragged in the grass, and
their leader piped on his slender pipe a melancholy tune.
On the litter lay what seemed little better than a damp
heap of fur; all that was left of Reepicheep. He was still
breathing, but more dead than alive, gashed with
innumerable wounds, one paw crushed, and, where his
tail had been, a bandaged stump.

"Now, Lucy," said Aslan.

Lucy had her diamond bottle out in a moment. Though
only a drop was needed on each of Reepicheep's wounds,
the wounds were so many that there was a long and
anxious silence before she had finished and the Master
Mouse sprang from the litter. His hand went at once to
his sword hilt, with the other he twirled his whiskers. He
bowed.

"Hail, Aslan!" came his shrill voice. "I have the honour
–" But then he suddenly stopped.

The fact was that he still had no tail – whether that
Lucy had forgotten it or that her cordial, though it could
heal wounds, could not make things grow again. Reepicheep became aware of his loss as he made his bow; perhaps it altered something in his balance. He looked over
his right shoulder. Failing to see his tail, he strained his
neck further till he had to turn his shoulders and his
whole body followed. But by that time his hind-quarters
had turned too and were out of sight. Then he strained his

neck looking over his shoulder again, with the same result. Only after he had turned completely round three times did he realize the dreadful truth.

"I am confounded," said Reepicheep to Aslan. "I am completely out of countenance. I must crave your indulgence for appearing in this unseemly fashion."

"It becomes you very well, Small One," said Aslan.

"All the same," replied Reepicheep, "if anything could

be done . . . Perhaps her Majesty?" and here he bowed to Lucy.

"But what do you want with a tail?" asked Aslan.

"Sir," said the Mouse, "I can eat and sleep and die for my King without one. But a tail is the honour and glory of a Mouse."

"I have sometimes wondered, friend," said Aslan, "whether you do not think too much about your honour."

"Highest of all High Kings," said Reepicheep, "permit me to remind you that a very small size has been bestowed on us Mice, and if we did not guard our dignity, some (who weigh worth by inches) would allow themselves very unsuitable pleasantries at our expense. That is why I have been at some pains to make it known that no one who does not wish to feel this sword as near his heart as I can reach shall talk in my presence about Traps or Toasted Cheese or Candles: no, Sir – not the tallest fool in Narnia!" Here he glared very fiercely up at Wimbleweather, but the Giant, who was always a stage behind everyone else, had not yet discovered what was being talked about down at his feet, and so missed the point.

"Why have your followers all drawn *their* swords, may I ask?" said Aslan.

"May it please your High Majesty," said the second Mouse, whose name was Peepiceek, "we are all waiting to cut off our own tails if our Chief must go without his. We will not bear the shame of wearing an honour which is denied to the High Mouse."

"Ah!" roared Aslan. "You have conquered me. You have great hearts. Not for the sake of your dignity, Reepicheep, but for the love that is between you and your people, and still more for the kindness your people showed me long ago when you ate away the cords that bound me on the Stone Table (and it was then, though you have long forgotten it, that you began to be *Talking* Mice), you shall have your tail again."

Before Aslan had finished speaking the new tail was in its place. Then, at Aslan's command, Peter bestowed the Knighthood of the Order of the Lion on Caspian, and Caspian, as soon as he was knighted, himself bestowed it on Trufflehunter and Trumpkin and Reepicheep, and made Doctor Cornelius his Lord Chancellor, and confirmed the Bulgy Bear in his hereditary office of Marshal of the Lists. And there was great applause.

After this the Telmarine soldiers, firmly but without taunts or blows, were taken across the ford and all put under lock and key in the town of Beruna and given beef and beer. They made a great fuss about wading in the river, for they all hated and feared running water just as much as they hated and feared woods and animals. But in the end the nuisance was over: and then the nicest parts of that long day began.

Lucy, sitting close to Aslan and divinely comfortable, wondered what the trees were doing. At first she thought they were merely dancing; they were certainly going round slowly in two circles, one from left to right and the other from right to left. Then she noticed that they kept throwing something down in the centre of both circles. Sometimes she thought they were cutting off long strands of their hair; at other times it looked as if they were breaking off bits of their fingers – but, if so, they had plenty of fingers to spare and it did not hurt them. But whatever they were throwing down, when it reached the ground, it became brushwood or dry sticks. Then three or four of the Red Dwarfs came forward with their tinder boxes and set light to the pile, which first crackled, and then blazed, and finally roared as a woodland bonfire on midsummer night ought to do. And everyone sat down in a wide circle round it.

Then Bacchus and Silenus and the Maenads began a dance, far wilder than the dance of the trees; not merely a dance for fun and beauty (though it was that too) but a magic dance of plenty, and where their hands touched, and where their feet fell, the feast came into existence – sides of roasted meat that filled the grove with delicious smell, and wheaten cakes and oaten cakes, honey and many-coloured sugars and cream as thick as porridge and as smooth as still water, peaches, nectarines, pomegranates, pears, grapes, strawberries, raspberries – pyramids and cataracts of fruit. Then, in great wooden cups and bowls and mazers, wreathed with ivy, came the wines; dark, thick ones like syrups of mulberry juice, and clear red ones like red jellies liquefied, and yellow wines

and green wines and yellow-green and greenish-yellow.

But for the tree people different fare was provided. When Lucy saw Clodsley Shovel and his moles scuffling up the turf in various places (which Bacchus had pointed out to them) and realized that the trees were going to eat *earth* it gave her rather a shudder. But when she saw the earths that were actually brought to them she felt quite different. They began with a rich brown loam that looked almost exactly like chocolate; so like chocolate, in fact, that Edmund tried a piece of it, but he did not find it at all nice. When the rich loam had taken the edge off their hunger, the trees turned to an earth of the kind you see in Somerset, which is almost pink. They said it was lighter and sweeter. At the cheese stage they had a chalky soil, and then went on to delicate confections of the finest gravels powdered with choice silver sand. They drank very little wine, and it made the Hollies very talkative: for the most part they quenched their thirst with deep draughts of mingled dew and rain, flavoured with forest flowers and the airy taste of the thinnest clouds.

Thus Aslan feasted the Narnians till long after the

sunset had died away, and the stars had come out; and the great fire, now hotter but less noisy, shone like a beacon in the dark woods, and the frightened Telmarines saw it from far away and wondered what it might mean. The best thing of all about this feast was that there was no breaking up or going away, but as the talk grew quieter and slower, one after another would begin to nod and finally drop off to sleep with feet towards the fire and good friends on either side, till at last there was silence all round the circle, and the chattering of water over stone at the Ford of Beruna could be heard once more. But all night Aslan and the

Moon gazed upon each other with joyful and unblinking eyes.

Next day messengers (who were chiefly squirrels and birds) were sent all over the country with a proclamation to the scattered Telmarines – including, of course, the prisoners in Beruna. They were told that Caspian was now King and that Narnia would henceforth belong to the Talking Beasts and the Dwarfs and Dryads and Fauns and other creatures quite as much as to the men. Any who

chose to stay under the new conditions might do so; but for those who did not like the idea, Aslan would provide another home. Anyone who wished to go there must come to Aslan and the Kings at the Ford of Beruna by noon on the fifth day. You may imagine that this caused plenty of head-scratching among the Telmarines. Some of them, chiefly the young ones, had, like Caspian, heard stories of the Old Days and were delighted that they had come back. They were already making friends with the creatures. These all decided to stay in Narnia. But most of the older men, especially those who had been important under Miraz, were sulky and had no wish to live in a country where they could not rule the roost. "Live here with a lot of blooming performing animals! No fear," they said. "And ghosts too," some added with a shudder. "That's what those there Dryads really are. It's not canny." They were also suspicious. "I don't trust 'em," they said. "Not with that awful Lion and all. He won't keep his claws off us long, *you'll* see." But then they were equally suspicious of his offer to give them a new home. "Take us off to his den and eat us one by one most likely," they muttered. And the more they talked to one another the sulkier and more suspicious they became. But on the appointed day more than half of them turned up.

At one end of the glade Aslan had caused to be set up two stakes of wood, higher than a man's head and about three feet apart. A third, and lighter, piece of wood was bound across them at the top, uniting them, so that the whole thing looked like a doorway from nowhere into nowhere. In front of this stood Aslan himself with Peter on his right and Caspian on his left. Grouped round them were Susan and Lucy, Trumpkin and Trufflehunter, the Lord Cornelius, Glenstorm, Reepicheep, and others. The children and the Dwarfs had made good use of the royal wardrobes in what had been the castle of Miraz and was now the castle of Caspian, and what with silk and cloth of gold, with snowy linen glancing through slashed sleeves, with silver mail shirts and jewelled sword-hilts, with gilt helmets and feathered bonnets, they were almost too bright to look at. Even the beasts wore rich chains about their necks. Yet nobody's eyes were on them or the children. The living and strokable gold of Aslan's mane outshone them all. The rest of the Old Narnians stood down each side of the glade. At the far end stood the

Telmarines. The sun shone brightly and pennants fluttered in the light wind.

"Men of Telmar," said Aslan, "you who seek a new land, hear my words. I will send you all to your own country, which I know and you do not."

"We don't remember Telmar. We don't know where it is. We don't know what it is like," grumbled the Telmarines.

"You came into Narnia out of Telmar," said Aslan. "But you came into Telmar from another place. You do not belong to this world at all. You came hither, certain generations ago, out of that same world to which the High King Peter belongs."

At this, half the Telmarines began whimpering, "There you are. Told you so. He's going to kill us all, send us right out of the world," and the other half began throwing out their chests and slapping one another on the back and whispering, "There you are. Might have guessed we didn't belong to this place with all its queer, nasty, unnatural creatures. We're of royal blood, you'll see." And even Caspian and Cornelius and the children turned to Aslan with looks of amazement on their faces.

"Peace," said Aslan in the low voice which was nearest to his growl. The earth seemed to shake a little and every living thing in the grove became still as stone.

"You, Sir Caspian," said Aslan, "might have known that you could be no true King of Narnia unless, like the Kings of old, you were a son of Adam and came from the world of Adam's sons. And so you are. Many years ago in that world, in a deep sea of that world which is called the South Sea, a shipload of pirates were driven by storm on an island. And there they did as pirates would: killed the natives and took the native women for wives, and made palm wine, and drank and were drunk, and lay in the shade of the palm trees, and woke up and quarrelled, and sometimes killed one another. And in one of these frays six were put to flight by the rest and fled with their women into the centre of the island and up a mountain, and went, as they thought, into a cave to hide. But it was one of the magical places of that world, one of the chinks or chasms between that world and this. There were many chinks or chasms between worlds in old times, but they have grown rarer. This was one of the last: I do not say *the* last. And so they fell, or rose, or blundered, or dropped right through, and found themselves in this world, in the Land of Telmar which was then unpeopled. But why it was unpeopled is a long story: I will not tell it now. And in Telmar their descendants lived and became a fierce and proud people; and after many generations there was a famine in Telmar and they invaded Narnia, which was then in some disorder (but that also would be a long story), and conquered it and ruled it. Do you mark all this well, King Caspian?"

"I do indeed, Sir," said Caspian. "I was wishing that I came of a more honourable lineage."

"You come of the Lord Aslan and the Lady Eve," said Aslan. "And that is both honour enough to erect the head of the poorest beggar, and shame enough to bow the shoulders of the greatest emperor on earth. Be content."

Caspian bowed.

"And now," said Aslan, "you men and women of Telmar, will you go back to that island in the world of men from which your fathers first came? It is no bad place. The race of those pirates who first found it has died out, and it is without inhabitants. There are good wells of fresh water, and fruitful soil, and timber for building, and fish in the lagoons; and the other men of that world have not yet discovered it. The chasm is open for your return; but this I must warn you, that once you have gone through, it will close behind you for ever. There will be no more commerce between the worlds by that door."

There was silence for a moment. Then a burly, decent-looking fellow among the Telmarine soldiers pushed forward and said:

"Well, I'll take the offer."

"It is well chosen," said Aslan. "And because you have spoken first, strong magic is upon you. Your future in that world shall be good. Come forth."

The man, now a little pale, came forward. Aslan and his court drew aside, leaving him free access to the empty doorway of the stakes.

"Go through it, my son," said Aslan, bending towards him and touching the man's nose with his own. As soon as the Lion's breath came about him, a new look came into the man's eyes – startled, but not unhappy – as if he were trying to remember something. Then he squared his shoulders and walked into the Door.

Everyone's eyes were fixed on him. They saw the three pieces of wood, and through them the trees and grass and sky of Narnia. They saw the man between the doorposts: then, in one second, he had vanished utterly.

From the other end of the glade the remaining Telmarines set up a wailing. "Ugh! What's happened to him? Do you mean to murder us? We won't go that way." And then one of the clever Telmarines said:

"We don't see any other world through those sticks. If

you want us to believe in it, why doesn't one of *you* go? All your own friends are keeping well away from the sticks."

Instantly Reepicheep stood forward and bowed. "If *my* example can be of any service, Aslan," he said, "I will take eleven mice through that arch at your bidding without a moment's delay."

"Nay, little one," said Aslan, laying his velvety paw ever so lightly on Reepicheep's head. "They would do dreadful things to you in that world. They would show you at fairs. It is others who must lead."

"Come on," said Peter suddenly to Edmund and Lucy. "Our time's up."

"What do you mean?" said Edmund.

"This way," said Susan, who seemed to know all about it. "Back into the trees. We've got to change."

"Change what?" asked Lucy.

"Our clothes, of course," said Susan. "Nice fools we'd look on the platform of an English station in *these*."

"But our other things are at Caspian's castle," said Edmund.

"No, they're not," said Peter, still leading the way into the thickest wood. "They're all here. They were brought down in bundles this morning. It's all arranged."

"Was that what Aslan was talking to you and Susan about this morning?" asked Lucy.

"Yes – that and other things," said Peter, his face very solemn. "I can't tell it to you all. There were things he wanted to say to Su and me because we're not coming back to Narnia."

"Never?" cried Edmund and Lucy in dismay.

"Oh, you two are," answered Peter. "At least, from what he said, I'm pretty sure he means you to get back some day. But not Su and me. He says we're getting too old."

"Oh, Peter," said Lucy. "What awful bad luck. Can you bear it?"

"Well, I think I can," said Peter. "It's all rather different from what I thought. You'll understand when it comes to your last time. But, quick, here are our things."

It was odd, and not very nice, to take off their royal clothes and to come back in their school things (not very fresh now) into that great assembly. One or two of the nastier Telmarines jeered. But the other creatures all cheered and rose up in honour of Peter the High King,

and Queen Susan of the Horn, and King Edmund, and
Queen Lucy. There were affectionate and (on Lucy's part)
tearful farewells with all their old friends – animal kisses,
and hugs from Bulgy Bears, and hands wrung by
Trumpkin, and a last tickly, whiskerish embrace with
Trufflehunter. And of course Caspian offered the Horn
back to Susan and of course Susan told him to keep it.
And then, wonderfully and terribly, it was farewell to

Aslan himself, and Peter took his place with Susan's
hands on his shoulders and Edmund's on hers and Lucy's
on his and the first of the Telmarine's on Lucy's, and so in
a long line they moved forward to the Door. After that
came a moment which is hard to describe, for the children
seemed to be seeing three things at once. One was the
mouth of a cave opening into the glaring green and blue
of an island in the Pacific, where all the Telmarines would
find themselves the moment they were through the Door.
The second was a glade in Narnia, the faces of Dwarfs

and Beasts, the deep eyes of Aslan, and the white patches on the Badger's cheeks. But the third (which rapidly swallowed up the other two) was the grey, gravelly surface of a platform in a country station, and a seat with luggage round it, where they were all sitting as if they had never moved from it – a little flat and dreary for a moment after all they had been through, but also, unexpectedly, nice in its own way, what with the familiar railway smell and the English sky and the summer term before them.

"Well!" said Peter. "We *have* had a time."

"Bother!" said Edmund. "I've left my new torch in Narnia."

The Voyage of the
Dawn Treader

TO GEOFFREY CORBETT

CONTENTS

Plan of the
Dawn Treader

FORECASTLE

POOP

tiller

poop deck

lookout man

hen coop

boat

hatch

Lucy's cabin

Drinian's cabin

stern cabin

Caspian's cabin

galley

quarters

starboard

port

CHAPTER ONE

THE PICTURE IN THE BEDROOM

THERE was a boy called Eustace Clarence Scrubb, and he almost deserved it. His parents called him Eustace Clarence and masters called him Scrubb. I can't tell you how his friends spoke to him, for he had none. He didn't call his Father and Mother "Father" and "Mother", but Harold and Alberta. They were very up-to-date and advanced people. They were vegetarians, non-smokers and tee-totallers and wore a special kind of underclothes. In their house there was very little furniture and very few clothes on beds and the windows were always open.

Eustace Clarence liked animals, especially beetles, if they were dead and pinned on a card. He liked books if they were books of information and had pictures of grain elevators or of fat foreign children doing exercises in model schools.

Eustace Clarence disliked his cousins the four Pevensies, Peter, Susan, Edmund and Lucy. But he was quite glad when he heard that Edmund and Lucy were coming to stay. For deep down inside him he liked bossing and bullying; and, though he was a puny little person who couldn't have stood up even to Lucy, let alone Edmund, in a fight, he knew that there are dozens of ways to give people a bad time if you are in your own home and they are only visitors.

Edmund and Lucy did not at all want to come and stay with Uncle Harold and Aunt Alberta. But it really couldn't be helped. Father had got a job lecturing in America for sixteen weeks that summer, and Mother was to go with him because she hadn't had a real holiday for ten years. Peter was working very hard for an exam and he was to spend the holidays being coached by old Professor Kirke in whose house these four children had had wonderful adventures long ago in the war years. If he had still been in that house he would have had them all to stay. But he had somehow become poor since the old days and was living in a small cottage with only one bedroom to spare. It would have cost too much money to take the other three all to America, and Susan had gone.

Grown-ups thought her the pretty one of the family and she was no good at school work (though otherwise very old

for her age) and Mother said she "would get far more out of a trip to America than the youngsters". Edmund and Lucy tried not to grudge Susan her luck, but it was dreadful having to spend the summer holidays at their Aunt's. "But it's far worse for me," said Edmund, "because you'll at least have a room of your own and I shall have to share a bedroom with that record stinker, Eustace."

The story begins on an afternoon when Edmund and Lucy were stealing a few precious minutes alone together. And of course they were talking about Narnia, which was the name of their own private and secret country. Most of us, I suppose, have a secret country but for most of us it is only an imaginary country. Edmund and Lucy were luckier than other people in that respect. Their secret country was real. They had already visited it twice; not in a game or a dream but in reality. They had got there of course by Magic, which is the only way of getting to Narnia. And a promise, or very nearly a promise, had been made them in Narnia itself that they would some day get back. You may imagine that they talked about it a good deal, when they got the chance.

They were in Lucy's room, sitting on the edge of her bed and looking at a picture on the opposite wall. It was the only picture in the house that they liked. Aunt Alberta didn't like it at all (that was why it was put away in a little back room upstairs), but she couldn't get rid of it because it had been a wedding present from someone she did not want to offend.

It was a picture of a ship – a ship sailing straight towards you. Her prow was gilded and shaped like the head of a dragon with wide-open mouth. She had only one mast and one large, square sail which was a rich purple. The sides of the ship – what you could see of them where the gilded wings of the dragon ended – were green. She had just run up to the top of one glorious blue wave, and the nearer slope of that wave came down towards you, with streaks and bubbles on it. She was obviously running fast before a gay wind, listing over a little on her port side. (By the way, if you are going to read this story at all, and if you don't know already, you had better get it into your head that the left of a ship when you are looking ahead, is *port*, and the right is *starboard*.) All the sunlight fell on her from that side, and the water on that side was full of greens and purples. On the other, it was darker blue from the shadow of the ship.

"The question is," said Edmund, "whether it doesn't make things worse, *looking* at a Narnian ship when you can't get there."

"Even looking is better than nothing," said Lucy. "And she is such a very Narnian ship."

"Still playing your old game?" said Eustace Clarence, who had been listening outside the door and now came grinning into the room. Last year, when he had been staying with the Pevensies, he had managed to hear them all talking of Narnia and he loved teasing them about it. He thought of course that they were making it all up; and as he was far too stupid to make anything up himself, he did not approve of that.

"You're not wanted here," said Edmund curtly.

"I'm trying to think of a limerick," said Eustace. "Something like this:

> "Some kids who played games about Narnia
> Got gradually balmier and balmier —"

"Well *Narnia* and *balmier* don't rhyme, to begin with," said Lucy.

"It's an assonance," said Eustace.

"Don't ask him what an assy-thingummy is," said Edmund. "He's only longing to be asked. Say nothing and perhaps he'll go away."

Most boys, on meeting a reception like this, would either have cleared out or flared up. Eustace did neither. He just hung about grinning, and presently began talking again.

"Do you like that picture?" he asked.

"For heaven's sake don't let him get started about Art and all that," said Edmund hurriedly, but Lucy, who was very truthful, had already said, "Yes, I do. I like it very much."

"It's a rotten picture," said Eustace.

"You won't see it if you step outside," said Edmund.

"Why do you like it?" said Eustace to Lucy.

"Well, for one thing," said Lucy, "I like it because the ship looks as if it was really moving. And the water looks as if it was really wet. And the waves look as if they were really going up and down."

Of course Eustace knew lots of answers to this, but he didn't say anything. The reason was that at that very moment he looked at the waves and saw that they did look very much indeed as if they were going up and down. He had only once been in a ship (and then only as far as the Isle of Wight) and had been horribly seasick. The look of the waves in the picture made him feel sick again. He turned rather green and tried another look. And then all three children were staring with open mouths.

What they were seeing may be hard to believe when you read it in print, but it was almost as hard to believe when you saw it happening. The things in the picture were moving. It didn't look at all like a cinema either; the colours were too real and clean and out-of-doors for that. Down went the prow of the ship into the wave and up went a great shock of spray. And then up went the wave behind her, and her stern and her deck became visible for the first time, and then disappeared as the next wave came to meet her and her bows went up again. At the same moment an exercise book which had been lying beside Edmund on the bed flapped, rose and sailed through the air to the wall behind him, and Lucy felt all her hair whipping round her face as it does on a windy day. And this was a windy day; but the wind was blowing out of the picture towards them. And suddenly with the wind came the noises – the swishing of waves and the slap of water against the ship's sides and the creaking and the over-all high steady roar of air and water. But it was the smell, the wild, briny smell, which really convinced Lucy that she was not dreaming.

"Stop it," came Eustace's voice, squeaky with fright and bad temper. "It's some silly trick you two are playing. Stop it. I'll tell Alberta – Ow!"

The other two were much more accustomed to adventures, but, just exactly as Eustace Clarence said "Ow," they both said "Ow" too. The reason was that a great cold, salt splash had broken right out of the frame and they were breathless from the smack of it, besides being wet through.

"I'll smash the rotten thing," cried Eustace; and then several things happened at the same time. Eustace rushed towards the picture. Edmund, who knew something about magic, sprang after him, warning him to look out and not to be a fool. Lucy grabbed at him from the other side and was dragged forward. And by this time either they had grown much smaller or the picture had grown bigger. Eustace jumped to try to pull it off the wall and found himself standing on the frame; in front of him was not glass but real sea, and wind and waves rushing up to the frame as they might to a rock. He lost his head and clutched at the other two who had jumped up beside him. There was a second of struggling and shouting, and just as they thought they had got their balance a great blue roller surged up round them, swept them off their feet, and drew them down into the sea. Eustace's despairing cry suddenly ended as the water got into his mouth.

Lucy thanked her stars that she had worked hard at her swimming last summer term. It is true that she would have got on much better if she had used a slower stroke, and also that the water felt a great deal colder than it had looked while it was only a picture. Still, she kept her head and kicked her shoes off, as everyone ought to do who falls into deep water in their clothes. She even kept her mouth shut and her eyes open. They were still quite near the ship; she saw its green side towering high above them, and people looking at her from the deck. Then, as one might have expected, Eustace clutched at her in a panic and down they both went.

When they came up again she saw a white figure diving off the ship's side. Edmund was close beside her now, treading water, and had caught the arms of the howling Eustace. Then someone else, whose face was vaguely familiar, slipped an arm under her from the other side. There was a lot of shouting going on from the ship, heads crowding together above the bulwarks, ropes being thrown. Edmund and the stranger were fastening ropes round her. After that followed what seemed a very long delay during which her face got blue and her teeth began chattering. In reality the delay was not very long; they were waiting till the moment when she could be got on board the ship without being dashed against its side. Even with all their best endeavours she had a bruised knee when she finally stood, dripping and shivering, on the deck. After her Edmund was heaved up, and then the miserable Eustace. Last of all came the stranger – a golden-headed boy some years older than herself.

"Ca – Ca – Caspian!" gasped Lucy as soon as she had breath enough. For Caspian it was; Caspian, the boy king of Narnia whom they had helped to set on the throne during their last visit. Immediately Edmund recognized him too. All three shook hands and clapped one another on the back with great delight.

"But who is your friend?" said Caspian almost at once, turning to Eustace with his cheerful smile. But Eustace was crying much harder than any boy of his age has a right to cry when nothing worse than a wetting has happened to him, and would only yell out, "Let me go. Let me go back. I don't *like* it."

"Let you go?" said Caspian. "But where?"

Eustace rushed to the ship's side, as if he expected to see the picture frame hanging above the sea, and perhaps a glimpse of Lucy's bedroom. What he saw was blue waves flecked with foam, and paler blue sky, both spreading without a break to the horizon. Perhaps we can hardly blame him if his heart sank. He was promptly sick.

"Hey! Rynelf," said Caspian to one of the sailors. "Bring

spiced wine for their Majesties. You'll need something to warm you after that dip." He called Edmund and Lucy their Majesties because they and Peter and Susan had all been Kings and Queens of Narnia long before his time. Narnian time flows differently from ours. If you spent a hundred years in Narnia, you would still come back to our world at the very same hour of the very same day on which you left. And then, if you went back to Narnia after spending a week here, you might find that a thousand Narnian years had

passed, or only a day, or no time at all. You never know till you get there. Consequently, when the Pevensie children had returned to Narnia last time for their second visit, it was (for the Narnians) as if King Arthur came back to Britain, as some people say he will. And I say the sooner the better.

Rynelf returned with the spiced wine steaming in a flagon and four silver cups. It was just what one wanted, and as Ludy and Edmund sipped it they could feel the warmth going right down to their toes. But Eustace made faces and spluttered and spat it out and was sick again and began to cry again and asked if they hadn't any Plumptree's Vitaminized Nerve Food and could it be made with distilled water and anyway he insisted on being put ashore at the next station.

"This is a merry shipmate you've brought us, Brother," whispered Caspian to Edmund with a chuckle; but before he could say anything more Eustace burst out again.

"Oh! Ugh! What on earth's *that*! Take it away, the horrid thing."

He really had some excuse this time for feeling a little surprised. Something very curious indeed had come out of the cabin in the poop and was slowly approaching them. You might call it – and indeed it was – a Mouse. But then it

was a Mouse on its hind legs and stood about two feet high. A thin band of gold passed round its head under one ear and over the other and in this was stuck a long crimson feather. (As the Mouse's fur was very dark, almost black, the effect was bold and striking.) Its left paw rested on the hilt of a sword very nearly as long as its tail. Its balance, as it paced gravely along the swaying deck, was perfect, and its manners courtly. Lucy and Edmund recognized it at once – Reepicheep, the most valiant of all the Talking Beasts of Narnia, and the Chief Mouse. It had won undying glory in the second Battle of Beruna. Lucy longed, as she had always done, to take Reepicheep up in her arms and cuddle him. But this, as she well knew, was a pleasure she could never have:

it would have offended him deeply. Instead, she went down on one knee to talk to him.

Reepicheep put forward his left leg, drew back his right, bowed, kissed her hand, straightened himself, twirled his whiskers, and said in his shrill, piping voice:

"My humble duty to your Majesty. And to King Edmund, too." (Here he bowed again.) "Nothing except your Majesties' presence was lacking to this glorious venture."

"Ugh, take it away," wailed Eustace. "I hate mice. And I never could bear performing animals. They're silly and vulgar and – and sentimental."

"Am I to understand," said Reepicheep to Lucy after a long stare at Eustace, "that this singularly discourteous person is under your Majesty's protection? Because, if not –"

At this moment Lucy and Edmund both sneezed.

"What a fool I am to keep you all standing here in your wet things," said Caspian. "Come on below and get changed. I'll give you my cabin of course, Lucy, but I'm afraid we have no women's clothes on board. You'll have to make do with some of mine. Lead the way, Reepicheep, like a good fellow."

"To the convenience of a lady," said Reepicheep, "even a question of honour must give way – at least for the moment –" and here he looked very hard at Eustace. But Caspian hustled them on and in a few minutes Lucy found herself passing through the door into the stern cabin. She fell in love with it at once – the three square windows that looked out on the blue, swirling water astern, the low cushioned benches round three sides of the table, the swinging silver lamp overhead (Dwarfs' work, she knew at once by its exquisite delicacy) and the flat gold image of Aslan the Lion on the forward wall above the door. All this she took in in a flash, for Caspian immediately opened a door on the starboard side, and said, "This'll be your room, Lucy. I'll just get some dry things for myself –" he was rummaging in one of the lockers while he spoke – "and then leave you to change. If you'll fling your wet things outside the door I'll get them taken to the galley to be dried."

Lucy found herself as much at home as if she had been in Caspian's cabin for weeks, and the motion of the ship did not worry her, for in the old days when she had been a queen in Narnia she had done a good deal of voyaging. The cabin was very tiny but bright with painted panels (all birds and beasts and crimson dragons and vines) and spotlessly clean. Caspian's clothes were too big for her, but she could manage. His shoes, sandals and sea-boots were hopelessly big but she did not mind going barefoot on board ship. When she had finished dressing she looked out of her window at the water rushing past and took a long deep breath. She felt quite sure they were in for a lovely time.

CHAPTER TWO

ON BOARD THE *DAWN TREADER*

"Aн, there you are, Lucy," said Caspian. "We were just waiting for you. This is my captain, the Lord Drinian."

A dark-haired man went down on one knee and kissed her hand. The only others present were Reepicheep and Edmund.

"Where is Eustace?" asked Lucy.

"In bed," said Edmund, "and I don't think we can do anything for him. It only makes him worse if you try to be nice to him."

"Meanwhile," said Caspian, "we want to talk."

"By Jove, we do," said Edmund. "And first, about time. It's a year ago by our time since we left you just before your coronation. How long has it been in Narnia?"

"Exactly three years," said Caspian.

"All going well?" asked Edmund.

"You don't suppose I'd have left my kingdom and put to sea unless all was well," answered the King. "It couldn't be better. There's no trouble at all now between Telmarines, Dwarfs, Talking Beasts, Fauns and the rest. And we gave those troublesome giants on the frontier such a good beating last summer that they pay us tribute now. And I had an excellent person to leave as Regent while I'm away – Trumpkin, the Dwarf. You remember him?"

"Dear Trumpkin," said Lucy, "of course I do. You couldn't have made a better choice."

"Loyal as a badger, Ma'am, and valiant as – as a Mouse," said Drinian. He had been going to say "as a lion" but had noticed Reepicheep's eyes fixed on him.

"And where are we heading for?" asked Edmund.

"Well," said Caspian, "that's rather a long story. Perhaps you remember that when I was a child my usurping uncle Miraz got rid of seven friends of my father's (who might have taken my part) by sending them off to explore the unknown Eastern Seas beyond the Lone Islands."

"Yes," said Lucy, "and none of them ever came back."

"Right. Well, on my coronation day, with Aslan's approval, I swore an oath that, if once I established peace in Narnia, I would sail east myself for a year and a day to find my father's friends or to learn of their deaths and avenge them if I could. These were their names – the Lord Revilian, the Lord Bern, the Lord Argoz, the Lord Mavramorn, the Lord Octesian, the Lord Restimar, and – oh, that other one who's so hard to remember."

"The Lord Rhoop, Sire," said Drinian.

"Rhoop, Rhoop, of course," said Caspian. "That is my main intention. But Reepicheep here has an even higher hope." Everyone's eyes turned to the Mouse.

"As high as my spirit," it said. "Though perhaps as small as my stature. Why should we not come to the very eastern end of the world? And what might we find there? I expect to find Aslan's own country. It is always from the east, across the sea, that the great Lion comes to us."

"I say, that *is* an idea," said Edmund in an awed voice.

"But do you think," said Lucy, "Aslan's country would be that sort of country – I mean, the sort you could ever *sail* to?"

"I do not know, Madam," said Reepicheep. "But there is this. When I was in my cradle, a wood woman, a Dryad, spoke this verse over me:

"Where sky and water meet,
Where the waves grow sweet,
Doubt not, Reepicheep,
To find all you seek,
There is the utter East.

"I do not know what it means. But the spell of it has been on me all my life."

After a short silence Lucy asked, "And where are we now, Caspian?"

"The Captain can tell you better than I," said Caspian, so Drinian got out his chart and spread it on the table.

"That's our position," he said, laying his finger on it. "Or was at noon today. We had a fair wind from Cair Paravel and stood a little north for Galma, which we made on the next day. We were in port for a week, for the Duke of Galma made a great tournament for His Majesty and there he unhorsed many knights –"

"And got a few nasty falls myself, Drinian. Some of the bruises are there still," put in Caspian.

"– And unhorsed many knights," repeated Drinian with a grin. "We thought the Duke would have been pleased if the King's Majesty would have married his daughter, but nothing came of that –"

"Squints, and has freckles," said Caspian.

"Oh, poor girl," said Lucy.

"And we sailed from Galma," continued Drinian, "and ran into a calm for the best part of two days and had to row, and then had wind again and did not make Terebinthia till the fourth day from Galma. And there their King sent out a warning not to land for there was sickness in Terebinthia, but we doubled the cape and put in at a little creek far from the city and watered. Then we had to lie off for three days before we got a south-east wind and stood out for Seven Isles. The third day out a pirate (Terebinthian by her rig) overhauled us, but when she saw us well armed she stood off after some shooting of arrows on either part –"

"And we ought to have given her chase and boarded her and hanged every mother's son of them," said Reepicheep.

"– And in five days more we were in sight of Muil, which, as you know, is the westernmost of the Seven Isles. Then we rowed through the straits and came about sundown into Redhaven on the isle of Brenn, where we were very lovingly feasted and had victuals and water at will. We left Redhaven six days ago and have made marvellously good speed, so that I hope to see the Lone Islands the day after tomorrow. The sum is, we are now nearly thirty days at sea and have sailed more than four hundred leagues from Narnia."

"And after the Lone Islands?" said Lucy.

"No one knows, your Majesty," answered Drinian. "Unless the Lone Islanders themselves can tell us."

"They couldn't in our days," said Edmund.

"Then," said Reepicheep, "it is after the Lone Islands that the adventure really begins."

Caspian now suggested that they might like to be shown over the ship before supper, but Lucy's conscience smote her and she said, "I think I really must go and see Eustace. Seasickness is horrid, you know. If I had my old cordial with me I could cure him."

"But you have," said Caspian. "I'd quite forgotten about it. As you left it behind I thought it might be regarded as one of the royal treasures and so I brought it – if you think it ought to be wasted on a thing like seasickness."

"It'll only take a drop," said Lucy.

Caspian opened one of the lockers beneath the bench and brought out the beautiful little diamond flask which

Lucy remembered so well. "Take back your own, Queen," he said. They then left the cabin and went out into the sunshine.

In the deck there were two large, long hatches, fore and aft of the mast, and both open, as they always were in fair weather, to let light and air into the belly of the ship. Caspian led them down a ladder into the after hatch. Here they found themselves in a place where benches for rowing ran from side to side and the light came in through the oar-holes and danced on the roof. Of course Caspian's ship was not that horrible thing, a galley rowed by slaves. Oars were used only when wind failed or for getting in and out of harbour and everyone (except Reepicheep whose legs were too short) had often taken a turn. At each side of the ship the space under the benches was left clear for the rowers' feet, but all down the centre there was a kind of pit which went down to the very keel and this was filled with all kinds of things – sacks of flour, casks of water and beer, barrels of pork, jars of honey, skin bottles of wine, apples, nuts, cheeses, biscuits, turnips, sides of bacon. From the roof – that is, from the under side of the deck – hung hams and strings of onions, and also the men of the watch off-duty in their hammocks. Caspian led them aft, stepping from bench to bench; at least, it was stepping for him, and something between a step and a jump for Lucy, and a real long jump for Reepicheep. In this way they came to a partition with a door in it. Caspian opened the door and led them into a cabin which filled the stern underneath the deck cabins in the poop. It was of course not so nice. It was very low and the sides sloped together as they went down so that there was hardly any floor; and though it had windows of thick glass, they were not made to open because they were under water. In fact at this very moment, as the ship pitched they were alternately golden with sunlight and dim green with the sea.

"You and I must lodge here, Edmund," said Caspian. "We'll leave your kinsman the bunk and sling hammocks for ourselves."

"I beseech your Majesty –" said Drinian.

"No, no shipmate," said Caspian, "we have argued all that out already. You and Rhince" (Rhince was the mate) "are sailing the ship and will have cares and labours many a night when we are singing catches or telling stories, so

you and he must have the port cabin above. King Edmund and I can lie very snug here below. But how is the stranger?"

Eustace, very green in the face, scowled and asked whether there was any sign of the storm getting less. But Caspian said, "What storm?" and Drinian burst out laughing.

"Storm, young master!" he roared. "This is as fair weather as a man could ask for."

"Who's that?" said Eustace irritably. "Send him away. His voice goes through my head."

"I've brought you something that will make you feel better, Eustace," said Lucy.

"Oh, go away and leave me alone," growled Eustace. But he took a drop from her flask, and though he said it was beastly stuff (the smell in the cabin when she opened it was delicious) it is certain that his face came the right colour a few moments after he had swallowed it, and he must have felt better because, instead of wailing about the storm and his head, he began demanding to be put ashore and said that at the first port he would "lodge a disposition" against them all with the British Consul. But when Reepicheep asked what a disposition was and how you lodged it (Reepicheep thought it was some new way of arranging a single combat) Eustace could only reply, "Fancy not knowing that." In the end they succeeded in convincing Eustace that they were already sailing as fast as they could towards the nearest land they knew, and that they had no more power of sending him back to Cambridge – which was where Uncle Harold lived – than of sending him to the moon. After that he sulkily agreed to put on the fresh clothes which had been put out for him and come on deck.

Caspian now showed them over the ship, though indeed they had seen most it already. They went up on the forecastle and saw the look-out man standing on a little shelf inside the gilded dragon's neck and peering through its open mouth. Inside the forecastle was the galley (or ship's kitchen) and quarters for such people as the boatswain, the carpenter, the cook and the master-archer. If you think it odd to have the galley in the bows and imagine the smoke from its chimney streaming back over the ship, that is because you are thinking of steamships where there is always a headwind. On a sailing ship the wind is coming from behind, and anything smelly is put as far forward as possible. They were taken up to the fighting top, and at first it was rather alarming to rock to and fro there and see the deck looking small and far away beneath. You realized that if you fell there was no particular reason why you should fall on board rather than in the sea. Then they were taken to the poop, where Rhince was on duty with another

man at the great tiller, and behind that the dragon's tail rose up, covered with gilding, and round inside it ran a little bench. The name of the ship was *Dawn Treader*. She was only a little bit of a thing compared with one of our ships, or even with the cogs, dromonds, carracks and galleons which Narnia had owned when Lucy and Edmund had reigned there under Peter as the High King, for nearly all navigation had died out in the reigns of Caspian's ancestors. When his uncle, Miraz the usurper, had sent the seven lords to sea, they had had to buy a Galmian ship and man it with hired Galmian sailors. But now Caspian had begun to teach the Narnians to be sea-faring folk once more, and the *Dawn Treader* was the finest ship he had built yet. She was so small that, forward of the mast, there was hardly any deck room between the central hatch and the ship's boat on one side and the hen-coop (Lucy fed the hens) on the other. But she was a beauty of her kind, a "lady" as sailors say, her lines perfect, her colours pure, and every spar and rope and pin lovingly made. Eustace of course would be pleased with nothing, and kept on boasting about liners and motor-boats and aeroplanes and submarines ("As if *he* knew anything about them," muttered Edmund), but the other two were delighted with the *Dawn Treader*, and when they returned aft to the cabin and supper, and saw the whole western sky lit up with an immense crimson sunset, and felt the quiver of the ship, and tasted the salt on their lips, and thought of unknown lands on the Eastern rim of the world, Lucy felt that she was almost too happy to speak.

What Eustace thought had best be told in his own words, for when they all got their clothes back, dried, next morning, he at once got out a little black notebook and a pencil and started to keep a diary. He always had this notebook with him and kept a record of his marks in it, for though he didn't care much about any subject for its own sake, he cared a great deal about marks and would even go to people and say, "I got so much. What did you get?" But as he didn't seem likely to get many marks on the *Dawn Treader* he now started a diary. This was the first entry.

"*7 August*. Have now been twenty-four hours on this ghastly boat if it isn't a dream. All the time a frightful storm has been raging (it's a good thing I'm not seasick). Huge waves keep coming in over the front and I have seen the boat nearly go under any number of times. All the others pretend to take no notice of this, either from swank or because Harold says one of the most cowardly things ordinary people do is to shut their eyes to Facts. It's madness to come out into the sea in a rotten little thing like this. Not much bigger than a lifeboat. And, of course, absolutely primitive indoors. No proper saloon, no radio, no bathrooms, no deck-chairs. I was dragged all over it yesterday evening and it would make anyone sick to hear Caspian showing off his funny little toy boat as if it was the *Queen Mary*. I tried to tell him what real ships are like, but he's too dense. E. and L., *of course*, didn't back me up. I suppose a kid like L. doesn't realize the danger and E. is buttering up C. as everyone does here. They call him a King. I said I was a Republican but he had to ask me what that meant! He doesn't seem to know anything at all. *Needless to say* I've been put in the worst cabin of the boat, a perfect dungeon, and Lucy has been given a whole room on deck to herself, almost a nice room compared with the rest of this place. C. says that's because she's a girl. I tried to make him see what Alberta says, that all that sort of thing is really lowering girls but he was too dense. Still, he might see that I shall be ill if I'm kept in that *hole* any longer. E. says we mustn't grumble because C. is sharing it with us himself to make room for L. As if that didn't make it more crowded and far worse. Nearly forgot to say that there is also a kind of Mouse thing that gives everyone the most frightful cheek. The others can put up with it if they like but I shall twist his tail pretty soon if he tries it on me. The food is frightful too."

The trouble between Eustace and Reepicheep arrived even sooner than might have been expected. Before dinner next day, when the others were sitting round the table waiting (being at sea gives one a magnificent appetite), Eustace came rushing in, wringing his hand and shouting out:

"That little brute has half killed me. I insist on it being kept under control. I could bring an action against you, Caspian. I could order you to have it destroyed."

At the same moment Reepicheep appeared. His sword

was drawn and his whiskers looked very fierce but he was as polite as ever.

"I ask your pardons all," he said, "and especially her Majesty's. If I had known that he would take refuge here I would have awaited a more reasonable time for his correction."

"What on earth's up?" asked Edmund.

What had really happened was this. Reepicheep, who never felt that the ship was getting on fast enough, loved to sit on the bulwarks far forward just beside the dragon's head, gazing out at the eastern horizon and singing softly

in his little chirruping voice the song the Dryad had made for him. He never held on to anything, however the ship pitched, and kept his balance with perfect ease; perhaps his long tail, hanging down to the deck inside the bulwarks, made this easier. Everyone on board was familiar with this habit, and the sailors liked it because when one was on look-out duty it gave one somebody to talk to. Why exactly Eustace had slipped and reeled and stumbled all the way forward to the forecastle (he had not yet got his sea-legs) I never heard. Perhaps he hoped he would see land, or perhaps he wanted to hang about the galley and scrounge something. Anyway, as soon as he saw that long tail hanging down – and perhaps it was rather tempting – he thought it would be delightful to catch hold of it, swing Reepicheep round by it once or twice upside-down, then run away and laugh. At first the plan seemed to work beautifully. The Mouse was not much heavier than a very large cat. Eustace had him off the rail in a trice and very

silly he looked (thought Eustace) with his little limbs all splayed out and his mouth open. But unfortunately Reepicheep, who had fought for his life many a time, never lost his head even for a moment. Nor his skill. It is not very easy to draw one's sword when one is swinging round in the air by one's tail, but he did. And the next thing Eustace knew was two agonizing jabs in his hand which made him let go of the tail; and the next thing after that was that the Mouse had picked itself up again as if it were a ball bouncing off the deck, and there it was facing him, and a horrid long, bright, sharp thing like a skewer was waving to and fro within an inch of his stomach. (This doesn't count as below the belt for mice in Narnia because they can hardly be expected to reach higher.)

"Stop it," spluttered Eustace, "go away. Put that thing away. It's not safe. Stop it, I say. I'll tell Caspian.

I'll have you muzzled and tied up."

"Why do you not draw your own sword, poltroon!" cheeped the Mouse. "Draw and fight or I'll beat you black and blue with the flat."

"I haven't got one," said Eustace. "I'm a pacifist. I don't believe in fighting."

"Do I understand," said Reepicheep, withdrawing his sword for a moment and speaking very sternly, "that you do not intend to give me satisfaction?"

"I don't know what you mean," said Eustace, nursing his hand. "If you don't know how to take a joke I shan't bother my head about you."

"Then take that," said Reepicheep, "and that – to teach you manners – and the respect due to a knight – and a Mouse – and a Mouse's tail –" and at each word he gave Eustace a blow with the side of his rapier, which was thin, fine dwarf-tempered steel and as supple and effective as a birch rod. Eustace (of course) was at a school where they didn't have corporal punishment, so the sensation was quite new to him. That was why, in spite of having no sea-legs, it took him less than a minute to get off that forecastle and cover the whole length of the deck and burst in at the cabin door – still hotly pursued by Reepicheep. Indeed it seemed to Eustace that the rapier as well as the pursuit was hot. It might have been red-hot by the feel.

There was not much difficulty in settling the matter once Eustace realized that everyone took the idea of a duel seriously and heard Caspian offering to lend him a sword, and Drinian and Edmund discussing whether he ought to be handicapped in some way to make up for his being so much bigger than Reepicheep. He apologized sulkily and went off with Lucy to have his hand bathed and bandaged and then went to his bunk. He was careful to lie on his side.

CHAPTER THREE

THE LONE ISLANDS

"LAND in sight," shouted the man in the bows.

Lucy, who had been talking to Rhince on the poop, came pattering down the ladder and raced forward. As she went she was joined by Edmund, and they found Caspian, Drinian and Reepicheep already on the forecastle. It was a coldish morning, the sky very pale and the sea very dark blue with little white caps of foam, and there, a little way off on the starboard bow, was the nearest of the Lone Islands, Felimath, like a low green hill in the sea, and behind it, further off, the grey slopes of its sister Doorn.

"Same old Felimath! Same old Doorn," said Lucy, clapping her hands. "Oh – Edmund, how long it is since you and I saw them last!"

"I've never understood why they belong to Narnia," said Caspian. "Did Peter the High King conquer them?"

"Oh no," said Edmund. "They were Narnian before our time – in the days of the White Witch."

(By the way, I have never yet heard how these remote islands became attached to the crown of Narnia; if I ever do, and if the story is at all interesting, I may put it in some other book.)

"Are we to put in here, Sire?" asked Drinian.

"I shouldn't think it would be much good landing on Felimath," said Edmund. "It was almost uninhabited in our days and it looks as if it was the same still. The people lived mostly on Doorn and a little on Avra – that's the third one; you can't see it yet. They only kept sheep on Felimath."

"Then we'll have to double that cape, I suppose," said Drinian, "and land on Doorn. That'll mean rowing."

"I'm sorry we're not landing on Felimath," said Lucy. "I'd like to walk there again. It was so lonely – a nice kind of loneliness, and all grass and clover and soft sea air."

"I'd love to stretch my legs now too," said Caspian. "I tell you what. Why shouldn't we go ashore in the boat and send it back, and then we could walk across Felimath and let the *Dawn Treader* pick us up on the other side?"

If Caspian had been as experienced then as he became later on in this voyage he would not have made this suggestion; but at the moment it seemed an excellent one. "Oh do let's," said Lucy.

"You'll come, will you?" said Caspian to Eustace, who had come on deck with his hand bandaged.

"Anything to get off this blasted boat," said Eustace.

"Blasted?" said Drinian. "How do you mean?"

"In a civilized country like where I come from," said Eustace, "the ships are so big that when you're inside you wouldn't know you were at sea at all."

"In that case you might just as well stay ashore," said Caspian. "Will you tell them to lower the boat, Drinian."

The King, the Mouse, the two Pevensies, and Eustace all got into the boat and were pulled to the beach of Felimath. When the boat had left them and was being rowed back they all turned and looked round. They were surprised at how small the *Dawn Treader* looked.

Lucy was of course barefoot, having kicked off her shoes while swimming, but that is no hardship if one is going to walk on downy turf. It was delightful to be ashore again and to smell the earth and grass, even if at first the ground seemed to be pitching up and down like a ship, as it usually does for a while if one has been at sea. It was much warmer here than it had been on board and Lucy found the sand

pleasant to her feet as they crossed it. There was a lark
singing.

They struck inland and up a fairly steep, though low,
hill. At the top of course they looked back, and there was
the *Dawn Treader* shining like a great bright insect and
crawling slowly north-westward with her oars. Then they
went over the ridge and could see her no longer.

Doorn now lay before them, divided from Felimath by a
channel about a mile wide; behind it and to the left lay
Avra. The little white town of Narrowhaven on Doorn was
easily seen.

"Hullo! What's this?" said Edmund suddenly.

In the green valley to which they were descending six or
seven rough-looking men, all armed, were sitting by a tree.

"Don't tell them who we are," said Caspian.

"And pray, your Majesty, why not?" said Reepicheep
who had consented to ride on Lucy's shoulder.

"It just occurred to me," replied Caspian, "that no one
here can have heard from Narnia for a long time. It's just
possible they may not still acknowledge our over-lordship.
In which case it might not be quite safe to be known as the
King."

"We have our swords, Sire," said Reepicheep.

"Yes, Reep, I know we have," said Caspian. "But if it is
a question of re-conquering the three islands, I'd prefer to
come back with a rather larger army."

By this time they were quite close to the strangers, one of
whom – a big black-haired fellow – shouted out, "A good
morning to you."

"And a good morning to you," said Caspian. "Is there
still a Governor of the Lone Islands?"

"To be sure there is," said the man, "Governor Gumpas.
His Sufficiency is at Narrowhaven. But you'll stay and
drink with us."

Caspian thanked him, though neither he nor the others much liked the look of their new acquaintance, and all of them sat down. But hardly had they raised their cups to their lips when the black-haired man nodded to his companions and, as quick as lightning, all the five visitors found themselves wrapped in strong arms. There was a moment's struggle but all the advantages were on one side, and soon everyone was disarmed and had their hands tied behind their backs — except Reepicheep, writhing in his captor's grip and biting furiously.

"Careful with that beast, Tacks," said the Leader. "Don't damage him. He'll fetch the best price of the lot, I shouldn't wonder."

"Coward! Poltroon!" squeaked Reepicheep. "Give me my sword and free my paws if you dare."

"Whew!" whistled the slave merchant (for that is what he was). "It can talk! Well I never did. Blowed if I take less than two hundred crescents for him." The Calormen crescent, which is the chief coin in those parts, is worth about a third of a pound.

"So that's what you are," said Caspian. "A kidnapper and slaver. I hope you're proud of it."

"Now, now, now, now," said the slaver. "Don't you start any jaw. The easier you take it, the pleasanter all round, see? I don't do this for fun. I've got my living to make same as anyone else."

"Where will you take us?" asked Lucy, getting the words out with some difficulty.

"Over to Narrowhaven," said the slaver. "For market day tomorrow."

"Is there a British Consul there?" asked Eustace.

"Is there a which?" said the man.

But long before Eustace was tired of trying to explain, the slaver simply said, "Well, I've had enough of this jabber. The Mouse is a fair treat but this one would talk the hind leg off a donkey. Off we go, mates."

Then the four human prisoners were roped together, not cruelly but securely, and made to march down to the shore. Reepicheep was carried. He had stopped biting on a threat of having his mouth tied up, but he had a great deal to say, and Lucy really wondered how any man could bear to have the things said to him which were said to the slave dealer by the Mouse. But the slave dealer, far from objecting, only said "Go on" whenever Reepicheep paused for breath, occasionally adding, "It's as good as a play," or, "Blimey, you can't help almost thinking it knows what it's saying!" or "Was it one of you what trained it?" This so infuriated Reepicheep that in the end the number of things he thought of saying all at once nearly suffocated him and he became silent.

When they got down to the shore that looked towards Doorn they found a little village and a long-boat on the beach and, lying a little further out, a dirty bedraggled looking ship.

"Now, youngsters," said the slave dealer, "let's have no fuss and then you'll have nothing to cry about. All aboard."

At that moment a fine-looking bearded man came out of one of the houses (an inn, I think) and said:

"Well, Pug. More of your usual wares?"

The slaver, whose name seemed to be Pug, bowed very low, and said in a wheedling kind of voice, "Yes, please your Lordship."

"How much do you want for that boy?" asked the other, pointing to Caspian.

"Ah," said Pug, "I knew your Lordship would pick on the best. No deceiving your Lordship with anything second rate. That boy, now, I've taken a fancy to him myself. Got kind of fond of him, I have. I'm that tender-hearted I didn't ever ought to have taken up this job. Still, to a customer like your Lordship —"

"Tell me your price, carrion," said the Lord sternly. "Do you think I want to listen to the rigmarole of your filthy trade?"

"Three hundred crescents, my Lord to your honourable Lordship, but to anyone else –"

"I'll give you a hundred and fifty."

"Oh please, please," broke in Lucy. "Don't separate us, whatever you do. You don't know –" But then she stopped for she saw that Caspian didn't even now want to be known.

"A hundred and fifty, then," said the Lord. "As for you, little maiden, I am sorry I cannot buy you all. Unrope my boy, Pug. And look – treat these others well while they are in your hands or it'll be the worse for you."

"Well!" said Pug. "Now who ever heard of a gentleman in my way of business who treated his stock better than what I do? Well? Why, I treat 'em like my own chidren."

"That's likely enough to be true," said the other grimly.

The dreadful moment had now come. Caspian was untied and his new master said, "This way, lad," and Lucy burst into tears and Edmund looked very blank. But Caspian looked over his shoulder and said, "Cheer up. I'm sure it will come all right in the end. So long."

"Now, missie," said Pug. "Don't you start taking on and spoiling your looks for the market tomorrow. You be a good girl and then you won't have nothing to cry *about*, see?"

Then they were rowed out to the slave-ship and taken below into a long, rather dark place, none too clean, where they found many other unfortunate prisoners; for Pug was of course a pirate and had just returned from cruising among the islands and capturing what he could. The children didn't meet anyone whom they knew; the prisoners were mostly Galmians and Terebinthians. And there they sat in the straw and wondered what was happening to Caspian and tried to stop Eustace talking as if everyone except himself was to blame.

Meanwhile Caspian was having a much more interesting time. The man who had bought him led him down a little lane between two of the village houses and so out into an open place behind the village. Then he turned and faced him.

"You needn't be afraid of me, boy," he said. "I'll treat you well. I bought you for your face. You reminded me of someone."

"May I ask of whom, my Lord?" said Caspian.

"You remind me of my master, King Caspian of Narnia."

Then Caspian decided to risk everything on one stroke.

"My Lord," he said, "I *am* your master. I am Caspian King of Narnia."

"You make very free," said the other. "How shall I know this is true?"

"Firstly by my face," said Caspian. "Secondly because I know within six guesses who you are. You are one of those seven lords of Narnia whom my Uncle Miraz sent to sea and whom I have come out to look for – Argoz, Bern, Octesian, Restimar, Mavramorn, or – or – I have forgotten the others. And finally, if your Lordship will give me a sword I will prove on any man's body in clean battle that I am Caspian the son of Caspian, lawful King of Narnia, Lord of Cair Paravel, and Emperor of the Lone Islands."

"By heaven," exclaimed the man, "it is his father's very voice and trick of speech. My liege – your Majesty –" And there in the field he knelt and kissed the King's hand.

"The moneys your Lordship disbursed for our person will be made good from our own treasury," said Caspian.

"They're not in Pug's purse yet, Sire," said the Lord Bern, for he it was. "And never will be, I trust. I have moved his Sufficiency the Governor a hundred times to crush this vile traffic in man's flesh."

"My Lord Bern," said Caspian, "we must talk of the state of these Islands. But first what is your Lordship's own story?"

"Short enough, Sire," said Bern. "I came thus far with my six fellows, loved a girl of the islands, and felt I had had enough of the sea. And there was no purpose in returning to Narnia while your Majesty's uncle held the reins. So I married and have lived here ever since."

"And what is this governor, this Gumpas, like? Does he still acknowledge the King of Narnia for his lord?"

"In words, yes. All is done in the King's name. But he would not be best pleased to find a real, live King of Narnia coming in upon him. And if your Majesty came before him alone and unarmed – well he would not deny his allegiance, but he would pretend to disbelieve you. Your Grace's life would be in danger. What following has your Majesty in these waters?"

"There is my ship just rounding the point," said Caspian. "We are about thirty swords if it came to fighting. Shall we not have my ship in and fall upon Pug and free my friends whom he holds captive?"

"Not by my counsel," said Bern. "As soon as there was a fight two or three ships would put out from Narrowhaven to rescue Pug. Your Majesty must work by a show of more power than you really have, and by the terror of the King's name. It must not come to plain battle. Gumpas is a chicken-hearted man and can be over-awed."

After a little more conversation Caspian and Bern walked down to the coast a little west of the village and there Caspian winded his horn. (This was not the great magic horn of Narnia, Queen Susan's Horn: he had left that at home for his regent Trumpkin to use if any great need fell upon the land in the King's absence.) Drinian, who was on the look-out for a signal, recognized the royal

horn at once and the *Dawn Treader* began standing in to
shore. Then the boat put off again and in a few moments
Caspian and the Lord Bern were on deck explaining the
situation to Drinian. He, just like Caspian, wanted to lay
the *Dawn Treader* alongside the slave-ship at once and
board her, but Bern made the same objection.

"Steer straight down this channel, captain," said Bern,
"and then round to Avra where my own estates are. But
first run up the King's banner, hang out all the shields, and
send as many men to the fighting top as you can. And
about five bowshots hence, when you get open sea on your
port bow, run up a few signals."

"Signals? To whom?" said Drinian.

"Why, to all the other ships we haven't got but which it
might be well that Gumpas thinks we have."

"Oh, I see," said Drinian rubbing his hands. "And
they'll read our signals. What shall I say? *Whole fleet
round the South of Avra and assemble at —?*"

"Bernstead," said the Lord Bern. "That'll do excel-
lently. Their whole journey — if there *were* any ships —

would be out of sight from Narrowhaven."

Caspian was sorry for the others languishing in the hold of Pug's slave-ship, but he could not help finding the rest of that day enjoyable. Late in the afternoon (for they had to do all by oar), having turned to starboard round the north-east end of Doorn and port again round the point of Avra, they entered into a good harbour on Avra's southern shore where Bern's pleasant lands sloped down to the water's edge. Bern's people, many of whom they saw working in the fields, were all freemen and it was a happy and prosperous fief. Here they all went ashore and were royally feasted in a low, pillared house overlooking the bay. Bern and his gracious wife and merry daughters made them good cheer. But after dark Bern sent a messenger over by boat to Doorn to order some preparations (he did not say exactly what) for the following day.

CHAPTER FOUR

WHAT CASPIAN DID THERE

NEXT morning the Lord Bern called his guests early, and after breakfast he asked Caspian to order every man he had into full armour. "And above all," he added, "let everything be as trim and scoured as if it were the morning of the first battle in a great war between noble kings with all the world looking on." This was done; and then in three boatloads Caspian and his people, and Bern with a few of his, put out for Narrowhaven. The king's flag flew in the stern of his boat and his trumpeter was with him.

When they reached the jetty at Narrowhaven, Caspian found a considerable crowd assembled to meet them. "This is what I sent word about last night," said Bern. "They are all friends of mine and honest people." And as soon as Caspian stepped ashore the crowd broke out into hurrahs and shouts of, "Narnia! Narnia! Long live the King." At the same moment – and this was also due to Bern's messengers – bells began ringing from many parts of the town. Then Caspian caused his banner to be advanced and his trumpet to be blown and every man drew his sword and set his face into a joyful sternness, and they marched up the street so that the street shook, and their armour shone (for it was a sunny morning) so that one could hardly look at it steadily.

At first the only people who cheered were those who had been warned by Bern's messenger and knew what was happening and wanted it to happen. But then all the children joined in because they liked a procession and had seen very few. And then all the schoolboys joined in because they also liked processions and felt that the more noise and disturbance there was the less likely they would be to have any school that morning. And then all the old women put their heads out of doors and windows and began chattering and cheering because it was a king, and what is a governor compared with that? And all the young women joined in for the same reason and also because Caspian and Drinian and the rest were so handsome. And then all the young men came to see what the young women were looking at, so that by the time Caspian reached the castle gates, nearly the whole town was shouting; and where Gumpas sat in the castle, muddling and messing about with accounts and forms and rules and regulations, he heard the noise.

At the castle gate Caspian's trumpeter blew a blast and cried, "Open for the King of Narnia, come to visit his trusty and well-beloved servant the governor of the Lone

Islands." In those days everything in the islands was done in a slovenly, slouching manner. Only the little postern opened, and out came a tousled fellow with a dirty old hat on his head instead of a helmet, and a rusty old pike in his hand. He blinked at the flashing figures before him. "Carn – seez – fishansy," he mumbled which was his way of saying, "You can't see his Sufficiency"). "No interviews without 'pointments 'cept 'tween nine 'n' ten p.m. second Saturday every month."

"Uncover before Narnia, you dog," thundered the Lord Bern, and dealt him a rap with his gauntleted hand which sent his hat flying from his head.

"'Ere? Wot's it all about?" began the doorkeeper, but no one took any notice of him. Two of Caspian's men stepped through the postern and after some struggling with bars and bolts (for everything was rusty) flung both wings of the gate wide open. Then the King and his followers strode into the courtyard. Here a number of the governor's guards were lounging about and several more (they were mostly wiping their mouths) came tumbling out of various door-ways. Though their armour was in a disgraceful condition, these were fellows who might have fought if they had been led or had known what was happening; so this was the dangerous moment. Caspian gave them no time to think.

"Where is the captain?" he asked.

"I am, more or less, if you know what I mean," said a languid and rather dandified young person without any armour at all.

"It is our wish," said Caspian, "that our royal visitation to our realm of the Lone Islands should, if possible, be an occasion of joy and not of terror to our loyal subjects. If it were not for that, I should have something to say about the state of your men's armour and weapons. As it is, you are pardoned. Command a cask of wine to be opened that your men may drink our health. But at noon tomorrow I wish to see them here in this courtyard looking like men-at-arms and not like vagabonds. See to it on pain of our extreme displeasure."

The captain gaped but Bern immediately cried, "Three cheers for the King," and the soldiers, who had understood about the cask of wine even if they understood nothing else, joined in. Caspian then ordered most of his own men to remain in the courtyard. He, with Bern and Drinian and four others, went into the hall.

Behind a table at the far end with various secretaries about him sat his Sufficiency, the Governor of the Lone Islands. Gumpas was a bilious-looking man with hair that had once been red and was now mostly grey. He glanced up as the strangers entered and then looked down at his papers saying automatically, "No interviews without appointments except between nine and ten p.m. on second Saturdays."

Caspian nodded to Bern and then stood aside. Bern and Drinian took a step forward and each seized one end of the table. They lifted it, and flung it on one side of the hall where it rolled over, scattering a cascade of letters, dossiers, ink-pots, pens, sealing-wax and documents. Then, not roughly but as firmly as if their hands were pincers of steel, they plucked Gumpas out of his chair and deposited him, facing it, about four feet away. Caspian at once sat down in the chair and laid his naked sword across his knees.

"My Lord," said he, fixing his eyes on Gumpas, "you have not given us quite the welcome we expected. I am the King of Narnia."

"Nothing about it in the correspondence," said the governor. "Nothing in the minutes. We have not been notified of any such thing. All irregular. Happy to consider any applications –"

"And we are come to enquire into your Sufficiency's conduct of your office," continued Caspian. "There are two points especially on which I require an explanation. Firstly I find no record that the tribute due from these Islands to the crown of Narnia has been received for about a hundred and fifty years."

"That would be a question to raise at the Council next month," said Gumpas. "If anyone moves that a commission of enquiry be set up to report on the financial history of the islands at the first meeting next year, why then . . ."

"I also find it very clearly written in our laws," Caspian went on, "that if the tribute is not delivered the whole debt has to be paid by the Governor of the Lone Islands out of his private purse."

At this Gumpas began to pay real attention. "Oh, that's quite out of the question," he said. "It is an economic impossibility – er – your Majesty must be joking."

Inside, he was wondering if there were any way of getting rid of these unwelcome visitors. Had he known that Caspian had only one ship and one ship's company with him, he would have spoken soft words for the moment, and hoped to have them all surrounded and killed during the night. But he had seen a ship of war sail down the straits yesterday and seen it signalling, as he supposed, to its consorts. He had not then known it was the King's ship for there was not wind enough to spread the flag out and make the golden lion visible, so he had waited further developments. Now he imagined that Caspian had a whole fleet at Bernstead. It would never have occurred to Gumpas that anyone would walk into Narrowhaven to take the islands with less than fifty men; it was certainly not at all the kind of thing he could imagine doing himself.

"Secondly," said Caspian, "I want to know why you have permitted this abominable and unnatural traffic in slaves to grow up here, contrary to the ancient custom and usage of our dominions."

"Necessary, unavoidable," said his Sufficiency. "An essential part of the economic development of the islands, I assure you. Our present burst of prosperity depends on it."

"What need have you of slaves?"

"For export, your Majesty. Sell 'em to Calormen mostly; and we have other markets. We are a great centre of the trade."

"In other words," said Caspian, "you don't need them. Tell me what purpose they serve except to put money into the pockets of such as Pug?"

"Your Majesty's tender years," said Gumpas, with what was meant to be a fatherly smile, "hardly make it possible that you should understand the economic problem involved. I have statistics, I have graphs, I have –"

"Tender as my years be," said Caspian, "I believe I understand the slave trade from within quite as well as your Sufficiency. And I do not see that it brings into the islands meat or bread or beer or wine or timber or cabbages or books or instruments of music or horses or armour or anything else worth having. But whether it does or not, it must be stopped."

"But that would be putting the clock back," gasped the governor. "Have you no idea of progress, of development?"

"I have seen them both in an egg," said Caspian. "We call it 'Going Bad' in Narnia. This trade must stop."

"I can take no responsibility for any such measure," said Gumpas.

"Very well, then," answered Caspian, "we relieve you of your office. My Lord Bern, come here." And before Gumpas quite realized what was happening, Bern was kneeling with his hands between the King's hands and taking the oath to govern the Lone Islands in accordance with the old customs, rights, usages and laws of Narnia. And Caspian said, "I think we have had enough of governors," and made Bern a Duke, the Duke of the Lone Islands.

"As for you, my Lord," he said to Gumpas, "I forgive you your debt for the tribute. But before noon tomorrow you and yours must be out of the castle, which is now the Duke's residence."

"Look here, this is all very well," said one of Gumpas's secretaries, "but suppose all you gentlemen stop play-acting and we do a little business. The question before us really is —"

"The question is," said the Duke, "whether you and the rest of the rabble will leave without a flogging or with one. You may choose which you prefer."

When all this had been pleasantly settled, Caspian ordered horses, of which there were a few in the castle, though very ill-groomed and he, with Bern and Drinian and a few others, rode out into the town and made for the slave market. It was a long low building near the harbour and the scene which they found going on inside was very much like any other auction; that is to say, there was a great crowd and Pug, on a platform, was roaring out in a raucous voice:

"Now, gentlemen, lot twenty-three. Fine Terebinthian agricultural labourer, suitable for the mines or the galleys. Under twenty-five years of age. Not a bad tooth in his head. Good, brawny fellow. Take off his shirt, Tacks, and let the gentlemen see. There's muscle for you! Look at the chest on him. Ten crescents from the gentleman in the corner. You must be joking, sir. Fifteen! Eighteen! Eighteen is bidden for lot twenty-three. Any advance on eighteen? Twenty-one. Thank you, sir. Twenty-one is bidden –"

But Pug stopped and gaped when he saw the mail-clad figures who had clanked up to the platform.

"On your knees, every man of you, to the King of Narnia," said the Duke. Everyone heard the horses jingling and stamping outside and many had heard some rumour of the landing and the events at the castle. Most obeyed. Those who did not were pulled down by their neighbours. Some cheered.

"Your life is forfeit, Pug, for laying hands on our royal person yesterday," said Caspian. "But your ignorance is pardoned. The slave trade was forbidden in all our dominions quarter of an hour ago. I declare every slave in this market free."

He held up his hand to check the cheering of the slaves and went on, "Where are my friends?"

"That dear little gel and the nice young gentleman?" said Pug with an ingratiating smile. "Why, they were snapped up at once –"

"We're here, we're here, Caspian," cried Lucy and Edmund together and, "At your service, Sire," piped Reepicheep from another corner. They had all been sold but the men who had bought them were staying to bid for other slaves and so they had not yet been taken away. The crowd parted to let the three of them out and there was great hand-clasping and greeting between them and Caspian. Two merchants of Calormen at once approached. The Calormen have dark faces and long beards. They wear flowing robes and orange-coloured turbans, and they are a wise, wealthy, courteous, cruel and ancient people. They bowed most politely to Caspian and paid him long compliments, all about the fountains of prosperity irrigating the gardens of prudence and virtue – and things like that – but of course what they wanted was the money they had paid.

"That is only fair, sirs," said Caspian. "Every man who has bought a slave today must have his money back. Pug, bring out your takings to the last minim." (A minim is the fortieth part of a crescent.)

"Does your good Majesty mean to beggar me?" whined Pug.

"You have lived on broken hearts all your life," said Caspian, "and if you *are* beggared, it is better to be a beggar than a slave. But where is my other friend?"

"Oh *him*?" said Pug. "Oh take *him* and welcome. Glad to have him off my hands. I've never seen such a drug in the market in all my born days. Priced him at five crescents in the end and even so nobody'd have him. Threw him in free with other lots and still no one would have him. Wouldn't touch him. Wouldn't look at him. Tacks, bring out Sulky."

Thus Eustace was produced, and sulky he certainly looked; for though no one would want to be sold as a slave, it is perhaps even more galling to be a sort of utility slave whom no one will buy. He walked up to Caspian and said, "I see. As usual. Been enjoying yourself somewhere while the rest of us were prisoners. I suppose you haven't even found out about the British Consul. Of course not."

That night they had a great feast in the castle of Narrowhaven and then, "Tomorrow for the beginning of our real adventures!" said Reepicheep when he had made his bows to everyone and went to bed. But it could not really be tomorrow or anything like it. For now they were preparing to leave all known lands and seas behind them and the fullest preparations had to be made. The *Dawn Treader* was emptied and drawn on land by eight horses over rollers and every bit of her was gone over by the most skilled shipwrights. Then she was launched again and victualled and watered as full as she could hold – that is to say for twenty-eight days. Even this, as Edmund noticed with disappointment, only gave them a fortnight's eastward sailing before they had to abandon their quest.

While all this was being done Caspian missed no chance of questioning all the oldest sea captains whom he could find in Narrowhaven to learn if they had any knowledge or

even any rumours of land further to the east. He poured out many a flagon of the castle ale to weather-beaten men with short grey beards and clear blue eyes, and many a tall yarn he heard in return. But those who seemed the most truthful could tell of no lands beyond the Lone Islands, and many thought that if you sailed too far east you would come into the surges of a sea without lands that swirled perpetually round the rim of the world – "And that, I reckon, is where your Majesty's friends went to the bottom." The rest had only wild stories of islands inhabited by headless men, floating islands, waterspouts, and a fire that burned along the water. Only one, to Reepicheep's delight, said, "And beyond that, Aslan country. But that's beyond the end of the world and you can't get there." But when they questioned him he could only say that he'd heard it from his father.

Bern could only tell them that he had seen his six companions sail away eastward and that nothing had ever been heard of them again. He said this when he and Caspian were standing on the highest point of Avra looking down on the eastern ocean. "I've often been up here of a morning," said the Duke, "and seen the sun come up out of the sea, and sometimes it looked as if it were only a couple of miles away. And I've wondered about my friends and wondered what there really is behind that horizon. Nothing, most likely, yet I am always half ashamed that I stayed behind. But I wish your Majesty wouldn't go. We may need your help here. This closing the slave market might make a new world; war with Calormen is what I foresee. My liege, think again."

"I have an oath, my lord Duke," said Caspian. "And anyway, what *could* I say to Reepicheep?"

CHAPTER FIVE

THE STORM AND WHAT CAME OF IT

It was nearly three weeks after their landing that the *Dawn Treader* was towed out of Narrowhaven harbour. Very solemn farewells had been spoken and a great crowd had assembled to see her departure. There had been cheers, and tears too, when Caspian made his last speech to the Lone Islanders and parted from the Duke and his family, but as the ship, her purple sail still flapping idly, drew further from the shore, and the sound of Caspian's trumpet from the poop came fainter across the water, everyone became silent. Then she came into the wind. The sail swelled out, the tug cast off and began rowing back, the first real wave ran up under the *Dawn Treader*'s prow, and she was a live ship again. The men off duty went below, Drinian took the first watch on the poop, and she turned her head eastward round the south of Avra.

The next few days were delightful. Lucy thought she was the most fortunate girl in the world, as she woke each morning to see the reflections of the sunlit water dancing on the ceiling of her cabin and looked round on all the nice new things she had got in the Lone Islands – seaboots and buskins and cloaks and jerkins and scarves. And then she would go on deck and take a look from the forecastle at a sea which was a brighter blue each morning and drink in an air that was a little warmer day by day. After that came breakfast and such an appetite as one only has at sea.

She spent a good deal of time sitting on the little bench in the stern playing chess with Reepicheep. It was amusing to see him lifting the pieces, which were far too big for him, with both paws and standing on tiptoes if he made a move near the centre of the board. He was a good player and when he remembered what he was doing he usually won. But every now and then Lucy won because the Mouse did something quite ridiculous like sending a knight into the danger of a queen and castle combined. This happened because he had momentarily forgotten it was a game of chess and was thinking of a real battle and making the knight do what he would certainly have done in its place. For his mind was full of forlorn hopes, death-or-glory charges, and last stands.

But this pleasant time did not last. There came an evening when Lucy, gazing idly astern at the long furrow or wake they were leaving behind them, saw a great rack of clouds building itself up in the west with amazing speed.

Then a gap was torn in it and a yellow sunset poured through the gap. All the waves behind them seemed to take on unusual shapes and the sea was a drab or yellowish colour like dirty canvas. The air grew cold. The ship seemed to move uneasily as if she felt danger behind her. The sail would be flat and limp one minute and wildly full the next. While she was noting these things and wondering at a sinister change which had come over the very noise of the wind, Drinian cried, "All hands on deck." In a moment everyone became frantically busy. The hatches were battened down, the galley fire was put out, men went aloft to reef the sail. Before they had finished the storm struck them. It seemed to Lucy that a great valley in the sea opened just before their bows, and they rushed down into it, deeper down than she would have believed possible. A great grey hill of water, far higher than the mast, rushed to meet them; it looked certain death but they were tossed to the top of it. Then the ship seemed to spin round. A cataract of water poured over the deck; the poop and forecastle were like two islands with a fierce sea between them. Up aloft the sailors were lying out along the yard desperately trying to get control of the sail. A broken rope stood out sideways in the wind as straight and stiff as if it was a poker.

"Get below, Ma'am," bawled Drinian. And Lucy, knowing that landsmen – and landswomen – are a nuisance to the crew, began to obey. It was not easy. The *Dawn Treader* was listing terribly to starboard and the deck sloped like the roof of a house. She had to clamber round to the top of the ladder, holding on to the rail, and then stand by while two men climbed up it, and then get down it as best she could. It was well she was already holding on tight for at the foot of the ladder another wave roared across the deck, up to her shoulders. She was already almost wet through with spray and rain but this was colder. Then she made a dash for the cabin door and got in and shut out for a moment the appalling sight of the speed with which they were rushing into the dark, but not of course the horrible confusion of creakings, groanings, snappings, clatterings, roarings and boomings which only sounded more alarming below than they had done on the poop.

And all next day and all the next it went on. It went on till one could hardly even remember a time before it had begun. And there always had to be three men at the tiller and it was as much as three could do to keep any kind of a course. And there always had to be men at the pump. And there was hardly any rest for anyone, and nothing could be cooked and nothing could be dried, and one man was lost overboard, and they never saw the sun.

When it was over Eustace made the following entry in his diary.

"*3 September*. The first day for ages when I have been able to write. We had been driven before a hurricane for thirteen days and nights. I know that because I kept a careful count, though the others all say it was only twelve. *Pleasant* to be embarked on a dangerous voyage with people who can't even count right! I have had a ghastly time, up and down enormous waves hour after hour, usually wet to the skin, and not even an *attempt* at giving us proper meals. Needless to say there's no wireless or even a rocket, so no chance of signalling anyone for help. It all proves what I keep on telling them, the madness of setting out in a rotten little tub like this. It would be bad enough even if one was with decent people instead of fiends in human form. Caspian and Edmund are simply brutal to me. The night we lost our mast (there's only a stump left now), though I was *not at all* well, they forced me to come on deck and work like a slave. Lucy shoved her oar in by saying that Reepicheep was longing to go only he was too small. I wonder she doesn't see that everything that little beast does is all for the sake of *showing off*. Even at her age

she ought to have that amount of sense. Today the beastly boat is level at last and the sun's out and we have all been jawing about what to do. We have food enough, pretty beastly stuff most of it, to last for sixteen days. (The poultry were all washed overboard. Even if they hadn't been, the storm would have stopped them laying.) The real trouble is water. Two casks seem to have got a leak knocked in them and are empty. (Narnian efficiency again.) On short rations, half a pint a day each, we've got enough for twelve days. (There's still lots of rum and wine but even *they* realize that would only make them thirstier.)

"If we could, of course, the sensible thing would be to turn west at once and make for the Lone Islands. But it took us eighteen days to get where we are, running like mad with a gale behind us. Even if we got an east wind it might take us far longer to get back. And at present there's no sign of an east wind – in fact there's no wind at all. As for rowing back, it would take far too long and Caspian says the men couldn't row on half a pint of water a day. I'm pretty sure this is wrong. I tried to explain that perspiration really cools people down, so the men would need less water if they were working. He didn't take any notice of this, which is always his way when he can't think of an answer. The others all voted for going *on* in the hope of finding land. I felt it my duty to point out that we didn't know there *was* any land ahead and tried to get them to see the dangers of *wishful thinking*. Instead of producing a better plan they had the cheek to ask me what I proposed. So I just explained coolly and quietly that I had been kidnapped and brought away on this *idiotic* voyage without my consent, and it was hardly *my* business to get *them* out of their scrape.

"*4 September*. Still becalmed. Very short rations for dinner and I got less than anyone. Caspian is very clever at helping and thinks I don't see! Lucy for some reason tried to make up to me by offering me some of hers but that *interfering prig* Edmund wouldn't let her. Pretty hot sun. Terribly thirsty all evening.

"*5 September*. Still becalmed and very hot. Feeling rotten all day and am sure I've got a temperature. Of course they haven't the sense to keep a thermometer on board.

"*6 September*. A horrible day. Woke up in the night *knowing* I was feverish and *must* have a drink of water. Any doctor would have said so. Heaven knows I'm the last person to try to get any unfair advantage but I never *dreamed* that this water-rationing would be meant to apply to a sick man. In fact I would have woken the others up and asked for some only I thought it would be selfish to wake them. So I got up and took my cup and tiptoed out of the Black Hole we slept in, taking great care not to disturb Caspian and Edmund, for they've been sleeping badly since the heat and the short water began. I always try to consider others whether they are nice to me or not. I got out all right into the big room, if you can call it a room, where the rowing benches and the luggage are. The thing of water is at this end. All was going beautifully, but before I'd drawn a cupful who should catch me but that *little spy* Reep. I tried to explain that I was going on deck for a breath of air (the business about the water had nothing to do with him) and he asked me why I had a cup. He made such a noise that the whole ship was roused. They treated me scandalously. I asked, as I think anyone would have, why Reepicheep was sneaking about the water cask in the middle of the night. He said that as he was too small to be any use on deck, he did sentry over the water every night so that one more man could go to sleep. Now comes their rotten unfairness: they all believed *him*. Can you beat it?

"I had to apologize or the dangerous little brute would have been at me with his sword. And then Caspian showed up in his true colours as a brutal tyrant and said out loud for everyone to hear that anyone found "stealing" water in future would "get two dozen". I didn't know what this meant till Edmund explained to me. It comes in the sort of books those Pevensie kids read.

"After this cowardly threat Caspian changed his tune and started being *patronizing*. Said he was sorry for me and that everyone felt just as feverish as I did and we must all make the best of it, etc., etc. Odious stuck-up prig. Stayed in bed all day today.

"*7 September*. A little wind today but still from the west.

Made a few miles eastward with part of the sail, set on what Drinian calls the jury-mast – that means the bowsprit set upright and tied (they call it "lashed") to the stump of the real mast. Still terribly thirsty.

"*8 September*. Still sailing east. I stay in my bunk all day now and see no one except Lucy till the two *fiends* come to bed. Lucy gives me a little of her water ration. She says girls don't get as thirsty as boys. I had often thought this but it ought to be more generally known at sea.

"*9 September*. Land in sight; a very high mountain a long way off to the south-east.

"*10 September*. The mountain is bigger and clearer but still a long way off. Gulls again today for the first time since I don't know how long.

"*11 September*. Caught some fish and had them for dinner. Dropped anchor at about 7 p.m. in three fathoms of water in a bay of this mountainous island. That idiot Caspian wouldn't let us go ashore because it was getting dark and he was afraid of savages and wild beasts. Extra water ration tonight."

What awaited them on this island was going to concern Eustace more than anyone else, but it cannot be told in his words because after September 11 he forgot about keeping his diary for a long time.

When morning came, with a low, grey sky but very hot, the adventurers found they were in a bay encircled by such cliffs and crags that it was like a Norwegian fjord. In front of them, at the head of the bay, there was some level land heavily overgrown with trees that appeared to be cedars, through which a rapid stream came out. Beyond that was a steep ascent ending in a jagged ridge and behind that a vague darkness of mountains which ran into dull-coloured clouds so that you could not see their tops. The nearer

cliffs, at each side of the bay, were streaked here and there
with lines of white which everyone knew to be waterfalls,
though at that distance they did not show any movement
or make any noise. Indeed the whole place was very silent
and the water of the bay as smooth as glass. It reflected
every detail of the cliffs. The scene would have been pretty
in a picture but was rather oppressive in real life. It was not
a country that welcomed visitors.

The whole ship's company went ashore in two boatloads and everyone drank and washed deliciously in the
river and had a meal and a rest before Caspian sent four
men back to keep the ship, and the day's work began.
There was everything to be done. The casks must be
brought ashore and the faulty ones mended if possible and
all refilled; a tree – a pine if they could get it – must be
felled and made into a new mast; sails must be repaired; a
hunting party organized to shoot any game the land might
yield; clothes to be washed and mended; and countless
small breakages on board to be set right. For the *Dawn
Treader* herself – and this was more obvious now that they
saw her at a distance – could hardly be recognized as the
same gallant ship which had left Narrowhaven. She looked
a crippled, discoloured hulk which anyone might have
taken for a wreck. And her officers and crew were no
better – lean, pale, red-eyed from lack of sleep, and dressed
in rags.

As Eustace lay under a tree and heard all these plans
being discussed his heart sank. Was there going to be no
rest? It looked as if their first day on the longed-for land
was going to be quite as hard work as a day at sea. Then a
delightful idea occurred to him. Nobody was looking –
they were all chattering about their ship as if they actually
liked the beastly thing. Why shouldn't he simply slip away?
He would take a stroll inland, find a cool, airy place up in

the mountains, have a good long sleep, and not rejoin
the others till the day's work was over. He felt it would
do him good. But he would take great care to keep the bay
and the ship in sight so as to be sure of his way back.

He wouldn't like to be left behind in this country.

He at once put his plan into action. He rose quietly from his place and walked away among the trees, taking care to go slowly and in an aimless manner so that anyone who saw him would think he was merely stretching his legs. He was surprised to find how quickly the noise of conversation died away behind him and how very silent and warm and dark green the wood became. Soon he felt he could venture on a quicker and more determined stride.

This soon brought him out of the wood. The ground began sloping steeply up in front of him. The grass was dry and slippery but manageable if he used his hands as well as his feet, and though he panted and mopped his forehead a good deal, he plugged away steadily. This showed, by the way, that his new life, little as he suspected it, had already done him some good; the old Eustace, Harold and Alberta's Eustace, would have given up the climb after about ten minutes.

Slowly, and with several rests, he reached the ridge. Here he had expected to have a view into the heart of the island, but the clouds had now come lower and nearer and a sea of fog was rolling to meet him. He sat down and looked back. He was now so high that the bay looked small beneath him and miles of sea were visible. Then the fog from the mountains closed in all round him, thick but not cold, and he lay down and turned this way and that to find the most comfortable position to enjoy himself.

But he didn't enjoy himself, or not for very long. He began, almost for the first time in his life, to feel lonely. At first this feeling grew very gradually. And then he began to worry about the time. There was not the slightest sound. Suddenly it occurred to him that he might have been lying there for hours. Perhaps the others had gone! Perhaps they had let him wander away on purpose simply in order to leave him behind! He leaped up in a panic and began the descent.

At first he tried to do it too quickly, slipped on the steep grass, and slid for several feet. Then he thought this had carried him too far to the left – and as he came up he had seen precipices on that side. So he clambered up again, as near as he could guess to the place he had started from, and began the descent afresh, bearing to his right. After that things seemed to be going better. He went very cautiously, for he could not see more than a yard ahead, and there was still perfect silence all around him. It is very unpleasant to have to go cautiously when there is a voice inside you saying all the time, "Hurry, hurry, hurry." For every moment the terrible idea of being left behind grew stronger. If he had understood Caspian and the Pevensies at all he would have known, of course, that there was not the least chance of their doing any such thing. But he had persuaded himself that they were all fiends in human form.

"At last!" said Eustace as he came slithering down a slide of loose stones (*scree*, they call it) and found himself on the level. "And now, where are those trees? There *is* something dark ahead. Why, I do believe the fog is clearing."

It was. The light increased every moment and made him blink. The fog lifted. He was in an utterly unknown valley and the sea was nowhere in sight.

CHAPTER SIX

THE ADVENTURES OF EUSTACE

AT that very moment the others were washing hands and faces in the river and generally getting ready for dinner and a rest. The three best archers had gone up into the hills north of the bay and returned laden with a pair of wild goats which were now roasting over a fire. Caspian had ordered a cask of wine ashore, strong wine of Archenland which had to be mixed with water before you drank it, so there would be plenty for all. The work had gone well so far and it was a merry meal. Only after the seond helping of goat did Edmund say, "Where's that blighter Eustace?"

Meanwhile Eustace stared round the unknown valley. It was so narrow and deep, and the precipices which surrounded it so sheer, that it was like a huge pit or trench. The floor was grassy though strewn with rocks, and here and there Eustace saw black burnt patches like those you see on the sides of a railway embankment in a dry summer.

About fifteen yards away from him was a pool of clear, smooth water. There was, at first, nothing else at all in the valley; not an animal, not a bird, not an insect. The sun beat down and grim peaks and horns of mountains peered over the valley's edge.

Eustace realized of course that in the fog he had come down the wrong side of the ridge, so he turned at once to see about getting back. But as soon as he had looked he shuddered. Apparently he had by amazing luck found the only possible way down – a long green spit of land, horribly steep and narrow, with precipices on either side. There was no other possible way of getting back. But could he do it, now that he saw what it was really like? His head swam at the very thought of it.

He turned round again, thinking that at any rate he'd better have a good drink from the pool first. But as soon as he had turned and before he had taken a step forward into the valley he heard a noise behind him. It was only a small noise but it sounded loud in that immense silence. It froze him dead-still where he stood for a second. Then he slewed round his neck and looked.

At the bottom of the cliff a little on his left hand was a low, dark hole – the entrance to a cave perhaps. And out of this two thin wisps of smoke were coming. And the loose stones just beneath the dark hollow were moving (that was the noise he had heard) just as if something were crawling in the dark behind them.

Something *was* crawling. Worse still, something was coming out. Edmund or Lucy or you would have recognized it at once, but Eustace had read none of the right books. The thing that came out of the cave was something he had never even imagined – a long lead-coloured snout, dull red eyes, no feathers or fur, a long lithe body that trailed on the ground, legs whose elbows went up higher than its back like a spider's, cruel claws, bat's wings that made a rasping noise on the stones, yards of tail. And the lines of smoke were coming from its two nostrils. He never said the word *Dragon* to himself. Nor would it have made things any better if he had.

But perhaps if he had known something about dragons he would have been a little surprised at this dragon's behaviour. It did not sit up and clap its wings, nor did it shoot out a stream of flame from its mouth. The smoke from its nostrils was like the smoke of a fire that will not last much longer. Nor did it seem to have noticed Eustace. It moved very slowly towards the pool – slowly and with many pauses. Even in his fear Eustace felt that it was an old, sad creature. He wondered if he dared make a dash for the ascent. But it might look round if he made any noise. It might come more to life. Perhaps it was only shamming. Anyway, what was the use of trying to escape by climbing from a creature that could fly?

It reached the pool and slid its horrible scaly chin down over the gravel to drink: but before it had drunk there came from it a great croaking or clanging cry and after a

few twitches and convulsions it rolled round on its side and
lay perfectly still with one claw in the air. A little dark
blood gushed from its wide-opened mouth. The smoke
from its nostrils turned black for a moment and then
floated away. No more came.

For a long time Eustace did not dare to move. Perhaps

this was the brute's trick, the way it lured travellers to their
doom. But one couldn't wait for ever. He took a step
nearer, then two steps, and halted again. The dragon
remained motionless; he noticed too that the red fire had
gone out of its eyes. At last he came up to it. He was quite
sure now that it was dead. With a shudder he touched it;
nothing happened.

The relief was so great that Eustace almost laughed out
loud. He began to feel as if he had fought and killed the
dragon instead of merely seeing it die. He stepped over it
and went to the pool for his drink, for the heat was getting

unbearable. He was not surprised when he heard a peal of thunder. Almost immediately afterwards the sun disappeared and before he had finished his drink big drops of rain were falling.

The climate of this island was a very unpleasant one. In less than a minute Eustace was wet to the skin and half blinded with such rain as one never sees in Europe. There was no use trying to climb out of the valley as long as this lasted. He bolted for the only shelter in sight – the dragon's cave. There he lay down and tried to get his breath.

Most of us know what we should expect to find in a dragon's lair, but, as I said before, Eustace had read only the wrong books. They had a lot to say about exports and imports and governments and drains, but they were weak on dragons. That is why he was so puzzled at the surface on which he was lying. Parts of it were too prickly to be stones and too hard to be thorns, and there seemed to be a great many round, flat things, and it all clinked when he moved. There was light enough at the cave's mouth to examine it by. And of course Eustace found it to be what any of us could have told him in advance – treasure. There were crowns (those were the prickly things), coins, rings, bracelets, ingots, cups, plates and gems.

Eustace (unlike most boys) had never thought much of treasure but he saw at once the use it would be in this new world which he had so foolishly stumbled into through the picture in Lucy's bedroom at home. "They don't have any tax here," he said, "And you don't have to give treasure to the government. With some of this stuff I could have quite a decent time here – perhaps in Calormen. It sounds the least phoney of these countries. I wonder how much I can carry? That bracelet now – those things in it are probably diamonds – I'll slip that on my own wrist. Too big, but not if I push it right up here above my elbow. Then fill my pockets with diamonds – that's easier than gold. I wonder when this infernal rain's going to let up?" He got into a less uncomfortable part of the pile, where it was mostly coins, and settled down to wait. But a bad fright, when once it is over, and especially a bad fright following a mountain walk, leaves you very tired. Eustace fell asleep.

By the time he was sound asleep and snoring the others had finished dinner and became seriously alarmed about him. They shouted, "Eustace! Eustace! Coo-ee!" till they were hoarse and Caspian blew his horn.

"He's nowhere near or he'd have heard that," said Lucy with a white face.

"Confound the fellow," said Edmund. "What on earth did he want to slink away like this for?"

"But we must do something," said Lucy. "He may have got lost, or fallen into a hole, or been captured by savages."

"Or killed by wild beasts," said Drinian.

"And a good riddance if he has, *I* say," muttered Rhince.

"Master Rhince," said Reepicheep, "you never spoke a word that became you less. The creature is no friend of mine but he is of the Queen's blood, and while he is one of our fellowship it concerns our honour to find him and to avenge him if he is dead."

"Of course we've got to find him (if we *can*)," said Caspian wearily. "That's the nuisance of it. It means a search party and endless trouble. Bother Eustace."

Meanwhile Eustace slept and slept – and slept. What woke him was a pain in his arm. The moon was shining in at the mouth of the cave, and the bed of treasures seemed to have grown much more comfortable: in fact he could hardly feel it at all. He was puzzled by the pain in his arm at first, but presently it occurred to him that the bracelet which he had shoved up above his elbow had become strangely tight. His arm must have swollen while he was asleep (it was his left arm).

He moved his right arm in order to feel his left, but stopped before he had moved it an inch and bit his lip in terror. For just in front of him, and a little on his right, where the moonlight fell clear on the floor of the cave, he saw a hideous shape moving. He knew that shape: it was a dragon's claw. It had moved as he moved his hand and became still when he stopped moving his hand.

"Oh, what a fool I've been," thought Eustace. "Of course, the brute had a mate and it's lying beside me."

For several minutes he did not dare to move a muscle. He saw two thin columns of smoke going up before his eyes, black against the moonlight; just as there had been smoke coming from the other dragon's nose before it died. This was so alarming that he held his breath. The two columns of smoke vanished. When he could hold his breath no longer he let it out stealthily; instantly two jets of smoke appeared again. But even yet he had no idea of the truth.

Presently he decided that he would edge very cautiously to his left and try to creep out of the cave. Perhaps the creature was asleep – and anyway it was his only chance. But of course before he edged to the left he looked to the left. Oh horror! there was a dragon's claw on that side too.

No one will blame Eustace if at this moment he shed tears. He was surprised at the size of his own tears as he saw them splashing on to the treasure in front of him. They also seemed strangely hot; steam went up from them.

But there was no good crying. He must try to crawl out from between the two dragons. He began extending his right arm. The dragon's fore-leg and claw on his right went through exactly the same motion. Then he thought he would try his left. The dragon limb on that side moved too.

Two dragons, one on each side, mimicking whatever he did! His nerve broke and he simply made a bolt for it.

There was such a clatter and rasping, and clinking of gold, and grinding of stones, as he rushed out of the cave that he thought they were both following him. He daren't look back. He rushed to the pool. The twisted shape of the dead dragon lying in the moonlight would have been enough to frighten anyone but now he hardly noticed it. His idea was to get into the water.

But just as he reached the edge of the pool two things happened. First of all it came over him like a thunder-clap that he had been running on all fours – and why on earth had he been doing that? And secondly, as he bent towards the water, he thought for a second that yet another dragon was staring up at him out of the pool. But in an instant he realized the truth. The dragon face in the pool was his own reflection. There was no doubt of it. It moved as he moved: it opened and shut its mouth as he opened and shut his.

He had turned into a dragon while he was asleep. Sleeping on a dragon's hoard with greedy, dragonish thoughts in his heart, he had become a dragon himself.

That explained everything. There had been no two dragons beside him in the cave. The claws to right and left had been his own right and left claw. The two columns of smoke had been coming from his own nostrils. As for the pain in his left arm (or what had been his left arm) he could now see what had happened by squinting with his left eye. The bracelet which had fitted very nicely on the upper arm of a boy was far too small for the thick, stumpy foreleg of a dragon. It had sunk deeply into his scaly flesh and there was a throbbing bulge on each side of it. He tore at the place with his dragon's teeth but could not get it off.

In spite of the pain, his first feeling was one of relief. There was nothing to be afraid of any more. He was a terror himself and nothing in the world but a knight (and not all of those) would dare to attack him. He could get even with Caspian and Edmund now –

But the moment he thought this he realized that he didn't want to. He wanted to be friends. He wanted to get back among humans and talk and laugh and share things. He realized that he was a monster cut off from the whole human race. An appalling loneliness came over him. He began to see that the others had not really been fiends at all. He began to wonder if he himself had been such a nice person as he had always supposed. He longed for their voices. He would have been grateful for a kind word even from Reepicheep.

When he thought of this the poor dragon that had been Eustace lifted up its voice and wept. A powerful dragon crying its eyes out under the moon in a deserted valley is a sight and a sound hardly to be imagined.

At last he decided he would try to find his way back to the shore. He realized now that Caspian would never have sailed away and left him. And he felt sure that somehow or other he would be able to make people understand who he was.

He took a long drink and then (I know this sounds shocking, but it isn't if you think it over) he ate nearly all the dead dragon. He was half-way through it before he realized what he was doing; for, you see, though his mind was the mind of Eustace, his tastes and his digestion were dragonish. And there is nothing a dragon likes so well as fresh dragon. That is why you so seldom find more than one dragon in the same county.

Then he turned to climb out of the valley. He began the climb with a jump and as soon as he jumped he found that he was flying. He had quite forgotten about his wings and it was a great surprise to him – the first pleasant surprise he had had for a long time. He rose high into the air and saw innumerable mountain-tops spread out beneath him in the moonlight. He could see the bay like a silver slab and the *Dawn Treader* lying at anchor and camp fires twinkling in the woods beside the beach. From a great

height he launched himself down towards them in a single glide.

Lucy was sleeping very soundly for she had sat up till the return of the search party in hope of good news about Eustace. It had been led by Caspian and had come back late and weary. Their news was disquieting. They had found no trace of Eustace but had seen a dead dragon in a valley. They tried to make the best of it and everyone assured everyone else that there were not likely to be more dragons about, and that one which was dead at about three o'clock that afternoon (which was when they had seen it) would hardly have been killing people a very few hours before.

"Unless it ate the little brat and died of him: he'd poison anything," said Rhince. But he said this under his breath and no one heard it.

But later in the night Lucy was wakened, very softly, and found the whole company gathered close together and talking in whispers.

"What is it?" said Lucy.

"We must all show great constancy," Caspian was saying. "A dragon has just flown over the tree-tops and lighted on the beach. Yes, I am afraid it is between us and the ship. And arrows are no use against dragons. And they're not at all afraid of fire."

"With your Majesty's leave —" began Reepicheep.

"No, Reepicheep," said the King very firmly, "you are *not* to attempt a single combat with it. And unless you promise to obey me in this matter I'll have you tied up. We must just keep close watch and, as soon as it is light, go down to the beach and give it battle. I will lead. King Edmund will be on my right and the Lord Drinian on my left. There are no other arrangements to be made. It will be light in a couple of hours. In an hour's time let a meal be served out and what is left of the wine. And let everything be done silently."

"Perhaps it will go away," said Lucy.

"It'll be worse if it does," said Edmund, "because then we shan't know where it is. If there's a wasp in the room I like to be able to see it."

The rest of the night was dreadful, and when the meal came, though they knew they ought to eat, many found that they had very poor appetites. And endless hours seemed to pass before the darkness thinned and birds began chirping here and there and the world got colder and wetter than it had been all night and Caspian said, "Now for it, friends."

They got up, all with swords drawn, and formed themselves into a solid mass with Lucy in the middle and Reepicheep on her shoulder. It was nicer than the waiting about and everyone felt fonder of everyone else than at ordinary times. A moment later they were marching. It grew lighter as they came to the edge of the wood. And there on the sand, like a giant lizard, or a flexible crocodile, or a serpent with legs, huge and horrible and humpy, lay the dragon.

But when it saw them, instead of rising up and blowing fire and smoke, the dragon retreated – you could almost say it waddled – back into the shallows of the bay.

"What's it wagging its head like that for?" said Edmund.

"And now it's nodding," said Caspian.

"And there's something coming from its eyes," said Drinian.

"Oh, can't you see," said Lucy. "It's crying. Those are tears."

"I shouldn't trust to that, Ma'am," said Drinian. "That's what crocodiles do, to put you off your guard."

"It wagged its head when you said that," remarked Edmund. "Just as if it meant No. Look, there it goes again."

"Do you think it understands what we're saying?" asked Lucy.

The dragon nodded its head violently.

Reepicheep slipped off Lucy's shoulder and stepped to the front.

"Dragon," came his shrill voice, "can you understand speech?"

The dragon nodded.

"Can you speak?"

It shook its head.

"Then," said Reepicheep, "it is idle to ask you your business. But if you will swear friendship with us raise your left foreleg above your head."

It did so, but clumsily because that leg was sore and swollen with the golden bracelet.

"Oh look," said Lucy, "there's something wrong with its leg. The poor thing – that's probably what it was crying about. Perhaps it came to us to be cured like in Androcles and the lion."

"Be careful, Lucy," said Caspian. "It's a very clever dragon but it may be a liar."

Lucy had, however, already run forward, followed by Reepicheep, as fast as his short legs could carry him, and then of course the boys and Drinian came, too.

"Show me your poor paw," said Lucy, "I might be able to cure it."

The dragon-that-had-been-Eustace held out its sore leg gladly enough, remembering how Lucy's cordial had cured him of sea-sickness before he became a dragon. But he was disappointed. The magic fluid reduced the swelling and eased the pain a little but it could not dissolve the gold.

Everyone had now crowded round to watch the treatment, and Caspian suddenly exclaimed, "Look!" He was staring at the bracelet.

CHAPTER SEVEN

HOW THE ADVENTURE ENDED

"Look at what?" said Edmund.

"Look at the device on the gold," said Caspian.

"A little hammer with a diamond above it like a star," said Drinian. "Why, I've seen that before."

"Seen it!" said Caspian. "Why, of course you have. It is the sign of a great Narnian house. This is the Lord Octesian's arm-ring."

"Villain," said Reepicheep to the dragon, "have you devoured a Narnian lord?" But the dragon shook his head violently.

"Or perhaps," said Lucy, "this *is* the Lord Octesian, turned into a dragon – under an enchantment, you know."

"It needn't be either," said Edmund. "All dragons collect gold. But I think it's a safe guess that Octesian got no further than this island."

"Are you the Lord Octesian?" said Lucy to the dragon, and then, when it sadly shook its head, "Are you someone enchanted – someone human, I mean?"

It nodded violently.

And then someone said – people disputed afterwards whether Lucy or Edmund said it first – "You're not – not Eustace by any chance?"

And Eustace nodded his terrible dragon head and thumped his tail in the sea and everyone skipped back (some of the sailors with ejaculations I will not put down in writing) to avoid the enormous and boiling tears which flowed from his eyes.

Lucy tried hard to console him and even screwed up her courage to kiss the scaly face, and nearly everyone said

"Hard luck" and several assured Eustace that they would all stand by him and many said there was sure to be some way of disenchanting him and they'd have him as right as rain in a day or two. And of course they were all very anxious to hear his story, but he couldn't speak. More than once in the days that followed he attempted to write it for them on the sand. But this never succeeded. In the first place Eustace (never having read the right books) had no idea how to tell a story straight. And for another thing, the muscles and nerves of the dragon-claws that he had to use had never learned to write and were not built for writing anyway. As a result he never got nearly to the end before the tide came in and washed away all the writing except the bits he had already trodden on or accidentaly swished out with his tail. And all that anyone had seen would be something like this — the dots are for the bits he had smudged out—

I WNET TO SLEE . . . RGOS AGRONS I MEAN DRANGONS CAVE CAUSE ITWAS DEAD AND AINING SO HAR . . . WOKE UP AND COU . . . GET OFFF MI ARM OH BOTHER . . .

It was, however, clear to everyone that Eustace's character had been rather improved by becoming a dragon. He was anxious to help. He flew over the whole island and found it was all mountainous and inhabited only by wild goats and droves of wild swine. Of these he brought back many carcasses as provisions for the ship. He was a very humane killer too, for he could dispatch a beast with one blow of his tail so that it didn't know (and presumably still doesn't know) it had been killed. He ate a few himself, of course, but always alone, for now that he was a dragon he liked his food raw but he could never bear to let others see him at his messy meals. And one day, flying slowly and wearily but in great triumph, he bore back to camp a great tall pine tree which he had torn up by the roots in a distant valley and which could be made into a capital mast. And in the evening if it turned chilly, as it sometimes did after the heavy rains, he was a comfort to everyone, for the whole party would come and sit with their backs against his hot sides and get well warmed and dried; and one puff of his fiery breath would light the most obstinate fire. Sometimes he would take a select party for a fly on his back, so that they could see wheeling below them the green slopes, the rocky heights, the narrow pit-like valleys and far out over the sea to the eastward a spot of darker blue on the blue horizon which might be land.

The pleasure (quite new to him) of being liked and, still more, of liking other people, was what kept Eustace from despair. For it was very dreary being a dragon. He shuddered whenever he caught sight of his own reflection as he flew over a mountain lake. He hated the huge batlike wings, the saw-edged ridge on his back, and the cruel, curved claws. He was almost afraid to be alone with himself and yet he was ashamed to be with the others. On the evenings when he was not being used as a hot-water bottle he would slink away from the camp and lie curled up like a snake between the wood and the water. On such occasions, greatly to his surprise, Reepicheep was his most constant comforter. The noble Mouse would creep away from the merry circle at the camp fire and sit down by the dragon's head, well to the windward to be out of the way of his smoky breath. There he would explain that what had happened to Eustace was a striking illustration of the turn of Fortune's wheel, and that if he had Eustace at his own house in Narnia (it was really a hole not a house and the dragon's head, let alone his body, would not have fitted in) he could show him more than a hundred examples of emperors, kings, dukes, knights, poets, lovers, astronomers, philosophers, and magicians, who had fallen from prosperity into the most distressing circumstances, and of whom many had recovered and lived happily ever afterwards. It did not, perhaps, seem so very comforting at the time, but it was kindly meant and Eustace never forgot it.

But of course what hung over everyone like a cloud was the problem of what to do with their dragon when they were ready to sail. They tried not to talk of it when he was there, but he couldn't help overhearing things like, "Would he fit all along one side of the deck? And we'd have to shift all the stores to the other side down below so as to balance," or, "Would towing him be any good?" or "Would he be able to keep up by flying?" and (most often of all), "But how are we to feed him?" And poor Eustace realized more and more that since the first day he came on board he had been an unmitigated nuisance and that he was now a greater nuisance still. And this ate into his mind, just as that bracelet ate into his foreleg. He knew that it only made it worse to tear at it with his great teeth, but he couldn't help tearing now and then, especially on hot nights.

*

About six days after they had landed on Dragon Island, Edmund happened to wake up very early one morning. It was just getting grey so that you could see the tree-trunks if they were between you and the bay but not in the other direction. As he woke he thought he heard something moving, so he raised himself on one elbow and looked about him: and presently he thought he saw a dark figure moving on the seaward side of the wood. The idea that at once occurred to his mind was, "Are we so sure there are no natives on this island after all?" Then he thought it was Caspian – it was about the right size – but he knew that Caspian had been sleeping next to him and could see that he hadn't moved. Edmund made sure that his sword was in its place and then rose to investigate.

He came down softly to the edge of the wood and the dark figure was still there. He saw now that it was too small for Caspian and too big for Lucy. It did not run away. Edmund drew his sword and was about to challenge the stranger when the stranger said in a low voice, "Is that you, Edmund?"

"Yes. Who are you?" said he.

"Don't you know me?" said the other. "It's me – Eustace."

"By jove," said Edmund, "so it is. My dear chap –"

"Hush," said Eustace and lurched as if he were going to fall.

"Hello!" said Edmund, steadying him. "What's up? Are you ill?"

Eustace was silent for so long that Edmund thought he was fainting; but at last he said, "It's been ghastly. You don't know . . . but it's all right now. Could we go and talk somewhere? I don't want to meet the others just yet."

"Yes, rather, anywhere you like," said Edmund. "We can go and sit on the rocks over there. I say, I *am* glad to see you – er – looking yourself again. You must have had a pretty beastly time."

They went to the rocks and sat down looking out across the bay while the sky got paler and paler and the stars disappeared except for one very bright one low down and near the horizon.

"I won't tell you how I became a – a dragon till I can tell the others and get it all over," said Eustace. "By the way, I didn't even know it *was* a dragon till I heard you all using the word when I turned up here the other morning. I want to tell you how I stopped being one."

"Fire ahead," said Edmund.

"Well, last night I was more miserable than ever. And that beastly arm-ring was hurting like anything –"

"Is that all right now?"

Eustace laughed – a different laugh from any Edmund had heard him give before – and slipped the bracelet easily off his arm. "There it is," he said, "and anyone who likes can have it as far as I'm concerned. Well, as I say, I was lying awake and wondering what on earth would become of me. And then – but, mind you, it may have been all a dream. I don't know."

"Go on," said Edmund, with considerable patience.

"Well, anyway, I looked up and saw the very last thing I expected: a huge lion coming slowly towards me. And one queer thing was that there was no moon last night, but there was moonlight where the lion was. So it came nearer and nearer. I was terribly afraid of it. You may think that, being a dragon, I could have knocked any lion out easily enough. But it wasn't that kind of fear. I wasn't afraid of it eating me, I was just afraid of *it* – if you can understand. Well, it came close up to me and looked straight into my eyes. And I shut my eyes tight. But that wasn't any good because it told me to follow it."

"You mean it spoke?"

"I don't know. Now that you mention it, I don't think it did. But it told me all the same. And I knew I'd have to do what it told me, so I got up and followed it. And it led me a long way into the mountains. And there was always this moonlight over and round the lion wherever we went. So at last we came to the top of a mountain I'd never seen before and on the top of this mountain there was a garden – trees and fruit and everything. In the middle of it there was a well.

"I knew it was a well because you could see the water bubbling up from the bottom of it: but it was a lot bigger than most wells – like a very big, round bath with marble steps going down into it. The water was as clear as anything and I thought if I could get in there and bathe it would ease the pain in my leg. But the lion told me I must undress first. Mind you, I don't know if he said any words out loud or not.

"I was just going to say that I couldn't undress because I hadn't any clothes on when I suddenly thought that dragons are snaky sort of things and snakes can cast their skins. Oh, of course, thought I, that's what the lion means. So I started scratching myself and my scales began coming off all over the place. And then I scratched a little deeper and, instead of just scales coming off here and there, my whole skin started peeling off beautifully, like it does after an illness, or as if I was a banana. In a minute or two I just stepped out of it. I could see it lying there beside me, looking rather nasty. It was a most lovely feeling. So I started to go down into the well for my bathe.

"But just as I was going to put my feet into the water I looked down and saw that they were all hard and rough and wrinkled and scaly just as they had been before. Oh, that's all right, said I, it only means I had another smaller suit on underneath the first one, and I'll have to get out of it too. So I scratched and tore again and this underskin peeled off beautifully and out I stepped and left it lying beside the other one and went down to the well for my bathe.

"Well, exactly the same thing happened again. And I thought to myself, oh dear, how ever many skins have I got to take off? For I was longing to bathe my leg. So I scratched away for the third time and got off a third skin, just like the two others, and stepped out of it. But as soon as I looked at myself in the water I knew it had been no good.

"Then the lion said – but I don't know if it spoke – "You will have to let me undress you." I was afraid of his claws, I can tell you, but I was pretty nearly desperate now. So I just lay flat down on my back to let him do it.

"The very first tear he made was so deep that I thought it had gone right into my heart. And when he began pulling the skin off, it hurt worse than anything I've ever felt. The only thing that made me able to bear it was just the pleasure of feeling the stuff peel off. You know – if you've ever picked the scab off a sore place. It hurts like billy-oh but it *is* such fun to see it coming away."

"I know exactly what you mean," said Edmund.

"Well, he peeled the beastly stuff right off – just as I thought I'd done it myself the other three times, only they hadn't hurt – and there it was lying on the grass: only ever so much thicker, and darker, and more knobbly-looking than the others had been. And there was I as smooth and soft as a peeled switch and smaller than I had been. Then he caught hold of me – I didn't like that much for I was very tender underneath now that I'd no skin on – and threw me into the water. It smarted like anything but only for a moment. After that it became perfectly delicious and as soon as I started swimming and splashing I found that all the pain had gone from my arm. And then I saw why. I'd turned into a boy again. You'd think me simply phoney if I told you how I felt about my own arms. I know they've no muscle and are pretty mouldy compared with Caspian's, but I was so glad to see them.

"After a bit the lion took me out and dressed me –"

"Dressed you. With his paws?"

"Well, I don't exactly remember that bit. But he did somehow or other: in new clothes – the same I've got on now, as a matter of fact. And then suddenly I was back here. Which is what makes me think it must have been a dream."

"No. It wasn't a dream," said Edmund.

"Why not?"

"Well, there are the clothes, for one thing. And you have been – well, un-dragoned, for another."

"What do you think it was, then?" asked Eustace.

"I think you've seen Aslan," said Edmund.

"Aslan!" said Eustace. "I've heard that name mentioned several times since we joined the *Dawn Treader*. And I felt – I don't know what – I hated it. But I was hating everything then. And by the way, I'd like to apologize. I'm afraid I've been pretty beastly."

"That's all right," said Edmund. "Between ourselves, you haven't been as bad as I was on my first trip to Narnia. You were only an ass, but I was a traitor."

"Well, don't tell me about it, then," said Eustace. "But who is Aslan? Do you know him?"

"Well – he knows me," said Edmund. "He is the great Lion, the son of the Emperor-beyond-the-Sea, who saved me and saved Narnia. We've all seen him. Lucy sees him most often. And it may be Aslan's country we are sailing to."

Neither said anything for a while. The last bright star had vanished and though they could not see the sunrise because of the mountains on their right, they knew it was going on because the sky above them and the bay before them turned the colour of roses. Then some bird of the parrot kind screamed in the wood behind them, they heard movements among the trees, and finally a blast on Caspian's horn. The camp was astir.

Great was the rejoicing when Edmund and the restored Eustace walked into the breakfast circle round the camp fire. And now of course everyone heard the earlier part of his story. People wondered whether the other dragon had killed the Lord Octesian several years ago or whether Octesian himself had been the old dragon. The jewels with which Eustace had crammed his pockets in the cave had disappeared along with the clothes he had then been wearing: but no one, least of all Eustace himself, felt any desire to go back to that valley for more treasure.

In a few days now the *Dawn Treader*, remasted, re-painted, and well stored, was ready to sail. Before they embarked Caspian caused to be cut on a smooth cliff facing the bay the words:

DRAGON ISLAND
DISCOVERED BY CASPIAN X, KING OF NARNIA, ETC.
IN THE FOURTH
YEAR OF HIS REIGN.
HERE, AS WE SUPPOSE, THE LORD OCTESIAN
HAD HIS DEATH

It would be nice, and fairly true, to say that "from that time forth Eustace was a different boy". To be strictly accurate, he began to be a different boy. He had relapses. There were still many days when he could be very tiresome. But most of those I shall not notice. The cure had begun.

The Lord Octesian's arm ring had a curious fate. Eustace did not want it and offered it to Caspian and Caspian offered it to Lucy. She did not care about having it. "Very well, then, catch as catch can," said Caspian and flung it up in the air. This was when they were all standing looking at the inscription. Up went the ring, flashing in the sunlight, and caught, and hung, as neatly as a well-thrown quoit, on a little projection on the rock. No one could climb up to get it from below and no one could climb down to get it from above. And there, for all I know, it is hanging still and may hang till that world ends.

CHAPTER EIGHT

TWO NARROW ESCAPES

EVERYONE was cheerful as the *Dawn Treader* sailed from Dragon Island. They had fair winds as soon as they were out of the bay and came early next morning to the unknown land which some of them had seen when flying over the mountains while Eustace was still a dragon. It was a low green island inhabited by nothing but rabbits and a few goats, but from the ruins of stone huts, and from blackened places where fires had been, they judged that it had been peopled not long before. There were also some bones and broken weapons.

"Pirates' work," said Caspian.

"Or the dragon's," said Edmund.

The only other thing they found there was a little skin boat, or coracle, on the sands. It was made of hide stretched over a wicker framework. It was a tiny boat, barely four feet long, and the paddle which still lay in it was in proportion. They thought that either it had been made for a child or else that the people of that country had been Dwarfs. Reepicheep decided to keep it, as it was just the right size for him; so it was taken on board. They called that land Burnt Island, and sailed away before noon.

For some five days they ran before a south-south-east wind, out of sight of all lands and seeing neither fish nor gull. Then they had a day when it rained hard till the afternoon. Eustace lost two games of chess to Reepicheep and began to get like his old and disagreeable self again, and Edmund said he wished they could have gone to America with Susan. Then Lucy looked out of the stern windows and said:

"Hello! I do believe it's stopping. And what's *that*?"

They all tumbled up to the poop at this and found that the rain had stopped and that Drinian, who was on watch, was also staring hard at something astern. Or rather, at several things. They looked a little like smooth rounded rocks, a whole line of them with intervals of about forty feet in between.

"But they can't be rocks," Drinian was saying, "because they weren't there five minutes ago."

"And one's just disappeared," said Lucy.

"Yes, and there's another one coming up," said Edmund.

"And nearer," said Eustace.

"Hang it!" said Caspian. "The whole thing is moving this way."

"And moving a great deal quicker than we can sail, Sire," said Drinian. "It'll be up with us in a minute."

They all held their breath, for it is not at all nice to be pursued by an unknown something either on land or sea. But what it turned out to be was far worse than anyone had suspected. Suddenly, only about the length of a cricket pitch from their port side, an appalling head reared itself out of the sea. It was all greens and vermilions with purple blotches – except where shell fish clung to it – and shaped rather like a horse's, though without ears. It had enormous eyes, eyes made for staring through the dark depths of the ocean, and a gaping mouth filled with double rows of sharp fish-like teeth. It came up on what they first took to be a huge neck, but as more and more of it emerged everyone knew that this was not its neck but its body and that at last they were seeing what so many people have foolishly wanted to see – the great Sea Serpent. The folds of its gigantic tail could be seen far away, rising at intervals from the surface. And now its head was towering up higher than the mast.

Every man rushed to his weapon, but there was nothing to be done, the monster was out of reach. "Shoot! Shoot!" cried the Master Bowman, and several obeyed, but the arrows glanced off the Sea Serpent's hide as if it was iron-plated. Then, for a dreadful minute, everyone was still, staring up at its eyes and mouth and wondering where it would pounce.

But it didn't pounce. It shot its head forward across the

ship on a level with the yard of the mast. Now its head was just beside the fighting top. Still it stretched and stretched till its head was over the starboard bulwark. Then down it began to come – not on to the crowded deck but into the water, so that the whole ship was under an arch of serpent. And almost at once that arch began to get smaller: indeed on the starboard the Sea Serpent was now almost touching the *Dawn Treader*'s side.

Eustace (who had really been trying very hard to behave well, till the rain and the chess put him back) now did the first brave thing he had ever done. He was wearing a sword that Caspian had lent him. As soon as the serpent's body was near enough on the starboard side he jumped on to the bulwark and began hacking at it with all his might. It is true that he accomplished nothing beyond breaking Caspian's second-best sword into bits, but it was a fine thing for a beginner to have done.

Others would have joined him if at that moment Reepicheep had not called out, "Don't fight! Push!" It was so unusual for the Mouse to advise anyone not to fight that, even in that terrible moment, every eye turned to him. And when he jumped up on to the bulwark, forward of the snake, and set his little furry back against its huge scaly, slimy back, and began pushing as hard as he could, quite a number of people saw what he meant and rushed to both sides of the ship to do the same. And when, a moment later, the Sea Serpent's head appeared again, this time on the port side, and this time with its back to them, then everyone understood.

The brute had made a loop of itself round the *Dawn Treader* and was beginning to draw the loop tight. When it got quite tight – snap! – there would be floating matchwood where the ship had been and it could pick them out of the water one by one. Their only chance was to push the loop backward till it slid over the stern; or else (to put the same thing another way) to push the ship forward out of the loop.

Reepicheep alone had, of course, no more chance of doing this than of lifting up a cathedral, but he had nearly killed himself with trying before others shoved him aside. Very soon the whole ship's company except Lucy and the Mouse (which was fainting) was in two long lines along the two bulwarks, each man's chest to the back of the man in front, so that the weight of the whole line was in the last man, pushing for their lives. For a few sickening seconds (which seemed like hours) nothing appeared to happen. Joints cracked, sweat dropped, breath came in grunts and gasps. Then they felt that the ship was moving. They saw that the snake-loop was further from the mast than it had been. But they also saw that it was smaller. And now the real danger was at hand. Could they get it over the poop, or was it already too tight? Yes. It would just fit. It was resting on the poop rails. A dozen or more sprang up on the poop. This was far better. The Sea Serpent's body was so low now that they could make a line across the poop and push side by side. Hope rose high till everyone remembered the high carved stern, the dragon tail, of the *Dawn Treader*. It would be quite impossible to get the brute over that.

"An axe," cried Caspian hoarsely, "and still shove." Lucy, who knew where everything was, heard him where she was standing on the main deck staring up at the poop. In a few seconds she had been below, got the axe, and was rushing up the ladder to the poop. But just as she reached the top there came a great crashing noise like a tree coming down and the ship rocked and darted forward. For at that very moment, whether because the Sea Serpent was being pushed so hard, or because it foolishly decided to draw the noose tight, the whole of the carved stern broke off and the ship was free.

The others were too exhausted to see what Lucy saw. There, a few yards behind them, the loop of Sea Serpent's body got rapidly smaller and disappeared into a splash. Lucy always said (but of course she was very excited at the moment, and it may have been only imagination) that she saw a look of idiotic satisfaction on the creature's face. What is certain is that it was a very stupid animal, for instead of pursuing the ship it turned its head round and began nosing all along its own body as if it expected to find the wreckage of the *Dawn Treader* there. But the *Dawn Treader* was already well away, running before a fresh breeze, and the men lay and sat panting and groaning all about the deck, till presently they were able to talk about it, and then to laugh about it. And when some rum had been served out they even raised a cheer; and everyone praised the valour of Eustace (though it hadn't done any good) and of Reepicheep.

After this they sailed for three days more and saw nothing but sea and sky. On the fourth day the wind changed to the north and the seas began to rise; by the afternoon it had nearly become a gale. But at the same time they sighted land on their port bow.

"By your leave, Sire," said Drinian, "we will try to get under the lee of that country by rowing and lie in harbour, maybe till this is over." Caspian agreed, but a long row against the gale did not bring them to the land before evening. By the last light of that day they steered into a natural harbour and anchored, but no one went ashore that night. In the morning they found themselves in the green bay of a rugged, lonely-looking country which sloped up to a rocky summit. From the windy north beyond that summit clouds came streaming rapidly. They lowered the boat and loaded her with any of the water casks which were now empty.

"Which stream shall we water at, Drinian?" said Caspian as he took his seat in the stern-sheets of the boat. "There seem to be two coming down into the bay."

"It makes little odds, Sire," said Drinian. "But I think it's a shorter pull to that on the starboard – the eastern one."

"Here comes the rain," said Lucy.

"I should think it does!" said Edmund, for it was already pelting hard. "I say, let's go to the other stream. There are trees there and we'll have some shelter."

"Yes, let's," said Eustace. "No point in getting wetter than we need."

But all the time Drinian was steadily steering to the starboard, like tiresome people in cars who continue at forty miles an hour while you are explaining to them that they are on the wrong road.

"They're right, Drinian," said Caspian. "Why don't you bring her head round and make for the western stream?"

"As your Majesty pleases," said Drinian a little shortly. He had had an anxious day with the weather yesterday, and he didn't like advice from landsmen. But he altered course; and it turned out afterwards that it was a good thing he did.

By the time they had finished watering, the rain was over and Caspian, with Eustace, the Pevensies, and Reepicheep, decided to walk up to the top of the hill and see what could be seen. It was a stiffish climb through coarse grass and heather and they saw neither man nor beast, except sea-gulls. When they reached the top they saw that it was a very small island, not more than twenty acres; and from this height the sea looked larger and more desolate than it did from the deck, or even the fighting top, of the *Dawn Treader*.

"Crazy, you know," said Eustace to Lucy in a low voice,

looking at the eastern horizon. "Sailing on and on into *that* with no idea what we may get to." But he only said it out of habit, not really nastily as he would have done at one time.

It was too cold to stay long on the ridge for the wind still blew freshly from the north.

"Don't let's go back the same way," said Lucy as they turned; "let's go along a bit and come down by the other stream, the one Drinian wanted to go to."

Everyone agreed to this and after about fifteen minutes they were at the source of the second river. It was a more interesting place than they had expected; a deep little mountain lake, surrounded by cliffs except for a narrow channel on the seaward side out of which the water flowed. Here at last they were out of the wind, and all sat down in the heather above the cliff for a rest.

All sat down, but one (it was Edmund) jumped up again very quickly.

"They go in for sharp stones on this island," he said, groping about in the heather. "Where is the wretched thing? . . . Ah, now I've got it . . . Hullo! It wasn't a stone at all, it's a sword-hilt. No, by jove, it's a whole sword; what the rust has left of it. It must have lain here for ages."

"Narnian, too, by the look of it," said Caspian, as they all crowded round.

"I'm sitting on something too," said Lucy. "Something hard." It turned out to be the remains of a mail-shirt. By this time everyone was on hands and knees, feeling in the thick heather in every direction. Their search revealed, one by one, a helmet, a dagger, and a few coins; not Calormen crescents but genuine Narnian "Lions" and "Trees" such as you might see any day in the market-place of Beaversdam or Beruna.

"Looks as if this might be all that's left of one of our seven lords," said Edmund.

"Just what I was thinking," said Caspian. "I wonder which it was. There's nothing on the dagger to show. And I wonder how he died."

"And how we are to avenge him," added Reepicheep.

Edmund, the only one of the party who had read several detective stories, had meanwhile been thinking.

"Look here," he said, "there's something very fishy about this. He can't have been killed in a fight."

"Why not?" asked Caspian.

"No bones," said Edmund. "An enemy might take the armour and leave the body. But who ever heard of a chap who'd won a fight carrying away the body and leaving the armour?"

"Perhaps he was killed by a wild animal," Lucy suggested.

"It'd be a clever animal," said Edmund, "that would take a man's mail shirt off."

"Perhaps a dragon?" said Caspian.

"Nothing doing," said Eustace. "A dragon couldn't do it. I ought to know."

"Well, let's get away from the place, anyway," said Lucy. She had not felt like sitting down again since Edmund had raised the question of bones.

"If you like," said Caspian, getting up. "I don't think any of this stuff is worth taking away."

They came down and round to the little opening where the stream came out of the lake, and stood looking at the deep water within the circle of cliffs. If it had been a hot day, no doubt some would have been tempted to bathe and everyone would have had a drink. Indeed, even as it was, Eustace was on the very point of stooping down and scooping up some water in his hands when Reepicheep and Lucy both at the same moment cried, "Look," so he forgot about his drink and looked.

The bottom of the pool was made of large greyish-blue stones and the water was perfectly clear, and on the bottom lay a life-size figure of a man, made apparently of gold. It lay face downwards with its arms stretched out above its head. And it so happened that as they looked at it, the clouds parted and the sun shone out. The golden shape was lit up from end to end. Lucy thought it was the most beautiful statue she had ever seen.

"Well!" whistled Caspian. "That was worth coming to see! I wonder, can we get it out?"

"We can dive for it, Sire," said Reepicheep.

"No good at all," said Edmund. "At least, if it's really gold – solid gold – it'll be far too heavy to bring up. And that pool's twelve or fifteen feet deep if it's an inch. Half a moment, though. It's a good thing I've brought a hunting spear with me. Let's see what the depth *is* like. Hold on to

my hand, Caspian, while I lean out over the water a bit." Caspian took his hand and Edmund, leaning forward, began to lower his spear into the water.

Before it was half-way in Lucy said, "I don't believe the statue is gold at all. It's only the light. Your spear looks just the same colour."

"What's wrong?" asked several voices at once; for Edmund had suddenly let go of the spear.

"I couldn't hold it," gasped Edmund, "it seemed so *heavy*."

"And there it is on the bottom now," said Caspian, "and Lucy is right. It looks just the same colour as the statue."

But Edmund, who appeared to be having some trouble with his boots – at least he was bending down and looking at them – straightened himself all at once and shouted out in the sharp voice which people hardly ever disobey:

"Get back! Back from the water. All of you. At once!!"

They all did and stared at him.

"Look," said Edmund, "look at the toes of my boots."

"They look a bit yellow," began Eustace.

"They're gold, solid gold," interrupted Edmund. "Look at them. Feel them. The leather's pulled away from it already. And they're as heavy as lead."

"By Aslan!" said Caspian. "You don't mean to say –?"

"Yes, I do," said Edmund. "That water turns things into gold. It turned the spear into gold, that's why it got so heavy. And it was just lapping against my feet (it's a good thing I wasn't barefoot) and it turned the toe-caps into gold. And that poor fellow on the bottom – well, you see."

"So it isn't a statue at all," said Lucy in a low voice.

"No. The whole thing is plain now. He was here on a hot day. He undressed on top of the cliff – where we were sitting. The clothes have rotted away or been taken by birds to line nests with; the armour's still there. Then he dived and –"

"Don't," said Lucy. "What a horrible thing."

"And what a narrow shave *we've* had," said Edmund.

"Narrow indeed," said Reepicheep. "Anyone's finger, anyone's foot, anyone's whisker, or anyone's tail, might have slipped into the water at any moment."

"All the same," said Caspian, "we may as well test it." He stooped down and wrenched up a spray of heather. Then, very cautiously, he knelt beside the pool and dipped it in. It was heather that he dipped; what he drew out was a perfect model of heather made of the purest gold, heavy and soft as lead.

"The King who owned this island," said Caspian slowly, and his face flushed as he spoke, "would soon be the richest of all the Kings of the world. I claim this land for ever as a Narnian possession. It shall be called Goldwater Island. And I bind all of you to secrecy. No one must know of this. Not even Drinian – on pain of death, do you hear?"

"Who are talking to?" said Edmund. "I'm no subject of yours. If anything it's the other way round. I am one of the four ancient sovereigns of Narnia and you are under allegiance to the High King my brother."

"So it has come to that, King Edmund, has it?" said Caspian, laying his hand on his sword-hilt.

"Oh, stop it, both of you," said Lucy. "That's the worst of doing anything with boys. You're all such swaggering, bullying idiots – oooh! –" Her voice died away into a gasp. And everyone else saw what she had seen.

Across the grey hillside above them – grey, for the heather was not yet in bloom – without noise, and without looking at them, and shining as if he were in bright sunlight though the sun had in fact gone in, passed with slow pace the hugest lion that human eyes have ever seen. In describing the scene Lucy said afterwards, "He was the size of an elephant," though at another time she only said, "The size of a cart-horse." But it was not the size that mattered. Nobody dared to ask what it was. They knew it was Aslan.

And nobody ever saw how or where he went. They looked at one another like people waking from sleep.

"What were we talking about?" said Caspian. "Have

I been making rather an ass of myself?"

"Sire," said Reepicheep, "this is a place with a curse on it. Let us get back on board at once. And if I might have the honour of naming this island, I should call it Deathwater."

"That strikes me as a very good name, Reep," said Caspian, "though now that I come to think of it, I don't know why. But the weather seems to be settling and I dare say Drinian would like to be off. What a lot we shall have to tell him."

But in fact they had not much to tell for the memory of the last hour had all become confused.

"Their Majesties all seemed a bit bewitched when they came aboard," said Drinian to Rhince some hours later when the *Dawn Treader* was once more under sail and Deathwater Island already below the horizon. "Something happened to them in that place. The only thing I could get clear was that they think they've found the body of one of these lords we're looking for."

"You don't say so, Captain," answered Rhince. "Well, that's three. Only four more. At this rate we might be home soon after the New Year. And a good thing too. My baccy's running a bit low. Good night, Sir."

CHAPTER NINE

THE ISLAND OF THE VOICES

AND now the winds which had so long been from the north-west began to blow from the west itself and every morning when the sun rose out of the sea the curved prow of the *Dawn Treader* stood up right across the middle of the sun. Some thought that the sun looked larger than it looked from Narnia, but others disagreed. And they sailed and sailed before a gentle yet steady breeze and saw neither fish nor gull nor ship nor shore. And stores began to get low again, and it crept into their hearts that perhaps they might have come to a sea which went on for ever. But when the very last day on which they thought they could risk continuing their eastward voyage dawned, it showed, right ahead between them and the sunrise, a low land lying like a cloud.

They made harbour in a wide bay about the middle of the afternoon and landed. It was a very different country from any they had yet seen. For when they had crossed the sandy beach they found all silent and empty as if it were an uninhabited land, but before them there were level lawns in which the grass was as smooth and short as it used to be in the grounds of a great English house where ten gardeners were kept. The trees, of which there were many, all stood well apart from one another, and there were no broken branches and no leaves lying on the ground. Pigeons sometimes cooed but there was no other noise.

Presently they came to a long, straight, sanded path with not a weed growing on it and trees on either hand. Far off at the other end of this avenue they now caught sight of a house – very long and grey and quiet-looking in the afternoon sun.

Almost as soon as they entered this path Lucy noticed that she had a little stone in her shoe. In that unknown place it might have been wiser for her to ask the others to wait while she took it out. But she didn't; she just dropped quietly behind and sat down to take off her shoe. Her lace had got into a knot.

Before she had undone the knot the others were a fair distance ahead. By the time she had got the stone out and was putting the shoe on again she could no longer hear them. But almost at once she heard something else. It was not coming from the direction of the house.

What she heard was a thumping. It sounded as if dozens of strong workmen were hitting the ground as hard as they could with great wooden mallets. And it was very quickly coming nearer. She was already sitting with her back to a tree, and as the tree was not one she could climb, there was really nothing to do but to sit dead still and press herself against the tree and hope she wouldn't be seen.

Thump, thump, thump . . . and whatever it was must be very close now for she could feel the ground shaking. But she could see nothing. She thought the thing – or things – must be just behind her. But then there came a thump on the path right in front of her. She knew it was on the path not only by the sound but because she saw the sand scatter as if it had been struck a heavy blow. But she could see nothing that had struck it. Then all the thumping noises drew together about twenty feet away from her and

The Voyage of the Dawn Treader

suddenly ceased. Then came the Voice.

It was really very dreadful because she could still see nobody at all. The whole of that park-like country still looked as quiet and empty as it had looked when they first landed. Nevertheless, only a few feet away from her, a voice spoke. And what it said was:

"Mates, now's our chance."

Instantly a whole chorus of other voices replied, "Hear him. Hear him. 'Now's our chance', he said. Well done, Chief. You never said a truer word."

"What I say," continued the first voice, "is, get down to the shore between them and their boat, and let every mother's son look to his weapons. Catch 'em when they try to put to sea."

"Eh, that's the way," shouted all the other voices. "You never made a better plan, Chief. Keep it up, Chief. You couldn't have a better plan than that."

"Lively, then, mates, lively," said the first voice. "Off we go."

"Right again, Chief," said the others. "Couldn't have a better order. Just what we were going to say ourselves. Off we go."

Immediately the thumping began again – very loud at first but soon fainter and fainter, till it died out in the direction of the sea.

Lucy knew there was no time to sit puzzling as to what these invisible creatures might be. As soon as the thumping noise had died away she got up and ran along the path after the others as quickly as her legs would carry her. They must at all costs be warned.

While this had been happening the others had reached the house. It was a low building – only two stories high – made of a beautiful mellow stone, many-windowed, and partially covered with ivy. Everything was so still that

Eustace said, "I think it's empty," but Caspian silently pointed to the column of smoke which rose from one chimney.

They found a wide gateway open and passed through it into a paved courtyard. And it was here that they had their first indication that there was something odd about this island. In the middle of the courtyard stood a pump, and

beneath the pump a bucket. There was nothing odd about that. But the pump handle was moving up and down, though there seemed to be no one moving it.

"There's some magic at work here," said Caspian.

"Machinery!" said Eustace. "I do believe we've come to a civilized country at last."

At that moment Lucy, hot and breathless, rushed into the courtyard behind them. In a low voice she tried to make them understand what she had overheard. And when they had partly understood it even the bravest of them did not look very happy.

"Invisible enemies," muttered Caspian. "And cutting us

off from the boat. This is an ugly furrow to plough."

"You've no idea what *sort* of creatures they are, Lu?" asked Edmund.

"How can I, Ed, when I couldn't see them?"

"Did they sound like humans from their footsteps?"

"I didn't hear any noise of feet — only voices and this frightful thudding and thumping — like a mallet."

"I wonder," said Reepicheep, "do they become visible when you drive a sword into them?"

"It looks as if we shall find out," said Caspian. "But let's get out of this gateway. There's one of these gentry at that pump listening to all we say."

They came out and went back on to the path where the trees might possibly make them less conspicuous. "Not that it's any good *really*," said Eustace, "trying to hide from people you can't see. They may be all round us."

"Now, Drinian," said Caspian. "How would it be if we gave up the boat for lost, went down to another part of the bay, and signalled to the *Dawn Treader* to stand in and take us aboard?"

"Not depth for her, Sire," said Drinian.

"We could swim," said Lucy.

"Your Majesties all," said Reepicheep, "hear me. It is folly to think of avoiding an invisible enemy by any amount of creeping and skulking. If these creatures mean to bring us to battle, be sure they will succeed. And whatever comes of it I'd sooner meet them face to face than be caught by the tail."

"I really think Reep is in the right this time," said Edmund.

"Surely," said Lucy, "if Rhince and the others on the *Dawn Treader* see us fighting on the shore they'll be able to do *something*."

"But they won't see us fighting if they can't see any

enemy," said Eustace miserably. "They'll think we're just swinging our swords in the air for fun."

There was an uncomfortable pause.

"Well," said Caspian at last, "let's get on with it. We must go and face them. Shake hands all round – arrow on the string, Lucy – swords out, everyone else – and now for it. Perhaps they'll parley."

It was strange to see the lawns and the great trees looking so peaceful as they marched back to the beach. And when they arrived there, and saw the boat lying where they had left her, and the smooth sand with no one to be seen on it, more than one doubted whether Lucy had not merely imagined all she had told them. But before they reached the sand, a voice spoke out of the air.

"No further, masters, no further now," it said. "We've got to talk with you first. There's fifty of us and more here with weapons in our fists."

"Hear him, hear him," came the chorus. "That's our Chief. You can depend on what he says. He's telling you the truth, he is."

"I do not see these fifty warriors," observed Reepicheep.

"That's right, that's right," said the Chief Voice. "You don't see us. And why not? Because we're invisible."

"Keep it up, Chief, keep it up," said the Other Voices. "You're talking like a book. They couldn't ask for a better answer than that."

"Be quiet, Reep," said Caspian, and then added in a louder voice, "You invisible people, what do you want with us? And what have we done to earn your enmity?"

"We want something that little girl can do for us," said the Chief Voice. (The others explained that this was just what they would have said themselves.)

"Little girl!" said Reepicheep. "The lady is a queen."

"We don't know about queens," said the Chief Voice.

("No more we do, no more we do," chimed in the others.) "But we want something she can do."

"What is it?" said Lucy.

"And if it is anything against her Majesty's honour or safety," added Reepicheep, "you will wonder to see how many we can kill before we die."

"Well," said the Chief Voice. "It's a long story. Suppose we all sit down?"

The proposal was warmly approved by the other voices but the Narnians remained standing.

"Well," said the Chief Voice. "It's like this. This island has been the property of a great magician time out of mind. And we all are – or perhaps in a manner of speaking, I might say, we were – his servants. Well, to cut a long story short, this magician that I was speaking about, he told us to do something we didn't like. And why not? Because we didn't want to. Well, then, this same magician he fell into a great rage; for I ought to tell you he owned the island and he wasn't used to being crossed. He was terribly downright, you know. But let me see, where am I? Oh yes, this magician then, he goes upstairs (for you must know he kept all his magic things up there and we all lived down below), I say he goes upstairs and puts a spell on us. An uglifying spell. If you saw us now, which in my opinion you may thank your stars you can't, you wouldn't believe what we looked like before we were uglified. You wouldn't really. So there we all were so ugly we couldn't bear to look at one another. So then what did we do? Well, I'll tell you what we did. We waited till we thought this same magician would be asleep in the afternoon and we creep upstairs and go to his magic book, as bold as brass, to see if we can do anything about this uglification. But we were all of a sweat and a tremble, so I won't deceive you. But, believe me or believe me not, I do assure you that we couldn't find anything in the way of a spell for taking off the ugliness. And what with time getting on and being afraid that the old gentleman might wake up any minute – I was all of a muck sweat, so I won't deceive you – well, to cut a long story short, whether we did right or whether we did wrong, in the end we see a spell for making people invisible. And we thought we'd rather be invisible than go on being as ugly as all that. And why? Because we'd like it better. So my little girl, who's just about your little girl's age, and a sweet child she was before she was uglified, though now – but least said soonest mended – I say, my little girl she says the spell, for it's got to be a little girl or else the magician himself, if you see my meaning, for otherwise it won't work. And why not? Because nothing happens. So my Clipsie says the spell, for I ought to have told you she reads beautifully, and there we all were as invisible as you could wish to see. And I do assure you it was a relief not to see one another's faces. At first, anyway. But the long and the short of it is we're mortal tired of being invisible. And there's another thing. We never reckoned on this magician (the one I was telling you about before) going invisible too. But we haven't ever seen him since. So we don't know if he's dead, or gone away, or whether he's just sitting upstairs being invisible, and perhaps coming down and being invisible there. And, believe me, it's no manner of use listening because he always did go about with his bare feet on, making no more noise than a great big cat. And I'll tell all you gentlemen straight, it's getting more than what our nerves can stand."

Such was the Chief Voice's story, but very much shortened, because I have left out what the Other Voices said. Actually he never got out more than six or seven words without being interrupted by their agreements and encouragements, which drove the Narnians nearly out of their minds with impatience. When it was over there was a very long silence.

"But," said Lucy at last, "what's all this got to do with us? I don't understand."

"Why, bless me, if I haven't gone and left out the whole point," said the Chief Voice.

"That you have, that you have," roared the Other Voices with great enthusiasm. "No one couldn't have left it out cleaner and better. Keep it up, Chief, keep it up."

"Well, I needn't go over the whole story again," began the Chief Voice.

"No. Certainly not," said Caspian and Edmund.

"Well, then, to put it in a nutshell," said the Chief Voice, "we've been waiting for ever so long for a nice little girl from foreign parts, like it might be you, Missie – that would go upstairs and go to the magic book and find the spell that takes off the invisibleness, and say it. And we all swore that the first strangers as landed on this island (having a nice little girl with them, I mean, for if they hadn't it'd be another matter) we wouldn't let them go away alive unless they'd done the needful for us. And that's why, gentlemen, if your little girl doesn't come up to scratch, it will be our painful duty to cut all your throats. Merely in the way of business, as you might say, and no offence, I hope."

"I don't see all your weapons," said Reepicheep. "Are they invisible too?" The words were scarcely out of his mouth before they heard a whizzing sound and next moment a spear had stuck, quivering, in one of the trees behind them.

"That's a spear, that is," said the Chief Voice.

"That it is, Chief, that it is," said the others. "You couldn't have put it better."

"And it came from my hand," the Chief Voice continued. "They get visible when they leave us."

"But why do you want *me* to do this?" asked Lucy.

"Why can't one of your own people? Haven't you got any girls?"

"We dursen't, we dursen't," said all the Voices. "We're not going upstairs again."

"In other words," said Caspian, "you are asking this lady to face some danger which you daren't ask your own sisters and daughters to face!"

"That's right, that's right," said all the Voices cheerfully. "You couldn't have said it better. Eh, you've had some education, you have. Anyone can see that."

"Well, of all the outrageous – " began Edmund, but Lucy interrupted.

"Would I have to go upstairs at night, or would it do in daylight?"

"Oh, daylight, daylight, to be sure," said the Chief Voice. "Not at night. No one's asking you to do that. Go upstairs in the dark? Ugh."

"All right, then, I'll do it," said Lucy. "No," she said, turning to the others, "don't try to stop me. Can't you see it's no use? There are dozens of them there. We can't fight them. And the other way there *is* a chance."

"But a magician!" said Caspian.

"I know," said Lucy. "But he mayn't be as bad as they make out. Don't you get the idea that these people are not very brave?"

"They're certainly not very clever," said Eustace.

"Look here, Lu," said Edmund. "We really can't let you do a thing like this. Ask Reep, I'm sure he'll say just the same."

"But it's to save my own life as well as yours," said Lucy. "I don't want to be cut to bits with invisible swords any more than anyone else."

"Her Majesty is in the right," said Reepicheep. "If we had any assurance of saving *her* by battle, our duty would

be very plain. It appears to me that we have none. And the
service they ask of her is in no way contrary to her
Majesty's honour, but a noble and heroical act. If the
Queen's heart moves her to risk the magician, I will not
speak against it."

As no one had ever known Reepicheep to be afraid of
anything, he could say this without feeling at all awkward.
But the boys, who had all been afraid quite often, grew
very red. None the less, it was such obvious sense that they
had to give in. Loud cheers broke from the invisible people
when their decision was announced, and the Chief Voice
(warmly supported by all the others) invited the Narnians
to come to supper and spend the night. Eustace didn't want
to accept, but Lucy said, "I'm sure they're not treacherous.
They're not like that at all," and the others agreed. And so,
accompanied by an enormous noise of thumpings (which
became louder when they reached the flagged and echoing
courtyard) they all went back to the house.

CHAPTER TEN

THE MAGICIAN'S BOOK

THE invisible people feasted their guests royally. It was
very funny to see the plates and dishes coming to the table
and not to see anyone carrying them. It would have been
funny even if they had moved along level with the floor, as
you would expect things to do in invisible hands. But they
didn't. They progressed up the long dining-hall in a series
of bounds or jumps. At the highest point of each jump a
dish would be about fifteen feet up in the air; then it would
come down and stop quite suddenly about three feet from

the floor. When the dish contained anything like soup or stew the result was rather disastrous.

"I'm beginning to feel very inquisitive about these people," whispered Eustace to Edmund. "Do you think they're human at all? More like huge grasshoppers or giant frogs, I should say."

"It does look like it," said Edmund. "But don't put the idea of the grasshoppers into Lucy's head. She's not too keen on insects; especially big ones."

The meal would have been pleasanter if it had not been so exceedingly messy, and also if the conversation had not consisted entirely of agreements. The invisible people agreed about everything. Indeed most of their remarks were the sort it would not be easy to disagree with: "What I always say is, when a chap's hungry, he likes some victuals," or "Getting dark now; always does at night," or even "Ah, you've come over the water. Powerful wet stuff, ain't it?" And Lucy could not help looking at the dark yawning entrance to the foot of the staircase – she could see it from where she sat – and wondering what she would find when she went up those stairs next morning. But it was a good meal otherwise, with mushroom soup and boiled chickens and hot boiled ham and gooseberries, redcurrants, curds, cream, milk, and mead. The others liked the mead but Eustace was sorry afterwards that he had drunk any.

When Lucy woke up next morning it was like waking up on the day of an examination or a day when you are going to the dentist. It was a lovely morning with bees buzzing in and out of her open window and the lawn outside looking very like somewhere in England. She got up and dressed and tried to talk and eat ordinarily at breakfast. Then, after being instructed by the Chief Voice about what she was to do upstairs, she bid goodbye to the others, said nothing, walked to the bottom of the stairs, and began going up them without once looking back.

It was quite light, that was one good thing. There was, indeed, a window straight ahead of her at the top of the first flight. As long as she was on that flight she could hear the *tick-tock-tick-tock* of a grandfather clock in the hall below. Then she came to the landing and had to turn to her left up the next flight; after that she couldn't hear the clock any more.

Now she had come to the top of the stairs. Lucy looked and saw a long, wide passage with a large window at the far end. Apparently the passage ran the whole length of the house. It was carved and panelled and carpeted and very many doors opened off it on each side. She stood still and couldn't hear the squeak of a mouse, or the buzzing of a fly, or the swaying of a curtain, or anything – except the beating of her own heart.

"The last doorway on the left," she said to herself. It did seem a bit hard that it should be the last. To reach it she would have to walk past room after room. And in any room there might be the magician – asleep, or awake, or invisible, or even dead. But it wouldn't do to think about that. She set out on her journey. The carpet was so thick that her feet made no noise.

"There's nothing whatever to be afraid of yet," Lucy told herself. And certainly it was a quiet, sunlit passage; perhaps a bit too quiet. It would have been nicer if there had not been strange signs painted in scarlet on the doors – twisty, complicated things which obviously had a meaning and it mightn't be a very nice meaning either. It would have been nicer still if there weren't those masks hanging on the wall. Not that they were exactly ugly – or not so very ugly – but the empty eye-holes did look queer, and if you let yourself you would soon start imagining that the masks were

doing things as soon as your back was turned to them.

After about the sixth door she got her first real fright. For one second she felt almost certain that a wicked little bearded face had popped out of the wall and made a grimace at her. She forced herself to stop and look at it. And it was not a face at all. It was a little mirror just the size and shape of her own face, with hair on the top of it and a beard hanging down from it, so that when you looked in the mirror your own face fitted into the hair and beard and it looked as if they belonged to you. "I just caught my own reflection with the tail of my eye as I went past," said Lucy to herself. "That was all it was. It's quite harmless." But she didn't like the look of her own face with that hair and beard, and went on. (I don't know what the Bearded Glass was for because I am not a magician.)

Before she reached the last door on the left, Lucy was beginning to wonder whether the corridor had grown longer since she began her journey and whether this was part of the magic of the house. But she got to it at last. And the door was open.

It was a large room with three big windows and it was lined from floor to ceiling with books; more books than Lucy had ever seen before, tiny little books, fat and dumpy books, and books bigger than any church Bible you have ever seen, all bound in leather and smelling old and learned and magical. But she knew from her instructions that she need not bother about any of these. For *the* Book, the Magic Book, was lying on a reading-desk in the very middle of the room. She saw she would have to read it standing (and anyway there were no chairs) and also that she would have to stand with her back to the door while she read it. So at once she turned to shut the door.

It wouldn't shut.

Some people may disagree with Lucy about this, but I

think she was quite right. She said she wouldn't have minded if she could have shut the door, but that it was unpleasant to have to stand in a place like that with an open doorway right behind your back. I should have felt just the same. But there was nothing else to be done.

One thing that worried her a good deal was the size of the Book. The Chief Voice had not been able to give her any idea whereabouts in the Book the spell for making things visible came. He even seemed rather surprised at her asking. He expected her to begin at the beginning and go on till she came to it; obviously he had never thought that there was any other way of finding a place in a book. "But it might take me days and weeks!" said Lucy, looking at the huge volume, "and I feel already as if I'd been in this place for hours."

She went up to the desk and laid her hand on the book; her fingers tingled when she touched it as if it were full of electricity. She tried to open it but couldn't at first; this, however, was only because it was fastened by two leaden clasps, and when she had undone these it opened easily enough. And what a book it was!

It was written, not printed; written in a clear, even hand, with thick downstrokes and thin upstrokes, very large, easier than print, and so beautiful that Lucy stared at it for a whole minute and forgot about reading it. The paper was crisp and smooth and a nice smell came from it; and in the margins, and round the big coloured capital letters at the beginning of each spell, there were pictures.

There was no title page or title; the spells began straight away, and at first there was nothing very important in them. They were cures for warts (by washing your hands in moonlight in a silver basin) and toothache and cramp, and a spell for taking a swarm of bees. The picture of the man with toothache was so lifelike that it would have set your

Cure for warts: wash in a silver basin by moonlight.

own teeth aching if you looked at it too long, and the golden bees which were dotted all round the fourth spell looked for a moment as if they were really flying.

Lucy could hardly tear herself away from that first page, but when she turned over, the next was just as interesting. "But I must get on," she told herself. And on she went for about thirty pages which, if she could have remembered them, would have taught her how to find buried treasure, how to remember things forgotten, how to forget things you wanted to forget, how to tell whether anyone was speaking the truth, how to call up (or prevent) wind, fog, snow, sleet or rain, how to produce enchanted sleeps and how to give a man an ass's head (as they did to poor Bottom). And the longer she read the more wonderful and more real the pictures became.

Then she came to a page which was such a blaze of pictures that one hardly noticed the writing. Hardly – but she *did* notice the first words. They were, *An infallible spell to make beautiful her that uttereth it beyond the lot of mortals*. Lucy peered at the pictures with her face close to the page, and though they had seemed crowded and muddlesome before, she found she could now see them quite clearly. The first was a picture of a girl standing at a reading-desk reading in a huge book. And the girl was dressed exactly like Lucy. In the next picture Lucy (for the girl in the picture was Lucy herself) was standing up with her mouth open and a rather terrible expression on her face, chanting or reciting something. In the third picture the beauty beyond the lot of mortals had come to her. It was strange, considering how small the pictures had looked at first, that the Lucy in the picture now seemed quite as big as the real Lucy; and they looked into each other's eyes and the real Lucy looked away after a few minutes because she was dazzled by the beauty of the other Lucy; though she could still see a sort of likeness to herself in that beautiful face. And now the pictures came crowding on her thick and fast. She saw herself throned on high at a great tournament in Calormen and all the Kings of the world fought because of her beauty. After that it turned from tournaments to real wars, and all Narnia and Archenland, Telmar and Calormen, Galma and Terebinthia, were laid waste with the fury of the kings and dukes and great lords who fought for her favour. Then it changed and Lucy, still beautiful beyond the lot of mortals, was back in England. And Susan (who had always been the beauty of the family) came home from America. The Susan in the picture looked exactly like the real Susan only plainer and with a nasty expression. And Susan was jealous of the dazzling beauty of Lucy, but that didn't matter a bit because no one cared anything about Susan now.

"I *will* say the spell," said Lucy. "I don't care. I will."

She said *I don't care* because she had a strong feeling that she mustn't.

But when she looked back at the opening words of the spell, there in the middle of the writing, where she felt quite sure there had been no picture before, she found the great face of a lion, of The Lion, Aslan himself, staring into hers. It was painted such a bright gold that it seemed to be coming towards her out of the page; and indeed she never was quite sure afterwards that it hadn't really moved a little. At any rate she knew the expression on his face quite well. He was growling and you could see most of his teeth. She became horribly afraid and turned over the page at once.

A little later she came to a spell which would let you know what your friends thought about you. Now Lucy had wanted very badly to try the other spell, the one that made you beautiful beyond the lot of mortals. So she felt that to make up for not having said it, she really would say this one. And all in a hurry, for fear her mind would change, she said the words (nothing will induce me to tell you what they were). Then she waited for something to happen.

As nothing happened she began looking at the pictures. And all at once she saw the very last thing she expected – a picture of a third-class carriage in a train, with two schoolgirls sitting in it. She knew them at once. They were Marjorie Preston and Anne Featherstone. Only now it was much more than a picture. It was alive. She could see the telegraph posts flicking past outside the window. Then gradually (like when the radio is "coming on") she could hear what they were saying.

"Shall I see anything of you this term?" said Anne, "or are you still going to be all taken up with Lucy Pevensie."

"Don't know what you mean by *taken up*," said Marjorie.

"Oh yes, you do," said Anne. "You were crazy about her last term."

"No, I wasn't," said Marjorie. "I've got more sense than that. Not a bad little kid in her way. But I was getting pretty tired of her before the end of term."

"Well, you jolly well won't have the chance any other term!" shouted Lucy. "Two-faced little beast." But the sound of her own voice at once reminded her that she was talking to a picture and that the real Marjorie was far away in another world.

"Well," said Lucy to herself, "I did think better of her than that. And I did all sorts of things for her last term, and I stuck to her when not many other girls would. And she knows it too. And to Anne Featherstone of all people! I wonder are all my friends the same? There are lots of other pictures. No. I won't look at any more. I won't, I won't' — and with a great effort she turned over the page, but not before a large, angry tear had splashed on it.

On the next page she came to a spell "for the refreshment of the spirit'. The pictures were fewer here but very beautiful. And what Lucy found herself reading was more like a story than a spell. It went on for three pages and before she had read to the bottom of the page she had forgotten that she was reading at all. She was living in the story as if it were real, and all the pictures were real too. When she had got to the third page and come to the end, she said, "That is the loveliest story I've ever read or ever shall read in my whole life. Oh, I wish I could have gone on reading it for ten years. At least I'll read it over again."

But here part of the magic of the Book came into play. You couldn't turn back. The right-hand pages, the ones ahead, could be turned; the left-hand pages could not.

"Oh, what a shame!" said Lucy. "I did so want to read it again. Well, at least I must remember it. Let's see . . . it was about . . . about . . . oh dear, it's all fading away again. And even this last page is going blank. This is a very queer book. How can I have forgotten? It was about a cup and a sword and a tree and a green hill, I know that much. But I can't remember and what *shall* I do?"

And she never could remember; and ever since that day what Lucy means by a good story is a story which reminds her of the forgotten story in the Magician's Book.

She turned on and found to her surprise a page with no pictures at all; but the first words were *A Spell to make hidden things visible*. She read it through to make sure of all the hard words and then said it out loud. And she knew at once that it was working because as she spoke the colours came into the capital letters at the top of the page and the pictures began appearing in the margins. It was like when you hold to the fire something written in Invisible Ink and the writing gradually shows up; only instead of the dingy colour of lemon juice (which is the easiest Invisible Ink) this was all gold and blue and scarlet. They were odd pictures and contained many figures that Lucy did not much like the look of. And then she thought, "I suppose I've made everything visible, and not only the Thumpers. There might be lots of other invisible things hanging about a place like this. I'm not sure that I want to see them all."

At that moment she heard soft, heavy footfalls coming along the corridor behind her; and of course she remembered what she had been told about the Magician walking in his bare feet and making no more noise than a cat. It is always better to turn round than to have anything creeping up behind your back. Lucy did so.

Then her face lit up till, for a moment (but of course she didn't know it), she looked almost as beautiful as that other Lucy in the picture, and she ran forward with a little cry of delight and with her arms stretched out. For what stood in the doorway was Aslan himself, The Lion, the highest of all High Kings. And he was solid and real and warm and he let her kiss him and bury herself in his shining mane. And from the low, earthquake-like sound that came from inside him, Lucy even dared to think that he was purring.

"Oh, Aslan," said she, "it was kind of you to come."

"I have been here all the time," said he, "but you have just made me visible."

"Aslan!" said Lucy almost a little reproachfully. "Don't make fun of me. As if anything *I* could do would make *you* visible!"

"It did," said Aslan. "Do you think I wouldn't obey my own rules?"

After a little pause he spoke again.

"Child," he said, "I think you have been eaves-dropping."

"Eavesdropping?"

"You listened to what your two schoolfellows were saying about you."

"Oh that? I never thought that was eavesdropping, Aslan. Wasn't it magic?"

"Spying on people by magic is the same as spying on them in any other way. And you have misjudged your friend. She is weak, but she loves you. She was afraid of the older girl and said what she does not mean."

"I don't think I'd ever be able to forget what I heard her say."

"No, you won't."

"Oh dear," said Lucy. "Have I spoiled everything? Do you mean we would have gone on being friends if it hadn't been for this – and been really great friends – all our lives perhaps – and now we never shall."

"Child," said Aslan, "did I not explain to you once

before that no one is ever told what *would have happened*?"

"Yes, Aslan, you did," said Lucy. "I'm sorry. But please —"

"Speak on, dear heart."

"Shall I ever be able to read that story again; the one I couldn't remember? Will you tell it to me, Aslan? Oh do, do, do."

"Indeed, yes, I will tell it to you for years and years. But now, come. We must meet the master of this house."

CHAPTER ELEVEN

THE DUFFLEPUDS MADE HAPPY

LUCY followed the great Lion out into the passage and at once she saw coming towards them an old man, barefoot, dressed in a red robe. His white hair was crowned with a chaplet of oak leaves, his beard fell to his girdle, and he supported himself with a curiously carved staff. When he saw Aslan he bowed low and said,

"Welcome, Sir, to the least of your houses."

"Do you grow weary, Coriakin, of ruling such foolish subjects as I have given you here?"

"No," said the Magician, "they are very stupid but there is no real harm in them. I begin to grow rather fond of the creatures. Sometimes, perhaps, I am a little impatient, waiting for the day when they can be governed by wisdom instead of this rough magic."

"All in good time, Coriakin," said Aslan.

"Yes, all in very good time, Sir," was the answer. "Do you intend to show yourself to them?"

"Nay," said the Lion, with a little half-growl that meant (Lucy thought) the same as a laugh. "I should frighten them out of their senses. Many stars will grow old and come to take their rest in islands before your people are ripe for that. And today before sunset I must visit Trumpkin the Dwarf where he sits in the castle of Cair Paravel counting the days till his master Caspian comes home. I will tell him all your story, Lucy. Do not look so sad. We shall meet soon again."

"Please, Aslan," said Lucy, "what do you call *soon?*"

"I call all times soon," said Aslan; and instantly he was vanished away and Lucy was alone with the Magician.

"Gone!" said he, "and you and I quite crestfallen. It's always like that, you can't keep him; it's not as if he were a *tame* lion. And how did you enjoy my book?"

"Parts of it very much indeed," said Lucy. "Did you know I was there all the time?"

"Well, of course I knew when I let the Duffers make themselves invisible that you would be coming along presently to take the spell off. I wasn't quite sure of the exact day. And I wasn't especially on the watch this morning. You see they had made me invisible too and being invisible always makes me so sleepy. Heigh-ho – there I'm yawning again. Are you hungry?"

"Well, perhaps I am a little," said Lucy. "I've no idea what the time is."

"Come," said the Magician. "All times may be soon to Aslan; but in my home all hungry times are one o'clock."

He led her a little way down the passage and opened a door. Passing in, Lucy found herself in a pleasant room full of sunlight and flowers. The table was bare when they entered, but it was of course a magic table, and at a word from the old man the tablecloth, silver, plates, glasses and food appeared.

"I hope that is what you would like," said he. "I have tried to give you food more like the food of your own land than perhaps you have had lately."

"It's lovely," said Lucy, and so it was; an omelette, piping hot, cold lamb and green peas, a strawberry ice, lemon-squash to drink with the meal and a cup of chocolate to follow. But the magician himself drank only wine and ate only bread. There was nothing alarming about him, and Lucy and he were soon chatting away like old friends.

"When will the spell work?" asked Lucy. "Will the Duffers be visible again at once?"

"Oh yes, they're visible now. But they're probably all asleep still; they always take a rest in the middle of the day."

"And now that they're visible, are you going to let them off being ugly? Will you make them as they were before?"

"Well, that's rather a delicate question," said the Magician. "You see, it's only *they* who think they were so nice to look at before. They say they've been uglified, but that isn't what I called it. Many people might say the change was for the better."

"Are they awfully conceited?"

"They are. Or at least the Chief Duffer is, and he's taught all the rest to be. They always believe every word he says."

"We'd noticed that," said Lucy.

"Yes – we'd get on better without him, in a way. Of course I could turn him into something else, or even put a spell on him which would make them not believe a word he said. But I don't like to do that. It's better for them to admire him than to admire nobody."

"Don't they admire *you*?" asked Lucy.

"Oh, not *me*," said the Magician. "They wouldn't admire *me*."

"What was it you uglified them for – I mean, what they call *uglified*?"

"Well, they wouldn't do what they were told. Their work is to mind the garden and raise food – not for me, as they imagine, but for themselves. They wouldn't do it at all if I didn't make them. And of course for a garden you want water. There is a beautiful spring about half a mile away up the hill. And from that spring there flows a stream which comes right past the garden. All I asked them to do was to take their water from the stream instead of trudging up to the spring with their buckets two or three times a day and tiring themselves out besides spilling half of it on the way back. But they wouldn't see it. In the end they refused point blank."

"Are they as stupid as all that?" asked Lucy.

The Magician sighed. "You wouldn't believe the troubles I've had with them. A few months ago they were all for washing up the plates and knives before dinner: they said it saved time afterwards. I've caught them planting boiled potatoes to save cooking them when they were dug up. One day the cat got into the dairy and twenty of them were at work moving all the milk out; no one thought of moving the cat. But I see you've finished. Let's go and look at the Duffers now they can be looked at."

They went into another room which was full of polished instruments hard to understand – such as Astrolabes, Orreries, Chronoscopes, Poesimeters, Choriambuses and Theodolinds – and here, when they had come to the window, the Magician said, "There. There are your Duffers."

"I don't see anybody," said Lucy. "And what are those mushroom things?"

The things she pointed at were dotted all over the level grass. They were certainly very like mushrooms, but far too big – the stalks about three feet high and the umbrellas about the same length from edge to edge. When she looked carefully she noticed too that the stalks joined the umbrellas not in the middle but at one side which gave an unbalanced look to them. And there was something – a sort of little bundle – lying on the grass at the foot of each stalk. In fact the longer she gazed at them the less like mushrooms they appeared. The umbrella part was not

really round as she had thought at first. It was longer than it was broad, and it widened at one end. There were a great many of them, fifty or more.

The clock struck three.

Instantly a most extraordinary thing happened. Each of the "mushrooms" suddenly turned upside-down. The little bundles which had lain at the bottom of the stalks were heads and bodies. The stalks themselves were legs. But not two legs to each body. Each body had a single thick leg right under it (not to one side like the leg of a one-legged man) and at the end of it, a single enormous foot – a broad-toed foot with the toes curling up a little so that it looked rather like a small canoe. She saw in a moment why they had looked like mushrooms. They had been lying flat on their backs each with its single leg straight up in the air and

its enormous foot spread out above it. She learned afterwards that this was their ordinary way of resting; for the
foot kept off both rain and sun and for a Monopod to lie
under its own foot is almost as good as being in a tent.

"Oh, the funnies, the funnies," cried Lucy, bursting into
laughter. "Did *you* make them like that?"

"Yes, yes. I made the Duffers into Monopods," said the

Magician. He too was laughing till the tears ran down his
cheeks. "But watch," he added.

It was worth watching. Of course these little one-footed
men couldn't walk or run as we do. They got about by
jumping, like fleas or frogs. And what jumps they made! –
as if each big foot were a mass of springs. And with what a
bounce they came down; that was what made the thumping noise which had so puzzled Lucy yesterday. For now
they were jumping in all directions and calling out to one
another, "Hey, lads! We're visible again."

"Visible we are," said one in a tasselled red cap who was

obviously the Chief Monopod. "And what I say is, when chaps are visible, why, they can see one another."

"Ah, there it is, there it is, Chief," cried all the others. "There's the point. No one's got a clearer head than you. You couldn't have made it plainer."

"She caught the old man napping, that little girl did," said the Chief Monopod. "We've beaten him this time."

"Just what we were going to say ourselves," chimed the chorus. "You're going stronger than ever today, Chief. Keep it up, keep it up."

"But do they dare to talk about you like that?" said Lucy. "They seemed to be so afraid of you yesterday. Don't they know you might be listening?"

"That's one of the funny things about the Duffers," said the Magician. "One minute they talk as if I ran everything and overheard everything and was extremely dangerous. The next moment they think they can take me in by tricks that a baby would see through – bless them!"

"Will they have to be turned back into their proper shapes?" asked Lucy. "Oh, I do hope it wouldn't be unkind to leave them as they are. Do they really mind very much? They seem pretty happy. I say – look at that jump. What were they like before?"

"Common little dwarfs," said he. "Nothing like so nice as the sort you have in Narnia."

"It *would* be a pity to change them back," said Lucy. "They're so funny: and they're rather nice. Do you think it would make any difference if I told them that?"

"I'm sure it would – if you could get it into their heads."

"Will you come with me and try?"

"No, no. You'll get on far better without me."

"Thanks awfully for the lunch," said Lucy and turned quickly away. She ran down the stairs which she had come up so nervously that morning and cannoned into Edmund at the bottom. All the others were there with him waiting, and Lucy's conscience smote her when she saw their anxious faces and realized how long she had forgotten them.

"It's all right," she shouted. "Everything's all right. The Magician's a brick – and I've seen *Him* – Aslan."

After that she went from them like the wind and out into the garden. Here the earth was shaking with the jumps and the air ringing with the shouts of the Monopods. Both were redoubled when they caught sight of her.

"Here she comes, here she comes," they cried. "Three cheers for the little girl. Ah! She put it across the old gentleman properly, she did."

"And we're extremely regrettable," said the Chief Monopod, "that we can't give you the pleasure of seeing us as we were before we were uglified, for you wouldn't believe the difference, and that's the truth, for there's no denying we're mortal ugly now, so we won't deceive you."

"Eh, that we are, Chief, that we are," echoed the others, bouncing like so many toy balloons. "You've said it, you've said it."

"But I don't think you are at all," said Lucy, shouting to make herself heard. "I think you look very nice."

"Hear her, hear her," said the Monopods. "True for you, Missie. Very nice we look. You couldn't find a handsomer lot." They said this without any surprise and did not seem to notice that they had changed their minds.

"She's a-saying," remarked the Chief Monopod, "as how we looked very nice before we were uglified."

"True for you, Chief, true for you," chanted the others. "That's what she says. We heard her ourselves."

"I did *not*," bawled Lucy. "I said you're very nice *now*."

"So she did, so she did," said the Chief Monopod, "said we were very nice then."

"Hear 'em both, hear 'em both," said the Monopods. "There's a pair for you. Always right. They couldn't have put it better."

"But we're saying just the opposite," said Lucy, stamping her foot with impatience.

"So you are, to be sure, so you are," said the Monopods. "Nothing like an opposite. Keep it up, both of you."

"You're enough to drive anyone mad," said Lucy, and gave it up. But the Monopods seemed perfectly contented, and she decided that on the whole the conversation had been a success.

And before everyone went to bed that evening something else happened which made them even more satisfied with their one-legged condition. Caspian and all the Narnians went back as soon as possible to the shore to give their news to Rhince and the others on board the *Dawn Treader*, who were by now very anxious. And, of course, the Monopods went with them, bouncing like footballs and agreeing with one another in loud voices till Eustace said, "I wish the Magician would make them inaudible instead of invisible." (He was soon sorry he had spoken because then he had to explain that an inaudible thing is something you can't hear, and though he took a lot of trouble he never felt sure that the Monopods had really understood, and what especially annoyed him was that they said in the end, "Eh, he can't put things the way our Chief does. But you'll learn, young man. Hark to *him*. He'll show you how to say things. There's a speaker for you!") When they reached the bay, Reepicheep had a brilliant idea. He had his little coracle lowered and paddled himself about in it till the Monopods were thoroughly interested. He then stood up in it and said, "Worthy and intelligent Monopods, you do not need boats. Each of you has a foot that will do instead. Just jump as lightly as you can on the water and see what happens."

The Chief Monopod hung back and warned the others that they'd find the water powerful wet, but one or two of the younger ones tried it almost at once; and then a few others followed their example, and at last the whole lot did the same. It worked perfectly. The huge single foot of a Monopod acted as a natural raft or boat, and when Reepicheep had taught them how to cut rude paddles for themselves, they all paddled about the bay and round the *Dawn Treader*, looking for all the world like a fleet of little canoes with a fat dwarf standing up in the extreme stern of each. And they had races, and bottles of wine were lowered down to them from the ship as prizes, and the sailors stood leaning over the ship's sides and laughed till their own sides ached.

The Duffers were also very pleased with their new name of Monopods, which seemed to them a magnificent name though they never got it right. "That's what we are," they bellowed, "Moneypuds, Pomonods, Poddymons. Just what it was on the tips of our tongues to call ourselves." But they soon got it mixed up with their old name of Duffers and finally settled down to calling themselves the Dufflepuds; and that is what they will probably be called for centuries.

That evening all the Narnians dined upstairs with the Magician, and Lucy noticed how different the whole top floor looked now that she was no longer afraid of it. The mysterious signs on the doors were still mysterious but now looked as if they had kind and cheerful meanings, and even the bearded mirror now seemed funny rather than frightening. At dinner everyone had by magic what everyone liked best to eat and drink, and after dinner the Magician did a very useful and beautiful piece of magic. He

laid two blank sheets of parchment on the table and asked
Drinian to give him an exact account of their voyage up to
date: and as Drinian spoke, everything he described came
out on the parchment in fine clear lines till at last each
sheet was a splendid map of the Eastern Ocean, showing
Galma, Terebinthia, the Seven Isles, the Lone Islands,
Dragon Island, Burnt Island, Deathwater, and the land of
the Duffers itself, all exactly the right sizes and in the right
positions. They were the first maps ever made of those seas
and better than any that have been made since without
magic. For on these, though the towns and mountains
looked at first just as they would on an ordinary map,
when the Magician lent them a magnifying glass you saw
that they were perfect little pictures of the real things, so
that you could see the very castle and slave market and
streets in Narrowhaven, all very clear though very distant,
like things seen through the wrong end of a telescope. The
only drawback was that the coastline of most of the islands
was incomplete, for the map showed only what Drinian
had seen with his own eyes. When they were finished the
Magician kept one himself and presented the other to
Caspian: it still hangs in his Chamber of Instruments at
Cair Paravel. But the Magician could tell them nothing
about seas or lands further east. He did, however, tell them
that about seven years before a Narnian ship had put in at
his waters and that she had on board the lords Revilian,
Argoz, Mavramorn and Rhoop: so they judged that the
golden man they had seen lying in Deathwater must be the
Lord Restimar.

Next day, the Magician magically mended the stern of
the *Dawn Treader* where it had been damaged by the Sea
Serpent and loaded her with useful gifts. There was a most
friendly parting, and when she sailed, two hours after
noon, all the Dufflepuds paddled out with her to the

harbour mouth, and cheered until she was out of sound of
their cheering.

CHAPTER TWELVE

THE DARK ISLAND

AFTER this adventure they sailed on south and a little
east for twelve days with a gentle wind, the skies being
mostly clear and the air warm, and saw no bird or fish,
except that once there were whales spouting a long way to
starboard. Lucy and Reepicheep played a good deal of
chess at this time. Then on the thirteenth day, Edmund,
from the fighting top, sighted what looked like a great dark
mountain rising out of the sea on their port bow.

They altered course and made for this land, mostly by
oar, for the wind would not serve them to sail north-east.
When evening fell they were still a long way from it and
rowed all night. Next morning the weather was fair but a
flat calm. The dark mass lay ahead, much nearer and
larger, but still very dim, so that some thought it was still a
long way off and others thought they were running into a
mist.

About nine that morning, very suddenly, it was so close
that they could see that it was not land at all, nor even, in
an ordinary sense, a mist. It was a Darkness. It is rather
hard to describe, but you will see what it was like if you
imagine yourself looking into the mouth of a railway
tunnel – a tunnel either so long or so twisty that you
cannot see the light at the far end. And you know what it
would be like. For a few feet you would see the rails and
sleepers and gravel in broad daylight; then there would

come a place where they were in twilight; and then, pretty
suddenly, but of course without a sharp dividing line, they
would vanish altogether into smooth, solid blackness. It
was just so here. For a few feet in front of their bows they

could see the swell of the bright greenish-blue water. Beyond that, they could see the water looking pale and grey as it would look late in the evening. But beyond that again, utter blackness as if they had come to the edge of moonless and starless night.

Caspian shouted to the boatswain to keep her back, and all except the rowers rushed forward and gazed from the bows. But there was nothing to be seen by gazing. Behind them was the sea and the sun, before them the Darkness.

"Do we go into this?" asked Caspian at length.

"Not by my advice," said Drinian.

"The Captain's right," said several sailors.

"I almost think he is," said Edmund.

Lucy and Eustace didn't speak but they felt very glad inside at the turn things seemed to be taking. But all at once the clear voice of Reepicheep broke in upon the silence.

"And why not?" he said. "Will someone explain to me why not."

No one was anxious to explain, so Reepicheep continued:

"If I were addressing peasants or slaves," he said, "I might suppose that this suggestion proceeded from cowardice. But I hope it will never be told in Narnia that a company of noble and royal persons in the flower of their age turned tail because they were afraid of the dark."

"But what manner of use would it be ploughing through that blackness?" asked Drinian.

"Use?" replied Reepicheep. "Use, Captain? If by use you mean filling our bellies or our purses, I confess it will be no use at all. So far as I know we did not set sail to look for things useful but to seek honour and adventure. And here is as great an adventure as ever I heard of, and here, if we turn back, no little impeachment of all our honours."

Several of the sailors said things under their breath

that sounded like "Honour be blowed", but Caspian said:

"Oh, *bother* you, Reepicheep. I almost wish we'd left you at home. All right! If you put it that way, I suppose we shall have to go on. Unless Lucy would rather not?"

Lucy felt that she would very much rather not, but what she said out loud was, "I'm game."

"Your Majesty will at least order lights?" said Drinian.

"By all means," said Caspian. "See to it, Captain."

So the three lanterns, at the stern, and the prow and the masthead, were all lit, and Drinian ordered two torches amidships. Pale and feeble they looked in the sunshine. Then all the men except some who were left below at the oars were ordered on deck and fully armed and posted in their battle stations with swords drawn. Lucy and two archers were posted on the fighting top with bows bent and arrows on the string. Rynelf was in the bows with his line ready to take soundings. Reepicheep, Edmund, Eustace and Caspian, glittering in mail, were with him. Drinian took the tiller.

"And now, in Aslan's name, forward!" cried Caspian. "A slow, steady stroke. And let every man be silent and keep his ears open for orders."

With a creak and a groan the *Dawn Treader* started to creep forward as the men began to row. Lucy, up in the fighting top, had a wonderful view of the exact moment at which they entered the darkness. The bows had already disappeared before the sunlight had left the stern. She saw it go. At one minute the gilded stern, the blue sea, and the sky, were all in broad daylight: next minute the sea and sky had vanished, the stern lantern – which had been hardly noticeable before – was the only thing to show where the ship ended. In front of the lantern she could see the black shape of Drinian crouching at the tiller. Down below her the two torches made visible two small patches of deck and gleamed on swords and helmets, and forward there was another island of light on the forecastle. Apart from that, the fighting top, lit by the masthead light which was only just above her, seemed to be a little lighted world of its own floating in lonely darkness. And the lights themselves, as always happens with lights when you have to have them at the wrong time of day, looked lurid and unnatural. She also noticed that she was very cold.

How long this voyage into the darkness lasted, nobody knew. Except for the creak of the rowlocks and the splash of the oars there was nothing to show that they were moving at all. Edmund, peering from the bows, could see nothing except the reflection of the lantern in the water before him. It looked a greasy sort of reflection, and the ripple made by their advancing prow appeared to be heavy, small, and lifeless. As time went on everyone except the rowers began to shiver with cold.

Suddenly, from somewhere – no one's sense of direction was very clear by now – there came a cry, either of some inhuman voice or else a voice of one in such extremity of terror that he had almost lost his humanity.

Caspian was still trying to speak – his mouth was too dry – when the shrill voice of Reepicheep, which sounded louder than usual in that silence, was heard.

"Who calls?" it piped. "If you are a foe we do not fear you, and if you are a friend your enemies shall be taught the fear of us."

"Mercy!" cried the voice. "Mercy! Even if you are only one more dream, have mercy. Take me on board. Take me, even if you strike me dead. But in the name of all mercies do not fade away and leave me in this horrible land."

"Where are you?" shouted Caspian. "Come aboard and welcome."

There came another cry, whether of joy or terror, and

then they knew that someone was swimming towards them.

"Stand by to heave him up, men," said Caspian.

"Aye, aye, your Majesty," said the sailors. Several crowded to the port bulwark with ropes and one, leaning far out over the side, held the torch. A wild, white face appeared in the blackness of the water, and then, after some scrambling and pulling, a dozen friendly hands had heaved the stranger on board.

Edmund thought he had never seen a wilder-looking man. Though he did not otherwise look very old, his hair was an untidy mop of white, his face was thin and drawn, and, for clothing, only a few wet rags hung about him. But what one mainly noticed were his eyes, which were so widely opened that he seemed to have no eyelids at all, and stared as if in an agony of pure fear. The moment his feet reached the deck he said:

"Fly! Fly! About with your ship and fly! Row, row, row for your lives away from this accursed shore."

"Compose yourself," said Reepicheep, "and tell us what the danger is. We are not used to flying."

The stranger started horribly at the voice of the Mouse, which he had not noticed before.

"Nevertheless you will fly from here," he gasped. "This is the Island where Dreams come true."

"That's the island I've been looking for this long time," said one of the sailors. "I reckoned I'd find I was married to Nancy if we landed here."

"And I'd find Tom alive again," said another.

"Fools!" said the man, stamping his foot with rage. "That is the sort of talk that brought me here, and I'd better have been drowned or never born. Do you hear what I say? This is where dreams – dreams, do you understand – come to life, come real. Not daydreams: dreams."

There was about half a minute's silence and then, with a great clatter of armour, the whole crew were tumbling down the main hatch as quick as they could and flinging themselves on the oars to row as they had never rowed before; and Drinian was swinging round the tiller, and the boatswain was giving out the quickest stroke that had ever been heard at sea. For it had taken everyone just that half-minute to remember certain dreams they had had – dreams that make you afraid of going to sleep again – and to realize what it would mean to land on a country where dreams come true.

Only Reepicheep remained unmoved.

"Your Majesty, your Majesty," he said, "are you going to tolerate this mutiny, this poltroonery? This is a panic, this is a rout."

"Row, row," bellowed Caspian. "Pull for all our lives. Is her head right, Drinian? You can say what you like, Reepicheep. There are some things no man can face."

"It is, then, my good fortune not to be a man," replied Reepicheep with a very stiff bow.

Lucy from up aloft had heard it all. In an instant that one of her own dreams which she had tried hardest to forget came back to her as vividly as if she had only just woken from it. So *that* was what was behind them, on the island, in the darkness! For a second she wanted to go down to the deck and be with Edmund and Caspian. But what was the use? If dreams began coming true, Edmund and Caspian themselves might turn into something horrible just as she reached them. She gripped the rail of the fighting top and tried to steady herself. They were rowing back to the light as hard as they could: it would be all right in a few seconds. But oh, if only it could be all right now!

Though the rowing made a good deal of noise it did not quite conceal the total silence which surrounded the ship.

Everyone knew it would be better not to listen, not to strain his ears for any sound from the darkness. But no one could help listening. And soon everyone was hearing things. Each one heard something different.

"Do you hear a noise like . . . like a huge pair of scissors opening and shutting . . . over there?" Eustace asked Rynelf.

"Hush!" said Rynelf. "I can hear *them* crawling up the sides of the ship."

"*It's* just going to settle on the mast," said Caspian.

"Ugh!" said a sailor. "There are the gongs beginning. I knew they would."

Caspian, trying not to look at anything (especially not to keep looking behind him), went aft to Drinian.

"Drinian," he said in a very low voice. "How long did we take rowing in? — I mean rowing to where we picked up the stranger."

"Five minutes, perhaps," whispered Drinian. "Why?"

"Because we've been more than that already trying to get out."

Drinian's hand shook on the tiller and a line of cold sweat ran down his face. The same idea was occurring to everyone on board. "We shall never get out, never get out," moaned the rowers. "He's steering us wrong. We're going round and round in circles. We shall never get out." The stranger, who had been lying in a huddled heap on the deck, sat up and burst out into a horrible screaming laugh.

"Never get out!" he yelled. "That's it. Of course. We shall never get out. What a fool I was to have thought they would let me go as easily as that. No, no, we shall never get out."

Lucy leant her head on the edge of the fighting top and whispered, "Aslan, Aslan, if ever you loved us at all, send us help now." The darkness did not grow any less, but she began to feel a little – a very, very little – better. "After all, nothing has really happened to us yet," she thought.

"Look!" cried Rynelf's voice hoarsely from the bows. There was a tiny speck of light ahead, and while they watched a broad beam of light fell from it upon the ship. It did not alter the surrounding darkness, but the whole ship was lit up as if by searchlight. Caspian blinked, stared round, saw the faces of his companions all with wild, fixed expressions. Everyone was staring in the same direction: behind everyone lay his black, sharply-edged shadow.

Lucy looked along the beam and presently saw something in it. At first it looked like a cross, then it looked like an aeroplane, then it looked like a kite, and at last with a whirring of wings it was right overhead and was an albatross. It circled three times round the mast and then perched for an instant on the crest of the gilded dragon at the prow. It called out in a strong sweet voice what seemed to be words though no one understood them. After that it spread its wings, rose, and began to fly slowly ahead, bearing a little to starboard. Drinian steered after it not doubting that it offered good guidance. But no one except Lucy knew that as it circled the mast it had whispered to her, "Courage, dear heart," and the voice, she felt sure, was Alsan's, and with the voice a delicious smell breathed in her face.

In a few moments the darkness turned into a greyness ahead, and then, almost before they dared to begin hoping, they had shot out into the sunlight and were in the warm, blue world again. And all at once everybody realized that there was nothing to be afraid of and never had been. They blinked their eyes and looked about them. The brightness

of the ship herself astonished them: they had half
expected to find that the darkness would cling to the white
and the green and the gold in the form of some grime or
scum. And then first one, and then another, began
laughing.

"I reckon we've made pretty good fools of ourselves,"
said Rynelf.

Lucy lost no time in coming down to the deck, where she
found the others all gathered round the newcomer. For a
long time he was too happy to speak, and could only gaze
at the sea and the sun and feel the bulwarks and the ropes,
as if to make sure he was really awake, while tears rolled
down his cheeks.

"Thank you," he said at last. "You have saved me from
. . . but I won't talk of that. And now let me know who you
are. I am a Telmarine of Narnia, and when I was worth
anything men called me the Lord Rhoop."

"And I," said Caspian, "am Caspian, King of Narnia,
and I sail to find you and your companions who were my
father's friends."

Lord Rhoop fell on his knees and kissed the King's hand.
"Sire," he said, "you are the man in all the world I most
wished to see. Grant me a boon."

"What is it?" asked Caspian.

"Never to bring me back there," he said. He pointed
astern. They all looked. But they saw only bright blue sea
and bright blue sky. The Dark Island and the darkness had
vanished for ever.

"Why!" cried Lord Rhoop. "You have destroyed it!"

"I don't think it was us," said Lucy.

"Sire," said Drinian, "this wind is fair for the south-
east. Shall I have our poor fellows up and set sail? And
after that, every man who can be spared, to his
hammock."

"Yes," said Caspian, "and let there be grog all round. Heigh-ho, I feel I could sleep the clock round myself."

So all afternoon with great joy they sailed south-east with a fair wind. But nobody noticed when the albatross had disappeared.

CHAPTER THIRTEEN

THE THREE SLEEPERS

THE wind never failed but it grew gentler every day till at length the waves were little more than ripples, and the ship glided on hour after hour almost as if they were sailing on a lake. And every night they saw that there rose in the east new constellations which no one had ever seen in Narnia and perhaps, as Lucy thought with a mixture of joy and fear, no living eye had seen at all. Those new stars were big and bright and the nights were warm. Most of them slept on deck and talked far into the night or hung over the ship's side watching the luminous dance of the foam thrown up by their bows.

On an evening of startling beauty, when the sunset behind them was so crimson and purple and widely spread that the very sky itself seemed to have grown larger, they came in sight of land on their starboard bow. It came slowly nearer and the light behind them made it look as if the capes and headlands of this new country were all on fire. But presently they were sailing along its coast and its western cape now rose up astern of them, black against the red sky and sharp as if it was cut out of cardboard, and then they could see better what this country was like. It had no mountains but many gentle hills with slopes like pillows. An attractive smell came from it – what Lucy called "a dim, purple kind of smell", which Edmund said (and Rhince thought) was rot, but Caspian said, "I know what you mean."

They sailed on a good way, past point after point, hoping to find a nice deep harbour, but had to content themselves in the end with a wide and shallow bay. Though it had seemed calm out at sea there was of course surf breaking on the sand and they could not bring the *Dawn Treader* as far in as they would have liked. They dropped anchor a good way from the beach and had a wet and tumbling landing in the boat. The Lord Rhoop remained on board the *Dawn Treader*. He wished to see no more islands. All the time that they remained in this country the sound of the long breakers was in their ears.

Two men were left to guard the boat and Caspian led the others inland, but not far because it was too late for exploring and the light would soon go. But there was no need to go far to find an adventure. The level valley which lay at the head of the bay showed no road or track or other sign of habitation. Underfoot was fine springy turf dotted here and there with a low bushy growth which Edmund and Lucy took for heather. Eustace, who was really rather good at botany, said it wasn't, and he was probably right; but it was something of very much the same kind.

When they had gone less than a bowshot from the shore, Drinian said, "Look! What's that?" and everyone stopped.

"Are they great trees?" said Caspian.

"Towers, I think," said Eustace.

"It might be giants," said Edmund in a lower voice.

"The way to find out is to go right in among them," said Reepicheep, drawing his sword and pattering off ahead of everyone else.

"I think it's a ruin," said Lucy when they had got a good

deal nearer, and her guess was the best so far. What they now saw was a wide oblong space flagged with smooth stones and surrounded by grey pillars but unroofed. And from end to end of it ran a long table laid with a rich crimson cloth that came down nearly to the pavement. At either side of it were many chairs of stone richly carved and with silken cushions upon the seats. But on the table itself there was set out such a banquet as had never been seen, not even when Peter the High King kept his court at Cair Paravel. There were turkeys and geese and peacocks, there were boars' heads and sides of venison, there were pies shaped like ships under full sail or like dragons and elephants, there were ice puddings and bright lobsters and gleaming salmon, there were nuts and grapes, pineapples and peaches, pomegranates and melons and tomatoes. There were flagons of gold and silver and curiously-wrought glass; and the smell of the fruit and the wine blew towards them like a promise of all happiness.

"I *say*!" said Lucy.

They came nearer and nearer, all very quietly.

"But where are the guests?" asked Eustace.

"We can provide that, Sir," said Rhince.

"Look!" said Edmund sharply. They were actually within the pillars now and standing on the pavement. Everyone looked where Edmund had pointed. The chairs were not all empty. At the head of the table and in the two places beside it there was something – or possibly three somethings.

"What are *those*?" asked Lucy in a whisper. "It looks like three beavers sitting on the table."

"Or a huge bird's nest," said Edmund.

"It looks more like a haystack to me," said Caspian.

Reepicheep ran forward, jumped on a chair and thence on to the table, and ran along it, threading his way as nimbly as a dancer between jewelled cups and pyramids of fruit and ivory salt-cellars. He ran right up to the mysterious grey mass at the end: peered, touched, and then called out:

"These will not fight, I think."

Everyone now came close and saw that what sat in those three chairs was three men, though hard to recognize as men till you looked closely. Their hair, which was grey,

had grown over their eyes till it almost concealed their faces, and their beards had grown over the table, climbing round and entwining plates and goblets as brambles entwine a fence, until, all mixed in one great mat of hair, they flowed over the edge and down to the floor. And from their heads the hair hung over the backs of their chairs so that they were wholly hidden. In fact the three men were nearly all hair.

"Dead?" said Caspian.

"I think not, Sire," said Reepicheep, lifting one of their hands out of its tangle of hair in his two paws. "This one is warm and his pulse beats."

"This one, too, and this," said Drinian.

"Why, they're only asleep," said Eustace.

"It's been a long sleep, though," said Edmund, "to let their hair grow like this."

"It must be an enchanted sleep," said Lucy. "I felt the moment we landed on this island that it was full of magic. Oh! do you think we have perhaps come here to break it?"

"We can try," said Caspian, and began shaking the nearest of the three sleepers. For a moment everyone thought he was going to be successful, for the man breathed hard and muttered, "I'll go eastward no more. Out oars for Narnia." But he sank back almost at once into a yet deeper sleep than before: that is, his heavy head sagged a few inches lower towards the table and all efforts to rouse him again were useless. With the second it was much the same. "Weren't born to live like animals. Get to the east while you've a chance – lands behind the sun," and sank down. And the third only said, "Mustard, please," and slept hard.

"*Out oars for Narnia*, eh?" said Drinian.

"Yes," said Caspian, "you are right, Drinian. I think our quest is at an end. Let's look at their rings. Yes, these are their devices. This is the Lord Revilian. This is the Lord Argoz: and this, the Lord Mavramorn."

"But we can't wake them," said Lucy. "What are we to do?"

"Begging your Majesties' pardons all," said Rhince, "but why not fall to while you're discussing it? We don't see a dinner like this every day."

"Not for your life!" said Caspian.

"That's right, that's right," said several of the sailors.

"Too much magic about here. The sooner we're back on board the better."

"Depend upon it," said Reepicheep, "it was from eating this food that these three lords came by a seven years' sleep."

"I wouldn't touch it to save my life," said Drinian.

"The light's going uncommon quick," said Rynelf.

"Back to ship, back to ship," muttered the men.

"I really think," said Edmund, "they're right. We can decide what to do with the three sleepers tomorrow. We daren't eat the food and there's no point in staying here for the night. The whole place smells of magic – and danger."

"I am entirely of King Edmund's opinion," said Reepicheep, "as far as concerns the ship's company in general. But I myself will sit at this table till sunrise."

"Why on earth?" said Eustace.

"Because," said the Mouse, "this is a very great adventure, and no danger seems to me so great as that of knowing when I get back to Narnia that I left a mystery behind me through fear."

"I'll stay with you, Reep," said Edmund.

"And I too," said Caspian.

"And me," said Lucy. And then Eustace volunteered also. This was very brave of him because never having read of such things or even heard of them till he joined the *Dawn Treader* made it worse for him than for the others.

"I beseech your Majesty –" began Drinian.

"No, my Lord," said Caspian. "Your place is with the ship, and you have had a day's work while we five have idled." There was a lot of argument about this but in the end Caspian had his way. As the crew marched off to the shore in the gathering dusk none of the five watchers, except perhaps Reepicheep, could avoid a cold feeling in the stomach.

They took some time choosing their seats at the perilous table. Probably everyone had the same reason but no one said it out loud. For it was really a rather nasty choice. One could hardly bear to sit all night next to those three terrible hairy objects which, if not dead, were certainly not alive in the ordinary sense. On the other hand, to sit at the far end, so that you would see them less and less as the night grew darker, and wouldn't know if they were moving, and perhaps wouldn't see them at all by about two o'clock – no, it was not to be thought of. So they sauntered round and round the table saying, "What about here?" and "Or perhaps a bit further on," or, "Why not on this side?" till at last they settled down somewhere about the middle but nearer to the sleepers than to the other end. It was about ten by now and almost dark. Those strange new constellations burned in the east. Lucy would have liked it better if they had been the Leopard and the Ship and other old friends of the Narnian sky.

They wrapped themselves in their sea cloaks and sat still and waited. At first there was some attempt at talk but it didn't come to much. And they sat and sat. And all the time they heard the waves breaking on the beach.

After hours that seemed like ages there came a moment when they all knew they had been dozing a moment before but were all suddenly wide awake. The stars were all in quite different positions from those they had last noticed. The sky was very black except for the faintest possible greyness in the east. They were cold, though thirsty, and stiff. And none of them spoke because now at last something was happening.

Before them, beyond the pillars, there was the slope of a low hill. And now a door opened in the hillside, and light appeared in the doorway, and a figure came out, and the door shut behind it. The figure carried a light, and this light was really all that they could see distinctly. It came slowly nearer and nearer till at last it stood right at the table opposite to them. Now they could see that it was a tall girl, dressed in a single long garment of clear blue which left her arms bare. She was bareheaded and her yellow hair hung down her back. And when they looked at her they thought they had never before known what beauty meant.

The light which she had been carrying was a tall candle in a silver candlestick which she now set upon the table. If there had been any wind off the sea earlier in the night it must have died down by now, for the flame of the candle burned as straight and still as if it were in a room with the windows shut and the curtains drawn. Gold and silver on the table shone in its light.

Lucy now noticed something lying lengthwise on the table which had escaped her attention before. It was a knife of stone, sharp as steel, a cruel-looking, ancient-looking thing.

No one had yet spoken a word. Then – Reepicheep first, and Caspian next – they all rose to their feet, because they felt that she was a great lady.

"Travellers who have come from far to Aslan's table," said the girl. "Why do you not eat and drink?"

"Madam," said Caspian, "we feared the food because we thought it had cast our friends into an enchanted sleep."

"They have never tasted it," she said.

"Please," said Lucy, "what happened to them?"

"Seven years ago," said the girl, "they came here in a ship whose sails were rags and her timbers ready to fall apart. There were a few others with them, sailors, and when they came to this table one said, 'Here is the good place. Let us set sail and reef sail and row no longer but sit down and end our days in peace!' And the second said, 'No, let us re-embark and sail for Narnia and the west; it may be that Miraz is dead.' But the third, who was a very masterful man, leaped up and said, 'No, by heaven. We are men and Telmarines, not brutes. What should we do but seek adventure after adventure? We have not long to live in any event. Let us spend what is left in seeking the unpeopled world behind the sunrise.' And as they quarrelled he caught up the Knife of Stone which lies there on the table and would have fought with his comrades. But it is a thing not right for him to touch. And as his fingers closed upon the hilt, deep sleep fell upon all the three. And till the enchantment is undone they will never wake."

"What is this Knife of Stone?" asked Eustace.

"Do none of you know it?" said the girl.

"I – I think," said Lucy, "I've seen something like it before. It was a knife like it that the White Witch used when she killed Aslan at the Stone Table long ago."

"It was the same," said the girl, "and it was brought here to be kept in honour while the world lasts."

Edmund, who had been looking more and more uncomfortable for the last few minutes, now spoke.

"Look here," he said, "I hope I'm not a coward – about eating this food, I mean – and I'm sure I don't mean to be rude. But we have had a lot of queer adventures on this voyage of ours and things aren't always what they seem. When I look in your face I can't help believing all you say: but then that's just what might happen with a witch too. How are we to know you're a friend?"

"You can't know," said the girl. "You can only believe – or not."

After a moment's pause Reepicheep's small voice was heard.

"Sire," he said to Caspian, "of your courtesy fill my cup with wine from that flagon: it is too big for me to lift. I will drink to the lady."

Caspian obeyed and the Mouse, standing on the table, held up a golden cup between its tiny paws and said, "Lady, I pledge you." Then it fell to on cold peacock, and in a short while everyone else followed its example. All were very hungry and the meal, if not quite what you wanted for a very early breakfast, was excellent as a very late supper.

"Why is it called Aslan's table?" asked Lucy presently.

"It is set here by his bidding," said the girl, "for those who come so far. Some call this island the World's End, for though you can sail further, this is the beginning of the end."

"But how does the food *keep*?" asked the practical Eustace.

"It is eaten, and renewed every day," said the girl. "This you will see."

"And what are we to do about the Sleepers?" asked Caspian. "In the world from which my friends come" (here he nodded at Eustace and the Pevensies) "they have a story of a prince or a king coming to a castle where all the people lay in an enchanted sleep. In that story he could not dissolve the enchantment until he had kissed the Princess."

"But here," said the girl, "it is different. Here he cannot kiss the Princess till he has dissolved the enchantment."

"Then," said Caspian, "in the name of Aslan, show me how to set about that work at once."

"My father will teach you that," said the girl.

"Your father!" said everyone. "Who is he? And where?"

"Look," said the girl, turning round and pointing at the door in the hillside. They could see it more easily now, for while they had been talking the stars had grown fainter and great gaps of white light were appearing in the greyness of the eastern sky.

CHAPTER FOURTEEN

THE BEGINNING OF THE END OF THE WORLD

SLOWLY the door opened again and out there came a figure as tall and straight as the girl's but not so slender. It carried no light but light seemed to come from it. As it came nearer, Lucy saw that it was like an old man. His silver beard came down to his bare feet in front and his silver hair hung down to his heels behind and his robe appeared to be made from the fleece of silver sheep. He looked so mild and grave that once more all the travellers rose to their feet and stood in silence.

But the old man came on without speaking to the travellers and stood on the other side of the table opposite to his daughter. Then both of them held up their arms before them and turned to face the east. In that position they began to sing. I wish I could write down the song, but no one who was present could remember it. Lucy said afterwards that it was high, almost shrill, but very beautiful, "A cold kind of song, an early morning kind of song." And as they sang, the grey clouds lifted from the eastern sky and the white patches grew bigger and bigger till it was all white, and the sea began to shine like silver. And long afterwards (but those two sang all the time) the east began to turn red and at last, unclouded, the sun came up out of the sea and its long level ray shot down the length of the table on the gold and silver and on the Stone Knife.

Once or twice before, the Narnians had wondered whether the sun at its rising did not look bigger in these seas than it had looked at home. This time they were certain. There was no mistaking it. And the brightness of its ray on the dew and on the table was far beyond any morning brightness they had ever seen. And as Edmund said afterwards, "Though lots of things happened on that trip which *sound* more exciting, that moment was really the most exciting." For now they knew that they had truly come to the beginning of the End of the World.

Then something seemed to be flying at them out of the very centre of the rising sun: but of course one couldn't look steadily in that direction to make sure. But presently the air became full of voices – voices which took up the same song that the Lady and her Father were singing, but in far wilder tones and in a language which no one knew. And soon after that the owners of these voices could be seen. They were birds, large and white, and they came by hundreds and thousands and alighted on everything; on the grass, and the pavement, on the table, on your shoulders, your hands, and your head, till it looked as if heavy snow had fallen. For, like snow, they not only made everything white but blurred and blunted all shapes. But Lucy, looking out from between the wings of the birds that covered her, saw one bird fly to the Old Man with something in its beak that looked like a little fruit, unless it was a little live coal, which it might have been, for it was too bright to look at. And the bird laid it in the Old Man's mouth.

Then the birds stopped their singing and appeared to be very busy about the table. When they rose from it again everything on the table that could be eaten or drunk had disappeared. These birds rose from their meal in their thousands and hundreds and carried away all the things that could not be eaten or drunk, such as bones, rinds, and shells, and took their flight back to the rising sun. But now, because they were not singing, the whir of their wings seemed to set the whole air a-tremble. And there was the table pecked clean and empty, and the three old Lords of Narnia still fast asleep.

Now at last the Old Man turned to the travellers and bade them welcome.

"Sir," said Caspian, "will you tell us how to undo the enchantment which holds these three Narnian Lords asleep."

"I will gladly tell you that, my son," said the Old Man. "To break this enchantment you must sail to the World's End, or as near as you can come to it, and you must come back having left at least one of your company behind."

"And what must happen to that one?" asked Reepicheep.

"He must go on into the utter east and never return into the world."

"That is my heart's desire," said Reepicheep.

"And are we near the World's End now, Sir?" asked Caspian. "Have you any knowledge of the seas and lands further east than this?"

"I saw them long ago," said the Old Man, "but it was from a great height. I cannot tell you such things as sailors need to know."

"Do you mean you were flying in the air?" Eustace blurted out.

"I was a long way above the air, my son," replied the Old Man. "I am Ramandu. But I see that you stare at one another and have not heard this name. And no wonder, for the days when I was a star had ceased long before any of you knew this world, and all the constellations have changed."

"Golly," said Edmund under his breath. "He's a *retired* star."

"Aren't you a star any longer?" asked Lucy.

"I am a star at rest, my daughter," answered Ramandu.

"When I set for the last time, decrepit and old beyond all that you can reckon, I was carried to this island. I am not so old now as I was then. Every morning a bird brings me a fire-berry from the valleys in the Sun, and each fire-berry takes away a little of my age. And when I have become as young as the child that was born yesterday, then I shall take my rising again (for we are at earth's eastern rim) and once more tread the great dance."

"In our world," said Eustace, "a star is a huge ball of flaming gas."

"Even in your world, my son, that is not what a star is but only what it is made of. And in this world you have already met a star: for I think you have been with Coriakin."

"Is he a retired star, too?" said Lucy.

"Well, not quite the same," said Ramandu. "It was not quite as a rest that he was set to govern the Duffers. You might call it a punishment. He might have shone for thousands of years more in the southern winter sky if all had gone well."

"What did he do, Sir?" asked Caspian.

"My son," said Ramandu, "it is not for you, a son of Adam, to know what faults a star can commit. But come, we waste time in such talk. Are you yet resolved? Will you sail further east and come again, leaving one to return no more, and so break the enchantment? Or will you sail westward?"

"Surely, Sire," said Reepicheep, "there is no question about that? It is very plainly part of our quest to rescue these three lords from enchantment."

"I think the same, Reepicheep," replied Caspian. "And even if it were not so, it would break my heart not to go as near the World's End as the *Dawn Treader* will take us. But I am thinking of the crew. They signed on to seek the seven lords, not to reach the rim of the Earth. If we sail east from here we sail to find the edge, the utter east. And no one knows how far it is. They're brave fellows, but I see signs that some of them are weary of the voyage and long to have our prow pointing to Narnia again. I don't think I should take them further without their knowledge and consent. And then there's the poor Lord Rhoop. He's a broken man."

"My son," said the star, "it would be no use, even though you wished it, to sail for the World's End with men unwilling or men deceived. That is not how great unenchantments are achieved. They must know where they go and why. But who is this broken man you speak of?"

Caspian told Ramandu the story of Rhoop.

"I can give him what he needs most," said Ramandu. "In this island there is sleep without stint or measure, and sleep in which no faintest footfall of a dream was ever heard. Let him sit beside these other three and drink oblivion till your return."

"Oh, do let's do that, Caspian," said Lucy. "I'm sure it's just what he would love."

At that moment they were interrupted by the sound of many feet and voices: Drinian and the rest of the ship's company were approaching. They halted in surprise when they saw Ramandu and his daughter; and then, because these were obviously great people, every man uncovered his head. Some sailors eyed the empty dishes and flagons on the table with regret.

"My lord," said the King to Drinian, "pray send two men back to the *Dawn Treader* with a message to the Lord Rhoop. Tell him that the last of his old shipmates are here asleep – a sleep without dreams – and that he can share it."

When this had been done, Caspian told the rest to sit down and laid the whole situation before them. When he had finished there was a long silence and some whispering until presently the Master Bowman got to his feet, and said:

"What some of us have been wanting to ask for a long time, your Majesty, is how we're ever to get home when we do turn, whether we turn here or somewhere else. It's been west and north-west winds all the way, barring an occasional calm. And if that doesn't change, I'd like to know what hopes we have of seeing Narnia again. There's not much chance of supplies lasting while we *row* all that way."

"That's landsman's talk," said Drinian. "There's always a prevailing west wind in these seas all through the late summer, and it always changes after the New Year. We'll have plenty of wind for sailing westward; more than we shall like from all accounts."

"That's true, Master," said an old sailor who was a Galmian by birth. "You get some ugly weather rolling up from the east in January and February. And by your leave, Sire, if I was in command of this ship I'd say to winter here and begin the voyage home in March."

"What'd you eat while you were wintering here?" asked Eustace.

"This table," said Ramandu, "will be filled with a king's feast every day at sunset."

"Now you're talking!" said several sailors.

"Your Majesties and gentlemen and ladies all," said Rynelf, "there's just one thing I want to say. There's not one of us chaps as was pressed on this journey. We're volunteers. And there's some here that are looking very hard at that table and thnking about king's feasts who were talking very loud about adventures on the day we sailed from Cair Paravel, and swearing they wouldn't come home till we'd found the end of the world. And there were some standing on the quay who would have given all they had to come with us. It was thought a finer thing then to have a cabin-boy's berth on the *Dawn Treader* than to wear a knight's belt. I don't know if you get the hang of what I'm saying. But what I mean is that I think chaps who set out like us will look as silly as – as those Dufflepuds – if we come home and say we got to the beginning of the world's end and hadn't the heart to go further."

Some of the sailors cheered at this but some said that that was all very well.

"This isn't going to be much fun," whispered Edmund to Caspian. "What are we to do if half those fellows hang back?"

"Wait," Caspian whispered back. "I've still a card to play."

"Aren't you going to say anything, Reep?" whispered Lucy.

"No. Why should your Majesty expect it?" answered Reepicheep in a voice that most people heard. "My own plans are made. While I can, I sail east in the *Dawn Treader*. When she fails me, I paddle east in my coracle. When she sinks, I shall swim east with my four paws. And when I can swim no longer, if I have not reached Aslan's country, or shot over the edge of the world in some vast cataract, I shall sink with my nose to the sunrise and Peepiceek will be head of the talking mice in Narnia."

"Hear, hear," said a sailor, "I'll say the same, barring the bit about the coracle, which wouldn't bear me." He added in a lower voice, "I'm not going to be outdone by a mouse."

At this point Caspian jumped to his feet. "Friends," he said, "I think you have not quite understood our purpose. You talk as if we had come to you with our hat in our hand, begging for shipmates. It isn't like that at all. We and

our royal brother and sister and their kinsman and Sir
Reepicheep, the good knight, and the Lord Drinian have an
errand to the world's edge. It is our pleasure to choose
from among such of you as are willing those whom we
deem worthy of so high an enterprise. We have not said
that any can come for the asking. That is why we shall now
command the Lord Drinian and Master Rhince to consider
carefully what men among you are the hardest in battle,
the most skilled seamen, the purest in blood, the most loyal
to our person, and the cleanest of life and manners; and to
give their names to us in a schedule." He paused and went
on in a quicker voice, "Aslan's mane!" he exclaimed. "Do
you think that the privilege of seeing the last things is to be
bought for a song? Why, every man that comes with us
shall bequeath the title of Dawn Treader to all his
descendants, and when we land at Cair Paravel on the
homeward voyage he shall have either gold or land enough
to make him rich all his life. Now – scatter over the island,
all of you. In half an hour's time I shall receive the names
that Lord Drinian brings me."

There was rather a sheepish silence and then the crew
made their bows and moved away, one in this direction
and one in that, but mostly in little knots or bunches,
talking.

"And now for the Lord Rhoop," said Caspian.

But turning to the head of the table he saw that Rhoop
was already there. He had arrived, silent and unnoticed,
while the discussion was going on, and was seated beside
the Lord Argoz. The daughter of Ramandu stood beside
him as if she had just helped him into his chair; Ramandu
stood behind him and laid both his hands on Rhoop's grey
head. Even in daylight a faint silver light came from the
hands of the star. There was a smile on Rhoop's haggard
face. He held out one of his hands to Lucy and the other to

Caspian. For a moment it looked as if he were going to say something. Then his smile brightened as if he were feeling some delicious sensation, a long sigh of contentment came from his lips, his head fell forward, and he slept.

"Poor Rhoop," said Lucy. "I *am* glad. He must have had terrible times."

"Don't let's even think of it," said Eustace.

Meanwhile Caspian's speech, helped perhaps by some magic of the island, was having just the effect he intended. A good many who had been anxious enough to *get* out of the voyage felt quite differently about being *left* out of it. And of course whenever any one sailor announced that he had made up his mind to ask for permission to sail, the ones who hadn't said this felt that they were getting fewer and more uncomfortable. So that before the half-hour was nearly over several people were positively "sucking up" to Drinian and Rhince (at least that was what they called it at my school) to get a good report. And soon there were only three left who didn't want to go, and those three were trying very hard to persuade others to stay with them. And very shortly after that there was only one left. And in the end he began to be afraid of being left behind all on his own and changed his mind.

At the end of the half-hour they all came trooping back to Aslan's Table and stood at one end while Drinian and Rhince went and sat down with Caspian and made their report; and Caspian accepted all the men but that one who had changed his mind at the last moment. His name was Pittencream and he stayed on the Island of the Star all the time the others were away looking for the World's End, and he very much wished he had gone with them. He wasn't the sort of man who could enjoy talking to Ramandu and Ramandu's daughter (nor they to him), and it rained a good deal, and though there was a wonderful feast on the Table every night, he didn't very much enjoy it. He said it gave him the creeps sitting there alone (and in the rain as likely as not) with those four Lords asleep at the end of the Table. And when the others returned he felt so out of things that he deserted on the voyage home at the Lone Islands, and went and lived in Calormen, where he told wonderful stories about his adventures at the End of the World, until at last he came to believe them himself. So you may say, in a sense, that he lived happily ever after. But he could never bear mice.

That night they all ate and drank together at the great Table between the pillars where the feast was magically renewed: and next morning the *Dawn Treader* set sail once more just when the great birds had come and gone again.

"Lady," said Caspian, "I hope to speak with you again when I have broken the enchantments." And Ramandu's daughter looked at him and smiled.

CHAPTER FIFTEEN

THE WONDERS OF THE LAST SEA

VERY soon after they had left Ramandu's country they began to feel that they had already sailed beyond the world. All was different. For one thing they all found that they were needing less sleep. One did not want to go to bed nor to eat much, nor even to talk except in low voices. Another thing was the light. There was too much of it. The sun when it came up each morning looked twice, if not three times, its usual size. And every morning (which gave Lucy the strangest feeling of all) the huge white birds, singing their song with human voices in a language no one knew, streamed overhead and vanished astern on their way to their breakfast at Aslan's Table. A little later they came flying back and vanished into the east.

"How beautifully clear the water is!" said Lucy to herself, as she leaned over the port side early in the afternoon of the second day.

And it was. The first thing that she noticed was a little black object, about the size of a shoe, travelling along at the same speed as the ship. For a moment she thought it was something floating on the surface. But then there came floating past a bit of stale bread which the cook had just thrown out of the galley. And the bit of bread looked as if it were going to collide with the black thing, but it didn't. It passed above it, and Lucy now saw that the black thing could not be on the surface. Then the black thing suddenly got very much bigger and flicked back to normal size a moment later.

Now Lucy knew she had seen something just like that happen somewhere else – if only she could remember where. She held her hand to her head and screwed up her face and put out her tongue in the effort to remember. At last she did. Of course! It was like what you saw from a train on a bright sunny day. You saw the black shadow of your own coach running along the fields at the same pace as the train. Then you went into a cutting; and immediately the same shadow flicked close up to you and got big, racing along the grass of the cutting-bank. Then you came out of the cutting and – flick! – once more the black shadow had gone back to its normal size and was running along the fields.

"It's our shadow! – the shadow of the *Dawn Treader*," said Lucy. "Our shadow running along on the bottom of the sea. That time when it got bigger it went over a hill. But in that case the water must be clearer than I thought! Good gracious, I must be seeing the bottom of the sea; fathoms and fathoms down."

As soon as she had said this she realized that the great silvery expanse which she had been seeing (without noticing) for some time was really the sand on the sea-bed and that all sorts of darker or brighter patches were not lights and shadows on the surface but real things on the bottom. At present, for instance, they were passing over a mass of soft purply green with a broad, winding strip of pale grey in the middle of it. But now that she knew it was on the bottom she saw it much better. She could see that bits of the dark stuff were much higher than other bits and were waving gently. "Just like trees in a wind," said Lucy. "And I do believe that's what they are. It's a submarine forest."

They passed on above it and presently the pale streak was joined by another pale streak. "If I was down there," thought Lucy, "that streak would be just like a road through the wood. And that place where it joins the other would be a crossroads. Oh, I do wish I was. Hallo! the forest is coming to an end. And I do believe the streak really was a road! I can still see it going on across the open sand. It's a different colour. And it's marked out with something at the edges – dotted lines. Perhaps they are stones. And now it's getting wider."

But it was not really getting wider, it was getting nearer. She realized this because of the way in which the shadow of the ship came rushing up towards her. And the road – she felt sure it was a road now – began to go in zig-zags. Obviously it was climbing up a steep hill. And when she held her head sideways and looked back, what she saw was very like what you see when you look down a winding road from the top of a hill. She could even see the shafts of sunlight falling through the deep water on to the wooded valley – and, in the extreme distance, everything melting away into a dim greenness. But some places – the sunny ones, she thought – were ultramarine blue.

She could not, however, spend much time looking back; what was coming into view in the forward direction was too exciting. The road had apparently now reached the top of the hill and ran straight forward. Little specks were moving to and fro on it. And now something most wonderful, fortunately in full sunlight – or as full as it can be when it falls through fathoms of water – flashed into sight. It was knobbly and jagged and of a pearly, or perhaps an ivory, colour. She was so nearly straight above it that at first she could hardly make out what it was. But everything became plain when she noticed its shadow. The sunlight was falling across Lucy's shoulders, so the shadow of the thing lay stretched out on the sand behind it. And by its shape she saw clearly that it was a shadow of towers and pinnacles, minarets and domes.

"Why! – it's a city or a huge castle," said Lucy to herself.

"But I wonder why they've built it on top of a high mountain?"

Long afterwards when she was back in England and talked all these adventures over with Edmund, they thought of a reason and I am pretty sure it is the true one. In the sea, the deeper you go, the darker and colder it gets, and it is down there, in the dark and cold, that dangerous things live – the squid and the Sea Serpent and the Kraken. The valleys are the wild, unfriendly places. The sea-people feel about their valleys as we do about mountains, and feel about their mountains as we feel about valleys. It is on the heights (or, as we would say, "in the shallows") that there is warmth and peace. The reckless hunters and brave knights of the sea go down into the depths on quests and adventures, but return home to the heights for rest and peace, courtesy and council, the sports, the dances and the songs.

They had passed the city and the sea-bed was still rising. It was only a few hundred feet below the ship now. The road had disappeared. They were sailing above an open park-like country, dotted with little groves of brightly-coloured vegetation. And then – Lucy nearly squealed aloud with excitement – she had seen People.

There were between fifteen and twenty of them, and all mounted on sea-horses – not the tiny little sea-horses which you may have seen in museums but horses rather bigger than themselves. They must be noble and lordly people, Lucy thought, for she could catch the gleam of gold on some of their foreheads and streamers of emerald- or orange-coloured stuff fluttered from their shoulders in the current. Then:

"Oh, bother these fish!" said Lucy, for a whole shoal of small fat fish, swimming quite close to the surface, had come between her and the Sea People. But though this spoiled her view it led to the most interesting thing of all.

Suddenly a fierce little fish of a kind she had never seen before came darting up from below, snapped, grabbed, and sank rapidly with one of the fat fish in its mouth. And all the Sea People were sitting on their horses staring up at what had happened. They seemed to be talking and laughing. And before the hunting fish had got back to them with its prey, another of the same kind came up from the Sea People. And Lucy was almost certain that one big Sea Man who sat on his sea-horse in the middle of the party had sent it or released it; as if he had been holdng it back till then in his hand or on his wrist.

"Why, I do declare," said Lucy, "it's a hunting party. Or more like a hawking party. Yes, that's it. They ride out with these little fierce fish on their wrists just as we used to ride out with falcons on our wrists when we were Kings and Queens at Cair Paravel long ago. And then they fly them – or I suppose I should say *swim* them – at the others. How –"

She stopped suddenly because the scene was changing. The Sea People had noticed the *Dawn Treader*. The shoal of fish had scattered in every direction: the People themselves were coming up to find out the meaning of this big, black thing which had come between them and the sun. And now they were so close to the surface that if they had been in air, instead of water, Lucy could have spoken to them. There were men and women both. All wore coronets of some kind and many had chains of pearls. They wore no other clothes. Their bodies were the colour of old ivory, their hair dark purple. The King in the centre (no one could mistake him for anything but the King) looked proudly and fiercely into Lucy's face and shook a spear in his hand. His knights did the same. The faces of the ladies were filled with astonishment. Lucy felt sure they had never seen a ship or a human before – and how should they, in seas beyond the world's end where no ship ever came?

"What are you staring at, Lu?" said a voice close beside her.

Lucy had been so absorbed in what she was seeing that she started at the sound, and when she turned she found that her arm had gone "dead" from leaning so long on the

rail in one position. Drinian and Edmund were beside her.

"Look," she said.

They both looked, but almost at once Drinian said in a low voice:

"Turn round at once, your Majesties – that's right, with our backs to the sea. And don't look as if we were talking about anything important."

"Why, what's the matter?" said Lucy as she obeyed.

"It'll never do for the sailors to see *all that*," said Drinian. "We'll have men falling in love with a sea-woman, or falling in love with the under-sea country itself, and jumping overboard. I've heard of that kind of thing happening before in strange seas. It's always unlucky to see *these* people."

"But we used to know them," said Lucy. "In the old days at Cair Paravel when my brother Peter was High King. They came to the surface and sang at our coronation."

"I think that must have been a different kind, Lu," said Edmund. "They could live in the air as well as under water. I rather think these can't. By the look of them they'd have surfaced and started attacking us long ago if they could. They seem very fierce."

"At any rate," said Drinian, but at that moment two sounds were heard. One was a plop. The other was a voice from the fighting top shouting, "Man overboard!" Then everyone was busy. Some of the sailors hurried aloft to take in the sail: others hurried below to get to the oars; and Rhince, who was on duty on the poop, began to put the helm hard over so as to come round and back to the man who had gone overboard. But by now everyone knew that it wasn't strictly a man. It was Reepicheep.

"Drat that mouse!" said Drinian. "It's more trouble than all the rest of the ship's company put together. If there is any scrape to be got into, in it will get! It ought to be put in irons – keel-hauled – marooned – have its whiskers cut off. Can anyone see the little blighter?"

All this didn't mean that Drinian really disliked Reepicheep. On the contrary he liked him very much and was therefore frightened about him, and being frightened put him in a bad temper – just as your mother is much angrier with you for running out into the road in front of a car than a stranger would be. No one, of course, was afraid of Reepicheep's drowning, for he was an excellent swimmer; but the three who knew what was going on below the water were afraid of those long, cruel spears in the hands of the Sea People.

In a few minutes the *Dawn Treader* had come round and everyone could see the black blob in the water which was Reepicheep. He was chattering with the greatest excitement but as his mouth kept on getting filled with water nobody could understand what he was saying.

"He'll blurt the whole thing out if we don't shut him up," cried Drinian. To prevent this he rushed to the side and lowered a rope himself, shouting to the sailors, "All right, all right. Back to your places. I hope I can heave a *mouse* up without help." And as Reepicheep began climbing up the rope – not very nimbly because his wet fur made him heavy – Drinian leaned over and whispered to him,

"Don't tell. Not a word."

But when the dripping Mouse had reached the deck it turned out not to be at all interested in the Sea People.

"Sweet!" he cheeped. "Sweet, sweet!"

"What are you talking about?" asked Drinian crossly. "And you needn't shake yourself all over *me*, either."

"I tell you the water's sweet," said the Mouse. "Sweet, fresh. It isn't salt."

For a moment no one quite took in the importance of this. But then Reepicheep once more repeated the old prophecy:

> "Where the waves grow sweet,
> Doubt not, Reepicheep,
> There is the utter East."

Then at last everyone understood.

"Let me have a bucket, Rynelf," said Drinian.

It was handed him and he lowered it and up it came again. The water shone in it like glass.

"Perhaps your Majesty would like to taste it first," said Drinian to Caspian.

The King took the bucket in both hands, raised it to his lips, sipped, then drank deeply and raised his head. His face was changed. Not only his eyes but everything about him seemed to be brighter.

"Yes," he said, "it is sweet. That's real water, that. I'm not sure that it isn't going to kill me. But it is the death I would have chosen – if I'd known about it till now."

"What do you mean?" asked Edmund.

"It – it's like light more than anything else," said Caspian.

"That is what it is," said Reepicheep. "Drinkable light. We must be very near the end of the world now."

There was a moment's silence and then Lucy knelt down on the deck and drank from the bucket.

"It's the loveliest thing I have ever tasted," she said with a kind of gasp. "But oh – it's strong. We shan't need to *eat* anything now."

And one by one everybody on board drank. And for a long time they were all silent. They felt almost too well and strong to bear it; and presently they began to notice another result. As I have said before, there had been too much light ever since they left the island of Ramandu – the sun too large (though not too hot), the sea too bright, the air too shining. Now, the light grew no less – if anything, it increased – but they could bear it. They could look straight up at the sun without blinking. They could see more light than they had ever seen before. And the deck and the sail and their own faces and bodies became brighter and brighter and every rope shone. And next morning, when the sun rose, now five or six times its old size, they stared hard into it and could see the very feathers of the birds that came flying from it.

Hardly a word was spoken on board all that day, till about dinner-time (no one wanted any dinner, the water was enough for them) Drinian said:

"I can't understand this. There is not a breath of wind. The sail hangs dead. The sea is as flat as a pond. And yet we drive on as fast as if there were a gale behind us."

"I've been thinking that, too," said Caspian. "We must be caught in some strong current."

"H'm," said Edmund. "That's not so nice if the World really has an edge and we're getting near it."

"You mean," said Caspian, "that we might be just – well, poured over it?"

"Yes, yes," cried Reepicheep, clapping his paws together. "That's how I've always imagined it – the World like a great round table and the waters of all the oceans endlessly pouring over the edge. The ship will tip up – stand on her head – for one moment we shall see over the edge – and then, down, down, the rush, the speed –"

"And what do you think will be waiting for us at the bottom, eh?" said Drinian.

"Aslan's country perhaps," said the Mouse, its eyes shining. "Or perhaps there isn't any bottom. Perhaps it goes down for ever and ever. But whatever it is, won't it be worth anything just to have looked for one moment beyond the edge of the world."

"But look here," said Eustace, "this is all rot. The world's round – I mean, round like a ball, not like a table."

"*Our* world is," said Edmund. "But is this?"

"Do you mean to say," asked Caspian, "that you three come from a round world (round like a ball) and you've never told me! It's really too bad of you. Because we have fairy-tales in which there are round worlds and I always loved them. I never believed there were any real ones. But I've always wished there were and I've always longed to live in one. Oh, I'd give anything – I wonder why you can get into our world and we never get into yours? If only I had the chance! It must be exciting to live on a thing like a ball. Have you ever been to the parts where people walk about upside-down?"

Edmund shook his head. "And it isn't like that," he added. "There's nothing particularly exciting about a round world when you're there."

CHAPTER SIXTEEN

THE VERY END OF THE WORLD

REEPICHEEP was the only person on board besides Drinian and the two Pevensies who had noticed the Sea People. He had dived in at once when he saw the Sea King shaking his spear, for he regarded this as a sort of threat or challenge and wanted to have the matter out there and then. The excitement of discovering that the water was now fresh had distracted his attention, and before he remembered the Sea People again Lucy and Drinian had taken him aside and warned him not to mention what he had seen.

As things turned out they need hardly have bothered, for by this time the *Dawn Treader* was gliding over a part of the sea which seemed to be uninhabited. No one except Lucy saw anything more of the People, and even she had only one short glimpse. All morning on the following day they sailed in fairly shallow water and the bottom was weedy. Just before midday Lucy saw a large shoal of fishes grazing on the weed. They were all eating steadily and all moving in the same direction. "Just like a flock of sheep," thought Lucy. Suddenly she saw a little Sea Girl of about her own age in the middle of them – a quiet, lonely-looking girl with a sort of crook in her hand. Lucy felt sure that this girl must be a shepherdess – or perhaps a fish-herdess – and that the shoal was really a flock at pasture. Both the fishes and the girl were quite close to the surface. And just as the girl, gliding in the shallow water, and Lucy, leaning over the bulwark, came opposite to one another, the girl looked up and stared straight into Lucy's face. Neither could speak to the other and in a moment the Sea Girl dropped astern. But Lucy will never forget her face. It did not look frightened or angry like those of the other Sea People. Lucy had liked that girl and she felt certain the girl had liked her. In that one moment they had somehow become friends. There does not seem to be much chance of their meeting again in that world or any other. But if ever they do they will rush together with their hands held out.

After that for many days, without wind in her shrouds or foam at her bows, across a waveless sea, the *Dawn Treader* glided smoothly east. Every day and every hour the light became more brilliant and still they could bear it. No one ate or slept and no one wanted to, but they drew buckets of dazzling water from the sea, stronger than wine and some- how wetter, more liquid, than ordinary water, and pledged one another silently in deep draughts of it. And one or two of the sailors who had been oldish men when the voyage began now grew younger every day. Everyone on board was filled with joy and excitement, but not an excitement that made one talk. The further they sailed the less they spoke, and then almost in a whisper. The stillness of that last sea laid hold on them.

"My Lord," said Caspian to Drinian one day, "what do you see ahead?"

"Sire," said Drinian, "I see whiteness. All along the horizon from north to south, as far as my eyes can reach."

"That is what I see too," said Caspian, "and I cannot imagine what it is."

"If we were in higher latitudes, your Majesty," said Drinian, "I would say it was ice. But it can't be that; not here. All the same, we'd better get men to the oars and hold the ship back against the current. Whatever the stuff is, we don't want to crash into it at this speed!"

They did as Drinian said, and so continued to go slower and slower. The whiteness did not get any less mysterious as they approached it. If it was land it must be a very strange land, for it seemed just as smooth as the water and on the same level with it. When they got very close to it Drinian put the helm hard over and turned the *Dawn Treader* south so that she was broadside on to the current and rowed a little way southward along the edge of the whiteness. In so doing they accidentally made the important discovery that the current was only about forty feet wide and the rest of the sea as still as a pond. This was good news for the crew, who had already begun to think that the return journey to Ramandu's land, rowing against stream all the way, would be pretty poor sport. (It also explained why the shepherd girl had dropped so quickly astern. She was not in the current. If she had been she would have been moving east at the same speed as the ship.)

And still no one could make out what the white stuff was. Then the boat was lowered and it put off to investigate. Those who remained on the *Dawn Treader* could see that the boat pushed right in amidst the whiteness. Then they could hear the voices of the party in the boat (clear across the still water) talking in a shrill and surprised way. Then there was a pause while Rynelf in the bows of the boat took a sounding; and when, after that, the boat came rowing back there seemed to be plenty of the white stuff inside her. Everyone crowded to the side to hear the news.

"Lilies, your Majesty!" shouted Rynelf, standing up in the bows.

"*What* did you say?" asked Caspian.

"Blooming lilies, your Majesty," said Rynelf. "Same as in a pool or in a garden at home."

"Look!" said Lucy, who was in the stern of the boat. She held up her wet arms full of white petals and broad flat leaves.

"What's the depth, Rynelf?" asked Drinian.

"That's the funny thing, Captain," said Rynelf. "It's still deep. Three and a half fathoms clear."

"They can't be real lilies – not what we call lilies," said Eustace.

Probably they were not, but they were very like them. And when, after some consultation, the *Dawn Treader* turned back into the current and began to glide eastward through the Lily Lake or the Silver Sea (they tried both these names but it was the Silver Sea that stuck and is now on Caspian's map) the strangest part of their travels began. Very soon the open sea which they were leaving was only a thin rim of blue on the western horizon. Whiteness, shot with faintest colour of gold, spread round them on every side, except just astern where their passage had thrust the lilies apart and left an open lane of water that shone like dark green glass. To look at, this last sea was very like the Arctic; and if their eyes had not by now grown as strong as eagles' the sun on all that whiteness – especially at early morning when the sun was hugest – would have been unbearable. And every evening the same whiteness made the daylight last longer. There seemed no end to the lilies. Day after day from all those miles and leagues of flowers there rose a smell which Lucy found it very hard to describe; sweet – yes, but not at all sleepy or overpowering, a fresh, wild, lonely smell that seemed to get into your brain and make you feel that you could go up mountains at a run or wrestle with an elephant. She and Caspian said to one another, "I feel that I can't stand much more of this, yet I don't want it to stop."

They took soundings very often but it was only several days later that the water became shallower. After that it went on getting shallower. There came a day when they had to row out of the current and feel their way forward at a snail's pace, rowing. And soon it was clear that the *Dawn Treader* could sail no further east. Indeed it was only by very clever handling that they saved her from grounding.

"Lower the boat," cried Caspian, "and then call the men aft. I must speak to them."

"What's he going to do?" whispered Eustace to Edmund. "There's a queer look in his eyes."

"I think we probably all look the same," said Edmund.

They joined Caspian on the poop and soon all the men were crowded together at the foot of the ladder to hear the King's speech.

"Friends," said Caspian, "we have now fulfilled the quest on which you embarked. The seven lords are all accounted for and as Sir Reepicheep has sworn never to return, when you reach Ramandu's Land you will doubtless find the Lords Revilian and Argoz and Mavramorn awake. To you, my Lord Drinian, I entrust this ship, bidding you sail to Narnia with all the speed you may, and above all not to land on the Island of Deathwater. And instruct my regent, the Dwarf Trumpkin, to give to all these, my shipmates, the rewards I promised them. They have been earned well. And if I come not again it is my will that the Regent, and Master Cornelius, and Trufflehunter the Badger, and the Lord Drinian choose a King of Narnia with the consent —"

"But, Sire," interrupted Drinian, "are you abdicating?"

"I am going with Reepicheep to see the World's End," said Caspian.

A low murmur of dismay ran through the sailors.

"We will take the boat," said Caspian. "You will have no need of it in these gentle seas and you must build a new one in Ramandu's island. And now —"

"Caspian," said Edmund suddenly and sternly, "you can't do this."

"Most certainly," said Reepicheep, "his Majesty cannot."

"No indeed," said Drinian.

"Can't?" said Caspian sharply, looking for a moment not unlike his uncle Miraz.

"Begging your Majesty's pardon," said Rynelf from the deck below, "but if one of us did the same it would be called deserting."

"You presume too much on your long service, Rynelf," said Caspian.

"No, Sire! He's perfectly right," said Drinian.

"By the Mane of Aslan," said Caspian, "I had thought you were all my subjects here, not my schoolmasters."

"I'm not," said Edmund, "and I say you can *not* do this."

"Can't again," said Caspian. "What do you mean?"

"If it please your Majesty, we mean *shall not*," said Reepicheep with a very low bow. "You are the King of Narnia. You break faith with all your subjects, and especially with Trumpkin, if you do not return. You shall not please yourself with adventures as if you were a private person. And if your Majesty will not hear reason it will be the truest loyalty of every man on board to follow me in disarming and binding you till you come to your senses."

"Quite right," said Edmund. "Like they did with Ulysses when he wanted to go near the Sirens."

Caspian's hand had gone to his sword hilt, when Lucy said, "And you've almost promised Ramandu's daughter to go back."

Caspian paused. "Well, yes. There is that," he said. He stood irresolute for a moment and then shouted out to the ship in general.

"Well, have your way. The quest is ended. We all return. Get the boat up again."

"Sire," said Reepicheep, "we do not *all* return. I, as I explained before –"

"Silence!" thundered Caspian. "I've been lessoned but I'll not be baited. Will no one silence that Mouse?"

"Your Majesty promised," said Reepicheep, "to be good lord to the Talking Beasts of Narnia."

"Talking beasts, yes," said Caspian. "I said nothing about beasts that never stop talking." And he flung down the ladder in a temper and went into the cabin, slamming the door.

But when the others rejoined him a little later they found him changed; he was white and there were tears in his eyes.

"It's no good," he said. "I might as well have behaved decently for all the good I did with my temper and swagger. Aslan has spoken to me. No – I don't mean he was actually here. He wouldn't fit into the cabin, for one thing. But that gold lion's head on the wall came to life and spoke to me. It was terrible – his eyes. Not that he was at all rough with me – only a bit stern at first. But it was terrible all the same. And he said – he said – oh, I can't bear it. The worst thing he could have said. You're to go on – Reep and Edmund, and Lucy, and Eustace; and I'm to go back. Alone. And at once. And what *is* the good of anything?"

"Caspian, dear," said Lucy. "You knew we'd have to go back to our own world sooner or later."

"Yes," said Caspian with a sob, "but this is sooner."

"You'll feel better when you get back to Ramandu's Island," said Lucy.

He cheered up a little later on, but it was a grievous parting on both sides and I will not dwell on it. About two o'clock in the afternoon, well victualled and watered (though they thought they would need neither food nor drink) and with Reepicheep's coracle on board, the boat pulled away from the *Dawn Treader* to row through the endless carpet of lilies. The *Dawn Treader* flew all her flags and hung out her shields to honour their departure. Tall and big and homelike she looked from their low position with the lilies all round them. And before she was out of sight they saw her turn and begin rowing slowly westward. Yet though Lucy shed a few tears, she could not feel it as much as you might have expected. The light, the silence, the tingling smell of the Silver Sea, even (in some odd way) the loneliness itself, were too exciting.

There was no need to row, for the current drifted them steadily to the east. None of them slept or ate. All that night and all next day they glided eastward, and when the third day dawned – with a brightness you or I could not bear even if we had dark glasses on – they saw a wonder ahead. It was as if a wall stood up between them and the

sky, a greenish-grey, trembling, shimmering wall. Then up
came the sun, and at its first rising they saw it through the
wall and it turned into wonderful rainbow colours. Then
they knew that the wall was really a long, tall wave – a
wave endlessly fixed in one place as you may often see at
the edge of a waterfall. It seemed to be about thirty feet

high, and the current was gliding them swiftly towards it.
You might have supposed they would have thought of their
danger. They didn't. I don't think anyone could have in
their position. For now they saw something not only
behind the wave but behind the sun. They could not have
seen even the sun if their eyes had not been strengthened by
the water of the Last Sea. But now they could look at the
rising sun and see it clearly and see things beyond it. What
they saw – eastward, beyond the sun – was a range of
mountains. It was so high that either they never saw the
top of it or they forgot it. None of them remembers seeing
any sky in that direction. And the mountains must really
have been outside the world. For any mountains even a
quarter of a twentieth of that height ought to have had ice
and snow on them. But these were warm and green and full

of forests and waterfalls however high you looked. And suddenly there came a breeze from the east, tossing the top of the wave into foamy shapes and ruffling the smooth water all round them. It lasted only a second or so but what it brought them in that second none of those three children will ever forget. It brought both a smell and a sound, a musical sound. Edmund and Eustace would never talk about it afterwards. Lucy could only say, "It would break your heart." "Why," said I, "was it so sad?" "Sad!! No," said Lucy.

No one in that boat doubted that they were seeing beyond the End of the World into Aslan's country.

At that moment, with a crunch, the boat ran aground. The water was too shallow now for it. "This," said Reepicheep, "is where I go on alone."

They did not even try to stop him, for everything now felt as if it had been fated or had happened before. They helped him to lower his little coracle. Then he took off his sword ("I shall need it no more," he said) and flung it far away across the lilied sea. Where it fell it stood upright with the hilt above the surface. Then he bade them goodbye, trying to be sad for their sakes; but he was quivering with happiness. Lucy, for the first and last time, did what she had always wanted to do, taking him in her arms and caressing him. Then hastily he got into his coracle and took his paddle, and the current caught it and away he went, very black against the lilies. But no lilies grew on the wave; it was a smooth green slope. The coracle went more and more quickly, and beautifully it rushed up the wave's side. For one split second they saw its shape and Reepicheep's on the very top. Then it vanished, and since that moment no one can truly claim to have seen Reepicheep the Mouse. But my belief is that he came safe to Aslan's country and is alive there to this day.

As the sun rose the sight of those mountains outside the world faded away. The wave remained but there was only blue sky behind it.

The children got out of the boat and waded – not towards the wave but southward with the wall of water on their left. They could not have told you why they did this; it was their fate. And though they had felt – and been – very grown-up on the *Dawn Treader*, they now felt just the opposite and held hands as they waded through the lilies. They never felt tired. The water was warm and all the time it got shallower. At last they were on dry sand, and then on grass – a huge plain of very fine short grass, almost level with the Silver Sea and spreading in every direction without so much as a molehill.

And of course, as it always does in a perfectly flat place without trees, it looked as if the sky came down to meet the grass in front of them. But as they went on they got the strangest impression that here at last the sky did really come down and join the earth – a blue wall, very bright, but real and solid: more like glass than anything else. And soon they were quite sure of it. It was very near now.

But between them and the foot of the sky there was something so white on the green grass that even with their eagles' eyes they could hardly look at it. They came on and saw that it was a Lamb.

"Come and have breakfast," said the Lamb in its sweet milky voice.

Then they noticed for the first time that there was a fire lit on the grass and fish roasting on it. They sat down and ate the fish, hungry now for the first time for many days. And it was the most delicious food they had ever tasted.

"Please, Lamb," said Lucy, "is this the way to Aslan's country?"

"Not for you," said the Lamb. "For you the door into Aslan's country is from your own world."

"What!" said Edmund. "Is there a way into Aslan's country from our world too?"

"There is a way into my country from all the worlds," said the Lamb; but as he spoke his snowy white flushed into tawny gold and his size changed and he was Aslan himself, towering above them and scattering light from his mane.

"Oh, Aslan," said Lucy. "Will you tell us how to get into your country from our world?"

"I shall be telling you all the time," said Aslan. "But I will not tell you how long or short the way will be; only that it lies across a river. But do not fear that, for I am the great Bridge Builder. And now come; I will open the door in the sky and send you to your own land."

"Please, Aslan," said Lucy. "Before we go, will you tell us when we can come back to Narnia again? Please. And oh, do, do, do make it soon."

"Dearest," said Aslan very gently, "you and your brother will never come back to Narnia."

"Oh, *Aslan*!!" said Edmund and Lucy both together in despairing voices.

"You are too old, children," said Aslan, "and you must begin to come close to your own world now."

"It isn't Narnia, you know," sobbed Lucy. "It's *you*. We shan't meet *you* there. And how can we live, never meeting you?"

"But you shall meet me, dear one," said Aslan.

"Are – are you there too, Sir?" said Edmund.

"I am," said Aslan. "But there I have another name. You must learn to know me by that name. This was the very reason why you were brought to Narnia, that by knowing me here for a little, you may know me better there."

"And is Eustace never to come back here either?" said Lucy.

"Child," said Aslan, "do you really need to know that? Come, I am opening the door in the sky." Then all in one moment there was a rending of the blue wall (like a curtain being torn) and a terrible white light from beyond the sky, and the feel of Aslan's mane and a Lion's kiss on their foreheads and then – the back bedroom in Aunt Alberta's home in Cambridge.

Only two more things need to be told. One is that Caspian and his men all came safely back to Ramandu's Island. And the three lords woke from their sleep. Caspian married

Ramandu's daughter and they all reached Narnia in the end, and she became a great queen and the mother and grandmother of great kings. The other is that back in our own world everyone soon started saying how Eustace had improved, and how "You'd never know him for the same boy": everyone except Aunt Alberta, who said he had become very commonplace and tiresome and it must have been the influence of those Pevensie children.